BECALMED

by Normandie Fischer

BECALMED BY NORMANDIE FISCHER
Published by Lighthouse Publishing of the Carolinas
2333 Barton Oaks Dr., Raleigh, NC, 27614

ISBN 978-1-938499-61-6
Copyright © 2013 by Normandie Fischer
Cover design by kateink.com

Available in print from your local bookstore, online, or from the publisher at:
www.lighthousepublishingofthecarolinas.com

For more information on this book and the author visit: www.normandiefischer.com

Library of Congress Cataloging-in-Publication Data
Normandie Fischer
Becalmed / Normandie Fischer 1st ed.

Printed in the United States of America

Lighthouse Publishing
of the Carolinas
www.lighthousepublishingofthecarolinas.com

Praise for Becalmed

With a voice that sings and characters that sail right into your heart, Fischer has crafted a story that will keep the pages turning, the heart twisting, and stick with you long after The End.

~Roseanna M. White, author of
Ring of Secrets and *Jewel of Persia*

Normandie Fischer's spirited tale enchants in the tradition of Maeve Binchy and Anne Rivers Siddons. Her Southern charm pours over the page like warm honey on a sweet bun. Each delicious morsel leaves you longing for more.

~D. D. Falvo, author

Normandie Fischer anchors her readers so she can set them on a course full of twists, turns, and unforgettable characters. She digs into the human condition and pulls life's richest moments out, allowing the reader a chance to sail away and dream the impossible.

~ Linda Glaz, literary agent and author

"Write about what you know" is what any good writer does. Normandie Fischer just does it better than most. On inland waterways and the open ocean, Normandie's characters chart a course for home through trials and temptations, for a chance at love and redemption. Becalmed is the story of one woman's journey to care for herself while caring for others, to be true to herself and true to another when what she hopes for will take a miracle or at least an act of God.

~ Jane Shealy, editor

Normandie Fischer brings the Carolina coast alive as her characters walk off the page to become your friends and enemies. She weaves her incredible sailing experience and love of the sea through a story that captures the reader's heart and holds it to the end.

~ David E. Stevens,
author of *The Resurrect Trilogy*

Smart and sassy with a Southern twang. Sailing with authentic lingo and imagery. Normandie Fischer delivers a spunky but lonely heroine who feels like she's running out of time in the love department. Intriguing characters and a timeless story of need and desire, *Becalmed* takes readers out on the rough seas of relationship and delivers them to a satisfying conclusion on stable shores.

~ Nicole Petrino-Salter, author of
The Famous One and *Breath of Life*

The author manages to pull you into the life of Tadie from the very first line, and continues to hold you captive with every line thereafter. Weaving a story that is both enchanting and real to life, this is a novel that will resonate with anyone who has known heartache, loss, and the sweeping joy of love's sweet arrival.

~ Susannah Friis, freelance writer
and speaker

Fischer has delivered a marvelous romance set in the sailing world of coastal North Carolina that intelligently includes the sometimes challenging reality of that life. In a delightful twist, the daughter of a widowed cruiser falls in love with a recreational sailor/professional jewelry designer before her father does, and tries to bring them together. But the adults in the novel just won't cooperate. Storms, damaged boats, a delightful seven-year-old, unwanted advances from an old flame, and two people searching for truth in their own lives, all work together to make *Becalmed* a wonderful read. Well done!

~ Patti Phillips, author of the crime
fiction blog, www.kerriansnotebook.com

Acknowledgements

If it takes a village to raise a child, it certainly takes an entire town to craft and publish a book. *Becalmed* wouldn't exist without the encouragement and help of my long-time critique partner, Jane Lebak, or my writing and editing friends, Amy Alessio, Linda Glaz, and Robin Patchen.

Many, many thanks to my agent, Terry Burns, for his friendship and faith. Thank you to Eddie Jones and everyone at Lighthouse Publishing of the Carolinas, including Andrea Merrell and Christy Miller, for pushing me to make this story the best it could be. How could I go wrong with another sailor at the helm of a publishing company? And Andrea has the patience of a saint as well as an excellent eye for detail.

I'm so grateful to my beloved Michael, who has always given me space and time to write. I love it that he "gets" me, and his encouragement and prayers kept me going when all those negative voices in my head tried to shout me down. My mother, Ella Meadows Giesey, continues to teach me so much about grace and love. Thank you, Mama. And to my darling children, Ariana Milton Scoville and Joshua Milton, who have always been my cheerleaders, I couldn't be more proud of the adults you have become. When my own world felt *becalmed*, you were there.

Dedication

To Sara Meadows, my beloved auntie.
I first loved sailing because of her. She was my aunt, fourteen
years my mother's senior. Named Sara, she was called Sister by
all of us, and Tadie by the town she knew ... a Southern thing. I
remember the way she wore her boat cap pulled low, the sleeves of
her loose shirt rolled above the elbow as she tacked past crab pots
and out the narrow channel from Sleepy Creek into Core Sound.
Her life made me wonder about small towns and single
women. Hence, this story.

Chapter One

Out here on the water between Shackleford Banks and the islands fronting Taylor Creek, the wind can turn as skittish as those barrier-island ponies. Some days, it blows up a stink as it whips through the Beaufort Inlet and across the low dunes of the Cape Lookout National Seashore. Other days, it just lies down flat.

Tadie Longworth didn't mind which way the wind played its tricks when she sailed alone. But with Hannah on board and the breeze a dimming memory, she cared. Her best friend sat forward in the cockpit, wilting like the edges of her floppy red hat as she poured bottled water down the front of her shirt.

"You want me to soak a towel?" Tadie asked. "Drape it over your legs to cool you?" She plucked at her own shirt, damp with salt water. "It helps."

Hannah fanned her face. "Just find us some wind," she said, elongating a sigh.

Tadie bit back a grin. Such a drama queen. Trust Hannah to milk even discomfort.

In the stillness, the loud rumble of an overtaking speedboat grabbed Tadie's attention. Fool. He had plenty of water to steer clear of them, but no, he'd rather throw a wake at *Luna's* beam as he flashed past in a blur of yellow.

Luna's sails snapped, whip-like. Tadie pushed away the wooden boom and scanned the horizon for some sign that a breeze might waft this way before Hannah cried mutiny. Yet even the gulls were silent, sitting placidly on glass.

A loud ringing from her satchel startled them both. Hannah, closest to the bag, dug out the cell phone and glanced at the screen before handing it over. "Don't recognize the number."

Tadie released the breath she'd been holding against images of an ambulance and Elvie Mae rushed to the hospital. Absurd flight of fancy. It was only a lumpectomy, after all, and not until Friday.

She spoke a hello, but the half-whisper that answered almost made her drop the phone. She hadn't heard that smooth, dream-shaper voice in years. Too surprised to hit the *End* button, she said, "Alex?"

"Who else?" The tone seemed amused. She could almost see his smirk, perhaps a brow lifted and lowered. "I'm back and I've missed you, Tadie. Missed *us*."

Cat's paws disturbed the water about a hundred yards out, but the only wind on board at the moment came from Alex's sigh—and from her own gathering ire, which sounded in her head like the whoosh of water past her ears during a deep dive.

Hannah's eyebrows nearly hit her hairline. "Alex?" she mouthed. "Matt's brother? *That* Alex?"

Tadie covered the phone's mike and frowned. "The one and only."

Hannah settled back against the cushion, the long nails of her left hand beating a nervous tattoo against her plastic water bottle.

Tadie whispered, "Shush now," before bringing the phone back to her ear.

Bored, that's what she'd been. Hot and bored. Why else would she have answered her phone, like Pavlov's dog responding to a bell? Now look where her curiosity had gotten her.

She corralled her frustration and spit it at Alex. *The creep.* "Us?

What *us*? The us you flicked off like so much dust sixteen years ago?" She'd thought they'd been in love, for heaven's sake. Promised.

"Now, Tadie, don't go rehashing that. We were good friends, even more than friends."

"And then? Poof! All gone."

"You know sometimes things happen beyond our control."

Was he delusional? "Zippers don't usually slide open without help. There was no immaculate conception."

Hannah hooted, then slapped her hand over her mouth.

"Look, I'm sorry," Alex said, a bit of a whine creeping in. Tadie had forgotten that whine. "I said so then," he continued. "I'm saying so now. But after all this time, I thought we could be friends again and take *Luna* out. We could swim off the shoals like we used to."

"That's not happening, Alex. Not in this lifetime."

"Don't tell me you don't sail anymore." He paused. "Or are you seeing someone? Hannah didn't mention anybody."

"Alex, you have a wife. Go play with her." She hit the End button, huffed, and pushed the tiller hard to port, trying to eke out enough momentum to shift *Luna* into that patch of breeze, and then pointed to the cleat near Hannah's back. "You want to loose that jib sheet? Hold it and be ready to pull in on the other when I give the word."

Hannah, roused from her half-recumbent position, uncleated the line. "Aye, aye, skipper. If you think we need to bother."

"I'm hoping so. If not, we'll improve our arm muscles with those paddles stuck there behind you."

Hannah sipped from her water bottle without comment. Then she slowly screwed on the cap, set the bottle in the cooler, and fluttered her painted nails toward the bag and Tadie's now silent phone. "You gonna tell me about that?"

Tadie ignored the question. "You didn't say Alex was already in Beaufort. Or that he might be on the prowl."

"I don't get him calling you, but I told you Matt needed help running the business and Alex was coming. He started back yesterday, after he and Bethanne got settled out at her parents' place on the

Straits."

"I'd like to know how he got my cell number."

"It wasn't me. Or Matt, not knowingly," Hannah said, tucking a loose strand of hair behind her ear. "I bet Matt's got you in his Rolodex at the office. He's got the world in that old thing."

Blowing out a loud breath, Tadie leaned down to peer under the boom at the water ahead and corrected course slightly. "You think something else is going on I should know about?"

"Like what?"

"Like some issue between him and Bethanne. You know Alex. He was a sneaky, conniving snake when he left the first time, and it doesn't look like he's shed that skin." Tadie's words slapped the air. She wished they could have connected with Alex.

Luna's bow crossed into the short wind waves, and a breeze caught the main.

"Jib," Tadie said, nodding toward the lee sheet.

Hannah grabbed the line and pulled it taut while Tadie settled their direction from the helm. At her nod, Hannah set the line in a quick-release cam cleat at the centerboard well. She could free it if things got dicey as they sometimes did in these waters, especially when *Luna* sailed near a headland where dunes or trees blocked or shifted the wind.

"You want I should leave it stuck here or cleat it?" Hannah asked, still holding the line's tail.

Tadie glanced from the water to the sky at their stern. An anvil-shaped cloud had formed over Shackleford Banks, but it shouldn't toss anything their way for a while. "Looks like a wind shift, probably from whatever's brewing on the Atlantic. Leave it while we see what happens."

The afternoon sun danced off the water, little diamond sparkles on the short waves. If a storm came, the water would turn ugly, from this silvery blue to a darkened pewter that spewed whitecaps.

"Will we beat it home?" Hannah nodded at the heaping cloud mass as she tightened the chin strap on her floppy hat so a gust couldn't grab it.

"If the wind behaves, easily."

"And if not?"

"Don't worry. I've run from a storm before. And you've been with me."

"And gotten soaked in the process."

"Trust me."

"Said the spider to the fly." Hannah reached back to readjust her cushion. Finally settled, she stretched her legs and wiggled red-painted toes that matched her fingernails and those hat stripes.

Tadie grinned at her friend's fascination with scarlet. "I think that was what the snake said to the boy."

"Kipling?"

"Probably Disney."

Hannah huffed, and she lowered her sunglasses down the bridge of her nose to show off a scowl.

Tadie wasn't buying it. "You remember the movie. We saw it together."

"Fine, the movie, the book. Whatever," Hannah said, fluttering again. "What I want to know is why Alex called you? He hasn't before, has he, when he and Bethanne came to town?"

A disgusted half-whistle was all Tadie could manage. "Never." She just wanted to forget the call—both Alex's tone and his words.

Hannah didn't let her. "What'd he say?"

"Loose the jib a little." Tadie let the main sheet slide through her fingers as she pointed them a little off the wind, heading north. "That's good. Right there." Then she answered Hannah's question. "Your esteemed brother-in-law wants to be friends again and go sailing with me. Lands, Hannah, we haven't been friends since we were nineteen."

Hannah's lips pursed. "Did he forget he's married?"

"Seems like it."

"But still ..."

"But still, *what*?"

"Well, I don't get it, looking back and all."

"Looking back's the problem, isn't it?" Tadie said. "My memory is exceptional when it comes to those days."

"I know he hurt you, but at least he did the right thing by Bethanne and the baby. And it's been a long time."

Tadie shot a glare Hannah's way. "What's got into you? Where's that solidarity, the old, 'How could he do that?' Weren't we both members of the We-Hate-Alex-for-Being-a-Scumbag Club?"

"I'm just saying ..."

"Is this all because he came home to help Matt? I mean, I know Matt loves his brother."

The hat shaded Hannah's face, but her silence seemed awfully loud.

"Hannah?"

"We need Alex. Matt says he gave up his job and his house in Connecticut just to come home and take up the slack at work. I'm counting on things being different now. On Matt getting well again."

Did she imagine a choke in Hannah's voice? The hint of tears? "Has something else happened, something with Matt's heart? Something you're not telling me?"

"No. Nothing."

Her friend's brittle laugh didn't sound like *nothing*. Tadie blinked.

"He keeps saying he's fine," Hannah said, "but I can tell. I can see it. And he won't slow down."

"Maybe with Alex working, things will ease up."

Hannah didn't answer, but she did suck on one long nail.

The growing breeze and a beam reach had propelled them toward the Beaufort waterfront and the anchored boats. Tadie eased the tiller to port and released more line as they entered the creek.

Luna was a flat-bottomed sharpie, a lovely little boat that sailed easily over shoals with the simple lifting of her centerboard, but she became tippy if unbalanced when a gust hit. She loved to gad about on an easy reach, and now that they'd come within the protection of the headland, she zipped forward.

Tadie checked out the various cruising boats that filled in spaces between long-time residents hooked to mooring balls. "Look, will you? That one's from Hong Kong."

And there bobbed another, a lovely cutter-rigged boat with a dark green hull. She tried to read its stern before she had to focus all her attention on the boat traffic ahead. The *Nancy-something*, out of Delaware. Gorgeous lines, with brightwork that made Tadie's fingers itch to touch the satiny varnish. So many of the big new boats were just plastic tubs, but this one had wooden caprails that someone maintained to perfection. Considering her own hard work on her much-smaller *Luna*, she knew there was love poured into that sailboat.

A little red-haired girl and a man—her daddy?—bobbed in a dinghy, looking as if they'd just come off that beauty. The man rowed them toward shore, while the child's chatter drifted across the water, turning into laughter when a motorboat's wake bucked their small boat, and the waves rolled under and headed toward *Luna*. The child waved at *Luna's* crew.

"Hey!" Tadie called, returning the wave as she pointed *Luna* across the wake. "Welcome to Beaufort!"

Hannah was still watching the pair when Tadie turned her sharpie's bow around and into the wind. The breeze spilled from the sails, and *Luna* glided gently up to her dock. Tadie grabbed a line she'd left looped on an outside piling, cleated it inboard, and tossed another line around the dock cleat.

Setting lines, cleaning up, and putting on sail covers took time, but eventually they were on the dock, carrying bags and cooler up to her house. "I've got sweet tea in the refrigerator. You want to sit out here or inside?" she asked Hannah.

"I can't stay. I've got a zillion things to do, especially if that storm's coming this way. We're due at the Straits house." With a sniff, Hannah began separating out her things. "Bethanne's cooking. I'm not looking forward to it."

Tadie couldn't imagine sitting through a dinner with either of them, but the fact of Alex's call festered like a red-ant sting. "If Alex calling me indicates some new and erratic behavior, do you think Matt ought to worry? I mean, can Matt trust him?"

Puckers appeared between Hannah's brows. "I don't see why not. Alex owns part of the business."

"I thought you said he sold his shares to Matt."

"Only half. That still leaves him with a quarter, so he's bound to want the company to do well."

Hating that she'd caused her friend more worry, Tadie hefted the small cooler into Hannah's trunk. "Of course. I'm just thrown off by that call, you know?"

"I get it."

"Let me know how the dinner goes."

Hannah slid behind the wheel. "I'll call."

Tadie watched until the car had backed out of the drive before she climbed her front steps and hipped open the door. If only she could fix things—make Matt better, send Alex back to Hartford, and see Elvie Mae cancer free.

She kicked off her sailing shoes and tucked them in the closet next to a pair of waders, then wandered barefoot into the living room and yanked open the drapes. The rings clicked against the brass rod, waking Ebenezer. The large tabby blinked once, licked his nearest paw, and settled back into the down cushion he'd appropriated.

"Hello to you too." Tadie scratched behind Eb's ear, sighing when he ignored her. She should have listened to Hannah and brought home a dog.

Her bare feet dragged across the oriental carpet that protected the old waxed floor from scuffs. She preferred the coolness of the bare wood and welcomed it when the rug ended. Her fingers trailed along the edge of the mahogany hall table and across the raised door panel into her silent kitchen as Alex's words hovered.

Closing her eyes, she whispered, "Breathe. You're happy. You *like* your life."

She did. She had her business and her house and her friends.

Certainly, loneliness and grief had laid her low as deaths multiplied around her, but she'd recovered. She'd even grown stronger. Or was that merely another delusion?

Once, time had crept. When had it decided to rush headlong at endings? When she was twenty? When thirty loomed on the horizon and then blipped on by, right off the radar screen?

"You're overreacting," she told the empty room, because her cat obviously wasn't interested. "It was only a phone call."

Tadie opened the refrigerator and stared inside before closing it when she couldn't remember what she'd wanted. She braced against the counter and stared unseeing out the back window.

The kettle. That was it. "Tea," she said, as if the spoken word would anchor her.

She set the kettle on the stove. But tearing open a new box of Earl Grey and collecting a cup and spoon provided no distraction at all. Imagining murder did.

A little shiver slithered up her spine.

She'd use her mama's silver carving knife, the one with the steel blade and the worked handle that lay in its felt-lined slot, honed and ready. All she had to do was lift it out, hunt up Alex, and plunge it deep into his throat. Blood would ooze. He'd raise a hand to beg forgiveness for stealing her youth and choke on the words. She'd toss her head and turn away.

Ha! Perhaps she should write murder mysteries instead of designing jewelry. Or take up wood carving so she'd have something physical on which to loose all this anger. Chips would fly, and she'd end up chiseling the wood down to toothpicks.

She blew a tickling hair off her nose. At her back, the kettle whistled. She poured boiling water into her mug and waited while the tea steeped.

If only she were happily married. A man on her arm—and in her bed—babies filling the rooms in this big empty house of hers. Then she could thumb her nose at the past. Instead, she languished here in her childhood home, morphing with each passing day into one of the town's odd, decrepit singles—a maiden aunt to nobody.

She had wanted more. Especially with Alex. Oh my, could that man touch things in her. His kiss ... But something, even with Alex, had always stopped her from going any further. Call her old-fashioned. Call her a fool.

Or, perhaps, the way things had turned out, call her smart. Only, now, here she was.

Why did he have to phone and get her stirred up again?

The tea bag landed silently in the trash, and the only sound was the slight clack of silver against ceramic as she mixed in a dollop of honey. Dinner didn't sound appetizing, but she plucked two truffles from her horde of Godiva. Balancing the full saucer in one hand, she flipped light switches with the other as she made her way upstairs. A breeze wafted in her open windows, stirring the curtains and dispelling the afternoon heat.

While her huge tub filled with orange-scented bubbles, she sipped tea and bit into the chocolate. Its raspberry filling oozed over her fingertips. Licking it off, she sighed, savoring another bite, another sip, before loosing a small smile. Yes ma'am. Spinsters had to take their pleasure where they could, and, as far as this spinster was concerned, chocolate and bubble baths ranked right up there on the decadence scale.

She laid a hand towel next to the book she'd been reading and lowered herself into the water. And wasn't this one of the blessings of being single? Doing what she wanted, when she wanted, how she wanted, with no man telling her to fetch and carry?

And no man to touch her or to take away the loneliness.

Stop it. Now.

She'd made the choice to be here, hadn't she? To say no to Alex and the others who had offered to take what she'd been reluctant to give. She needed to get over herself.

Easier said than done.

She tried to focus on the story in front of her. The book's sleuth had become almost a friend, cheered on through mystery after mystery.

Her gaze lifted from the page. Somehow, the heroine's London antics seemed trite. Tadie set the book aside and sank deeper until bubbles covered her breasts. Finally, prune-fingered, she climbed out and rubbed most of her body dry before slipping into the lightest of her sleep shirts. She retrieved her book and collapsed onto the cool sheets of her bed.

Maggie, the heroine, dashed madly through a foggy London. Tadie tried to follow her meanderings up one street and down another, but when the phone jangled in her ear, she reached for it before realizing she should have checked the caller ID.

"What?"

"Hey, it's me."

"Ah, Hannah." It must be the story making her so jumpy, the story and her day. "I thought you were dining out."

"Bethanne was delayed at the Dunes Club. I suggested we try for another night, but she just talked right over me. We're to go at eight, which means she'll serve at nine. *Nine?* Does she think this is the big city?"

"Poor Hannah. Have a snack."

"I've fixed us both some scrambled eggs and toast so Matt could take his blood pressure medicine. Anyway, I called because of that little girl we saw, the one with the cute father. Leastwise, I assume it was her father."

Tadie's eyes closed as she slid into a reclining position. Cute father, cute daughter. Wasn't that the truth? "Mmm, yes."

"Woohoo! I knew it. I saw you looking."

"Stop it. They have a gorgeous boat. It made me dream of the cruising life." How could she not wish—just for a moment—that she had been aboard that lovely sailboat? She tried to stifle a sigh. "I imagine the mother was below taking a nap."

"There's no telling." Teasing laughter lingered in Hannah's voice. "He could be a single parent. Maybe divorced."

"Not likely. I can't imagine a man taking on the work of sailing and managing a child on a boat like that, not all by himself."

"Maybe they were just out for a quick sail."

"That's not a quick-sailing boat." Tadie longed to see the boat's insides, the homey comforts that child's mother would have insisted on before she'd go cruising.

"I'm thinking you ought to take *Luna* out again tomorrow."

"You think?" Tadie wiggled farther down on the mattress, but something—a wrinkle, a pea—poked at her right buttock. She flipped to her left side and resettled the phone at her ear.

"I wouldn't mind keeping you company on a sail-by. We could see who's on board, you know, just to be friendly."

"Hannah, stop. I'm not desperate enough to go chasing sailboats or sailors. Have fun at dinner."

She disconnected, swung her legs off the bed, and padded over to the window. The sky's purplish-grey cast a gloom on the creek. Squinting, she searched the shadows where *Luna*'s white-tipped mast bobbed against the darker water. Was that a heron on the dock with its neck retracted in a swooping curve? Headlights from a passing car raked the nearby marsh, rendering the rest invisible.

Katydids chirped as they'd done many evenings, back when she used to wait and dream. Alex's image superimposed itself on the fleeting picture of a perfect boat. Blue eyes flashed from under too-long lashes. His easy smile had made her believe, if only in his presence, that they had a future, that she was beautiful. She'd fended him off in the back seat of his Chevy and behind the dunes, because some part of her had wondered and doubted. She'd had a mirror, hadn't she?

And boys lied.

Chapter Two

The sun beat on the overhead bimini, and not a breath of air bent around the island to cool the *Nancy Grace*. Sweat trickled down Will Merritt's neck, slithered between his shoulder blades, and glued him to his T-shirt. He lifted his cap to swipe at his brow, first with his right arm, then with his left, and went back to studying the street map of Beaufort. Yesterday afternoon they'd taken a cab several miles to the Food Lion. He supposed today they'd have to hit the chandleries the same way.

Jilly napped behind him in the bimini's shade, her knees tucked up on the cockpit cushions, her red hair spilling from the rubber bands he'd used on her pigtails. Either he or the heat had worn her out this morning.

This time of year, with hurricane season upon them, they should be putting miles between them and here. Nothing he could do about it now, not with the engine alarm signaling trouble. His dipstick had come up clean, but he'd noticed reddish oil in the bilge. Red, as opposed to black, meant a transmission issue. Probably the oil cooler had blown a tube, letting the oil seep out into the cooling water, but he wouldn't know for certain until he took things apart. He sighed. He could handle it, but he hated that it forced this detour.

"Punkin?" Will said, gently shaking his daughter's thin shoulder.

She knuckled her eyes. "Time?"

"We need to go into town."

Her small hands brushed at stray hairs as she slid from the cushion. "Can we get ice cream?"

"After shopping," he said, patting his buttoned pocket. "I have a few items to buy before I tackle the repairs."

"I'm ready. But first I need to use the head."

He followed her below to make sure all hatches were closed. He'd learned the hard way that leaving one open was like putting out the welcome mat for rain, even on a cloudless day. Odd thing about clouds. They could materialize from nowhere—unless you happened to want their shade.

He bent to pick up one of the *mola*-covered pillows that had fallen under the table, probably knocked off when he'd been messing with the engine compartment doors. A quick stab of longing pierced him. He saw again the Panamanian market stall and Nancy's fingers tracing bright panels of color. "Someday," his brand-new wife had said, her beautiful eyes dancing as she leaned into him, "someday we'll sail to the San Blas and buy directly from the Indians." Later, she'd dreamt of this boat and their sailing life, the three of them roaming the world. Now there were only two.

"Don't think about it," he whispered, hefting his backpack over one shoulder.

Hadn't that been his mantra since he'd lost her? Concentrate on the task at hand. Don't think about the past—or the might-have-beens.

All he had to do was fix the leak and point the *Nancy Grace* north. One step at a time. He could do that. He and Jilly.

And there she was, the light of his world, shrugging into her life jacket. "Daddy, do you think we'll see that lady again? The one in the pretty little boat?"

"It had good lines, didn't it?" Will smiled, ignoring the sailor for the boat. "Seemed like a sweet goer." The sight of a female sailor must have thrilled Jilly, whose own mother used to toss her hair in the wind and laugh. Nancy's joy at being alive and on the water had affected everyone in her sphere. Lord, how he missed her.

"The lady said, 'Welcome to Beaufort.' And the other lady in the big hat waved at us. This must be a nice place."

Will hoped so. Some places were, and some seemed to wish cruisers would keep on sailing to the next port.

He held the dinghy steady as Jilly backed down the boarding ladder. At the dinghy dock, she scrambled out onto the wooden planks and cleated the painter for him, then handed over her life vest. The boat wobbled as he put one foot on the boards. "Got it," he said with a quick look at the dinghy to make sure all was secure, and a glance out to where the *Nancy Grace* bobbed gracefully at anchor.

"Come on, Daddy. She's not going anywhere."

Will laughed and tugged gently at a pigtail. Jilly freed her hair with an exaggerated sigh. "You always worry the anchor's going to drag."

"I shouldn't, should I? Not with a first mate like you helping me set it."

They strolled hand-in-hand down the main street, past the tour boats—one painted with a serious set of shark teeth—and on past the dockmaster's office. A touristy sort of town, with small shops full of clothes, knick-knacks, and souvenirs, it had lots for Jilly to investigate.

"Whoa, Daddy, look at that. It must have sneaked in last night." She danced up on her toes and pointed to a huge yacht with three decks, one with slanted, darkened windows.

"That's some boat." Big yachts meant big bucks. Marinas weren't for the likes of him and Jilly, not if they wanted to keep the kitty full without him having to take too many consulting jobs. He had work offered to him, but it would mean staying someplace for a while and hooking back up to the world of airports and the Internet.

Heat bounced off the asphalt, so moisture-laden he didn't even need to sweat to feel the drips form. Jilly's idea started to sound good. Ice cream and some shade. He should have insisted she wear her boat cap and put on more sunscreen.

"Maybe we could fortify ourselves with something cold before we hit the chandleries. What do you say?"

"Yes, oh yes!" His daughter tugged him forward, up the wooden steps into the cool darkness of the ice cream shop. They ordered their usual—a mint chocolate chip, two scoops please, and a raspberry sherbet, one scoop.

"Look at that, Daddy. Can we go in there tomorrow?" Jilly pointed to a sign for the Rocking Chair Bookstore. "I bet it's nice. I need more books."

"We'll put it on our list of things to do."

Jilly's greenish eyes sparkled as she licked and bit into a chocolate chip. "You know what we need?"

Will shook his head, waiting.

"A better freezer on the boat, so we could take ice cream with us."

"We could. But then having it wouldn't be so special, would it?"

She seemed to think about that as she caught a drip with her tongue. "I guess not."

They flopped to the ground under one of the few trees that fronted the boardwalk. When a man in a flashy, flowered shirt scurried past, they followed his progress toward the wharf-front restaurant and a squawking, sun-visored woman.

"Uh-oh, he's in the doghouse," Jilly said.

Will whooped. "Where'd you hear that?"

"Aunt Liz. She said it about Uncle Dan if he came home late. Did Mommy ever put you in the doghouse?"

"If she did, she never told me."

"Oh." Jilly licked again, pressing the last scoop into the cone with her tongue. "When Aunt Liz said it, she was angry. I think it meant she wasn't going to be nice to Uncle Dan."

"Your mommy never got that angry."

"Because you weren't late."

"Well, I was sometimes. But I always called her to explain."

Jilly wiped her lips with the back of her hand. "That made it okay."

"Here. Use another napkin, or you're going to be all sticky."

"I already am. We need some water."

"Soon as you finish."

He found a public restroom and waited while Jilly cleaned up.

Bouncing out to the sidewalk again—how did she manage a bounce in this heat?—she pointed across the street toward the Maritime Museum. "You promised we could see what they have, the pirate stuff, like on the poster. You said so yesterday."

"I know I did." He glanced at his watch. "Tell you what. We'll ask them if there's a taxi stand in town."

"We used a taxi yesterday. You just stuck out your arm."

"But that was luck. I don't see any driving past now, do you? And we can't walk all the way to the West Marine."

"Can I look at some of the museum stuff?"

"Fifteen minutes."

"Thirty?"

"Twenty."

Jilly's smile widened, and she hopped ahead of him up the museum steps. She scanned the pirate exhibit while he chatted with the fellow at the information desk. Soon, she was tugging at his shirt. "Daddy, a book, please ... for when you're busy? We didn't have time to go to that other place. I mean, we're here, so could I?"

Will shooed her ahead, waited as she browsed, then let her count out her recent earnings—as first mate, she received a stipend for certain chores on board—to pay for a story about old Blackbeard himself.

Back on the sidewalk, she skipped toward the corner, her hair flapping at her shoulders. The heat, which made him long for a tall iced something, still hadn't fazed her. "At least," he said, squinting as he wiped fog from his dark lenses, "you can't complain about boredom tomorrow."

She slowed and turned toward him, her freckles crinkling along her nose. "I know. You'll be busy working, and I'll be getting smarter." She stepped off the curb into a blind spot just as tires screeched and a shiny green BMW convertible lurched toward her, its side mirror homing like a heat-seeking missile.

Chapter Three

Will yanked Jilly hard against him as the convertible barely braked. Her bony shoulders shook, and his own heart threatened to pound through his ribs. He glared past her. "You fool!" he yelled at the driver, who probably couldn't hear over the blaring music.

Will wanted to chase the fellow down and beat the snot out of him. Instead, he took a deep breath and smoothed his hand over his daughter's head. "You okay, kiddo?"

She turned to look after the nasty piece of work, her breath catching as the car took the corner and the driver's flashy sunglasses stared in their direction.

"The taxi stand is down a couple of blocks." Taking her hand, reminding himself that he shouldn't squeeze too tightly—in spite of wanting to pick her up and hang on for dear life—he stepped into the now-quiet street. "Let's case the shop windows on the way and hope we never see that cretin again."

Distracted, Jilly looked up at him. "I know that word."

"You do, huh?"

"It's a fancy way of calling him a dumb jerk. Right?" She danced up on the other curb, let go of his hand, and shuffled backward. "Am I right? Am I?"

"Close enough. Who taught you that one, Miss Dictionary?"

"Oh, Daddy." She giggled, sidling close enough to grab his hand again. "*You* did."

The clothing stores did not seem to interest Jilly, though she did stop to look at a hat she declared would be perfect for Tubby, her favorite bear. "But it's okay. We don't need it."

Which was a relief to Will, because Jilly's animal collection already took up much of the V-berth.

They passed a pub-like restaurant, and Jilly braked in front of a plate-glass window full of the odd and interesting.

"Daddy, look. Don't you just *love* that frog?" A large green toad sculpted of painted metal looked ready to devour the over-sized fly perched at the tip of its tongue. The eyes were spirals of metal with penny-sized pupils bulging toward the fly.

Will had to admit the thing had charm.

"Can we go in, just for a second? Please?"

"Sure, punkin." What did a few more minutes matter?

He helped her with the door. The jingle that sounded their entrance brought a hello from a silver-haired lady in a flowing green dress. "Come in," she said, smiling at them both, but concentrating on Jilly. "I see you met Jasper."

"Is that his name?" Jilly peered back toward the window.

The lady nodded. "Jasper Toad. And what's yours?"

"Jilly." She pointed to her father. "And my daddy's name is Will."

"I'm Isa," the lady said, holding out her hand first to Jilly, then to Will. "I'm very pleased to meet you both." She turned back to Jilly. "Would you like to see Jasper's friends?"

Jilly's eyes brightened. "Oh, yes."

The jade lady glided toward some shelves at the back of the store where a menagerie of metal animals held court. "These just came in. Aren't they wonderful?"

"Daddy, come here." Jilly pulled him to her side. "Look at the fish." A ribbed construction with brass scales and a mouth that resembled a small-toothed barracuda stood on its own pedestal. "Does he have a name?"

"I don't know," Isa said. "Why don't you ask him?"

Jilly did. They waited, the two adults watching as Jilly bent close to the metal object. Will bit his lip to stifle a grin.

Finally, Jilly's hand flew to her mouth. "Oh, dear, we goofed." She giggled. "Her name's Penelope. She's a girl fish."

Isa's eyes twinkled, but she spoke seriously to the sculpture. "I'm sorry. How do you do, Penelope?" She turned to Jilly. "I'm glad you found that out. Imagine if I'd gone on referring to her as a him?"

Jilly nodded. "I'm sure she forgives us. Otherwise, she wouldn't have told us her name at all, would she?" She looked up at Will.

He merely shrugged. Shrugging seemed safe.

Fortunately, Isa took up the slack. "You're absolutely right, Jilly. I can't tell you how grateful I am. My bosses will be pleased."

"Oh," Jilly said, looking around. "This isn't your store?"

Will's gaze followed the sweep of Isa's hand.

"Well, you know," she said, "I sometimes feel as if it is. But to tell the truth, two wonderful ladies merely allow me to work in this magical place." She indicated a shelf of pottery. "Those are Hannah's. She's one of the store's owners." Turning toward the front of the shop, she motioned with her hand. "Come, let me show you Tadie's work."

Jilly leaned back against Will as Isa reached into a glass case and pulled out a lacy necklace with a ruby or some other deep red jewel at its center. Jilly's fingers hovered just above the gem.

Isa nodded. "You may touch it."

Gently, his daughter ran a finger over the surface of the gem and the gold that surrounded it. "It's beautiful. Like a fairy necklace, but big enough for a lady."

"Now look in the glass there," Isa said. "See that ring and the other pieces? Some are silver, some gold."

Will leaned in behind Jilly as her nose touched the glass.

"Tadie must be a very nice lady."

"Why do you say that?" Isa asked.

Will watched, fascinated.

"She makes things my mommy would have liked." Jilly turned to Will. "Wouldn't Mommy have liked that necklace?"

Will couldn't have said anything if his life depended on it.

Isa must have noticed, because she directed Jilly's attention back to the array in front of them. "Would you like to try on something?"

Jilly pointed to one of the smaller rings, a simple setting in silver with a stone the color of her own green eyes. She had just slipped it on her finger when the bells jingled over the door, and a dark-haired man in jeans entered. Will recognized him immediately.

Isa looked up and smiled. "Be with you in a minute."

Either the creep was blind, or he wanted to pretend their earlier encounter hadn't nearly killed Jilly. With a casual wave at Isa, the man wandered just as casually toward them, keeping his sunglasses in place, even though the store's lights weren't overly bright.

Will guarded his expression so Jilly wouldn't see the anger he wanted to unleash, but she evidently hadn't noticed the man. When the ring spun around on her finger, she slipped it over her thumb, holding it up so everyone could admire it. "Pretty," she said as the stone's facets refracted the light. "Daddy, do you think we could buy something of Tadie's when I grow up?"

Will was about to answer when the stranger cleared his throat and took a step closer. "Speaking of Tadie," he said, drawing everyone's attention, "is she coming in today?"

Jilly sucked in an audible breath and sidled closer to Will, hiding her face in his shirt. He held her close with one hand. His other hand fisted.

Isa stepped around the counter. Her back straightened perceptibly, and her frigid glare reminded Will of his elementary school principal. He wanted to applaud. "She comes in when she wants. May I give her a message?"

"I'd like to surprise her." The creep's gaze traveled around the store. "She's done well for herself, hasn't she?" When he nodded toward the case, those dark lenses seemed to probe Jilly. "These hers?"

Jilly trembled at Will's back.

Just let the fellow say something to her. Just let him do something *remotely* threatening.

Isa's lips thinned. "Why don't I tell her who was asking." She didn't make it a question.

The man raised his palm and his eyebrows along with it. "No need. I'll check back later." With a dismissive salute he sauntered out of the shop.

Will unclenched his free hand. It itched.

"Hmm," was all Isa said.

Jilly slid the ring off and handed it back to Isa. "Thank you for showing it to me, Mrs. Isa."

"You're welcome, but it's just Isa."

"I like your name."

"And I like yours."

Taking one last look at the closed door, Jilly pressed toward the glass case, her hands resting on top as she examined its contents. "How old is she? Tadie, I mean."

"She's not as young as you, nor nearly as old as I am."

"I'm seven. And almost a half."

"Then she's much older." Isa seemed to study Will for a moment. "I'd guess she and Hannah are more your daddy's age."

"Aren't you and my daddy the same age?"

With a tinkling laugh that sounded like the bells over the door, Isa said, "You little darling. No, I think I'm old enough to be your daddy's big sister, if not his mother."

Jilly's jaw dropped open and her eyes rounded. "Oh, *not* his mother."

"Why not?"

"That would make you as old as my grandmother, and you can't be."

"Why ever not? Don't you like your grandmother?"

"I like her a lot. But she's so *old*."

"Well, of course, I wouldn't want to be *that* old."

Will coughed and put a hand on Jilly's shoulder. "Now that we've settled the age issue, perhaps you'd like to move on to another topic."

He mouthed, *I'm sorry,* to Isa.

Isa's hand fluttered, reminding Will of a butterfly's wing that settled instead of taking flight.

"I hope you and your daddy will come back to see me whenever you're in town," Isa said, leaning toward Jilly before turning to include Will in her invitation. "It's fun to meet someone who likes Jasper and his friends."

"When we're not busy working on the boat, we'll come, won't we, Daddy?" Jilly said, glancing back at the toad. "We've got to get her fixed so we can go to Baltimore."

"Baltimore, is it? And what will you be doing in Baltimore?"

"Our friends are supposed to meet us there. Only, something's wrong on the boat. So we can't go until it gets fixed."

"If you need information," Isa said, "I'm pretty sure we have a list of parts places and phone numbers somewhere. Tadie will be in either this afternoon or tomorrow. She'll know where it is."

"You certainly make a stranded cruiser feel welcome. I'd love to see the list." He patted Jilly's head. "Good thing you wanted to stop in here, First Mate."

Jilly beamed.

"She's indispensable," Will said, holding the door for his daughter.

"I can see that."

Back on the street, Jilly asked, "What's indispensable?"

"You. It means I can't do without you."

She reached for his hand. "You're indispensable too."

"So, Miss-Most-Important-Person-in-My-Life," he said, glancing at his watch, "what do you say? Let's grab that cab, go to West Marine, and see if we can find what we need. We'll come back to have an early dinner in town."

"Could we? A hamburger would be lovely."

Oh, Jilly. Will touched her soft cheek. Sometimes she was so like her mother. He could almost hear Nancy's low voice whispering through Jilly. "Lovely," Nancy used to say. "That would be lovely." He knew Jilly's mimic was unintentional, but the pang of loss felt like the scrape of a blade on raw flesh. He looked out over the water for a moment so she wouldn't see the flash in his eyes.

Will was pretty sure a *ka-ching* went off in the cabbie's mental cash register at the prospect of a trip to West Marine, all the way on the far side of Morehead City. Jilly didn't seem to mind. She wiled away the drive by discussing their promised dinner.

"Can we go to that place we saw, Daddy? That place next to the shop with Jasper and Penelope?"

Will dipped his head as if considering the matter. "It did look very much like a restaurant where a person could get a real hamburger."

"With fries and ketchup?"

"Absolutely."

"And a soda?"

His eyes narrowed, and he exaggerated a frown. "Soda?" He cleared his throat. "You mean, one of those terrible-for-you-full-of-sugar drinks that the crew of the *Nancy Grace* has forsworn?"

Her eyes widened as she nodded.

Touching one finger to his cheek, he raised his brows. "Madam First Mate, do you consider this the sort of day that requires an exception to the no-soda rule?"

Jilly straightened her spine even more and mimicked his finger on the cheek for a moment before her head bopped back up. "I do, Captain, sir."

Will peered down his nose at the skinny creature next to him, who seemed ready to burst into giggles. "Then," he said stiffly, "I so order it."

That sent Jilly over the edge. "Oh, Daddy, you are so funny."

* * * * *

Will rowed them back to the *Nancy Grace*, the oars sliding into the still water with barely a splash, pressing them forward, up and in, up and in, occasionally slapping the surface when he missed a beat.

Their trip to West Marine had proved fruitless, which meant another day's delay. But they'd had fun, and that's what mattered. That had to be what mattered.

Jilly brushed her teeth and climbed into bed. She said goodnight to her animals while she combed out her hair. Laying her comb aside, she expelled a deep, loud sigh, apparently for his benefit. "Daddy," she called. "You haven't heard my prayers."

He sat on the edge of her bunk. Enough light filtered in the open hatch that he could see her expression as she waited with her hands folded, ready.

"Dad-dy." She drew out the word in rebuke. When he smiled and bowed his head, she began. "Dear God, thank you for the soda and the hamburger. And thank you for that pretty store. And for telling me Penelope's name. Please bless Isa." She popped open her eyes. "Is it okay if I call her Isa?"

"It doesn't feel polite enough?"

Jilly gave her head a quick shake.

"Well, I think it's polite to do what she asked."

Jilly shut her eyes and bowed her head again. "Sorry, God. I'm back. Would you please tell Mommy I love her and miss her? She's doing okay, isn't she? And please bless Daddy and Nana and Pop-pop and Auntie Liz and Uncle Dan and, oh yes, bless Andrew and Daffy and I don't remember the big brother's name, but bless him too. And help Daddy figure out what's wrong with the motor thing and help us get to Baltimore in time to play with them again. You know we promised—"

"No, we said we'd try. Remember?"

"I know. Cruisers never travel by schedule. Okay, but, God, if you could get us there in time, it would be lovely, and I'd thank you a whole bunch."

She looked up at Will through her lashes, pressed her eyes closed, and said a quick, "Amen." When she opened them again, she held up her arms.

He leaned in and let them circle his neck. She smelled slightly of little-girl sweat. He'd have to see about showers tomorrow. "Goodnight," he whispered, kissing her cheek.

"Goodnight, Daddy."

"Don't let the bedbugs bite."

She smiled that precious smile so like Nancy's and turned on her side, tucking her knees up and hugging Tubby.

"Love you, punkin," he said as he stepped over the sill and into the salon.

He turned down the lamp and headed up to the cockpit. Sounds drifted across the water—music from someplace on shore, laughter, a shout or two, pots clanging on a large ketch anchored nearby. A slight breeze blew across the water, cooling the evening air.

Jilly wanted to get to Baltimore. After that they were supposed to head over to the Eastern Shore where her Aunt Liz had a home. But Liz reminded him so much of Nancy, sometimes the hurt was more than he could bear.

Maybe they'd get north in time. And maybe not.

Disappointment was something Jilly had learned early— disappointment and pain. He'd done his best to make it up to her.

He just hoped he was doing enough.

Chapter Four

Squawking ducks woke Tadie. Ducks, seagulls, sometimes even a pelican plopping out in the creek, acted as her alarm most mornings, although today it would have been the shimmering heat if the ducks hadn't started things so early. Not even the hint of a breeze sifted through the screens. Yesterday's thunderhead had dropped rain east of here, up around Davis, and had made a spectacle of itself shooting lightning out over the banks, but only oppressive humidity drenched Beaufort.

She flicked the switch on her bedroom coffeemaker, curbing her impatience as it dripped to fill one cup. Stirring, sipping, she sighed. Was anything better than a strong cup of coffee, brewed just right and colored to a creamy topaz? She carried her cup to the bed and watched the light brighten as the world came awake. An outboard *varoomed* to a start someplace on the creek—a fisherman or perhaps one of the dinghies from an anchored yacht.

Eb wandered in from his night's roam through the house and leapt up next to her, nudging her free hand with his head. She stroked down his back once. "Good morning to you too," she said as he settled at her hip.

The coffee's aroma filled the room until the heady scent of

jasmine eventually took its place. Mornings like this, the heavy air held fragrances close to home, which was why her mama had planted jasmine to lace up the trellis out front. Mama had called it the perfume of the gods, and though the flowers only released their scent at night, it lingered.

Tadie eased away from Ebenezer, who uncurled and rolled toward the spot she'd vacated on the sheet. "Spoiled cat," she said as she headed to the shower.

She'd just turned off the water when the phone pealed. She grabbed a towel, walked to the bedside table, and checked the caller ID.

"Got your coffee yet?" Hannah asked.

Tadie smoothed the towel on her bed and lay on it to drip-dry, relishing the feel of dampness on her flesh as the fan blades above her bed whirred methodically. "That and a shower. This might be the last cool moment I spend today."

"Call the electrician."

"I'd better. I dread even having to go to the Food Lion."

"Least it's air conditioned. Why you put up with your mama's antiquated ways is beyond me. If you'd listened last year when I told you to get a new system installed, you wouldn't be moaning now."

Tadie finger-combed wet hair away from her face. "I should have, but it was too soon. You know?"

"I suppose." Hannah's sigh sounded loud, as if she'd rearranged the receiver before breathing into it. Tadie heard a spoon click against porcelain. That explained it. Hannah, who sometimes added so much sugar her spoon ought to stand upright, was multitasking.

"That's better," Hannah said after a slurping sip. "Now, before you go brave the heat, I've got to tell you about the Straits house."

"Ah. The dinner."

"You okay hearing this?"

"I'd better get used to it. He's not leaving town just because I want him to."

"First thing, I told Matt he needed to get home early, but that didn't happen. I don't get him. He got his brother down here so he wouldn't have to work so much, and still he goes in at seven and works all hours. What's Alex going to think?"

At the mention of Alex's name, Tadie turned on her stomach and pulled the towel over her exposed flesh. "Maybe Matt can work inside and Alex out," she said after rearranging the towel to make sure nothing showed.

"Maybe, but Doc says Matt needs to avoid anxiety and follow orders, or his old heart might not make it."

"Are you sure that's what he said? I mean, forty-one's way too young to have an old heart."

"Especially when we're not so many years behind."

"I'm counting on at least forty good ones left."

"Why stop there? Why not fifty?"

"Mama and Daddy." Saying their names together made Tadie's throat constrict. She hated remembering all at once like that. Easing into it was one thing, but thinking how quickly they'd gone after her brother Bucky's death was another. Four years total, and now she was the only one left.

"It won't happen to you. Don't even think about it. Anyway, I've got to convince Matt to follow the doctor's orders to lose weight and take his meds. He's got to be proactive if he wants to get better."

"Amen to that. No more heart attacks."

"I refuse to let that man die. I told him flat out he can't leave us to turn into doddering old biddies, keeping each other company as we rock on our porches and gossip about the neighbors."

"Lord, preserve us."

She thought back to their old taunt. "Oo-oo, girl, you're gonna turn into another Miss Etta." Miss Etta was Tadie's next-door neighbor and just a little scary. She used to chase her daughter's chickens, her wispy hair flying as she waved a broom and screeched until Juniper corraled her mama onto the porch and her rocker. Not too many years ago, Juniper had also taken to creaking in that chair and watching the world pass along Front Street. But Juniper didn't do broom handles, and the chickens were long gone.

"You tell Matt to be good," she said. "Is Alex actually helping?"

"He'd better be. The place is a stress factory. You wouldn't think logging would be so hard, but Matt makes it that way. He can't keep his fingers out of all the pies they've got going, and he wants everything to happen his way. You know Matt."

"Got to be the boss."

"Exactly. And speaking of people being bored, it seems Bethanne's already begging Alex to get her a place in New Bern so she can leave the Straits house for weekends."

"I bet that went over well." Tadie tried to keep her voice light, but her fingers clutched the receiver, picturing Bethanne the last time she'd seen her, years ago, strutting around, eyes glinty and her smile all Cheshire-like.

"She finished redoing the house, got rid of all her mama's beach furniture, and replaced everything with heavy antiques. Lord love her, the place didn't used to be so bad. Now it's like a mausoleum. Anyway, she's done with that and gone to spending days playing bridge and sunbathing at the Dunes Club. When winter hits, she'll go batty." A cup clinked as if against its saucer. "I need you to come and play buffer at dinner on Friday."

Had Hannah actually suggested she join them? "You know that won't work," Tadie said with an edge to her voice. "Anything else, I'm there for you, but I'm not putting myself in front of, between, or anywhere around the two of them—not if I can help it."

"I figured you'd say that. I can't beg or bribe?"

"Nope. Not for love nor money. If he hadn't called the other day, maybe. I hadn't given him a thought for ages. But calling put him over the top on the creep list and got me dwelling on things I don't want to think about."

Like missing out on all she'd never see or feel from this side of marriage. But she wasn't about to say those things aloud.

Hannah heaved an exaggerated sigh. "I know. Bethanne makes me want to stuff a rag in her mouth. I already had to deal with her by myself last night. I'm not sure I can stand a repeat so soon. Matt's the one who invited them, bless his little heart. I wanted to wring his neck when I heard him tell them to come."

"Why don't you take them out? You could let a waiter be the buffer since I won't."

"You think?"

"Take them to Aqua. Or Front Street Grill. If you hit either of them late enough and reserve a table near the bar, you won't hear a thing Bethanne says."

"Girl, you're bad. Didn't I hear something about a new chef at Aqua?"

"You did. And Isa says she's living up to her press." Tadie narrowed her eyes at the thought of Alex and Bethanne snuggled in one of those booths, enjoying tapas and wine.

At least she wouldn't have to witness it.

"I'll see what Matt says. Anyway, I'm hoping they'll move up to New Bern. She's pushing for it."

"I guess New Bern's got enough Northerners to keep her happy."

"They can all go complain together," Hannah said. "They'll tell each other how awful the South is and ask why we don't do things right."

"Can't you just hear it?"

"Matt asked her once why her parents stayed if they hated it so much. Why they didn't just move back where they came from."

"And what did she say?"

"That they could afford it, and the weather suited. Then—and, honey, I remember the moment because I wanted to toss my drink right on that frosted hair she was so busy patting—if she didn't put on her superior smile and go on about what they could make of the town if only enough educated people moved in. As if nobody south of the Mason-Dixon went to college." Hannah mumbled something that sounded like *dratted Yankees.* "Why the heck don't they do us all a favor and go home?"

"Please, yes." Tadie almost felt sorry for Hannah, but not enough to sit down to dinner with Matt's kin. "For your sake, I wish I could help you. Friday wouldn't work anyway because it's Elvie's surgery."

"I'm sorry. I'd completely forgotten."

"If they find it's spread ..."

"Don't say it."

Tadie wiggled on the towel, the phone cradled at her neck, watching the sunlight dapple the wall. If only Friday were over with, Alex long gone, and she could take *Luna* out—this time alone—with only the water beneath and the sky above, with no need to think and no need to speak.

* * * * *

Errands forced her into a sundress. She patted her cheeks just thinking about the heat index with all that humidity hanging on and the forecasters expecting it to hit a hundred degrees by noon. What the county needed was a good drenching.

As she loaded her grocery cart, she imagined herself barricaded behind the air-conditioned walls of her studio. She'd stay cool—and go stir crazy.

Hannah was right. It was past time to call George Harding over at Miller Electric and see about getting a whole-house unit.

Her mama had been the one who'd hated air conditioning. Tadie could just hear Caroline Longworth's soft voice drawling instructions as she fanned herself and rocked languidly on the big front porch. Her mother had lived in a pretend world, where all things were lovely and all people good. Where gentleness reigned and mint juleps, sipped in frosted glasses, were the perfect elixir. Miss Caroline would wave at folk who'd stop to stare at their big house and turn to ask whoever was sitting out there with her, "Should we offer them tea?" She never realized the passersby were merely gawking tourists impressed by the white columns and imposing façade of the house her great-granddaddy had built.

After stacking the last can on the pantry shelves, Tadie let Eb back inside and dialed to retrieve her messages. Alex's voice surprised her. "Sorry I missed you at the shop yesterday. Perhaps this afternoon?"

She suppressed a curse as she punched *Delete*. Would he never let her be? She itched to chuck the phone across the room. It would thud on impact and the plastic would shatter, making a lovely cracking sound—and putting a hole in the plaster. Of course, when James came to fix it, he'd raise those bushy grey eyebrows and ask a question or two.

It was too bad cursing and chucking had been bred right out of her.

She set the kettle on to boil. Speaking of James, there he was, rattling around with the hose out back, watering the wilting vegetable garden as she'd asked. She could have turned on the hose herself, but that would only upset him. Now that her daddy was dead, James hated accepting a paycheck, said he didn't do enough to warrant one.

Which is why she hadn't sold her daddy's Lincoln. Nor simplified the garden.

Summer days when James handed over more tomatoes than anyone could use—or zucchini or peppers or beans—Elvie Mae just smiled her sweet smile and said, "Ain't these gonna make a goodly supply?" And when the extra jars Elvie put up got hauled over to the women's shelter, she said, "Your daddy'd be mighty proud."

Darling Elvie Mae. Tadie felt herself tearing and wiped at her eyes. If James couldn't think straight about the parched garden, he must be really worried.

While the tea steeped, she distracted herself with thoughts of phones and folk who shouldn't be using them to call other folk. The nerve of that Alex. As if he could just smile his smile and speak his cajoling words and think that was it, she'd come running.

Not *this* woman. Not even if Alex Morgan were the last man in Beaufort.

Stepping off the porch and out from under the oak tree's canopy, she felt the full force of that August furnace. And there was James, hoeing around the tomato plants, hatless as usual. She'd told him to find inside work on days like this, but he'd answered the same as always. "Sun don't hurt me none, Miss Sara. Sun and rain, they each got a time and a place. God be seein' to that."

The remembered cadence of his words rolled over her, the sound of his deep baritone, which had barely weakened with the passing years. James would never call her anything but her given name. Just like her mama.

On first hearing Bucky use the nickname with his little-boy lisp, Mama'd tilted her head and squinted, trying to make sense of it. "But you're Sara. I remember."

Daddy'd patted Mama's hand, but he'd gone back and forth, fitting the name to his audience. Didn't matter to him. As for James, he'd stood staunchly with Mama. "Miss Sara, your mama wants to call you what she named you and I ain't arguing. Not with you or your little brother. No sense distressin' Miz Caroline."

In the garden, James passed a blue bandana over his brow and picked up the hoe. He began the upswing, saw her coming, and the hoe stopped its arc. "Hey there, Miss Sara."

"Good morning." She tried to put a lilt in her voice, tried to overcome the heat and the thing they didn't want to mention. "Thought you might like something cold," she said, handing him a tall plastic cup filled with water and ice cubes. "I put a pitcher of sweet tea on the back porch. You get thirsty again, you can fill up there."

"You didn't need to do that, Miss Sara. I could fix it myself."

"I know Elvie Mae's the one who reminds you to drink when you're out here, and she's probably not feeling up to it today. So you come help yourself."

"Mighty grateful to you."

"How's her headache?"

"'Bout the same. Seems she's frettin' more'n she lets on."

Tadie laid a hand on his shoulder. She was surprised to feel bones protruding where there'd always been muscle. James couldn't be older than sixty.

She shook off those thoughts and lifted her hand, speaking briskly as if that gave the words authority. "She'll be fine." They just had to get through the next few days. Surely, the surgery would show the lump encapsulated and not spread to her lymph nodes—or elsewhere.

"Yes ma'am. The good Lord's watchin' out for her. I know that."

"When's Rita coming?"

"In time for her mama's surgery. Only got the one day off, even it being Friday, 'cause she's supposed to help depose some folk for her boss the next mornin'."

"I'm sorry."

"Don't make no sense to me, but she's that way." James kicked at a furrow and stomped it flat. Seeming surprised that he'd mashed it, he shook his head and loosened the dirt again with the hoe.

Fidgeting wasn't like James. "Fly her into New Bern," Tadie said. "And take the Lincoln to bring her to the hospital. The surgery's not until ten. You'll make it back in plenty of time." She brushed a wisp of damp hair off her forehead. "You stop your worrying, James. I'll be there with Elvie. Don't you imagine I won't. Think how much Rita's going to need to see her daddy with his big smile waiting there for her. They'll be sticking Elvie with a needle, making her drowsy. You won't miss much. And all the time, I'll be right there holding her hand."

"I sure thank you, Miss Sara."

"It'll give Rita more time with Elvie after the surgery. And I'll take care of the ticket. I'm just grateful they reinstated flights to Raleigh."

"You don't need to do that, Miss Sara. I got the money."

"Let me do it this time. Rita's family to me too."

James looked away, but not before Tadie saw the glistening in his eyes. "She thinks the world of you."

Tadie felt her own tears hovering. "Elvie Mae will be just fine." She cleared her throat. "If there's anything there, they'll get it. She has a good doctor."

James nodded. "She does that. And a lot of prayers. I got to remember that."

Chapter Five

It was after two o'clock when Tadie pushed open the door to Down East Creations and set her box of finished pieces on the counter.

The bells brought Isa from behind the jewelry case. "I'm not a happy camper, Tadie. I just sold your periwinkle necklace to a very undeserving woman from Charlotte. I kept imagining it with my new blouse. Wouldn't it have been perfect?" She twirled, modeling the gauzy peasant blouse and bright turquoise skirt.

Long and lithe, Isa Wellington looked more like a leftover hippie than a math teacher who'd decided to move out of Wilmington, Delaware. The moving out of Delaware part didn't seem all that strange. Either Tadie or Hannah would have done the same thing. But Hannah, who'd barely squeaked through Algebra II, never could wrap her mind around the fact that someone who looked like Isa could actually enjoy math enough to teach it.

"You don't want to let anything go."

"I know. I wish I could find a place at home for every single piece in this shop, especially yours and Hannah's. And Stefan's. I seem to like each new thing you bring in better than the last. I'm hopeless."

"At least you sell them."

"I tried putting spells on my favorites, but that didn't work.

All I have to do is covet something and it takes on a life of its own, reaching out to grab a buyer." A very dramatic sigh escaped Isa's lips. "No matter how I try to shoo customers away or at least try to get them interested in something else, they hone in on just that item, and there I am, writing up a sales slip." Her silver hair fell forward over her shoulders, and she loosed a second sigh. "It's very discouraging."

"But a good thing for us." Tadie looked around. "So where are those mugs you said I should see?"

Isa waved her toward the back of the store. "I'm not sure about that glaze. The colors look muddied."

Examining one of the tall stoneware pieces, Tadie saw exactly what Isa meant. She replaced it and selected another. "You think Carolyn was having an off day?"

"If so, she's been having a lot of them lately."

"If only her glazes were as polished as her wheel work."

Isa turned away from the shelf. "What did you bring?"

"Hope you like them," Tadie said, handing over the necklace, bracelet, and earrings she'd crafted from a weave of gold and silver.

Isa oohed. "These are gorgeous. I bet I could have kept the periwinkles if we'd had these earlier."

As Isa made room in the glass case, Tadie glanced to the wall where Stefan Ward's watercolors hung. "Did you sell the one of the shrimp boat at dusk?"

"I did. We hang a new one, I get attached to it, and before I can take my next breath, out the door it goes."

"If he'd only relocated earlier," Tadie said, grinning at her friend, "we might have turned a profit the first month we opened."

"And probably shut down some store in Michigan."

"Montana."

"That's right. I was thinking water, not mountains. Didn't he sail down?"

Tadie spoke over her shoulder as she headed to her office. "He bought the boat someplace in New England. Newport, I think."

"And stopped here, like a lot of us." Isa followed, pausing in the doorway. "Speaking of sailors, the cutest little redhead came in with her father who, by the way, is not hard on the eyes either. He needs to fix his boat before they head north. Don't we have a list of suppliers?"

"Oh, were they here? I saw them rowing to shore, and you're right. She's adorable." Tadie opened a drawer and flipped through her files until she found the list.

Isa took it from her. "That poor man's trying to get things ready for them to meet friends in Baltimore."

"I'm glad we can help."

"When I told Jilly—that's the little girl—about you and your work, she said she wants one of your rings."

Tadie had just clicked to open a file in her accounting program, so it took a moment for Isa's words to register. "My rings? Is her daddy going to commission one?"

"Maybe when she's older."

She typed in the date, said, "Okay," and expected Isa to leave. When the other woman just stood there, Tadie looked up. "What?"

"She's such a winning little thing. I wish you could have heard what she said about your pieces. Something about knowing you're a nice person."

"That's sweet. Were you singing my praises?"

"That wasn't it. She said your jewelry was the sort of thing her mother would have liked. I think her mother must be dead. It's very sad." Isa started to turn away and then paused. "Oh, and there was some fellow in here asking about you. Drop-dead gorgeous, let me tell you, but something about him bothered that little girl and her daddy. I thought he was rude. Pretty face, lousy manners."

Drop-dead gorgeous and asking about her? Rude and gorgeous? Well, Alex's message had said he'd been here. Tadie closed her eyes, took a deep breath, and set her fingers to the keyboard.

Later, waiting for the computer to shut down, she gathered her notes and stacked them in the to-do box. Working with numbers had helped some, but she still felt jittery. Too bad she'd brought her car when what she needed was exercise. She took one last look around, grabbed her bag and hat, and closed the office door behind her.

Isa glanced up. "Those last customers walked away with Hannah's salad bowl. At this rate, Hannah'd better cleave to that wheel."

"She'll be glad. It'll keep her mind off Matt."

Isa slipped the receipt into the drawer. "I know she's worried about him. Any more news?"

"Not that I've heard."

"Well, Jilly and her daddy ought to be returning soon to get that list." Isa's eyes danced as she pointed toward the metal animals in the back. "She told me what Jamie's fish is called."

"You mean the kind of fish?"

"Its name. Seems Jamie made a she-fish named Penelope."

"Sounds like Jilly has quite an imagination."

"I think she heard the fish speak to her."

"I-sa."

The way she said Isa's name must have raised the older woman's hackles, because she tilted up her chin. "Jilly heard *something*."

"I'm sure your young friend has a wonderful imagination. Children often think they hear voices grown-ups can't."

"Anything's possible," Isa said with an expressive shrug.

"What? Do you also believe in ghosts?"

"Sure, don't you?"

Tadie grunted out a half-laugh. "You must enjoy the town's annual ghost walk." Noticing the light in Isa's eyes, she said, "Look, I know a lot of folk do it in fun, but Elvie drummed into my head that ghosts aren't something we ought to mess around with."

"Well, honey, the church and its teachings are something I'm not messing with anymore. So, I'm open to alternatives."

She'd forgotten about Isa's ex-husband, a pillar of whatever church they'd attended up north. And an abuser. Wishing she'd kept her mouth shut, she turned to leave as bells tinkled over the door.

The child's hair danced to a stop off the sides of her head, and her sneakers squeaked on the floor. She was all bright colors: red hair, pink T-shirt, yellow shorts and socks. "Oh, it's you," she said to Tadie, her eyes sparkling and her voice chirping like an excited bird.

"Hey there," Tadie said, answering with a smile and setting her things on the counter. "I'm glad to see you again."

The father approached more sedately, nodding first at Isa and then in her direction.

"This is the jewelry lady, Jilly," Isa said, gesturing. "Will, Sara Longworth."

Tadie held out her hand and felt a sailor's calluses in Will's strong grip. She pictured him hauling line, his brown hair blowing, his eyes squinting against the sun. Startled that a simple handshake could provoke such images, she cleared her throat and looked from father to child. The little girl's cat-like eyes appeared huge in her face.

"Isa tells me you're on your way to Baltimore," Tadie said, glad words finally made it past her lips. "I hope you'll enjoy Beaufort for a little while first."

"It's pretty here." Jilly pulled at her father's shirt. "See? I told you she was a nice lady."

"And you were right." He looked back at Tadie. "Was that a sharpie you were sailing?"

"Eighteen feet on deck, three feet of bowsprit."

"I know sharpies from the Connecticut waters. And we saw some in your museum."

"A local yard built *Luna*. Who built your boat?"

Jilly piped in. "A man designed her just for us."

When her daddy tweaked her nose with a grin that mirrored the child's, Tadie felt an absurd pang. "How fun for you," she said, before pretending to be distracted by something on the counter.

Isa pulled the list from her pocket and handed it to Will. "Tadie found this for you."

Jilly scooted up close to Isa and whispered, "Is her name Sara or Tadie?"

Overhearing, Tadie answered the child. "Sara's my real name, but I've been Tadie to most of the folk around here since my little brother first said it in front of the other kids. Of course, to my mother I was always Sara. There aren't many left who still call me that."

"Is your mother dead?" Jilly asked, still whispering.

Tadie bent low. "Yes, Jilly, she is."

"Mine is too. And Tadie's a pretty name, but I like Sara. It sounds like you."

Tadie straightened slowly. "It does?"

"To me it does."

Isa stepped forward and smoothed a stray hair out of the child's face. "Why do you think so?"

"Because of the necklace."

Isa's "Aha!" made Tadie wonder if she'd missed something. "Do you know what the name Sara means?" Isa asked.

Jilly shook her head.

"Princess," Isa said, as if proud of the fact. Tadie squinted at her, wishing she knew how to shush her friend.

Jilly's eyes widened. "It does?" At Isa's nod, the child returned her gaze to Tadie. "Then that's why."

Tadie laughed self-consciously. "You think I'm a princess?"

"Magical," Jilly said.

Will nudged his daughter's shoulder, turning her toward him. "Sweetie, I think you're making Ms. Longworth uncomfortable. Remember?"

Jilly's head bowed, and she seemed suddenly fascinated by her sneakers. Finally, she spoke in that soft little voice. "I don't always have to say everything I think. I'm sorry."

Oh, dear, she'd embarrassed the child. "It's okay." When Jilly still didn't look up, Tadie bit her lower lip, wishing she knew what to do. She mouthed at Will, *May I?*

He nodded.

She bent slightly, extending a hand. "Jilly, come here, will you? Just for a minute?"

Jilly looked up at her father. When he nodded, she slipped her hand in Tadie's and followed to a window seat, climbing up next to Tadie and focusing intently with such trust that Tadie wished she'd left well enough alone.

But she had to say something. "You know what I think, Jilly?"

The child shook her head.

"I think you have a special gift."

Jilly's eyes widened, big and green and surrounded by pale lashes. "You do?"

Tadie nodded, dredging up a confidence she didn't feel. It should have been Isa over here—Isa, who was so good with children. "I think you have the gift of seeing the heart of things." She turned to include Will. "Am I right? Does this young lady see with her heart?" She thought she caught a sudden gleam in Will's eyes.

"She does indeed."

Jilly piped up with, "My mommy knew stuff. She was special."

Tadie squeezed Jilly's hand. "I'm sure she was. And do you know why I'm so sure?"

Jilly watched her with those round eyes.

"Because your mommy had you, and *you* are special."

Jilly's little arms flew around Tadie's neck, and she clung tightly. Tadie clung right back.

Heaven help her. Was it possible to fall in love this quickly? She couldn't let it happen. Jilly and her daddy would fix their boat and leave. Tears threatened as she loosened Jilly's arms.

On a deep breath, she stood, pulling the child to her feet. "Okay. So." She tried for a light note. "The thing is, I'm not a real princess—which you'd know if you lived here and knew me better. Right, Isa?"

"Well ... "

"Isa?"

"Right. No princess."

"But you may call me anything you wish. Is that a deal?"

Jilly's head bobbed, but after a moment's pause, she said, "Could you pretend to be a princess so I can call you Princess Sara?"

"Jilly, sweetheart, no," Will said. "Isn't there enough excitement in your life as it is? I mean, how many girls get to be first mate on the *Nancy Grace*?"

"That was my mama's name. Nancy Grace Fillmore Merritt." Jilly squared her thin little shoulders and lifted her chin. "The Fillmore is from my grandpa. The Merritt's from us." She pointed from her daddy to herself.

"Is Jilly your real name?" Isa asked.

"Don't you think," Tadie said, "we've had enough with real names and nicknames?"

Isa waved her quiet. "I want to know."

Will answered, a slight quiver at his lips. "Jilly is Gillian Grace."

The quiver distracted Tadie. No, no. Not good. She slid her focus back to his daughter.

"My real name is spelled with a *G* but my nickname has a *J* because Mommy said people would say it easier that way. And I'm named Gillian after my mommy's grandmother." She stopped for breath. "You already know where I got the Grace."

"Lovely names." Isa turned her shoulder toward Tadie, fluttering fingers behind her back. Tadie glared at them, but she didn't interrupt when Isa continued. "It's a funny thing about the South and names. As soon as I got here, I discovered that nicknames don't come in the normal way, from shortening a too-long or too-fancy one."

"Like I'm Jilly."

"Exactly. Did you know there are men called Bubba and Tee and Bo wandering this very town?"

Jilly's pigtails slapped against her jaw when she shook her head. Tadie risked a glance at the child's father, who seemed as mesmerized by this recital as his daughter. Isa's story only gained momentum. "Look at Tadie's name. Does it sound anything like Sara? I tell you, Jilly, this is a fascinating place for curious people."

"It is?"

"Yes ma'am. Why, over at the library, there's actually a woman named Teensy. Now, how did she get named that? She's not tiny at all, but she's not fat either."

Jilly giggled and put her hand over her mouth.

"And I heard one of our customers call his wife Saso."

Jilly looked from Isa to Tadie. "It's okay if you call me anything you want—Jilly or Gillian or even Grace."

Tadie tilted her head. "I like them all, but perhaps calling you Jilly would be easiest."

Jilly seemed to think about that. "Then maybe I'll call you Tadie."

"It would be less confusing. I'll know right away you're speaking to me."

"You mean because your mommy isn't around to call you Sara."

"Exactly."

Jilly slid up close to Tadie. "Will you sail over to see us on our boat?"

"How about as soon as we get a decent breeze?"

Will waved the list. "We'll be on board when we're not out provisioning. Thank you again for this." He glanced over at Jilly. "And for everything."

Tadie and Isa watched the pair walk out the door and past the shop window. Setting her sun hat on her head, Tadie looked at Isa. "An amazing child."

"Certainly precocious and loving. Her mother must have been something."

With one more glance out the window at an apparently empty sidewalk, Tadie said, "Jilly makes me wish I'd known her." They might have been friends, she and that other woman who'd sailed. Who'd been a cruising mother. And wife.

How very sad for them.

"Will seems like an interesting sort." Isa leaned on the counter, resting her chin in her palm. "But he rather pales next to Jilly, doesn't he?"

"I know exactly what you mean. I can see the child clearly, but the father's face has already blurred. Poor man."

Isa's lips twitched.

Tadie turned and headed out the door, curious about that twitch. What did Isa mean by it? No telling, of course. But still ...

* * * * *

After dinner, Tadie wandered out to the dock to watch the sun set. Ibis trailed toward their roosts. A couple of pelicans dove *ker-plunk* for fish. Boats slipped up the creek, heading to the anchorage or dockside, their engines breaking the quiet but without force, the low RPM barely producing a wake. Where had they been? She imagined the stories their owners could tell. Light glowed from the portholes on a number of boats, including the one that belonged to Will and his daughter. It would be fun to sail out there now, just to be friendly—to see how they lived, what they cooked, and what they did on board that gorgeous boat.

The slap of oars on water brought her head around. She waved. "Hey, Mr. Bobby, how're you doing?"

"Hey, Tadie," her two-doors-down neighbor called. "Glorious evening."

"Sure is."

He tied up at his dock and hefted a bag from the old wooden rowboat he said kept him young. Bobby Simons was the kind of seventy-nine-year-old she'd like to become—agile and quick-witted, although his hair had thinned to nothing, and he had a slight limp from a car accident years ago. The screen door slammed behind him, and he called out a greeting to his daughter, Angie, who'd come home when her mama died, saying she'd sure rather live with her daddy than with that poor excuse for a husband she'd left behind.

What a picture Bobby and Angie made, not a thing about them alike except their sense of humor, which Bobby said was what had saved them both all these years. Angie laughed, declaring she hated to leave the house because it took too much effort to haul all her extra weight out the door and load it into the car. Still, she'd do it, mostly to go to the CVS Pharmacy or the Food Lion once a week. At least there she could lean over the cart, and if something needed fetching, Bobby'd just scoot off and bring it to her. Bobby was as proud of Angie as if she'd been homecoming queen, saying nobody could cook as fine a meal. Besides—and here Tadie could hear him cackle with glee—who else was gonna try to beat him at chess or cribbage?

A light came on in Bobby's living room, and Tadie turned back in time to see a gull land on a nearby piling. The gulls made a mess of her dock with the shells they cracked for dinner, and they were a loud bunch, always squawking and cawing, but they seemed proud and fearless with their black and yellow beaks and pink legs. Bucky'd called them greedy so-and-sos as he shot picture after picture of them swooping after whatever he'd just tossed in the water. But they sure photographed well. At least she had his pictures left to remember that sweet, sweet boy. Their bright, shining star.

Tadie swiped at the tears she couldn't help. *Oh, Bucky.*

Soon, darkness folded over the creek, and mosquitoes forced her inside. After letting Ebenezer out and in again, she took a long shower, washed down the bathroom, put away laundry she'd brought up earlier, and finally climbed in bed at nine thirty. She clicked on one of Prokofiev's works in the CD player. Too rousing. Debussy's *Nocturnes* came up next, perfect go-to-sleep music. If she could only get comfortable. The wrinkles irritated her, so she sat up and smoothed out the fitted sheet. The seam in her nightgown rubbed a line in her hip. She straightened it and turned on her back. Her skin itched. She scooted around, trying to scratch the illusive spot.

Ebenezer hopped off the bed and padded downstairs. She couldn't blame him.

Throwing off the sheet, she hoped for a breeze. The fan's whir only stirred the heavy, hot air. What in the world was wrong with her?

Another CD clicked on. *Baroque Music for Relaxing.* The supposedly soothing instrumentals were not performing as described.

Nothing was performing as described.

She felt ... empty. No, half full. As if she needed more.

But more what?

She reached down and pulled the sheet up to her neck, glaring at the dark. No one better say she needed a man. She'd known a few of those, including one momentary fiancé, and there was no way she needed another one. Men were messy and complicated—or boring—

and before long, the ones she wanted to keep either ran off or died.

Lord, have mercy, but this was not the way she wanted to feel every time she faced darkness and bed. "You up there, God? I could use some help here," she said, thinking this new focus of hers was probably the first step to becoming what she most feared. Didn't crazy folk worry a thing to death until it became their only reality?

She was on a slippery, downhill slope, sure as anything.

Chapter Six

Will aimed both cabin fans toward the motor hole, with the sweat rag handy to wipe his face when the drips got near his eyes. Jilly sheltered from the sun in her bunk, trying to read, while her own fan puffed air, swirling the heat and not accomplishing much else.

He'd found the leak and would go hunting for more parts later, but right now he needed to put things back together so they could hightail it out of threatening weather if they had to. Only a fool sat at anchor with no means of escape, and escape meant having a working engine.

They'd been back to visit Isa just before Down East closed, to thank her and Tadie for the list of suppliers. As Jilly'd hoped, this really was a friendly place. Isa's invitation for Jilly to stay at the store while he went on a supply run had his daughter bouncing on her toes and pleading for him to agree.

So that was on this afternoon's schedule. It would get Jilly out of the heat and give him a chance to take a rental car around town to visit more parts stores without having her pull on his pocket all the time, asking to get a drink or ice cream, go to the bathroom, or buy pizza.

He tightened another nut, which for some reason reminded him of last night's dream. *Fool.* Why should a simple job like this bring back *that* memory?

He shook his head, swiped again at the drops of sweat slipping through his eyebrows. Man, he had to get over this stuff. But Nancy had seemed so real, lying next to him in the bunk and wanting to talk. So he had. He'd told her about Jilly's leap forward in reading this year and how he trusted their baby with so many things.

"Too many," he'd whispered. "I know. Too many."

She'd listened and touched his forehead like she used to, running her fingers through his hair, brushing it back. He could swear he felt her—felt the slight scrape of fingernails across his skin, felt breath on his cheek, and then her kiss.

Her kiss.

Why'd he have to wake? And why so soon?

He banged the wrench against the metal block and cursed. *Why?*

His gut clenched, and he pressed a fist against it, trying to shut out the pain and the need. *Please. Tell me why.*

Jilly's voice roused him, calling from her cabin. "Daddy! You almost done?"

He sniffed and straightened. "Almost. One more nut to tighten."

That finished, he lifted himself out of the hole and closed the floorboards. A little cleaner on his hands, a quick wash, and they could go. At least he had something to do this afternoon. He didn't think he could bear sitting. Waiting. Thinking.

He ducked his head into Jilly's cabin. She had one leg crossed over the other knee, Tubby tucked nearby, and a book resting on her chest. He smiled and cleared his throat so he wouldn't startle her with his words. "You want to spread some peanut butter while I clean up?"

She dropped the book and bounced off her bunk. "And then the store?"

"And then the store."

"Okay!"

* * * * *

The days moved as languidly as the air. Hot and windless weather had trapped Tadie in her studio, where she soldered fittings to pieces that needed repair. Last night had been so hot she'd made a bed on the couch in the studio and slept there with the window air conditioner on high—until Ebenezer had scratched on the door, wanting in. Still, with him settled on a cushion nearby, her mind had relaxed and sleep had returned.

Now, she grabbed a muffin and headed to the hospital, freeing James to go fetch Rita. She held Elvie Mae's hand until the nurses wheeled her down to surgery.

The novel she'd brought to keep her company failed after three measly pages. Sticking it back in her bag, she flipped through the magazines on the table next to her seat—news, farming, fishing, or decorator journals. She picked up *Newsweek*.

Every so often, a doctor came through the doorway, his mask lowered over a loose shirt, his matching pants baggy like pajamas, a cap still covering his hair. He called out a name and spoke in hushed tones to the anxious family.

Tadie looked up each time someone pushed open either door—the one families used or the one reserved for medical staff. Finally, James stood holding the door for Rita to pass into the room.

The fluorescent ceiling lights exaggerated James's wrinkles and darkened the circles under his eyes to black. Had he looked this haggard yesterday?

She tossed aside the magazine and stood to pull the young woman into a fierce hug. "Rita, love." To both, she said, "They took her down early. She told me to make sure you two don't worry."

"The good Lord's watching." James patted Rita's hand and let loose a crooked smile.

"She'll be just fine, Daddy. She's strong."

"That's right, sugar. She sure is."

Tadie, noting Rita's crisp khakis and the orange-and-red silk top, smoothed back unruly hair and tried not to compare the silk to her own pale blue cotton. "You sure don't look like someone who just got off a plane, counselor. Love the colors." They were perfect with Rita's café au lait complexion.

Rita glanced around at the beige-pink walls. "Sure better than the paint they slathered in here. Why on earth don't hospitals hire a decorator?"

"Looks like they be trying to make folk sick, don't it?" James said, his effort at a grin still coming up lopsided.

Surely this whole thing was a scare for nothing, and that lump would be just a big mess of extra tissue, the needle biopsy a mistake. Tadie couldn't imagine any other truth right now. She reached across the table and touched Rita's hand. Rita clasped hers in return.

"I can't believe you had Daddy come get me in the Lincoln."

"Hurt your image, counselor?"

"Sure does. Good thing we don't have any clients from New Bern. They'd think I'm on the take."

"Drugs, at least."

"And what would that make me?" James peered over the reading glasses he'd donned so he could see what he was looking at in a farm magazine.

"The drug lord, Daddy. Cruising around in your posh car—"

"Picking up a gorgeous young thing at the airport," Tadie said.

James threw an arm around Rita's shoulders. "You sure are some gorgeous thing all right, sugar, and ain't I the lucky one? You look just like your mama when she was a girl."

Tadie watched James cuddle his grown-up daughter, and a familiar ache spread in her chest. All these years without—no, she wasn't going to let her mind go there. "I'm going to get something to drink. Can I bring you anything?"

"No, thanks, Miss Sara."

Rita shook her head. "Daddy stopped at Dunkin' Donuts in Havelock so I could refuel. I'm set."

Tadie's feet carried her to the vending machine and outside to the shade of a live oak tree. A train clackety-clacked through the center of town. She listened to its slow progress, imagining it offloading something at the port, onloading something else. There was always some huge, foreign-flagged ship waiting at the pier.

The heat began to refocus her thoughts. Sweat trickled down her chest and stuck tendrils of hair to the back of her neck. She held the cold bottle to one cheek and then the other.

Why had she come out here? To get away from thoughts of scalpels and the fact that people could die from a doctor's mistake no matter how simple the procedure?

Please, no.

She stood there, watching the cars, timing the stoplight changes, until she couldn't stand the heat any longer. The blast of cool air against her damp skin brought a momentary shiver, but now that she was back inside the hospital, she had to smother a panicky feeling that this visit would end as badly as so many others had.

People died. Families disappeared.

She paused in the empty hall outside the waiting room and gulped in stale, contaminated hospital air, pressing against her stomach until the spasm passed. When she pushed open the door, all she saw was James exiting the other way. A doctor must have fetched them.

Such an early meeting didn't look good. If everything were okay, the doctor would have said Elvie Mae was doing fine and left it at that. It must really be bad.

Tadie returned to the hall and paced, peeking her head in at every pass until she finally saw them.

Rita walked right into her embrace. "Oh, Tadie," she said, bursting into tears.

"It's okay, love. Whatever it is, we'll deal with it." She grabbed a tissue for Rita, who blew loudly.

James shuffled slowly back to his seat. "They took out the lump in her left breast. Of course, we knew they'd do that, but they went after a bunch more. Radical, they called it, didn't they?" He turned to his daughter. At her nod, he continued. "They took stuff around the lump."

"Lymph nodes?"

"That's right. He said they'll test those."

"He thinks it's all out," Rita said, glancing at the notes she held. "It looked intact. Isolated, he said, but they won't know for sure until they test to see if it had clean margins. And see if the lymph nodes are cancer-free. It was hard to hear. Once he said he didn't have real answers, I just wanted to get up and go be with her."

James rubbed fingers down his face, pausing to cover his mouth before dropping both hands to his lap. "I thought they'd know more."

The sadness in his voice hit Tadie, and she bit hard on her bottom lip to keep the tears at bay. Reaching out to both of them, she touched James's arm and squeezed Rita's free hand.

James stared at the door, probably thinking of Elvie Mae back there, waking without him.

"When will they be sure?" she asked Rita, whose fingers clutched hers right back, pinching where the stones in Tadie's ring caught flesh.

Rita let go. "We have an appointment for Tuesday."

"Can't he make an educated guess?"

James wiped his forehead, letting the handkerchief trace across his eyes. "Won't say."

"But he thinks he got all of it, right?" Tadie's voice cracked. She cleared her throat and tried again. "Right?"

James nodded. "Somethin' like."

Digging for another tissue, Rita sniffed. "Please, yes."

"Okay then. Let's hold on to that." Tadie needed to help them figure out how to get through the next bit. "Elvie's strong. No cancer's going to defeat her."

James's eyes held a little more spark when he looked back at her. "You're right, Miss Sara. Elvie's a fighter. And she's got faith, stronger than mine. But now we've got to help her win."

"We will. You know we will."

"Daddy, I'm going in to sit with Mama. I want to be there when she wakes up."

"That's good, sugar. I'll be in soon."

James watched Rita walk down the corridor. "It's going to kill

Rita to leave her mama right now."

"I'll get her back to New Bern. You stay here with Elvie. It's you she'll be needing."

James patted Tadie's hand. "Thank you, Miss Sara. You're a mighty good friend."

"Family, James. Family."

"Yes ma'am. Family."

Chapter Seven

Tadie steered down Highway 70, quiet until Rita was ready to talk. The traffic worsened as they passed Newport and approached Cherry Point Marine Corps Air Station.

Finally, at the intersection with Highway 101, Rita let out a long breath. "This has to be hard on Daddy. They've been together such a long time."

Tadie flicked her signal to change into the left lane. "I remember when I first heard about your daddy coming to work for us." Out of the corner of her eye, she noticed Rita's fingers unlocking.

"Mama has her version, Daddy his. I'd like to hear yours." Rita paused. "Please?"

She remembered the day Elvie Mae—her black braids flapping and her white apron strings dangling loose and threatening to trip her—had come squealing in to tell her James was coming to be their chauffeur and gardener. "I guess I was eight, maybe nine. Your mama was a grown woman of almost twenty-three, your daddy a good ten years older. I can't remember when your mama first started working for mine—helping your granny out in the kitchen or with the dusting. She took over after your granny broke her hip."

Rita's breath hitched. "Nana had bone cancer, didn't she?"

"I'm sorry. I'd forgotten that." They'd come to another light. Tadie reached over and gave a quick squeeze to Rita's limp fingers. "But one doesn't necessarily mean the other. You know that."

Rita nodded. "Go on."

"Well, your mama was a tiny little thing with that beautiful butterscotch coloring like yours. She kept her hair slicked in those braids with bright plastic barrettes. You've seen pictures. And her laugh. It's still beautiful, but as a little girl, I thought she was like a fairy. Her laugh danced in the air and made everyone around her smile. So the day she bounced in with her good news, I remember clapping my hands right along with her. She had that effect. I giggled and told her I'd always wanted to say, 'Home, James,' like in the movies. We had so much fun."

"You ever wonder if Daddy would rather have been something other than a gardener and chauffeur? He's not educated, but he's smart."

"He is that. Did you ever ask him?"

"Yeah, and he just smiled. Told me he had a good life, working for good people. Said he was glad to help Mr. Samuel and Miss Caroline." After a moment, Rita asked, "Did Mr. Samuel really need a driver back then? How many people in Beaufort had a chauffeur?"

"You'd be surprised, especially among the older folk. As for Daddy, I think his eyesight plagued him from an early age. So, yes, James made life a whole lot easier for him. Especially driving at night. Mama wouldn't get behind a wheel and was deathly afraid every time Daddy tried to convince her to learn. As far as the gardening, Mama loved plants, but she never could grow anything."

"But he'd been places—in the Army."

"Yes, but once he met your mama, that was that. There weren't many jobs in Carteret County in those days for someone who didn't work the water or big machines."

"She could have gone off with him someplace where he could have gotten more education, done better for himself. Why didn't she?"

"I don't know, but I think it had to do with my mama. Elvie knew she was needed right here. You remember how Mama was."

"We all loved Miss Caroline."

Tadie acknowledged that with a nod. "When your granny got sick, Mama was lost. But Elvie—she could make her smile like no one else. Well, no one except my daddy. Elvie and Mama had a real bond."

"I've wondered about this more times than I can tell you. I even asked my mama once. But between the two of them, my parents are the smilingest people I know. When they don't want to answer something, they just smile at you. It's frustrating."

"You're right about that. Many's the time I've seen it myself."

"What about you?" Rita's voice had lost its hint of a whine, and she asked as if the question had just occurred to her. "Do you ever think about leaving Beaufort?"

Tadie hesitated, because this wasn't something she felt comfortable discussing. "I don't normally let myself think about it. I came home because I had to."

"I guess. But now?"

"Now, I have the shop and my work. I have a good life."

"But haven't you wanted more? You used to talk about travel, about going back to Europe for a year or two."

Tadie noticed the speedometer needle had slipped past sixty. Backing off, she felt the tension in her right leg tighten, threatening a charley horse. She reached down to squeeze the muscle.

"You okay?" Rita asked.

"I'm fine. I didn't sleep well last night."

"Mama?"

"Yeah."

"Maybe when she recovers, you can take that trip."

"Maybe." But she didn't see how, not with all these obligations.

Besides, did she still want to go?

On the long drive home, all she could think about was a shower and bed. Some hotshot barreled past her once she got to 101, a fool who should have known better. A mile or so later, she passed his car parked on the shoulder in front of blue flashing lights, and she smiled for the first time in hours. But the smile faded quickly and didn't make her feel any better.

Worry about Elvie Mae segued into thoughts of the supper at Hannah's. Maybe Hannah would drop some arsenic in her guests' wine.

With a sigh, she whispered, "Sorry, God." Really, she needed to quit imagining murder and mayhem. She'd been raised better than that.

* * * * *

Although the water cleansed Tadie's skin of dirt and sweat, she couldn't scrub away the knot in her stomach. She wanted to call Hannah, but Hannah was getting ready for guests. A phone call might prompt her to badger Tadie into joining them.

Tadie could tell Hannah no, say she wanted to go back to the hospital to sit with Elvie. Or she could repeat that she never wanted to see Alexander Morgan again—although she did wish she could be a fly on the wall. But that was pure nosiness. Hannah would hoot and tell her to get her sorry ass dressed and over there. And then Tadie would have to act horrified that Hannah had said *ass* instead of something more refined, mimicking either Hannah's mother or her own. Or, she'd have to rebuke Hannah for calling hers *sorry* when the only sorry thing about it was a little more width and a few more curves than either of them had enjoyed in those teen years when the joke first started.

The memory amused her. Back when their bodies had just begun to mature, Hannah had decided they ought to practice sashaying so they could wiggle their way down the waterfront and impress the boys working boats for their families. Tadie's sashay had brought Hannah to her knees, doubled over with laughter. They'd never been a match for Bethanne's practiced swish when she first showed up in town.

Drawing her mother's gold-handled brush through her damp hair, Tadie tried to picture her younger self—the one who'd loved to sail and dream and hadn't yet had her heart broken. But all she remembered was sitting in front of this same mirror, her own brush in hand, trying to tame the untamable.

* * * * *

If she knew one thing back then, she knew plain. All she had to do in those early years was stare into that silvered glass, and she'd see it staring right back at her.

It wasn't fair. Some quirk of genetic roulette had landed her with a nondescript oval face and masses of unruly brownish hair that alternated between light and dark, streaked and not, depending on how much time she spent in the sun. Nothing like her mother's soft blonde curls or elegant profile. That same gene game had won Tadie a pair of big, almond-shaped eyes and set them to lording it over high cheek bones and a strong jaw. While these features made girls drool over her brother, Bucky, they looked ridiculous on her. And those eyebrows. Who else had such dark winged things, tamed only by plucking? Her nose was straight, but too short. Her mouth smiled wide enough to meet her ear lobes when she got to laughing. Her hair always broke free from clips or bands and wouldn't stay neat and in place, no matter how many pins Elvie Mae stuck in when she set it, and in spite of the best permanent wave Hairdo Beauty School and Salon had to offer.

But then, she was Samuel Ellis Longworth's daughter, and there wasn't much she could do about her bloodline. The Longworth genes made women ogle her daddy and her brother. Lucky them. On her, they repelled the boys or made them treat her like one of the guys.

And that's how it was—until she hit eleventh grade. That year, Alexander Morgan took notice. Alex had black wavy hair with a long thatch on top that he had to brush off his forehead—or flick off when he knew girls were watching. And his eyes. The first time Tadie had seen those eyes of sea-blue with hints of green, like two miniature Caribbeans, her heart had flipped. From then on, every time she walked past Cape Lookout Travel Center and caught a glimpse of the poster showing the sea around Antigua, she yearned to sail on that green-blue water with Alex Morgan.

Alex wasn't just gorgeous, he was smart—maybe the smartest boy in French Four. He and Tadie had vied for top honors since middle school, with Alex winning in math and science, Tadie in the humanities. But that was fine with Tadie. She was going to be a writer. Or an artist.

Alex listened. He asked her opinion about things, important things like life and art and the future. Early on, she'd figured out most boys liked to hear their own voice best. Alex seemed different.

She and Alex talked after class, at lunch, sometimes on the walk home when he got out of Chemistry Lab early enough to catch up to her, and when Tadie's best friend Hannah wasn't hanging on her arm. He even started going to youth group at church just to see her, but he stopped not long after their first date. Between him, Hannah, and his brother Matt, they got her more interested in going boating or to a movie most Sunday nights. She followed along because it felt so fine to walk around with her arm tucked in Alex's.

The first time Alex asked her out, they went to Atlantic Beach, drove bumper cars, and had triple ice cream cones. The same flavor—chocolate almond with a scoop of vanilla in between. The second time was to an old Cary Grant movie, *North by Northwest* or *Charade*, she didn't remember which, only that it was scary. She could still feel the prickles that scooted all over her skin when their elbows brushed on the armrest, and she didn't move hers away.

Alex kissed her late one June night as the lightning bugs flitted and flashed their tails and the crickets fiddled as if trying to wake the dead. From the large porch, she could hear her little sharpie creak against its mooring lines down at the dock when the canned laughter from Miss Etta's TV quieted. Miss Etta didn't like wearing her hearing aid, but her daughter Juniper came early to turn it off and get Miss Etta ready for bed.

Alex turned her to face him and settled his hands on either side of her face. When he rubbed one thumb lightly along her jaw, her legs went weak, nearly folding when his lips brushed hers. For the second kiss, he pulled her over to the porch swing, and it was a good thing she was sitting, or she'd have been flat on her back from fainting.

That second kiss and the next made Tadie wonder where Alex had acquired such polish. Her only other experience had been back in tenth grade when pimply Greg Matthews caught her behind a dune at a church cookout and slobbered all over her. She'd wanted to puke.

"I'll love you forever," Alex had promised between kisses. She'd almost believed him, even though the words were probably spoken in hope of a reward.

In her senior year, she kept the reward at bay, as much for practical as for moral reasons. She could hear Elvie's voice, warning her to hold herself apart until she married. And she still had a plain face and unruly hair and a mirror that told the truth. Did Alex, when he said she was beautiful?

They sailed and played and fought for valedictorian of their graduating class at East Carteret High School. Tadie won by four-tenths of a point.

* * * * *

Sleep swallowed her thoughts eventually, but morning happened. It always did.

The first call of the day came as she stood wrapped in a towel, still wet from her shower. She let it go to voice mail. When she'd pulled on shorts and a tee, she retrieved the message. A strange voice vaulted over the line, assaulting her with a sugary, "Tadie, hey, this is Bethanne Morgan. How're you doing?" The voice paused for a moment. Tadie's fingers tightened to a stranglehold on the phone. "Hannah was telling us all about your jewelry last night, and I'd love to see some of it. May I come by? After all, we're practically family. Call me."

Tadie sat down abruptly. Alex's wife. What was it with those two, calling her out of the blue? Sixteen years of silence, and now she was bombarded by both of them.

And *family*? Hah!

Twenty minutes later, she rinsed her mug and put it in the dishwasher. Her breakfast had glued itself in a ball just under her diaphragm. She wanted to yell at someone, but at whom? Ghosts?

The house had never seemed so empty. Even Eb had vanished to some cool haunt.

She peered out the open window. The breeze was still too light to sail. Maybe this afternoon. Until then, she should see if Elvie needed anything. Maybe she'd make those brownies Elvie loved.

Tadie had dozens of chores she ought to tackle, designs to finish, clasps to solder. Instead, she picked up the phone and hit speed dial. Hannah's rumpled voice answered on the third ring.

"What's your sister-in-law up to?" Tadie asked. "Why does she want to see my studio?"

Hannah answered with a moan. "Do you know what time I got to bed last night? It's Saturday."

"I know it's Saturday. Bethanne called me at eight-thirty this morning, wanting to come over."

"Lord, love her. She must be bored."

"Thanks."

Tadie heard rustling. "Hold on a minute," Hannah said. Water splashed against porcelain, followed by the sound of gargling. Finally, Hannah came back with, "That's better. Okay, look, you know she doesn't like you. Or any of us, for that matter. She's probably worried about Alex."

"So she wants to visit me? That makes a lot of sense." What was this, some alternate universe they'd slipped into, with no one acting as expected?

Tadie could feel a bout of dermatitus coming on. The doctor said nerves would make it flare, and hers felt as rickety as they had at Bucky's memorial service. She touched her neck, the last place she'd seen a breakout, but her skin felt smooth.

For now.

"I think she wants to case the opposition," Hannah said, the humor in her voice upping Tadie's mad.

"Honey, I stopped being the opposition at nineteen. That's old news."

"Yeah, well, you were right. All's not happy in their world."

"You could have fooled me. Are you sure Matt needs Alex here?"

Hannah's grunt sounded over the airwaves. "I'd like to say no. Bethanne was an absolute pill last night. If I hadn't been so concerned with other things, I'd have pointed at the door and sent them both home to learn some manners."

"I'm listening."

"I went all out, you know? Mostly because I hated them coming and figured I wouldn't give her anything to whine about. Magnolia-blossom centerpiece, pan-fried flounder in lemon-caper butter, mozzarella on tomatoes with basil, my cheese biscuits. But that didn't stop her."

Tadie puffed a pillow behind her back, changing hands and ears as she tried to get comfortable. "What happened?"

"It seems the Straits house is so far in the boonies, it takes an hour to get to New Bern or the club, and thirty minutes to get to our mediocre grocery stores. That's bad enough, but the traffic is terrible. Maniacs drive the potholed roads, and fools pass on curves."

"Lands, Hannah, who knew Carteret County was such a mess?"

"I know. I wanted to slap her. And Alex either ignored her or lit into her when she shot snide remarks his way. It was not fun."

"I'm sorry. You should have taken them to a restaurant like I suggested. Then you could have escaped before dessert."

"I haven't told you the worst of it."

When she didn't continue, Tadie said, "What? What happened?"

"I'm scared."

Tadie's blood pumped double-time as she imagined the worst. "Why?"

"Matt had another episode yesterday. He didn't want me to say anything, and he wouldn't go to the doctor. I think it scared him so much, he decided the best way to deal with it was not to, so he drank himself silly last night."

"That's not like him."

"No. Stupid man. But I am absolutely furious with Alex for plying him with liquor. He knows I won't buy the hard stuff. I guess he showed me when he brought over a bottle and did the honors."

"Does he know how sick Matt's been?"

"Of course. That's why he's here. And I didn't sleep a wink, worried something would happen if I turned my back."

"I am so sorry. How's he doing now?"

"Snoring like the drunk he was last night."

"So that's what kept you awake."

"Hah."

"Anything I can do? You going to sit there and watch him all day or what?"

"He made plans to go golfing with Alex. If he feels up to it, I guess I'll head to the shop for a couple of hours. I have a set of soup bowls ready to go."

"The new green glaze?"

"Yes ma'am. Came out real nice."

"Isa's going to be thrilled. We've got to get Carolyn's stuff off the shelf."

"I know. I saw it."

"You want to be the one to tell her?"

Hannah shuddered audibly. "No way. She'll think I'm jealous."

"I hate doing the dirty work."

"Ah, but you're so good at it."

Chapter Eight

"I sold a cup." Jilly watched from the settee as her daddy fiddled with engine stuff. Pretty soon it would be time to make dinner. Daddy had promised a surprise, but he wouldn't say what.

He stuck his head up. "Only one?" He didn't wait for her to answer before he ducked back down.

She tried anyway. "It was one of those big cups, a mug. You can buy them one at a time. And, besides, they're all painted different."

"Mmm ..."

"You could buy one. There's still some left. You'd like them."

No answer.

"Hannah makes them. They're pretty."

That got her an eye, long enough for Daddy to say, "Hannah?" He grabbed a screwdriver and a rag. It was full of goop.

"Remember how Isa told us Hannah makes pots and stuff? She's Tadie's friend and Isa's boss. One of them. Tadie's the other."

"Mmm ... hmm."

"I met Hannah today. She's the lady in the hat. The one who was sailing with Tadie when we first saw her, remember? Hannah's nice. Almost as nice as Tadie, but different."

The rag flopped over the top of the engine, and Daddy crawled so he was lying on his side. It looked too tight to fit, but he'd done it before.

Jilly wiggled closer to the other end of the settee so she could see him better. "Hannah told Isa I could get paid."

She would have thought her daddy'd answer that one. It was a big thing, earning money. Leaning out and over so maybe he could hear her better, she said, "Real money. A whole fifty cents an hour."

"Drat it!"

Jilly's eyes rounded for a moment before she figured he hadn't been *dratting* the money. He slithered back until he had space to sit up, and she saw what had gotten him mad. She couldn't help it. She giggled as he wiped something sticky off his face with his shirt. It didn't do so good as a rag.

Jilly clambered up to fetch the roll of paper towels. "Here."

"Thanks. What a mess." He scrubbed his face and used another for his hands.

"You almost finished?"

Her daddy sort-of laughed. "Not even close."

"But—"

"Hungry?"

Jilly nodded hard.

That got him out of the hole and the floorboards down to cover it. It also got him headed to the shower. "I'll be quick."

Sometimes Daddy knew quick, and sometimes he didn't. She sure hoped tonight was one when he knew, because her tummy was talking loud.

She wandered to the companionway steps, but not outside. She couldn't go outside without her daddy. Just to the steps. She could sit on the top one and peek out at the water and the other boats. Sometimes you could see fun stuff happening when nobody knew you were looking.

It wasn't dark yet, but somebody on another boat played a guitar. Wouldn't a guitar be fun to learn? Her daddy had given her a flute, but since he didn't know how to play it, she sure couldn't learn. That was the problem with going to school with just your daddy as teacher. If he didn't know something, how was she supposed to?

A big pelican flopped in, head first. Silly thing. Pelicans were funny birds.

It was okay, school on the boat, because she got to go places. And be with her daddy. Nobody was better than her daddy.

But it would be fun to stop sometimes and maybe do some land things, like learning guitar.

"Hey, punkin, what you doing?"

She scooted back down. "Watchin' pelicans."

"What about dinner?"

"I'm ready. What's the surprise?"

"Get your town shoes on. I'm taking you out."

Her eyes got round, and she could feel her mouth drop open. She shut it fast, and bouncing on her toes, said, "Out? Really? Where?"

"I don't know. Do you have any preferences?"

"You mean like where we went before? The hamburger place?"

"Like that. Or we could get all fancy and try someplace else."

"No, I like that one. I could have another burger."

"Or maybe spaghetti?"

"Do they do spaghetti?"

"Can't see why they wouldn't. It looks like a place that knows spaghetti from burgers. I also remember seeing pizza on the menu."

"Pizza! Let's have pizza!"

Jilly hurried to get ready, because she sure didn't want her daddy to change his mind. By the time she'd pulled on her lifejacket, he had the dinghy ready and the motor on. Motors were better if you went out at night, so you could get out of the way if somebody was coming. The dinghy had a little red and green light, but sometimes people went too fast. Not her daddy. But some people.

She looked at the outside of the restaurant this time, just to check the name. Daddy helped her say it. "Clawson's."

They sat in a booth. Jilly loved booths. The place had lots of wood and lots of noise, but she liked watching all the people.

And look who just came in!

"Daddy?" She reached over to get his attention, because he hadn't seen the grown-ups standing next to them. Jilly had. And she couldn't stop grinning.

* * * * *

A voice at Will's shoulder said, "Jilly, hey. Is this your daddy?"

He glanced from the woman to his daughter and back. "I'm Will Merritt."

"Hannah Morgan," she said, extending her hand.

Jilly bobbed in her seat. "Miss Hannah's the pottery lady, Daddy. Tadie's friend. The hat lady. I told you."

She had? Will didn't remember seeing the woman before, hat or no hat.

Hannah turned as an older man joined her. "And this is my husband, Matt." With a nod at each, she finished the introductions.

"We're having pizza." Jilly's eyes glittered. "You want some pizza too?"

Hannah glanced at her husband, who shrugged and said, "Sure, why not? Unless Will would rather not share."

Will liked the crinkle in the other man's eyes, the way his hand settled on his wife's hip. "We'd love to have you join us."

Jilly scooted out of her place and pressed in next to Will without a word.

Hannah took a seat. "You sweetie. Thanks."

"The glass is clean," Jilly said, pointing to her water. "I didn't touch it."

Their server appeared with more napkin-wrapped stainless and two more menus. When they'd chosen the pizza and ordered, the waitress asked if it would be on one check or two.

"One. Here." Matt pointed to himself.

"You don't have to do that," Will said.

"Why not? You included us. It's the least we can do."

Hannah patted her husband's hand and grinned at Will. "Don't deprive him. He likes to be generous."

"See, Daddy?" Jilly said. "I told you Hannah was nice."

When had they discussed Hannah? To cover his confusion, he said, "As is her husband."

"He doesn't remember." Jilly leaned forward to speak across the table, using her best grown-up voice. "Sometimes Daddy doesn't listen when he's working. He was in the motor hole, and something squirted him and got him dirty. That's when I told him about my money. I guess he didn't hear."

"Money?" Will asked. How had he missed the mention of money?

"I told you," Jilly said, still speaking to Hannah, who laughed and explained their arrangement.

Will watched closely as they ate and chatted. Figuring out that the Morgans were good people relieved his last reservation about Jilly spending time at Down East Creations. And wasn't she excited about this new adventure?

Later, he tucked Jilly in for the night, listening to her prayers and bending to kiss her now sweet-smelling forehead.

"This is a nice place, Daddy. It's okay if you don't get the motor thing fixed right away. I like it here."

"What about Baltimore?"

"The kids won't stay there very long. They'll be gone, like everyone. Everyone on a boat, I mean." She settled Tubby under her arm. "But here, people stay. Did you know Hannah and Tadie have been best friends since they were younger than me?"

"Than I, but no, I didn't know that."

"I don't have a best friend, except you and Tubby."

"Well, punkin, maybe sometime soon we ought to stop someplace and make friends."

Her eyes, which had been heavy lidded, opened wide. "Like here?"

Will shook his head. "They have hurricanes here. We need to get the boat fixed and go where the hurricanes aren't so bad."

"How come the people who live here can stay and we can't? Do the hurricanes only get strangers?"

"Of course not," Will said, lightly pinching her cheek. "If we lived in a place with lots of hurricanes, we'd figure out how to cope. But we don't need to bother when we don't live here."

She started to argue again, but Will laid his hand over hers and bent for another kiss. "Close your eyes and dream sweet dreams. And don't let the bedbugs bite."

"Thank you for the pizza."

"I had fun too. Go to sleep."

"I'm gonna pray about staying someplace. Okay?"

"Sure. You should pray about everything."

She should. Of course she should. Just as long as she didn't pray that they stay here.

He switched off her light and wandered out into the cockpit, but the still night invited mosquitoes. As they zoomed in and found their target on his flesh, he retreated below.

See? Mosquitoes and hurricanes. Obviously, they needed to leave. And soon.

Jilly wanted a best friend. Fine, just not in Beaufort. Besides, wherever they landed, she'd eventually tire of it.

He'd have to work harder at finding boats with kids. And figure out where to plant their feet for longer than a couple of days at a time.

Chapter Nine

"I saw him again," Hannah said, her voice breathy over the phone line. "Just now."

"You saw him who?" Tadie stretched on the bed, mimicking Eb's languid pose. She'd hoped for a laugh. She didn't get one.

"The cruiser. Will. The one with the gorgeous boat and the little girl, Jilly. Matt was feeling so much better that we walked down to Clawson's. Shared a pizza with them."

That got Tadie sitting up straighter. "You did? And how was it?"

"I can't believe you didn't tell me how delightful he is."

"I didn't know. How could I?"

"Well, you met them. Jilly said so."

"I spent all of ten minutes with them. I can't gauge the man's personality by that."

"Of course you can. He's got great eyes. And a deep laugh. Matt likes him."

Settling back against her pillows, Tadie smiled. "That's high praise."

"It is. So, when shall we go invade their space?"

"Invade what space?"

"The boat, silly. They said we could come by. You've got the only transportation out there."

"I think he's busy working on it. We'd better wait."

"And then they'll sail away. Waiting is *so* not a good idea."

"They're going to sail away, whatever we do."

"Maybe not. They don't have to, you know?"

"Sure they do. They're on the way to Baltimore."

"Maybe."

"Goodnight, Hannah."

Hannah's teasing laugh lingered, as did her words, although Tadie tried not to give them brain space. No, the *Nancy Grace* would sail away, taking Will and Jilly far from Beaufort. No sense getting worked up about it. That's the way things were.

* * * * *

Tadie managed to make it to the early communion service Sunday morning, the first one she'd been to in months, and stopped to see Elvie Mae on the way home. Now she was trying to distract herself as she waited for the tide, but the words on the page of her book began to blur long before the phone rang. She didn't bother to mark her place, just checked the caller ID, saw it was Rita, and answered.

"How did things go yesterday?" she asked.

"You wouldn't believe it," Rita said. "The witnesses can't keep their stories straight, so who knows what'll happen at trial."

"Maybe it won't get that far." Tadie yawned.

"Maybe. You napping?"

"Just resting while the tide comes in."

"Wish I were there to play with you. Did you see Mama?"

"On my way back from church. She was all smiles. You know your mama."

"Yeah, I do." Rita paused. Tadie heard a heavy exhale and the words, "I'm gonna give my notice tomorrow."

"Whoa. You're moving back? Your daddy know this yet?"

"You're the first I've told. I was thinking maybe you could help soften him up."

"Soften up *James*? With him so proud of you there in Raleigh? How do you propose I do that?"

"I don't know. Tell him I won't have any trouble finding a job there."

Tadie snorted. "You think?"

"I won't, because I'm not going to keep practicing this sort of law. This isn't me. It isn't what I signed on for."

Tadie waited, not sure where this was going.

"Look," Rita said, following the word with a distracted, "Hold on a sec." A click sounded, as if she were closing a door, followed by the clop of hard soles on stairs. "Okay. Sorry. I'm off to meet Martin, the doctor I was telling you about. Anyway, I bet I can find something in Morehead or even New Bern, where I can help at the other end. You know, before the wife gets herself killed or the kids get dropped out the window."

"Your folks aren't going to want you quitting just because your mama's sick. You know that."

"I'm doing it anyway. I've got to be there." The clopping stopped, and keys jingled.

"I agree. Come on home."

"You'll talk to Daddy?"

"I'll talk to him. Can't guarantee he'll listen. Anyway, you come stay in the big house until you get settled someplace else. Eb and I could use the company."

"It's not as if I haven't been hanging out in the big house since I could first crawl up those back steps." Tadie could almost hear Rita's smile. "You know how I always felt about your family, especially your daddy. Remember how his library always smelled of old leather and cigar smoke?"

"Yes ma'am. I still smell those cigars sometimes."

The sun had filtered through the tall windows of that room for years, settling on the Persian carpets until it bleached out a whole section. Mama used to stare at that faded area and say Daddy ought to draw the drapes, but he liked watching the dust dance in the light. To distract Mama, he'd wrap his arm around her and make her giggle.

"You two used to sit in there," Rita said, "reading or playing chess, and I'd come knocking on the door with a message from my mama. Your daddy would twinkle his eyes at me and say, 'Little Bit, you come on back when you've told your mama what she wants to know. I've got just the book for you.'"

The memory elicited a warmth that had nothing to do with the heat outside. "You were so short, your feet dangled off the couch." Tadie shifted and got up to check out the window. "Tide's almost in."

Rita wouldn't be distracted. She must be worried if she needed to reminisce so much. Tadie sat back down as the younger woman continued. "It meant a lot to me that you didn't mind your daddy inviting this little colored girl to invade your sanctuary. I read every book you and Mr. Samuel picked out for me."

"Daddy sure was proud of you."

"Not many white folk would have paid for somebody not their kin—somebody the wrong color—to go to university."

"Like I said, you made him proud. Besides, I don't think we knew you were black."

Rita's bark of laughter warmed Tadie's heart. "Honey, I didn't either. I used to think we were all just different shades. My daddy was the dark chocolate, your mama, the vanilla ice cream. Daddy said I was like a delicious piece of toffee he wanted to gobble up."

"Come summer, when Bucky and I spent all that time outside, there wasn't much difference between you and me."

"I know it. Of course, Bucky was light, like your mama."

"I envied my little brother's blond hair and light eyes. It wasn't fair at all."

"Well, at least you never had that nasty Lovell boy call you a *nigger*. When was that?"

"You were pretty young. I'll never forget you running in the house, weeping your little eyes out, asking your mama what that boy meant."

"It shook my world pretty bad, but you and your daddy just kept on treating me the same. There's nothing any of us wouldn't do for you."

"You all are family, Rita. You know it."

"And my daddy's gonna kill me."

"Honey, your daddy has never laid a hand on you. He's not going to start now that you're grown up."

"Maybe. And maybe not."

* * * * *

Had she really said she'd get in the middle between Rita and James? She supposed it came with always wanting to fix things, but hadn't she learned yet it was best to let folks sort out their own problems?

She hadn't. She'd probably go to the grave sorting through other people's messes. Folk had always come to her, even way back in elementary school. Take it to Tadie, she'll help. Ask Tadie. She'll do it.

"Too bad," she said to Eb, who was polishing the floor with his swishing tail, "it didn't make me an expert at solving my own problems."

Well, she wasn't going to say anything to James until they got Elvie home. He had enough to worry about without thinking Rita was throwing her life away, which was exactly what James would say.

Tadie changed into shorts and a T-shirt, grabbed sunscreen, her hat, and a long-sleeved shirt. On the way out, she picked up a water bottle and a jar of cashews. What she needed was time on the water. It had been a long, windless few days.

She'd just stepped onto her dock when a green sports car pulled to a stop at the curb and Alex climbed out. She kept moving.

"Well, lookee here." The sound of shoes on the wooden boards followed her. "Hey, you going sailing?"

She turned long enough to glare in his direction. "Alexander Morgan, was I not perfectly clear the other day?"

He lifted his sunglasses and grinned. "You mean when you said you want me to leave you alone?"

"That's it. Seemed perfectly clear to me." And wasn't she pleased that his looks held absolutely no appeal?

"Well, honey, I don't think I can do that." He dropped the glasses back in place and kept walking toward her.

"Go be with your wife, Alex. And get off my dock. You're no longer welcome here."

She continued on down to her little boat, dropped in her supplies, and eased into the cockpit. Alex came up behind her to loose the dock lines. She ignored him as she hoisted sail.

"I'd be happy to keep you company. I miss our sails together."

She stowed her shirt and pulled a cushion from under the stern decking before glancing up at him. "You know something, Alex? I don't. I don't miss anything about those days. So you just go away." She flicked her hands at him as if trying to shoo a fly. "Toss me the lines, please."

He seemed unfazed by her rejection as he threw the dock lines into the boat. Tadie pushed off, tightened sheets, and scooted out into the creek. She did not look back.

The breeze was just aft of the beam, propelling *Luna* smoothly out of the creek. After she'd trimmed the sails, she barely had to hold *Luna's* tiller, so she sat back and scanned the horizon for signs of life on the water. When it was time, she tacked toward the banks. The sun now shone directly on her without the sail to block it. Adjusting her cap, she dug for her water bottle.

One of the smaller Cape Lookout ferries zoomed past, leaving a wake that rocked *Luna*, bouncing her boom as she bashed down the far side of the swell. A family was on board, the daughter young, much like Jilly.

Which reminded her. Hadn't she promised to sail over to see their boat? She'd make it casual, unhurried. And without Hannah to smirk and hike her eyebrows, she could pull it off.

She gybed and headed back toward the anchorage, feeling a sense of anticipation that grew as *Luna* zipped among boats anchored here for a night or a week—or even longer. She sighed as she passed one with La Rochelle, France, painted on it. The one from Hong Kong had already upped anchor and slipped away.

North, probably. Maybe Maine. Wouldn't Maine be fun in the summer?

Well, she'd only get there if she made it happen. She could drive up. Charter a boat to go whale watching. Stop in Newport. Cape Cod. Take a ferry to Nantucket or Martha's Vineyard.

It just took doing. Getting off her duff and making a plan.

Living on the wild side.

Chapter Ten

The *Nancy Grace* sat tucked between a large ketch and a smaller wooden sloop out of Galveston. Tadie brought *Luna* alongside and pointed into the wind so the sails luffed.

"Ahoy, *Nancy Grace*. Anyone home?" She grabbed the boarding ladder, holding *Luna* steady.

Through the open companionway hatch, she heard an excited little voice say something before Will's head appeared.

"Hello, there. Would you like to tie up and come on board?"

"I would, but I thought I'd invite you and Jilly to join me for a short sail first."

As she spoke, Jilly squeezed past her daddy. "Can we ... plea-eese? You can work later."

He yanked at a pigtail. "Okay, squirt. Get your life jacket. I have to wash my hands and close the engine hatch."

"Do you have any water you can bring? Just for yourselves. I've got cashews."

A few minutes later, Will handed down the bottles of water and a bag of pretzels. He helped Jilly clamber down the ladder into *Luna*. Tadie pointed the child to a cushion and suggested she sit forward, to port of the centerboard well. Will climbed in and held the ladder while Tadie returned to the tiller. At her nod, he pushed them off. Without direction from Tadie, he took care of the jib sheet, adjusting it as she found her point of sail.

"What a pretty boat." Jilly ran her hands over the varnished rail, her eyes shining.

"Thank you," Tadie said. "Where would you like to explore? The wonderful thing about a boat that draws only six inches with her board up is that we can slip into all sorts of places."

Jilly looked at her daddy before saying, "How about up to the lighthouse? Can we see dolphins? I love dolphins."

"We might. You never know what we'll see. But I think Cape Lookout would work better when we have all day. Besides, on an incoming tide, we'd have a hard time making it around the hook. I have to pay attention to the currents."

"'Cause you don't have a motor."

"Yes ma'am. Now, if the wind blows from exactly the right quarter and with enough force, the current isn't such an issue. But most of the time, *Luna* only likes to take to the Cape going with the flow. I remember once waiting too long to come back, and it didn't matter what I did, *Luna* wasn't going to behave."

Jilly's eyes rounded. "What did you do?"

"Well, if Billy Doyle from over Harkers Island way hadn't been heading home about that time, I would've had to wait out the tide. That's why I always take plenty of water and a jacket or long shirt with me."

"What did Billy Doyle do?"

"He tossed me a line and towed *Luna* around past the riptide that cuts through there."

"Those smelly motors come in handy sometimes, don't they?" Will said.

The teasing look in his eyes elicited the same in Tadie's. "I sure hate to admit it, but Billy saved me several hours of kicking my heels on the banks."

Checking out *Luna's* rounded transom, he asked, "Have you ever thought about an electric motor, maybe on a bracket?"

"I have, but I like the challenge of trying to sail everywhere. It was my fault I got caught on the wrong side of the tide, and it sure taught me a lesson I haven't forgotten."

When Jilly asked what she'd do if a storm came, Tadie tried to sound soothing and make light of something that obviously frightened the child. "I check the weather and stay home if the weatherman suggests anything bad, or if I see clouds building. But around here, there's always someone like Billy willing to lend a hand. Worst case, I could go over to the lighthouse and get help from the rangers. This whole area is a national park. Did you know that?"

Jilly shook her head.

"Years ago, folk lived over on Shackleford or had fishing camps there, but a storm took out most of the houses. Then, a while back, they decided to keep this place from turning into another Nags Head or Atlantic Beach, full of houses and people, crowded and busy with no place left for wildlife. They made these banks federal parkland. Now the rangers protect the birds that use the dunes for nesting and the wild ponies that still roam out here."

"That's a good thing."

"It certainly is." Tadie checked ahead. "It's about time to tack. You want to help me?"

Jilly's head bobbed.

"Come sit up here, just on the other side of the tiller. Do you know the difference between steering with a tiller and a wheel?"

Jilly said, "Un-unh," as she scrambled up on the stern and stared at the tiller Tadie held.

"When you're steering the *Nancy Grace*, you turn the wheel the way you want to go, don't you?" Jilly nodded. "Well, with a tiller, you push it in the opposite direction. Can you find the wind?"

Jilly looked around, as if searching for it.

"Look at the sail, sweetie. See how the boom hangs over the boat on that side—the starboard side? The wind is pushing it over, so that means the wind is coming from there." Tadie pointed to port. "Does that make sense?"

The girl nodded again.

"Where would we point the bow if we want to go into the wind?" As Jilly's finger pointed left, Tadie said, "Excellent. Which way do we push the tiller to make the bow go that way?"

Jilly pointed right.

"Good. That will make the bow come around *into* the wind. You got that?"

Again Jilly's head bounced as she reached for the tiller.

"Just one more thing," Tadie said. "We don't want to keep the bow pointed straight into the wind, do we?"

"Nope. That would put us in irons, wouldn't it, Daddy?"

"Yes ma'am."

"And how do you know that term, young lady?"

"'Cause we've been in irons before on the *Nancy Grace*."

"I'm afraid so," Will admitted. "When Jilly's daddy wasn't paying enough attention to what he was doing."

"We've all been there." Tadie nodded to Jilly, who placed her hand on the tiller. "Push the tiller hard toward me until *Luna's* bow comes right around and goes *through* the wind to the other side, then you can ease the tiller back to the center. You've seen your daddy tack your boat, right?"

"And I've helped."

"I'm sure you have. A first mate is indispensable on a boat."

"Daddy," Jilly said proudly, "that's our word."

"It is indeed."

"Indispensable?" Tadie asked, pleased to have hit a chord.

"Yep."

"Okay, Miss Indispensable, let's see what you can do." Tadie pointed at the tiller. "Remember the commands?"

"Ready about?" Jilly called loudly.

Will took hold of the jib sheet. "Ready."

"Hardy Lee!" Jilly shouted, making Tadie laugh.

"Go for it. Hard-a-lee." *Luna's* bow began to turn. "Mind your head," she told them, pushing Jilly's down slightly so the swinging boom wouldn't clunk into her. "Ease the tiller back toward the center, gently. Excellent. You're a natural."

"Daddy, did you see that? I tacked the boat all by myself."

"You did, didn't you? And I imagine in that one maneuver you learned more about sailing than you've been able to learn on the *Nancy Grace* in the year we've been cruising."

Tadie adjusted the main sheet. "You sail her for a while, okay?" she told Jilly.

Jilly gripped the tiller for all she was worth.

When the main began to luff slightly, Tadie laid her hand over Jilly's to guide her. "See how a slight movement will bring her back on course? Keep your eye on the wind—where it's coming from—and on how much sail you have out. Shall I give you another short lesson?"

Jilly soaked up the information until she could recite the points of sail with faultless accuracy.

Will beamed at his daughter. "Your mother and I both learned on a small boat like this."

"I know. I'm going to learn to be as good a sailor as you are."

"I'm glad. Then you can be captain of the *Nancy Grace,* and I'll be your mate."

Jilly laughed as she turned to Tadie. "Isn't my daddy funny?"

"He is that," Tadie said, glancing from one to the other.

Will handed around the pretzel bag, but Jilly was too engrossed in her job.

"Not yet." She turned back to Tadie. "Don't you worry about getting stuck out here?"

"You mean becalmed?"

Jilly looked to her daddy.

"No wind," Will said.

"What do you do if you're way out and it stops blowing?"

Tadie looked from Jilly to her daddy. "Do you always start your engine when there isn't any wind, or do you sometimes just drift along, enjoying the water and the stillness until the wind comes up again?"

"Not often," Will answered. "We're usually in a hurry to get into port, because I never enter a new anchorage after dark. I don't want to take any risks with the cargo I carry."

"He means me," Jilly said, pointing to her chest.

"Precious cargo indeed," Tadie said. "I never go so far that I can't get home before dark, unless I'm pretty sure of finding help, like at the Cape. When the wind dies, I've got options. I can toss out an anchor on one of the shoals and either wait until the breeze returns or accept a tow from a passing boat." She pointed to the oar resting behind Will. "Or I paddle home. It takes some time, but it's excellent exercise. And I've rarely been out when there wasn't at least a breath of air."

"*Luna* probably moves in a lot less wind than we need for the *Nancy Grace*." Will shifted position, reaching for a bottled water, which he lifted in question. "Tadie? Jilly?"

"I'll take one," Tadie said. "And there's a jar of cashews behind you in that bag."

He passed out the water. "Do you often have crew?" Will asked as he dug for the nuts.

"Sometimes Hannah comes or another friend of mine, Rita. But not so much anymore." She glanced ahead. "Shall we tack again?"

At the end of that maneuver, Jilly asked if her daddy could drive some.

"Of course he may."

"You don't mind?" Will asked.

"Not at all. Frankly, it will be fun for me."

And it was. Tadie couldn't remember the last time someone else had taken the tiller for her or enjoyed doing it as much as Will seemed to. He got that same rapt look on his face that she recognized from catching herself at it, and every time he glanced over at either her or Jilly, a smile lit his face. It was the company that made it so much fun, Tadie decided, wishing these two wanted to stay a while. She hated growing fond of people only to have them move on.

* * * * *

The sun slanted low in the sky as *Luna* meandered up Taylor's Creek. They hadn't paid proper attention to the dying wind, and by the time they realized it had slowed, they were ghosting along at about a knot and a half—barely enough to waft them home. At least they'd been able to come in on a reach. If the faint breeze had been on the nose, *Luna* would have needed all their shoulder and arm power on the oars, and Jilly would have seen firsthand what no wind meant on a motorless boat.

After they dropped sails and tied up to the *Nancy Grace*, using cushions as fenders, Will asked, "You want to take potluck with us?"

"Daddy doesn't like to cook. He says I need to learn how."

"Aha! I see a purpose behind this invitation." Tadie ignored Will's murmured disclaimer as he held out sail ties. "So, Miss Jilly, why don't you and I try to scrounge enough for a meal?"

"She means to gather, collect," Will said, before Jilly could ask for a definition.

Ah, yes, the child might not understand. "Sorry. I forget."

"It's okay. Daddy uses big words so I can learn them. I like words."

"I like words too," Tadie said, stifling another pang. This family had way too much charm.

Jilly led the way up the ladder and barely waited for Tadie's feet to hit the cabin sole before she grabbed her hand and pulled her forward.

Will waved them toward the galley. "Scrounge away, ladies. Use anything you find. I'll be exceedingly grateful."

Tadie dug through the small refrigerator and pulled out eggs, cheese, and green onions. In a locker, Jilly helped her unearth a can of refried beans, along with salsa and an unopened package of flour tortillas.

"*Huevos rancheros,* coming up," Tadie said and put Jilly to work.

When they gathered at the salon table, Will eyed the plates. "You're hired. Anytime you want to come for a meal, just say the word. I'll even shop to order."

Tadie worked to hide the pleasure she felt at his words. She handed out paper towels for napkins. "I hope they're cooked properly. I'm not exactly an authentic Mexican chef."

Will scooped beans with some of the heated tortilla. "Could have fooled me."

"Jilly was a great help."

"I stirred the beans and put in the cheese," Jilly said, smoothing her napkin over her knees. "And the onions. Tadie chopped those."

"Excellent, ladies. This hungry man thanks you."

When Will volunteered to clean up after dinner, Jilly again grabbed Tadie's hand. "You wanna see my cabin?"

"I do."

"You've seen the head," Jilly said, waving at it as they passed. "Don't you like my shower? And this is where my daddy reads his charts. He's got electronic and paper. And radar, too, so we won't be surprised. That's daddy's workroom in there. It's kinda little. And this is my cabin. I get the V-berth. Isn't it grand?"

Tadie slid her hand over the smooth planking on the walls, as Jilly climbed the little step to her bunk to pull a bear from the menagerie. "This is Tubby. I've had him forever."

"Hey, Tubby, glad to meet you," Tadie said, touching the glass nose.

"Daddy's bed is back there." Jilly danced toward the aft cabin. "See, he has a nice bunk too. And he has a little bathroom—I mean, head—all his own."

A double Pullman berth extended along the port side with the same lovely wood cabinetry that offered lots of storage. Everything was ship-shape.

Out the hatch over his bed, Tadie could see sky. She imagined lying there, studying the stars.

"She's a wonderful boat. How does she sail?" Tadie asked, backing out of the cabin. Anything to take her mind off that bunk and the idea of starlight. She was pitiful. Plain pitiful.

"Ah, the sailor asking." Will's words made her blush. Well, not his words, but her thoughts. "She's a lot of fun," he said. "Mostly because she tracks well and has a sea-kindly motion."

"We love her," Jilly said.

"I understand. I love *Luna*. Now, dear people, I really must take myself and *Luna* home."

"There's no wind," Jilly said. "How're you going to get there?"

"It's not far. I've got to keep those muscles strong."

Will stood up. "Don't be absurd. I'll tow you home with our dinghy. I have one of those noisy things we sometimes use."

"You don't need to."

"It will be my pleasure." Will laid his hand on Jilly's head. "Okay, punkin, you get ready for bed, and I'll be back in a few minutes. You know the rules."

"No going on deck without you."

"Good girl."

As Will climbed the companionway steps, Tadie bent toward the child. "Thanks for all your help sailing *Luna* today. Perhaps you and your daddy can come with me some other time."

"And you'll come out with us? When Daddy fixes what's wrong?"

"I'd love to." Tadie reached for the child to give her a quick hug, and Jilly's arms grabbed hold and tightened. "Goodnight, sweet girl. Sleep tight and don't let the bed bugs bite."

Jilly sucked in a breath. "That's what my daddy always says."

Oh, glory. There was way too much about this child to love. "I had someone who tucked me in with those words when I was little," she said. Not her own daddy, but Elvie Mae.

One more hug and she excused herself to help Will launch his dinghy from the davits. "My dock's about two blocks up from where you tie the dinghy. There's a tee with solar-powered lights on the pilings at the end."

Will nodded and held *Luna* close for Tadie to climb on board. He rigged a bridle off his stern and tied the bow line to it. Tadie tightened down *Luna's* boom before grabbing the tiller as Will started the dinghy's motor.

She steered in Will's wake, hoping he could see her wave of encouragement when he turned to check on her. He pulled her right up to the dock and cut his motor early to keep the tow line free of his propeller. After she came alongside, he grabbed the spring line and helped ready *Luna* for the night.

Tadie held out her hand. "Thank you for the tow."

"You shouldn't thank me." He clasped her fingers, and she felt a strange tingling sensation. His teeth gleamed white as he smiled. "You're the one who has given us a perfect afternoon and evening. Thank you. Jilly and I will both remember that sail for a long time."

"I love the idea of helping another young girl enjoy *Luna* just as I did when I was her age. Perhaps you'll be here long enough for us to go again."

"Who knows?" He dropped her hand as if he'd just noticed it still rested in his. "Goodnight."

"Goodnight, Will."

She heard the outboard's hum long after she'd lost sight of his silhouette. As other sounds intruded—the lap of water against a piling, a car door slamming in the distance—she felt again the tingling in her hand and wiped her palm down the side of her shorts.

Chapter Eleven

The if-onlys surely did hurt sometimes. Small arms, an eager face, a child's laughter. Was that the *more* she wanted? Until Jilly, Tadie hadn't thought so.

Stop it.

It was early yet, too early for bed. She wandered into her studio and pulled out a tray of gemstones. Sometimes, fingering various pieces and setting one next to another helped her see patterns, arrangements for the stones, whether to use gold or silver, make it layered or simple. Some of her most productive time was spent just letting her mind wander.

She touched a piece of tourmaline and picked up some oddly shaped amber. Perhaps the amber would be next, after she'd finished the piece she was working on. A necklace. Silver in contrast to the golden highlights. Abstract, definitely.

After making a quick sketch, she jotted notes and set them aside. Restlessness wouldn't let her work. She picked up her water glass, hunting up a distraction as she glanced around the studio from the couch she'd set up under the side windows, to her workbenches, to the interior walls that held Bucky's pictures.

Oh, how she missed her dear, kind, fun-loving little brother.

She'd hung some of his earlier and artier pictures within easy view, shots of gulls and boats and life in Beaufort. But on the wall to her left were others, the last he'd taken. Or that he'd ever take. They were haunting pictures of an alien people in an alien world, people whose eyes stared out and reminded her of the place that had claimed him.

His journal and camera had returned home weeks after his casket. It had been hard to read his words at first, and then there'd come a day when that's all Tadie and her parents wanted to do. Read and remember.

And see what he'd seen.

Bucky talked about befriending an old man named Mustafa, whose son-in-law had slaughtered his wife, Mustafa's daughter, after discovering she'd offered a drink of water to a soldier. She'd interacted with a man not of her family and had to be punished.

Off with her head.

Tadie touched the photos, tracing the deep lines in a face that had to be Mustafa's. A few days after he'd posed for Bucky, the Afghan police had stilled his smile, knocked out his front teeth, and broken his spine. Bucky and a couple of his friends had hauled Mustafa to an American-built hospital. He'd lived, but barely.

Tadie opened the drawer that held Bucky's notes.

You won't believe the mess over here, all because these Islamic fundamentalists think their way is the only one.

He'd probably cleaned up his language because he knew their daddy would read the letter out loud to Mama.

They've taken away the basic freedoms—especially from women, who are treated like slaves and worse. Can you believe it? They're not allowed to go to a male doctor without a man from their family acting as chaperone. Turns out, a lot of them die. And if you don't worship Allah, bang—you're dead. What a way to make converts. It's crazy.

The news out of Iran would have fueled Bucky's frustration, with the talk of a twelfth Imam and world conversion through jihad. Kill yourself along with the infidels and enter the fast track to paradise—

along with the promise of seventy virgins. What did they offer female suicide bombers? Seventy husbands? Seventy nothings?

Closing her eyes, Tadie sucked in a breath and released it slowly.

Let it out, let it go. Breathe in, push out the anger.

She ought to stuff those photos out of sight in a drawer. But how, when they'd been Bucky's last?

"Helping the people gives my life meaning," he'd once said.

Had Mustafa's daughter left any children? If so, had any been daughters?

A photograph of ragged urchins bending over rubble brought Jilly's precious face to mind. Sweet Jilly, who had the freedom to become whatever she wanted because she was born here and not there.

Tadie turned to peer out the window. Look at her, living in this incredible place. A choked sob escaped, fighting the tears and startling Ebenezer. "Sorry," she said as he rolled over and curled up again on the studio couch, his back toward her.

She heard the back door open and Hannah's voice call, "Yoo-hoo!"

"In here."

Hannah's tap-tap meant heels, not walking shoes. Tadie checked her friend's opened-toed sandals as the other woman approached.

Hannah picked up one of the amber beads. "Whatcha doing?"

"Not much. You?"

"I went to the CVS to pick up a refill Matt forgot. You been to the new one yet? Then I dropped by the Piggly Wiggly for milk ... hey, you've been crying."

Tadie waved a hand toward Bucky's wall. "Just remembering." The pounding behind her eyes hadn't eased. "I should do something. Something real and meaningful—more than making jewelry and running a shop."

"But you're good at those things."

"And who am I helping? Whose life am I touching?"

Hannah bent forward, squinting at her. "You think you can bring Bucky back that way or make his death count somehow?"

Maybe that was it. She took a minute to decide whether this was a reason to weep or find humor. "I'm a mess."

"You are," Hannah said. "But I'm not saying you don't have the right to be."

"I was getting all philosophical because the world's falling apart, and Bucky's dead because of it." Hannah's hand slid down her forearm, eking out the first hint of calm Tadie had felt since entering her studio. "He talked about helping those people," she said. "I wish I could too. But I'm not a doctor. Or a politician."

"No."

"So I thought ... this is crazy, but I wondered ... " She turned back toward the window, breaking contact and immediately longing again for her friend's hand, for someone's touch. "I thought of adopting a war orphan. Maybe more than one."

She could almost hear Hannah's thoughts. Hadn't Hannah and Matt tried to adopt a child or two? And then they hadn't.

She should have remembered. "It was just foolishness. You want a cup of decaf tea?"

"Maybe a glass. With lots of ice."

Hannah didn't stay long. At the door, she pulled Tadie into a hug and said, "I'll help. If you decide you want to adopt and fill up this house, I'll help."

Locking up, Tadie thought of Hannah's words. Maybe she'd adopt an orphanage full and change the world twenty kids at a time.

She rested her forehead on her palms. *An orphanage?*

Her hand hit the light switches as she climbed to her room. What she needed was a candle, a bath, a good book, and music. Especially music.

Fine, so her escape had a routine to it. If it worked, who cared?

That elicited a groan. Because, honey, there wasn't anyone else *to* care, now was there?

She didn't even look to see what was in the CD changer. When the music turned out to be Respigi's *Fountains of Rome*, she released a little more of the tension that had tightened her muscles. She turned the water on full blast, poured in the bubble bath, and let the foam build while she picked out a Dorothy Sayer mystery that she'd meant to get to. Tucking it and a towel on the tub's edge, she lit a candle and slipped into the water.

* * * * *

Air-conditioning day. Glory. Tadie opened the door to George and his crew, who were going to install two house units and one in the apartment over the garage.

"George, you'll make sure they put the apartment's thermostat low enough for Elvie to reach, won't you? She's a tiny little thing. She's never been much more than five feet, and she's probably less than that now."

"We'll take care of it."

Tuesday morning, Tadie woke to cool. Blessed, blessed cool.

"Thank you, George," she told the kitchen as she tidied up before punching in the numbers for Miller Electric.

"Feelin' better, are you, Tadie?" George asked with what sounded like a chuckle.

"Yes sir. I'll probably *keep* feeling better until I get my next electric bill."

That brought a guffaw from the other end of the line. "Well, comfort costs. You know that."

"Sometimes. But it sure costs a whole lot more for you on your stink potter than for me on *Luna.*"

"Ouch. That was a low blow. You hear how much diesel's going for these days?"

"Horrible, I know. You better get yourself a sail."

"Not in this life. So, how's Matt? I saw Hannah a couple of days ago. She said he's not doing so good."

"They're watching it."

"Guess that's why Alex's back."

"Guess so."

"Okay, well, I'm glad you like the system. If you have any problems, give me a call, hear? I'll get prices on a lift for the apartment. How soon you need it?"

"I'm still thinking about it, with those steps being so steep. There's no rush, but it's bound to come in handy at some point."

"I saw one you could sit or stand in that could go right up next to those steps. We could get my nephew to build you a gate at the top. If Elvie or James ever need a wheelchair, they can just ride in, up, and out."

"Would it hold up to salt air?"

"One I'm thinking of would. Good sturdy thing."

"Then find out about it, will you? Elvie will be able to walk now. But the surgery got me thinking."

"I'll be in touch," George said.

Tadie sure liked living in a place where she knew most everyone, or at least their brothers or sisters or cousins. She'd gone to school with both George's first and second wife. The first had died early, but before she'd gone, she'd told George he ought to marry her best friend, Velma. He'd obeyed.

Remembering the image of a satisfied Velma and a stunned George on their wedding day, Tadie refilled Eb's water bowl and collected her car keys. When she got to the hospital, the nurse said Elvie was napping and James had retreated to the cafeteria.

Tadie went through the line to get an iced tea before pulling up a chair. "What did the doctor say?"

The black circles under his eyes seemed to have faded some. He swallowed a bite and rinsed it down with tea. "Doc said they couldn't find none of that cancer in the lymph nodes they took. Leastways, ones they tested."

"I'm so glad. It's what we thought, isn't it? What they expected?" At his nod, she asked, "So, what's next? Is she all well? I mean, we don't have to worry anymore, do we?"

"They're wanting to do that radiation, maybe chemotherapy on her, just to be on the safe side, Doc says. She says no."

"Lord, love her."

"Maybe you can talk some sense into her, Miss Sara."

Tadie sighed. Where did people get the idea she had all this power? First Rita, now James. And he should know better. "When have I ever been able to tell Elvie what to do about anything? When that woman makes up her mind, there's no moving her."

James hung his head on a slow nod. "You'd be right about that. She's like a rock buried deep. Takes a big plow to move her stubbornness out the way."

"You said they got all the cancer cells. So maybe it's okay not to go through all that mess chemo makes of the body."

"It's the just-in-case that's got me."

Tadie patted his rough hand. "I know."

His plate overflowed with food, but James stilled his fork and sat staring at the mashed potatoes he normally loved. Watching him, Tadie changed the subject and mentioned Rita's plan.

James didn't say much at first. He scowled, but his fork plowed through the potatoes. After downing a few more sips of tea, he looked her right in the eye. "You think she means it?"

"She said so."

"'Bout not liking this lawyering?"

"Yes sir. But maybe she'll go back to it one day."

He nodded. "Maybe. I don't want her quittin' just because she thinks I can't do for her mama."

"She knows you can. And she knows I'm here. But think about it from her point of view. Elvie's surgery made Rita take stock of what's important. And spending time with her mama is number one. Rita's a smart girl. She'll do fine at whatever she tries."

"Well," he said, scooping up a fork full of green beans. "I'll be happy to see her. Always am. And Elvie'll be beside herself."

"That's reason enough then."

Tadie stood and hugged James. "You want help getting Elvie home?"

"You're a good girl, but we'll do fine."

* * * * *

Tadie opened the shop door to see Stefan Ward unwrapping two more paintings to replace their dwindling supply. He glanced up from under heavy grey-spattered brows and ran a hand through his thick mane of salt-and-pepper hair. "Hey, Tadie. Brought you two watercolors."

She studied the wispy clouds and brightly hued skies. "Looking good."

"I've moved to the beach," he said. "Doing some ocean scenes for a change."

Isa's hand caressed the frame of a sunrise over the sea. "Every one of your paintings is more beautiful than the last. I wish I could own each one you've brought us, because I never tire of studying them."

A blush crept up Stefan's cheek. Surely he'd heard compliments before and plenty of them, but he looked like a hungry puppy, devouring Isa's words.

"Jilly helped in here again this morning," Isa said, not looking at Stefan.

"Good for her. I'm glad it's working out." Tadie turned toward her office. "Stefan, nice to see you again."

She flicked on the computer and logged in receipts until the numbers swam, merging with images of red hair and childish smiles. As she headed home, the sun's reflection on the water almost blinded her, all whitened silver broken only by an occasional ripple of blue. Her sundress swung against her legs, the air swirling beneath it and across her face. The briny odor of the sea had replaced the marsh smells that floated across the creek and lingered on airless days.

Alex's convertible zipped down a side street as she neared her house. Her feet pounded up her front steps and she glanced over her shoulder, checking in both directions as she slipped the key in the lock.

Then she slowed her movements. This was absurd. No one could bother her in her own home, not unless she let him.

She grabbed a glass of iced water and drifted into her studio, picking up and replacing various items before she turned to go upstairs. Minutes later, the rumble of her stomach sent her back down again.

A cobweb caught the light above the kitchen doorway. She attacked it with a dust mop, flicking on the television as she passed. It droned in the background while she poked around in the refrigerator, finally pulling out salad mixings and the last of a boiled chicken breast.

Ebenezer watched from beside his bowl. "Enjoy," she said, dropping in a few pieces of the chicken. "That's all you get."

The weatherman's voice noted local conditions as she tossed greens and sliced bites of chicken, reaching for the olive oil and a shaker of salt. He mentioned a storm in the Atlantic, which might become the first big hurricane of the season. She carried her salad to the couch.

The storm's predicted path appeared on the screen. Only one of the models suggested it might head northwest instead of only west. Good for the Southeast, bad for the Caribbean. August was prime time for storms, and they'd been mighty lucky this year. Best if any big blow held off and let Will and Jilly move the *Nancy Grace* out of town.

Chapter Twelve

Jilly's tummy felt like it wanted to bounce right out of her. She'd spent yesterday morning with Isa at the shop, but her daddy didn't want to go into town just yet, so she had to hang around and wait for him. Waiting was no fun. She'd finished her new book days ago and started on a harder one called *The Railroad Children*. It was okay, but she really had to think while she read it. It would probably get better. And easier once she figured things out.

She stuck her head down the engine hole to watch her daddy loosen a nut. Why were those things called nuts? They didn't look like peanuts or walnuts or even her favorite, pecans. So how come? It didn't make sense.

"Hey, punkin," her daddy said, looking sideways at her. "What's up?"

"You almost finished?"

"As much as I can do today."

"Did you call the parts man again?"

"I did. He said the new heat exchanger should be in by tomorrow at the latest."

"Didn't he say that yesterday?"

Her daddy wiped his hands on an oily rag. "And Friday he

promised it would be here Monday. Then Tuesday. I'd go someplace else if I hadn't given him a deposit on the thing." He pushed himself back up and onto the cabin sole. "I'm sorry about the holdup, kiddo. I know you wanted to get going."

"It's okay. We can stay. I like helping Isa in the shop. Yesterday she even let me write things on something she called a in—"

"Invoice?"

Jilly raised her palm and squinched her eyes. "In-in-*ventory*!" Her eyes popped open. "That's where she finds out what she's sold and what she hasn't. Did you know that?"

"I think I did. But maybe not exactly the kind of inventory you were using. That's another new word for your list."

Jilly's pigtails bobbed. "And I got to use the one you taught me, you know, the egrets-and-cows word?"

"I remember. How did you get to use it?"

"Well, Isa said her working for Hannah and Tadie is that thing. Something good for all of them. So, I told her how you'd said the cattle egrets eat the bugs that bother the cows, so everybody's happy."

Sliding his tool bag into the cupboard, her daddy glanced back over his shoulder. Jilly tried not to catch his eye, 'cause she was thinking as hard as she could to remember before he asked. It was sym-something. She remembered that much. Sym-bol? No. Sym-pathy? No.

She bit her lip and kept her eyes on her swinging legs.

"Up you go," he said. "Let me close the hatch."

Maybe he wouldn't make her say it.

"So, do you remember the egret and cow word? Or did you just let Isa use it?"

"I remember. Sort of. "

"Yes?"

She blinked up at him. "It starts with sym."

"It does indeed. Do you remember the next sound?"

Jilly shook her head.

"B."

"Symbee … " All of a sudden, it flashed right there. Yes! She made a power jab with her fist as she shouted out, "Symbiotic!"

Her daddy grabbed her and swung her around the small cabin, knocking over the water jug in the process. "You did it. What a girl."

Jilly's arms clung to his neck, and she pressed her cheek against his ear. Nobody could hug like her daddy.

When tomorrow came, they would have to get a taxi to go to the store for the part. They were good walkers, she and her daddy, but this store was too far. He said cruisers had to be good walkers, 'cause getting a cab all the time would break the bank. The times they got to ride in taxis were pretty fun, especially if they found one with an interesting driver.

* * * * *

And that's what they got the next day. The guy was huge and had a wrinkle across his nose. She wondered if it had been broken and not put back together right. His arms were the biggest things Jilly had ever seen, like tree trunks. She thought his shirt sleeves might bust right off if he moved wrong. His hair was all crinkly, like on a lot of black men, and his eyes kind of crinkled too.

As soon as she climbed in, he said, "Morning, missy. Where you and your daddy want to be goin' this fine day?"

Her daddy told him, and they started off, the driver chatting and asking if they were some of them people lived on a boat. He got real excited when he heard they were.

"Closest I ever come to going out on the water was in a little skiff my cousin had. He took me and Willy huntin' crabs. 'Bout near scared the living daylights out of us, 'cause we'd never learnt to swim. No sir, Momma didn't cotton to us going near the water, so that was the last time I did."

"You mean you don't like to go in the ocean?" Jilly asked, appalled.

"Not me. I aim to keep these two feet planted squarely on this here ground."

"Oh my. I'm sorry."

He laughed. "No need to be sorry, missy. I ain't. Not one bit."

Her daddy said, "Wait for us, please," to the driver, and then he held the door so she could go first into the parts place.

It was dark, mostly because the windows were really dirty, and the man behind the counter was skinny with not very nice eyes. The smell of him made her nose itch, a sort of sticky-sweet *uck*, along with smoke. Smoke was nasty.

"Sorry, Mr. Merritt. They promised, but you know how suppliers are. Say one thing, mean another. If that heat exchanger doesn't get here tomorrow, I'll send one of my boys over to Jacksonville." He leaned over the counter, his arms jutting like two hairy sticks out of the blue work shirt that had his name on the pocket: *Billy W.*

"I'd appreciate it," her daddy said. "I need to get the engine working again. So, by tomorrow before closing?"

"Sure thing," Billy W. said. "That is, if the hurricane don't come this way."

Daddy halted and jerked his head around. "Hurricane?"

"Didn't know as you'd heard or not. Thought you'd have mentioned it if you had. I know how you fellas are, always listening to your weather radios. I've got friends come in here—"

"What hurricane? Where's it heading?"

"That's just it. They ain't quite got that figured out. That tropical storm down there was heading kinda toward the Gulf. Seems it changed course, and in the process it stayed over the warm water long enough to graduate to bein' called a hurricane. Hurricane Delia."

"It's a bit early in the season, isn't it?"

"We get 'em anytime mid-August on. My daddy always said that in a hot year, you're gonna have your share. Don't know that's gospel, but it was to him. Anyway, we've had some scorchers all the way up the coast. Probably heated up the water. Sucked the storm this way."

Jilly looked up at her daddy. His forehead was wrinkled and his eyes sort of squinty, like he wasn't sure if the man was crazy or not.

"So where's it headed?"

The man scratched his head and loosened white flakes. They dropped to his shoulders, and a few hit the counter, but the counter was so dusty, he probably didn't notice.

"Someplace between Savannah and Norfolk," he said. "Least, that's what they're saying. Now, my bet is Norfolk. It's their turn, 'cause we've had Floyd and Isabelle. Irene not long ago, though that knocked folk for a loop all over the place. Anyway, I figure this one's bound to turn north, only not so far up as New Jersey. They got smacked with Sandy. So, percentages."

"Sure hope you're right." Daddy held the door for her.

Jilly didn't like the sound of that at all. A hurricane? Here? Daddy'd said that's why he wouldn't stay in Beaufort A hurricane coming now would really set him off.

His brow was still wrinkled when they climbed into the cab. "What are we going to do?" she asked.

"Well, the first thing is to listen to the radio. Then maybe we'll take the computer to that coffee place that has Wi-Fi."

The driver turned around. "You folks talkin' about that there storm down in the Caribbean? Delia? Hope it don't come here."

"You and me both."

"Daddy, I wish we had the Weather Channel."

He tweaked her nose. "So we could watch those guys standing in the rain, telling us what's happening while they look as if they'll blow away?"

Jilly nodded. "If it comes here, maybe they'll come too. You think?"

"Probably. But I don't imagine we have to worry about a hurricane. What are the chances?"

Jilly bit her lip. She knew all about those *chances*. She knew her daddy said it to make her feel better, but bad things happened. She didn't know why. They just did.

Chapter Thirteen

Tadie would have to write this off as a particularly unproductive day. She'd stared out the window as clouds built to the southeast. She'd fiddled with stones and broken a link while soldering a clasp to the chain. Oh, she'd managed to dust the downstairs rooms, but that didn't count because she'd just have to tackle those same surfaces in another day or two.

She was back in her studio, about to turn on the soldering torch, when Eb showed up, his tail twitching.

She looked at her watch. "Already?" she asked, knowing the answer.

"Coming," she told him. Of course, she was coming. Eb had trained her well.

He darted ahead into the kitchen, waiting like a sentinel while she filled his bowl. She watched as he sniffed at the dry food before turning to glare at her.

"Eat. That's all you're getting. You heard what your doctor said last time we went for your check up. You, sir, are fat. And I'm not to give you so much people-food."

Eb turned his back on her.

"It's for your own good."

The back door opened and Rita poked her head in. "He giving you trouble again?"

"Look at you," Tadie said, pulling Rita through the door and giving her a hug. "Can't believe you're here already."

"I'm taking vacation in lieu of notice, on account of the hurricane. Here," Rita said, setting a wrapped package on the counter. "I picked up flounder at Fishtowne."

"I appreciate it. You been up to see your mama yet?"

"Going now. I think I'll stay there at least tonight."

"You're welcome here any time."

"Thanks. Talk to you later."

Tadie turned on the Weather Channel and pulled out a cast iron skillet. A little oil, a dab of butter, a little salt, a hot pan. There was nothing better.

She listened as she browned the filet. Hurricane scares were a fact of life in coastal Carolina, but when a bad one hit, it could be devastating. They'd never faced the trouble New Orleans had because they weren't built the same. The dunes and barrier islands helped Beaufort, and with all the low-lying country round about, there was more room for the storm surge to spread out. Her own home had weathered more than a century of hurricanes. Isabelle hit some areas with severe flooding, and Irene made a mess with trees down all over the place. Seems FEMA had run out of aid money, so they'd best hope this one blew itself out and headed east.

She needed to haul *Luna* and make sure the shutters were ready to close, especially that one on the south side. They'd never boarded up the shop, but this year she would. And she had to stock up.

Isa couldn't stay at her new place on the beach, not in a big storm. Good thing this house had lots of extra rooms.

Tadie was forking bites of food when Hannah phoned. "We're getting ready, just in case," she said. "I'm putting Alex to work tomorrow. He'd better earn his keep if he's planning to live with us for any length of time."

"Did you forget to tell me something?" Tadie asked, her fork stilled.

"What? Oh, didn't I mention he and Bethanne split?"

"First I've heard."

"They had some big confrontation, and Alex moved in this afternoon. I just hope it won't be for long."

"I imagine you do. Can't he find a rental?"

Hannah sighed loudly, sounding exasperated. "He hasn't had time to look, and Bethanne closed up the house. Matt had to invite him."

"I'm sure it's only temporary. Alex won't like it any more than you do."

"Except here he won't be paying rent."

"There is that." Tadie laughed, but without much humor. When they said goodnight, her thoughts went to Alex and his non-marriage. Maybe that's why he'd been hovering. Well, he'd better not get any ideas. He hadn't wanted her then, and he sure wasn't going to get her now.

* * * * *

Will had been listening to NOAA weather radio every hour, and they'd just announced that Delia would center-punch the coast as a Category Three hurricane. He worked madly to get things ready so all he'd have to do was install the stupid cooler when it got here—if it got here. At this point, that didn't look promising.

They were talking about Delia having the potential to strengthen while it slithered closer to land. Great. He wished he could have hightailed it up the Ditch to some hurricane hole, but without a functioning oil cooler, he didn't have that option.

He looked at his watch. Five-fifteen. There wasn't a boatyard in town open at this hour, and he needed somewhere to haul out that was close enough for a quick limp. The engine would work in short spurts if he reinstalled the old, leaking heat exchanger and poured oil in every few minutes. But he couldn't go far. And he'd need an extra pair of hands other than Jilly's.

Jilly lay curled on the V-berth, trying to be good. He could hear her discussing something with Tubby, perhaps a secret she didn't want him to hear. He worried sometimes because she never whined or complained anymore. Not that he wanted her to misbehave, but he wasn't sure this kind of perfection in a kid was normal. He'd read about children worrying when they lost a parent, figuring that if they weren't perfect, the other one might go away too.

He bit the tip of his pen as he stared at clouds forming to the south. Should he do something different? Maybe talk to her about it or find a counselor?

He climbed to the top of the companionway and let the questions swirl out and up.

What should I do?

If only Nancy were here to tell him. Or if God would.

Nothing came except waves slapping gently against the hull, the occasional splash of a pelican, a dog barking from a nearby boat. Jilly was a happy child, and if she were better behaved and more mature than the average seven-year-old, he should rejoice. He'd read that home-schooled kids grew up faster than their peers. That had to be it.

Besides, he had more pressing things to think about, like a hurricane spiraling up the coast.

* * * * *

Jilly's tummy did a flip when Tadie breezed into the shop with curly hair sticking out all over the place. She sucked once more before pulling the straw from her mouth and called, "Hi!"

"Good morning, ladies. You look mighty cool."

"You," Isa said, eyeing her boss from shoes to hair, "look as if you've been jogging for miles."

That didn't sound nice. Trying to fix it, Jilly turned to Tadie. "I think you look pretty. You always do."

"Thanks." Tadie pushed stray hairs off her face. "Sure is hot out there. I walked, so it's a good thing I'm not trying to impress you two, isn't it? With this mop, that's not happening."

"I love your curls," Jilly said. She did. Tadie had perfect hair. Not red and straight.

"When they act like curls, they're fine."

"You know what?" Jilly said, bouncing up on her stool. "My daddy's gotta find someplace to put our boat so the hurricane won't hurt her. Isa gave him some places."

"Wonderful. I need to do the same thing with *Luna*. And, if you ladies will help me, I'd like to make the shop a little more hurricane-proof. Isa, can you bring a pen and paper?"

Jilly climbed off the stool and followed Tadie outside, ready for her assignment. "What can I do?"

"Here, take this." Tadie handed her a tape measure. "You hold this end, okay? Hold it right there. Good girl."

She pushed the end of the tape where Tadie had said, and Isa wrote the numbers down for the big windows and the glass door. Then they went back inside where it was cool.

"The previous owner of my condo always closed up the place," Isa told them, "so all I have to do is get the boards out of storage and find some strong man to put them up."

"My daddy can do it. He's very strong."

"I bet he is, sweetie. But I imagine he's going to be a bit preoccupied."

"Which reminds me ..." Tadie said.

Jilly could tell Tadie was talking to Isa, but Isa ducked down behind the counter to pick up something. Jilly leaned around to look. It was the pen.

When Isa stood back up, Tadie said the thing she had started. "If they evacuate the beach, you come stay with me. I have loads of room."

Tadie's house? Jilly slammed her eyes shut for a quick *Please, God*, before opening them to hear Isa say yes. Of course, Isa said yes. Jilly's tummy bounced and she stared hard at her sneakers.

What if Tadie just went away and didn't say anything about people on a boat—people who needed a place in the storm?

Someone cleared her throat. Maybe Jilly was supposed to look up and pay attention. She peeked.

"I have a very big house," Tadie said, looking straight at her. "It's much too big for one person—or even two. If you and your daddy need a place to stay, you can come to my house with Isa."

She'd said it! Tadie had said it. Jilly could feel her grin get really wide, because who could help smiling when someone did *exactly* what you'd prayed? "Oh, yes, please," she whispered.

"Only if your daddy wants to."

"He will. I know he will."

Tadie didn't stay long enough to be there when Jilly's daddy got back, but he'd fixed things so the *Nancy Grace* could get out of the water. Jilly was back on her stool, listening when he told Isa he needed help moving to the boatyard. "And then you and I," he said, talking to Jilly now, "will get to live on land for a week or so. What do you think of that?"

Jilly started to tell him about Tadie's house, but he was back talking to Isa and not looking. "I've got to get there by this evening so they can haul us, because they're not going to pull any more boats after today. The news isn't looking good. We'll get some heavy winds at the very least—which will land Jilly and me in a hotel."

Isa shook her head. "You can always try, but our motels fill up fast when people hear the word hurricane. Everybody from the beach starts booking rooms if they don't have family inland. They probably already have."

Jilly couldn't wait any longer. She reached out to grab her daddy's arm and make him look at her. "We *have* someplace to stay."

"We do?"

Finally, Isa helped out. "Tadie invited us all to her place," she said. "I live over on Atlantic Beach, so she said I should come—"

"Us too, Daddy!"

His brows rose as he looked from one to the other. "Us too? Just like that?"

Jilly's head bobbed up and down.

"We barely know her," he said. "We can't impose like that."

"She has a gigantic house, Daddy. She said so. She said it's way too big for one or even two. I guess she gets lonely in there."

"I think you're absolutely right, Jilly." Isa's hand rested on her shoulder. It felt good. Like Isa was saying she was on Jilly's side and not to worry. "I think Tadie would love an excuse to have a house party like in the old days."

"Doesn't that sound like *so* much fun, Daddy? We can go, can't we?"

He didn't look real happy. "We'll see. I'll have to talk to Tadie about it. Besides, the hurricane may hit someplace else entirely or even behave itself and head to sea. Let's not go off half-cocked until we know more, okay?"

"But we're still going to put the *Nancy Grace* in the boatyard?"

"Yes ma'am."

"Then we might need a place to stay."

"If the storm comes, yes."

Jilly crossed her fingers behind her back. "Okay."

"About moving the boat," Daddy said to Isa. "Do you happen to know anyone I could hire to give me a hand?"

"What about me, Daddy?"

He grabbed a pigtail and tugged, grinning down at her. "I'll need you to help me drive her, no doubt about that, but we need an adult at the wheel while I'm below pouring in oil every few minutes. I bought out the store."

Isa looked like she was thinking. Then she held up a finger. "Let me go make a call." A minute later, she stuck her head out of the office. "Is your dinghy at the dock?"

Daddy nodded. Jilly tugged at his hand, but before she could say anything, Isa came out.

"Tadie's going to meet you at your dinghy."

"Tadie?" Her voice sounded squeaky, but she didn't care.

"Yes ma'am." Isa grinned down at her. Isa was so nice. "I asked her for the name of someone who could help, and she gave me hers." Isa turned to Daddy. "Is that okay with you?"

Jilly held her breath.

"I hate to bother her."

"Oh pooh. She'll love it."

* * * * *

It didn't take Tadie ten minutes to get her things together and head down Front Street toward their rendezvous at the dinghy dock. She longed to be able to whistle. This was a whistling moment. Her feet felt light, as if she'd added insoles to her boat shoes.

Jilly bounded down the sidewalk to meet her. "Hello! Isn't this going to be fun?"

"Yes ma'am, it certainly is." She waved at Will, trying to contain her excitement. She was thrilled to be going on that lovely boat, even if the distance traveled would be less than a mile. "Where are we headed?"

"Up to Fowler's Yard. Ever been there?"

"Nope."

She climbed down into the dinghy and helped Jilly buckle on her lifejacket as Will started the outboard. No one said much on the way out, but Jilly seemed as excited as Tadie.

At the *Nancy Grace*, she helped Will hoist the motor and stow the dinghy on deck. "If you'll stand with Jilly at the wheel," Will said, "I'll add oil and start the engine."

It chugged to life. Will hoisted and stowed the anchor, then dashed below again to add more oil.

"I can't check the level while we're underway," he said when he came back on deck. "I hope that's enough to get us there. Anyway, let me get the lines and fenders out while you head to that marker at the end of town." He pointed first to the marker, then down to the chart. "Fowlers is just inside there, this side of the bridge."

"I've got it."

Tadie allowed Jilly to steer, correcting when necessary. Will made one more trip below as they neared the harbor entrance before he took the wheel and used the VHF to check back in with the marina.

"Can you handle the lines, Tadie? And Jilly, be ready to help me. Someone will be waiting at the dock."

"Aye, aye, Captain," they chorused.

It all went very smoothly. Tadie tossed the bow line to waiting hands and went aft for the stern line. Will had already stowed the sails and bimini, so he needed only to secure the dinghy and take down his dodger once the boat was on the hard. The travel lift looked ready to haul them.

Will spoke before she could. "Thanks for coming to our rescue."

"I enjoyed it. What's your plan if the storm comes here? Have you booked a room?"

Jilly didn't give her daddy a chance to answer. "Not yet."

"Then why don't you plan to stay with Isa and me?"

"Seems like a huge imposition."

"Not at all. We'll have fun."

Jilly leaned back against his legs and grabbed his hands at her shoulders. "We *want* to come," Jilly said. "Don't we, Daddy?"

"Certainly, if the storm comes this way. I'm sure Jilly would enjoy your house more than a hotel, even if we could find one. Isa seemed skeptical that we would."

Tadie stopped at the boarding ladder. "It's settled then. I'll look forward to hearing from you. Do you have my number?"

Will raised a finger as a gesture to wait and went below. Jilly bounced impatiently on the balls of her feet.

"Did you get your boat safe?" Jilly asked. "You want us to come and help?"

"Thank you. I have help lined up, but I certainly appreciate the offer."

"Ready." Will jotted down the number Tadie gave him and asked, apparently as an afterthought, "You have a ride home?"

"Isa," she said, on her way down the ladder.

Will's voice followed her with an, "Okay then."

She punched in Isa's number as she walked toward the marina office. She'd wait there or even start walking out to the access road. It was fine. Will was obviously preoccupied.

Well, who wouldn't be, getting his boat ready to haul? It had nothing to do with her.

Of course not.

Chapter Fourteen

Tadie flipped on the lamp next to the sofa and snuggled into the deep cushions with the Dorothy Sayer mystery she'd been trying to read. She was determined to get past the second chapter, but so far it hadn't hooked her interest. The new air-conditioning unit hummed unobtrusively. If it got much cooler, she'd need a sweater.

Imagine, a sweater in August.

The doorbell startled her. Who would come visiting at this hour— and come to the front door?

He stood with his feet slightly apart, hands tucked in the pockets of his jeans, the collar of his white oxford shirt open. His dark hair had a silvery sheen, but his face remained slightly in shadow as he looked down at her. The years vanished, and a younger Alex had come to take her walking with him in the fading summer light.

"Hey, Tadie." He spoke her name with the same caress he'd used way back when.

She stared, unable to move or find any words.

"I came to check on you. We got Matt's house battened down. Thought you might need help with yours."

"My house?" She cleared her throat to get rid of that croaky sound.

This was Alex, the man she despised. She took a deep breath, released it slowly, and backed away to close the door. "I'm fine. Thanks for asking."

He extended his hand, stopping her. "Haven't you heard the latest report? They projected a course that could hit us sooner rather than later."

"Last I heard, it was stalled down south, picking a target."

"So, what do you need done? What about *Luna*?"

"She's scheduled for tomorrow."

"Tide's high." He glanced out toward the water. "There's enough light and no wind. How about we get her out now? You still have the trailer?"

"A newer one."

"Yeah? Bearings go bad?"

Tadie grunted assent. She'd been taken by surprise. That had to be it. And by his concern for *Luna*.

She left the door open while she turned to get her shoes. She hated letting him help, but wouldn't she be cutting off her nose if she turned away an offer now?

Besides, it fit, him thinking about her boat, knowing what needed doing. He'd always been like that before. Before ...

She shook her head. She had to stop worrying about those years. They'd been in love, he'd broken her heart, but that was a long time ago. Now he was just Hannah's brother-in-law coming over to help Hannah's best friend—who'd been *his* best friend once, or so he'd said.

Where were those stupid shoes? She'd kicked them off hours ago. Where had she put them?

"I'll hitch up the trailer while you're getting ready," Alex called.

She headed to the kitchen. No shoes. She bent to look under the kitchen couch. "Have you seen my shoes?" she asked when Eb stuck his head down there too. He wiggled under, but all they found were dust bunnies. Her studio? Bedroom? She plodded upstairs.

Fine, they'd disappeared. Forget them.

She pulled an old pair of walking shoes from the back of the closet and stuffed her feet into them. Passing her dresser mirror, she caught a glimpse of her fly-away hair and paused to recapture it behind her head. No, she wasn't doing it for Alex. Alex was a thing of the past. Besides, even if he and Bethanne were separated, he was still a married man.

Married, got it?

Yes ma'am. Never going to forget that one.

He parked Matt's truck at the boat ramp and then got in her car to drive back to her dock. "You got two oars?"

"In the barn."

He left her and went to fetch them. The tails of his shirt hung untucked. She turned away.

"Good time to be doing this," he said, climbing down into the boat. "I imagine we're seeing the calm before the storm."

She had the lines ready to cast off when he pushed them toward the piling. They retrieved the spring lines and took their old positions, with Tadie on the starboard side, Alex on the port.

Her muscles strained as she tried to keep up with the strokes of the port-side oar. She wouldn't let Alex get ahead and turn *Luna's* bow off the rhumb line.

Fifteen minutes later they were at the landing. It took them another hour to get *Luna* ready, to bag the sails and lines, and to pull the boat onto her trailer. Tadie focused on the task at hand so she wouldn't hear his laugh when a turnbuckle got loose and sent the stay flying out of reach—or notice how their hands seemed to remember motions—or how their feet found the spot to stand, the best position to support the lowering mast. They'd done this together countless times.

Suddenly, another face appeared and that voice spoke in Tadie's head. Her daddy was calling her to set the cushion under the mast's rigging so it wouldn't mar the deck, telling her to watch her fingers so they wouldn't get pinched. It was her daddy who'd taught her to sail, to haul and ready *Luna.* They'd launched her together so many times, Samuel Ellis with some bit of wisdom cloaked in a story.

But he'd toss her no more lines, tell her no more sailing yarns. And her darling Bucky—Bucky would never again tell his big sister how to set the fenders off *Luna's* side.

Neither her daddy nor Bucky had chosen to leave. Alex had.

Keep focused. Keep the anger working.

Dark was almost upon them and the light over the barn door left some things in shadow. With Tadie giving the cues, Alex backed the trailer into its space. He uncoupled it from the hitch, locked it down, and helped her pull the doors closed. "We need to wash down the wheels."

"I'll get it in the morning, when I can see what I'm doing."

He nodded.

"Thanks so much."

He reached toward her just as the light at the garage apartment illuminated the stairs. James came out onto the landing.

"That you down there, Miss Sara?"

"Hey, James. Just putting *Luna* away."

Alex walked around to the side of the barn and called up, "How're you doing, James? It's me, Alex."

Silence. Then, "What you doin' here, Alex Morgan?"

Tadie could picture his squint and James wielding his sword.

"Just helping Tadie get her boat in. The storm's coming, you know."

"Yeah, I know 'bout it. I thought I'd be helpin' her in the morning."

She should have foreseen this. "I still need you to help me with the shutters, especially that loose one. How's Elvie?"

"She's just fine. Restin' while Rita's gone to the store. We thank you, Miss Sara, for gettin' all them supplies in. The only thing we didn't have was ginger ale. You know how Elvie loves her ginger ale when nothin' else feels good goin' down."

"I'm sorry I didn't think about getting some this morning. Good thing you've got Rita there. You'll send her over to visit soon, won't you?"

"Yes ma'am. I'll do that. You be wantin' her to stay with you for the storm?"

"No, thank you. I've got Isa and some boat-folk coming. Did I bring up enough candles?"

"Got plenty. We'll fill up the tub sometime tomorrow, so there'll be water, food, and candles. Can't want for much more, except folk you love around you. Ain't that right, Miss Sara?"

Tadie smiled, though James couldn't see her. "You've got it right there."

"So, Alex Morgan, you goin' on home to your family 'bout now?"

Tadie could barely make out Alex's features in the barn's light. She thought he looked rueful as he answered. "I am. Back to my brother's place."

"That'll be good. You stay there with that wife of yours, you hear?"

"Goodnight, James," Alex said. "Say 'hey' to Elvie Mae for me."

James ignored him. "Goodnight, Miss Sara," he said before harrumphing and heading back inside.

Tadie held out her hand to Alex. "Thanks again. I appreciate it."

"I could come in for coffee or something, by way of payment."

"I think not."

Alex kept hold of her hand instead of shaking it. "Bethanne moved back with her family. To be honest, I think she met someone at the Dunes Club."

"I'm sorry." Tadie pulled her hand free, tucking it with her other one behind her back. Her heart pounded, a fact she did not appreciate.

"I'm not sorry," he said softly.

"I've got to go." She backed toward the porch. "I suppose I'll see you around."

His teeth showed white in the gloom. "I'm counting on it."

She didn't watch him walk toward his car, but turned and fled up the backporch steps. So, his marriage had ended. Good—or bad— depending on how you wanted to look at it. Her daddy used to say what started badly usually ended badly. Alex's marriage qualified on both ends.

She plopped back on the couch and put her feet up. Why had she felt more vulnerable tonight? The answer had to be *Luna*. Her boat was like her baby. And anyone who cared about *Luna* had an advantage.

She grimaced. "That's just sick," she told her toes as they wiggled in front of her.

"No, it isn't. It's normal," her toes—or her other self—argued back.

She dropped her feet to the floor and rested her head in her hands. She *really* needed to get a life if a man could get to her just because he cared about her boat. She didn't even *like* Alex Morgan, no matter what they'd been before. Probably because of what they'd been and then weren't.

Maybe it was a hormonal imbalance. Early menopause? She cringed at the idea. She was way too young.

But she'd heard of celibate women shutting down early. She ought to see her doctor. She could ask for some kind of medication or maybe something herbal—something that would get her back on track.

A knock on the back door made her jump. Alex hadn't returned, had he? Perhaps he'd forgotten something. Maybe dropped something in the barn. She flipped on the porch light and opened the back door.

"I wanted to make sure you're okay." Rita entered the house and bent to run her hand along Eb's back. "He sure is getting big."

"All the kitten's gone out of him, and the heat's made him lazy."

"So, are you?"

"Fine? Sure. Your daddy worried?"

Rita nodded, obviously embarrassed. "Daddy said Alex was here."

"He was, but he's gone now. You want anything? Tea? Water? Come sit down."

"I'll sit a moment, but Mama and Daddy have been plying me with food and drink. You know them."

"Don't I ever. Since Elvie stopped cooking here, I've lost at least ten pounds." She glanced over at Eb. "They seem to have landed on him."

"Mama sits at the table and tries to spoon food onto my plate as if I'm ten." Rita followed her to the couch. "The apartment feels really comfortable. Thanks for getting it cooled. That window unit they had didn't quite make it to the bedrooms."

"I should have done it a lot earlier. How's your mama feeling?"

"She's got to get her strength back and have some physical therapy for her arm—where they took the lymph nodes—but the doctor thinks the prognosis is good."

Tadie tucked a pillow at her back and kicked off her shoes before propping her feet on the coffee table. It felt so good to relax and not have to do anything but visit with a friend. "I'm so glad you've come," she said, closing her eyes for a moment. "It's got to be making Elvie happy, and happy will go a long way in her recovery."

"She's always been my rock."

"Anything I can do, you'll let me know, right?"

"I will. Same for you." It sounded as if Rita's shoes had joined hers on the floor. "Let me know if you need a friend to talk to. I mean, this has to be confusing, having Alex back in town."

Tadie's eyes snapped open at that. "I don't even like him. Just because he helped with my boat doesn't change things."

Rita angled her head. "It sounds like you're protesting rather strongly."

"Divorced or not ..."

"Is he?"

"Not yet. But no matter, he can't come back into my life. Not that way. No man can do what he did and keep my respect."

"You go, girl."

"Yes ma'am. I aim to. So, what about you? Tell me more about this doctor of yours."

Rita studied her resting hands. When she lifted her head, her eyes glinted with mischief. "Did I mention he's white?"

Tadie's hand flew to her mouth. "White? Oh, my goodness, Rita!" She couldn't help it. A hoot broke loose. "I can hear your daddy now. You know he's not going to be happy, don't you? Elvie won't care, but

James? He may be the sweetest man in the world but, honey, you're the apple of his eye. Seems to me he may have something to say on the subject."

The dancing left Rita's eyes, and she loosed a deep sigh. "He's a bit of a snob, isn't he?"

"None better. A little bit of 'everyone in his place.'"

"So how come he sent me to school so I wouldn't be stuck in a certain *place*? How's that supposed to work? I can go to school with the white folk, have white girlfriends, but I can't kiss a white boy?"

"Maybe he's just worried you won't be accepted by the man's family. What's his name?"

"Martin. Dr. Martin Levinson."

"Oh, Rita, no. Jewish too?" More laughter bubbled out. As it waned, Tadie pressed palms to her cheeks to try to cool them. "What were you thinking? Honey, this is going to be a hard one."

"He doesn't look Jewish."

"And you don't look black. A lot that's going to help, as much as church means to your folks. They're going to want you there with them. I love you to pieces, but you're double-dosing your daddy with this one."

Rita's feet slid back into her sandals, and she stood quickly, beginning to pace the length of the kitchen.

"You think he's the one?" Tadie asked, fascinated by this turn of events.

"I don't know. How does a person know?"

"Don't ask me. Obviously, I haven't a clue."

Rita snapped a grin Tadie's way before stopping her march and bracing herself against a counter, her eyes all dreamy. "I look at Martin and think how good he is, and not just to me. In the little things—remembering what I like, what makes me laugh. He's caring to everyone, and—" her grin turned wicked "—Lord, have mercy, Tadie, he's so cute, he makes my toes curl."

Curling toes sounded good. It'd been a long time since Tadie's toes had done anything but balance her walk. "How'd he feel about your move home?"

"That's another thing. He's been totally supportive, even helped me pack. But the day he hugged me good-bye, I swear he had tears in his eyes."

"You're only a few hours away."

Rita nodded, her tone way past dreamy now. "I know."

"Well, it seems to me—who's not the expert, remember—he certainly fits all the romantic images I've ever had of the perfect mate."

"Except he's white. And Jewish."

"Well, yes. But maybe—" Tadie laced the words with a chuckle "—you could keep that a secret."

Rita couldn't seem to find the humor as she pushed away from the counter. "The white thing's going to fall apart as soon as they meet him."

"You think?"

Rita waved her off. "But the other? You know me, my mouth's going to open and out it'll come when I'm least ready. And I can hear Daddy now. Once he gets past the color issue, the whole unequally yoked thing is going to raise its ugly head."

"Then you'll have to be patient and see what happens. I guess if it's supposed to be, things will work out."

Sighing, as if that were all she could eke out, Rita headed toward the door. "I'll let Daddy know you're fine. And we'll be over to help do whatever's left in the morning."

As Rita's steps receded, Tadie turned toward the sink and held a glass under the faucet, barely noticing when the liquid spilled over her fingers and down the drain. Suddenly, the old emptiness felt like a burn needing salve.

She flicked off lights on her way upstairs. Some nights, being alone with only echoes and a lazy cat for company just didn't cut it.

Chapter Fifteen

The sky darkened to slate as Delia grew and gained momentum, twirling toward Cape Lookout just as Hurricane Irene had. Tadie looked over at Eb, who seemed to be polishing his toes. "How come my forebears didn't pick Brunswick, Georgia, or someplace like that to settle—some coastal town that doesn't get hurricanes? We might have liked Georgia."

Instead, her spit of land sucked those storms right in like a magnet dragging in iron.

The porch furniture was in the barn and all the planters under cover. James had fixed the loose shutters and closed all but those over the sink.

"I'll do those two at the last minute," Tadie told him. "You go fill up that tub of yours. Pots and pans too. You got your windows covered?"

"Yesterday. Elvie insisted. Didn't want me climbin' a ladder in the wind or rain."

"Good for her. The shop windows are being secured, so there's not much left to do but wait."

"I hear they been evacuating the beaches since yesterday. I been down to check on Mr. Bobby and Miss Angie. All's ready at their house, 'ceptin' they needed more candles. I took some extras you'd brought us. Miss Juniper's gone off with family, I guess. Her house is empty."

"Thanks for checking. This one's coming fast, isn't it? I'd better find out when Isa will arrive."

"Company'll ease the time."

Isa was out and about, away from her phone. Tadie dialed Hannah's number. "Everything okay there?"

"It is. Except I'm hoping the hurricane will blow Alex somewhere else."

Tadie smiled at the disgust in Hannah's voice. "He's getting to you?"

"Who remembered he could be so pouty? Land sakes, all he talks about is the raw deal he's getting from Bethanne, how he gave her so much, now look at what she's doing. Matt doesn't need this and, frankly, I don't either. Alex actually had the gall to suggest Matt do some of the heavy work yesterday."

"I'm sorry. All I can say is he was a big help hauling *Luna*. I appreciate you sending him."

"I didn't." The disgust now sounded like a good mad coming on. "Didn't even know he'd gone until he said so afterward, even though he went off with Matt's truck. Don't give him any points for altruism. He was pretty pleased with himself."

"I must have misunderstood."

"All I can say is, watch out for him."

"Yes ma'am. You can count on that. You know how I feel."

Replacing the receiver, Tadie grabbed her keys and headed out to see if anything needed doing at the shop. There, the man she'd hired had just about finished nailing boards and plywood in front of the windows.

She headed back home, checking the neighborhood as she passed. Shut down and boarded up.

Best thing she could do was use up the fresh and frozen vegetables that would spoil when the electricity shut down, as it always did during a storm. She was adding broth to the pot of soup when Will called. She didn't give herself time to think about that flurry of excitement his words created. She turned off the stove, wiped her hands, and headed out again.

The *Nancy Grace* stood at the end of a row of boats, just down from one that still had its roller furling and bimini up. Tadie hoped the fellows scurrying around with last minute tie-downs were planning to deal with that one.

Jilly, decked out in her slicker to ward off the few raindrops that had begun to fall, called down from the companionway steps where she stood guard. "Watch the ladder. It's wobbly. Daddy's almost ready."

"Permission to come aboard?" Tadie called up to Jilly.

Jilly turned and poked her head back inside. "Daddy, Tadie asked permission to come aboard. Can I say yes?"

Will's laughter came from below. Jilly's head swiveled back and her little voice shouted out, "Permission granted!"

Once on board, Tadie gave her hand to Jilly, who pulled her down into the salon. "I've packed Tubby. Is that okay?"

"Of course. I'll be happy to have him." To Will, she said, "Anything I can do to help?"

"I think we're ready," he said, adding the soft cooler he'd packed to the bags on deck.

They made it back to the house just as the rain began to fall in earnest. Scurrying inside, they shed their wet coats and hung them on hooks in the pantry.

Isa sat on the chintz couch at the far end of the big kitchen, watching the news. "I made myself at home," she called. "I wondered if you two would come. Aren't we going to have a grand party?" She pointed to Jilly's backpack with the bear's head poking out. "And who is that?" When Jilly introduced Tubby, Isa told her how important friends were. "And it looks like he's a good one."

"He is. He's been my friend forever."

Tadie turned the soup back on low as the others gathered to

watch a television meteorologist discuss satellite overlays on the big weather map. "When do they expect landfall?" she asked.

Isa looked up from examining Jilly's bear. "Tomorrow morning. I wish it would turn right and head someplace else, like the middle of the Atlantic. They're calling it a Category Three, but what'll it be by the time it lands after sucking up all that Gulf Stream heat?"

Tadie got to her feet and tried to sound cheerful. "We'll be fine. The shutters are closed, except for those two, and maybe you can help there, Will. The boats are all secured, and the shop's boarded. Isa? Is your condo set?"

As Will pulled on his slicker and slipped out the back door, Isa answered with a twinkle in her eye. "My neighbor and I worked together. You won't believe who he is." She paused, waiting until Tadie's brows rose in question. "Stefan Ward."

"No!"

"Isn't that a surprise? There he was, hauling boards in yesterday to take care of his new place, which happens to be a couple of balconies over from mine."

"Isa, that's a hoot." Tadie didn't mention the blush she'd caught on Stefan's face, but the memory provoked a smile as she checked on her soup. "It looks as if we'll have a feast. Will brought a cooler, and I see one that must be yours. The candles are out and ready, and I've put flashlights by the beds. Have I forgotten anything?"

Jilly piped up. "Where do you want us to sleep? It's almost time for Tubby's nap."

"Oh dear, I'm not being much of a hostess, am I? As soon as your daddy comes back, we'll head upstairs."

* * * * *

Tadie kept an eye on the child as Jilly ran her hand along the polished banister and occasionally peeked over the side to the hall below.

"It sure is a long way down," Jilly said.

Resting a hand on the child's shoulder, Tadie felt the soft swish of hair brush against her fingers. "Just be careful and you'll be fine."

At the top landing, Will set down the bags and looked at his daughter. "No sliding down the banister, young lady."

"You mean like Eloise? Tadie, do you know about Eloise?"

"The little girl who lived in a hotel?"

Jilly's head bobbed.

"I loved reading her stories when I was your age."

"My favorite was when Eloise went to Paris," Isa said.

Jilly clapped. "You know her too? I haven't read the Paris one yet."

"We'll have to see about that, won't we, Tadie?"

"We will." Tadie held out her hand and led the way through the first door on the left, flipping on the light as she entered. "I've put you in here, Jilly. My mother used this for her sitting room. Through that door is the dressing room and bath. Will, you can use that stool for Jilly's case."

The décor was very feminine, soft shades of yellow, with billowy curtains over windows that opened to the garden when they weren't barricaded behind shutters. A chaise longue covered in yellow and white silk stripes nestled in one corner, with a tall writing desk against a far wall. An old brass chest stood at the end of a ruffly bed piled high with satin pillows.

Touching the bedspread, Jilly turned with wide eyes. "I get to sleep here?"

"Yes ma'am. Right here." She caught Jilly staring at the portrait over the fireplace. "My father commissioned that painting of my mother shortly after they were married."

Jilly studied the woman who looked down at them with that sweet, innocent smile. "Her yellow hair matches the room. What was her name?"

"Caroline Longworth."

"She's the one who called you Sara."

"She did."

"And," Isa said, following them on the walk-through, "she also collected many of the beautiful stones Tadie uses in her jewelry."

Jilly showed Tubby the bed, settling him on the white coverlet. "She must have been a happy person."

"In her own way, probably happier than most."

Ebenezer picked that moment to join them. He paused in the doorway, sat on his haunches, and waited.

"A cat!" Jilly left the bedside and eased toward Eb. "Can I pet it?"

Tadie scooped up Eb and brought him near. "This is Ebenezer. Eb for short. He's very lazy, which means he's also very cuddly."

Jilly reached out a hand to stroke the cat. "Does he sleep with you?"

"When he's not roaming. Cats like the night, so he goes off to investigate after he knows I'm tucked in." Tadie turned to Will as she lowered Eb to the floor. "If you don't want him checking you out in the middle of the night, I'd suggest you shut your doors."

"He can come in with me." Jilly continued her stroking.

"He's safe," Tadie said. "He's too indolent to be much trouble."

"Another word for lazy," Will explained when Jilly looked up with a question in her eyes.

Isa's delicate laughter filled the room. "He's a typical cat, Jilly. Independent as well as very lazy."

Tadie led the way into a large dressing room and from there to the bath. "These are your towels, Jilly," she said, pointing to some light yellow ones. "The blue are for your daddy." At the connecting door, Jilly wiggled under her outstretched arm, followed by Eb. "I've put you here, Will. This was my parents' bedroom."

"I'm flattered," Will said. "Thank you."

The furniture in the master suite was massive, with a lot of curly maple and walnut pieces. Muted beige and splashes of burgundy on the wing chair and pillows picked up the dark wine colors of the huge Oriental rug. A marble fireplace stood at the far end.

"I see why your mother needed the sitting room," Isa said. "She obviously decorated this for your father."

"It was very much him. He spent hours reading in that chair, even into the night when my mother had one of her spells and wanted to be alone but not far away."

Will picked up a photo from a low bookcase. "Your father?" he asked. "Very distinguished."

"He was wonderful."

Jilly looked up at her daddy, then at Tadie. "Was he old when he died?"

"Much, much older than yours." Tadie could almost hear Jilly's sigh. She extended her hand again. "Let me show you the rest of the house."

Tadie pointed toward the front. "That's my room, the one Eb is staking out. Next is another bathroom. And here is yours, Isa."

"Lovely." Isa set her bag inside as Jilly peeked past her at the room. This one also held Caroline's touch—mostly white with blue and purple chintz pillows on the bed and chair.

"What about your brother? Where did he sleep?" Jilly asked as she looked around the hall.

"Upstairs."

"You mean there's *another* upstairs? It's all so big. I've never seen bedrooms with fireplaces."

"Would you like to check out the attic?"

At Jilly's nod, everyone trooped up the back stairs. The room at the top extended the length of the house. "Bucky had a darkroom here along with his bath," she said, opening the door to a room at the back of the space. "Daddy had this opened up and changed from servants' quarters, adding those skylights. But we still wanted attic storage space, so that's what those duck-under rooms are for." She pointed to small doors opening off the main room.

Jilly wrinkled her brow. "Duck-under?"

"Look in one. You'll see. The eaves come so low you've got to stoop to get to the things at the back. They're great for little people. We used to play hide and seek in them."

Isa glanced at her watch. "I think it's time for some of the goodies I brought. Shall I fix a plate of cheeses while you freshen up or whatever?"

"Can I help?" Jilly asked. "I love cheese."

"May I?" Will corrected.

"Sorry. *May* I help?"

"You certainly may," Isa said, waving Jilly forward.

Outside, the wind picked up momentum. Although the evening still held no hint of violence, Tadie shivered, knowing what would follow.

Chapter Sixteen

Jilly pouted when Will pointed her upstairs to bed. Tadie couldn't blame her, poor little thing. Her first hurricane. But Will was adamant.

"Will you come hear my prayers, Tadie?" The long lashes fell and lifted.

Tadie almost swooned as she accompanied the child upstairs. For the first time in her life, she tucked covers up around a child, felt small arms circle her neck for a goodnight kiss, and listened to a child's voice thank God for every single thing and person she could think of.

"And, God, please take good care of all the boats tonight, but especially ours and Tadie's. You know how much we love them, and the *Nancy Grace* is pretty much all Daddy and I have left of Mommy. And even if Tadie's boat doesn't make her remember her mommy, she loves it." She peeked up at Tadie. "Is that okay?"

"Very okay." Tadie smoothed the freshly brushed hair around Jilly's forehead—hair that Jilly had asked her to tame.

Snap went Jilly's eyes again. "And, God, an extra-special thank you for letting us stay in this beautiful house with Tadie and Isa. Will you tell Mommy where I am? I bet she'd like to know. And help Eb not be scared of the hurricane. Amen."

Then there was another hug, with thin arms pulling Tadie

down, with sweet lips kissing her cheek. How would she make social conversation after that?

She couldn't. Returning to the kitchen where Isa and Will camped in front of the television, she announced, "Early to bed for me tonight. Things may get rowdy before too long."

Isa rose to her feet. "I'm with you," she said, following Tadie up the stairs.

Will, remaining below, called behind them. "I'll be up soon. Good night, ladies."

"You go ahead and use the bath first," Tadie told Isa as they said goodnight.

She closed her door and began the process of getting ready for bed, the soft scent of little girl lingering in her nostrils. She'd finished her own ablutions and had climbed between her sheets when she heard the click of a door closing across the hall.

She would not think of Will sitting in her daddy's chair to ease out of his shoes. And she surely wouldn't imagine him climbing into her daddy's bed.

She just wouldn't.

* * * * *

The wind began to howl in earnest sometime after midnight, waking Eb. He circled her feet in search of comfort, but a crack of something breaking outside brought him to her shoulder. He nudged her chin, and his fur tickled her nose. She backed away. The rattle of his purr competed with wind noises.

Had Will been in to check on Jilly yet?

She wished ...

No. None of that.

But how was she supposed to be immune to such a child? Every time she looked at that little snip of a nose with its smattering of freckles and that red hair, she wanted to hug Jilly so hard there'd be no escaping—ever.

If she kept on this way, she'd weep through the night instead of sleep.

"Daddy, I miss you," she whispered to the dark.

Branches from the old pecan tree scraped the shutters at the side of the house. She'd meant to have all six pruned before now. Why did she remember they needed trimming only when the wind threatened to do it for her? It wouldn't be nearly as kind. Her mama's birdbath and stone bench sat under one of the old trees. Maybe James had remembered to take off the top part of the bath so it couldn't blow off and shatter.

This was her first hurricane since Samuel Longworth's death, the first she'd had to get through without his humor and calm steadiness.

She blinked, as if she could see him standing at the foot of her bed in his silk dressing gown with his unlit pipe in his hand, come for a cozy chat. He hadn't smoked the pipe in years, but he liked to carry it around and sometimes fit it to his lips for the memory of it, the lingering scent.

Edging around, he'd sit in the place she patted, asking, "What's on your mind, lovey?" He'd say something reassuring about Elvie, tell her how proud he was of their young Rita. He'd laugh at the thought of Rita's Jewish doctor. The rebel in him, the part of him that fit here in the South and yet didn't, mostly because he'd seen so much and been so many places in his youth, would like that Rita had a mind of her own.

A tear slid down her cheek. "Daddy, do you see what's happening with that child? What am I going to do?"

Was that his voice whispering? She heard or maybe only remembered his words. *Loving's a good thing. Don't mind the risk. Just keep your head on straight.*

"I know. I'll try."

He laughed—didn't he?—at the fix Alex had gotten himself into. *Serves him right. He's the one who messed in Bethanne's garden. Now he'd better figure out how to tend those flowers they grew.*

She smiled at his absurd metaphor.

It's what he'd have wanted—her smile. He always used to pick something off-the-wall like that, knowing she caught the words intended. She could have said them for him. Instead, they played the game.

"In the beginning, I wished it on him," she said to the image that felt real. "I wanted his marriage to be a mess so he'd come back to me."

I know, baby. I was here, remember?

"He's started coming after me again. You saw him help me bring in *Luna*."

A nod, his compassionate eyes looking down at her. But he didn't tell her what to do. He wouldn't have, even if he'd really been here.

This was something she'd have to figure out on her own.

* * * * *

The crack of splitting wood woke her. She spent a few moments identifying the sounds. Had a whole tree fallen or merely a limb? Her bedside clock was dark, so she fumbled for the flashlight and pointed the beam at her watch. Almost five-twenty.

The old house shuddered as the wind barreled through town, its howl frighteningly eerie. *Please, let no one be out there unprotected.*

A door opened and closed across the landing. Probably Jilly climbing in bed with her daddy. Wouldn't it be lovely to have someone with whom to snuggle when storms got bad? Eb had vacated his post next to her. He was undoubtedly shivering under a couch while the storm raged.

Thunderstorms had scared her mama so much that Tadie had to comfort her when Daddy was gone. At night, he always held her mama close, merely speaking a soft word to his daughter before telling her how brave she was and then sending her back to bed. He never knew Tadie had wished—more than once—that there'd been room enough in the big bed for her too.

Why all these morose thoughts? Didn't she have something better to do than lie here having a pity party?

She wished she could call Hannah. Hannah would tell her some absurd story and they'd laugh. At least, Hannah would have before all the trouble with Matt.

She flicked off the flashlight and listened to the dark night raging around her, wishing she were on better terms with God.

Chapter Seventeen

The stillness jarred Tadie awake, forcing her off the bed to see what was wrong. She flicked on a flashlight against the shuttered dark, then dressed in jeans and a top, gathered her hair into a clip, and slipped into the bathroom to brush her teeth with water from the pitcher she'd put there yesterday. She found Will awake in a big wing chair, Jilly asleep in his lap, and a twelve-inch taper burning beside them.

She pointed to the back of the house. Will nodded and slipped out from under Jilly's limp form. He tucked the afghan over her shoulders and followed Tadie to the back porch.

Considering the force unleashed in the last hours, things didn't look too bad in the yard. As she'd expected, limbs lay strewn everywhere. A couple inches of water stood near the barn, but that was probably from overly saturated ground, not flooding.

"I want to find out what made that loud crack in the night," she said, heading for the steps.

He extended a restraining hand and stopped her. "I don't think the eye is going to last very long, not the way that thing came through here."

He was right. Almost on his words, rain slashed from the opposite direction. Ducking through the door, Tadie shook off the drops that had collected in her hair. "You know what happens around here when a storm comes in from the south?" She took his silence for interest.

"The wind blows the water straight up the sounds, giving us really low tides. A northerly wind blows it right back, flooding the low areas. You watch the tides, especially down east, in a northerly wind. Even without a storm surge, the water can wash out the roads."

"High tide was at nine-thirty."

Tadie glanced at her watch. "Ten-twenty. It's outgoing, but just barely. Let's hope the storm doesn't stall."

"Daddy?" a sleepy voice called from the other room.

"Right here, punkin."

"What's happening? Is it daytime yet?"

"It is. See it through the cracks over there?"

Tadie aimed her flashlight toward the table, looking for matches and additional candles. "Let's light this place up a bit. What do you say? Make it more festive."

Jilly jumped off the chair. "I'll help."

"Come on over here and hold this for me," Tadie said, handing her the flashlight. "Aim it there so I can see."

They lit candles on the mantle. "That's better. Now you can help me light some in the kitchen, and we'll do something about food."

"Where's Eb?" Jilly asked, looking around the room.

"He'll come out when he smells breakfast."

* * * * *

Isa padded in as Tadie picked up the steaming kettle. "Thank goodness for gas stoves. Does this mean we actually get a cup of coffee?" Tadie watched her sniff her way to a carafe, through which a lovely brew dripped. "Ah ..."

"You may also have your choice of breakfast, as long as I don't have to bake it or toast it. This new oven has electronic gauges. Don't they plan for outages anymore when they design stoves?"

"They think we prefer a button to a knob. And a machine to do our thinking for us. I hate them. They always go on the fritz or jam or just turn recalcitrant." Isa turned to Jilly, touching the top of her head with a light tap. "How are you this loud morning, Miss Jilly?"

"What's recalcitrant?"

"Stubborn. Which I bet you never are."

"Never, ever. You know what? We're going to play cards after breakfast. Tadie said they always used to play Slapjack during hurricanes. Have you ever played Slapjack before?"

Isa lowered herself into the chair next to Jilly. "I think I have. The name sounds vaguely familiar."

"I haven't. But Tadie says it's really easy to learn."

"I recall having my hand slapped a few times."

Jilly fisted her hands and pulled them to her chest as if getting them out of harm's way. "Who hit you?"

"My sister. She was a wicked player. She won all the games."

"That's not very nice."

"I agree completely." Isa looked around. "Where's your daddy?"

"Upstairs. He said he'd only be a minute, but it's been a lot longer."

Tadie turned from minding the coffee. "Maybe he fell asleep."

"I woke him up a lot. He says I kick and sometimes I fling my arm in his face. I don't think I do. I never feel it. Don't you think I'd feel it if I was beating him up like he says?"

"Absolutely," Isa said. "Your father must be miserably mistaken."

Tadie, never having slept in a bed with anyone else—not even Hannah on sleepovers, because they always had twin beds when they were young—hadn't a clue.

Will's head poked around the entry. "Are you talking about me?"

Jilly hopped over and hugged him. "You didn't go back to bed. Tadie thought maybe you did, because I kept you up all night."

He ruffled Jilly's hair, which hung down past her shoulders in a riot of red. "Just getting presentable for breakfast. Now," he said, turning to Tadie, "what can I do to help?"

"Bacon anyone? And how about eggs?"

"Bacon," Jilly said. "We never get bacon. Daddy says it stinks up the boat."

"Well, then, let's skizzle up a mess of bacon that will otherwise spoil, and I'll scramble eggs. Do you like those?"

"What's skizzle?" Jilly asked.

"Ah. Elvie Mae always said she was going to skizzle up a mess of something when she meant she'd fry it up without a lot of fat in the pan. Maybe a pat of butter when she wanted to brown meat or fish."

"But bacon's got fat," Jilly said.

"Right. But I'm not adding more."

That seemed to satisfy the child. "Can I help?" Jilly asked.

"You can pull a chair over, and maybe your daddy can take care of the bread." Tadie pointed toward the loaf. "We can't make toast, so we'll have bread and butter with strawberry preserves Elvie put up last spring."

"I'll get the plates and set the table," Isa said.

Breakfast was cooked, served, eaten, and plates wiped clean, all by candlelight. Eb's new best friend added a dab or two of egg to his cat food. Several times they heard loud creaks and groans, a snap or two from the trees, and metal screeching, but nothing huge hit the house.

Ignoring the potential havoc, about which she could do nothing, Tadie concentrated instead on trying to slap the most jacks—within reason.

When Eb walked over Jilly's legs before leaping up to the couch pillow, she said, "Silly cat," and turned back to the game. She soon crowed, "Mine!" when three other palms hovered a fraction too long above the pile.

"Look at all the cards you've collected," Isa said, raising her brows. "Are you certain you've never played this game?"

Jilly shook her head as she collected her stack. "That's all four. Now what do we do?"

"Seems to me," Tadie said, "we have to declare you the queen of Slapjack and find something else to play."

"What else is there?"

"See that stack? I got those out for us to choose from. Can you read the titles?"

"Monopoly and Scrabble. What's that?"

"A word game. You might like Monopoly better. I also have checkers and chess, but we can save those for when the laws of attrition begin to work on this group."

"What?"

Tadie explained. "Have you ever heard of survival of the fittest?"

"Like with the wild horses? The strong one gets to make the babies."

Isa's brows shot up. "What have you been teaching this child, Will?"

Tadie wondered the same thing. "That's right, Jilly. The law of attrition applies to all the weak males who get so worn down they fall out of competition."

"Like me winning all the jacks."

"You show yourself the strong one, and eventually one or two of us may fall away from pure exhaustion."

"Or from always losing," Will said, stacking the cards.

"I suppose we could go file our nails." Isa began to braid her long hair. As she pulled the tail into a band, she glanced over her shoulder at Jilly. "The losers, that is. The attrited."

"Good word." Will gave her a thumbs-up. "Care to conjugate it in verb form?"

"I won't even try," Tadie said. "Of course, instead of filing our nails, we could roam the room, gossiping about the others."

"Elizabeth Bennett and what's his name's sister, you know, the one who wanted Mr. Darcy for herself." Isa leaned forward, looking pleased.

"Caroline Bingley."

Tadie couldn't remember when she'd last had this much fun on land. The hurricane had brought all these guests under her roof and given an excuse for her first house party. And here was Isa, relaxed and adding so much to the group.

"I take it we have two Jane Austen fans?" Will said.

Isa looked surprised. "He recognizes the references. Amazing."

"Jilly's mother. My mother. Jilly's aunt."

"Women of taste, obviously," Tadie said, pulling the board games from a cupboard near the stairs. "Austen is popular now, but Isa and I have long been official members of the Jane Austen fan club."

Isa nodded. "In my case, forever."

"Have you bought any of her novels for Jilly?" Tadie asked as she lowered herself to the floor and opened the Monopoly box.

Will ran his finger down Jilly's nose. "In about six years, she might enjoy reading Miss Austen. Right now, Blackbeard captivates her."

"And wild horses," Tadie said.

"And breeding practices," Isa threw in.

Jilly rolled her eyes. "You guys."

"I'll tell you what, Miss Jilly," Tadie said, "if you keep in touch and let me know where I can find you, I will send you the complete works of Jane Austen for your fourteenth birthday. Every young woman must own a set."

Jilly's eyes lit. "That would be lovely." She turned to her father. "We can do that, can't we? Always tell Tadie where we are?"

"Of course we can."

"But I won't be fourteen for a long time."

Isa waved her hand in the air. "It will come upon you sooner than you can imagine."

* * * * *

They played Monopoly and then played Monopoly some more. Mid-game, Tadie popped corn on the stove top.

"You can do it like that instead of in a microwave?" Will asked, only to be swatted by Isa.

They sipped hot chocolate and ate more of Tadie's soup while Jilly racked up properties, including Boardwalk. Fortunately for the rest of them, Isa bought Park Place on her next turn. Will and Tadie breathed a collective sigh as their pieces continued to land on one or the other.

When Jilly begged to buy the coveted property from Isa, she received a firm negative. "You'd break me with one hotel," Isa said.

Jilly extended her lower lip, but her eyes sparkled as she pretended to pout. "Well, this way neither of us can make money on them."

"Hold on a minute. Don't get greedy." Will forked over the rent money as he landed on the houseless property.

Landing on the last of the purple low-rent properties, Tadie let out a, "Woohoo. Hotels coming up."

"Won't help much," Will said, examining her rental amount.

"I know. But it didn't cost much either."

Eventually, hotels dotted the landscape, and everyone seemed to owe money to someone. When Will raked in the stash in the middle of the board, he escaped debt and proudly bought two more houses.

Isa counted her paltry change. She had a long way around the board and a lot of rents to pay before she'd hit *Go* again and could add two hundred to the measly amount tucked under her side of the board. "Ladies," she said, "I'm going broke. I propose we call Will the winner and be done with it."

"You mean *quit*?" Jilly asked.

"Did I say the wrong thing?"

The edge of Will's finely carved lips curled in what certainly looked like a smirk. "Perhaps Isa has a broken nail," he said, his eyes dancing as he returned Tadie's bemused stare.

Isa held up her fingers and examined the ends. "Here goes that law, Jilly. Right in front of your eyes."

"Ah," Will said, winking at Tadie before turning his gaze toward Isa. "The first to go. What does that say about you, my dear Isa?"

She picked up a cushion. "I assume you're referring to the fact that I won't be lead stallion this year. If I weren't afraid of catching this on fire, it would be in your face, Will Merritt."

"Thank God for small favors."

"You're teasing, aren't you? Both of you?" Jilly asked, a worried frown wrinkling her nose and forehead.

Tadie reached out a hand. "Of course they are. Grown-up silliness."

As she spoke, Will grabbed Jilly, bringing her up on his lap and tickling her until her squeals of "Daddddy!" forced him to quit. He turned her to his chest and wrapped his strong arms around her in a hug.

Tadie watched, mesmerized. When she glanced up, she saw Isa staring, not at Will and Jilly, but at her.

Chapter Eighteen

The rain continued long after the heavy winds abated. When Rita called from the apartment to check on them, Tadie picked up the hall phone, the only one in the house not dependent on electricity.

"We're fine," Tadie said. "If you get bored with the older folk, you can come play with us. We've exhausted Slapjack and Monopoly—which was an all-day affair—and now Isa has a puzzle set out on a card table in the living room. I think Will's going to help her, but that may not keep Jilly going for long."

"Daddy's done the same thing over here. He loves that tropical puzzle you gave him, when was it? A couple of Christmases ago? Mama's lounging around, watching us try to match pieces of identical blue."

"You okay with cooking and everything?"

"Doing well, thanks. I peeked out a little while ago. The old oak out back lost its good swinging limb. But it may have needed to come down anyway."

"Won't we be lucky if that's all we lost? I haven't been out yet."

"Hold on a sec, Tadie. What, Daddy?"

Tadie heard James say something before Rita came back on. "Daddy says not to worry about the cars. There was a little water, but not deep enough to hurt much. He'll get them washed down as soon as the electricity comes back."

"Thank him, will you? What about Isa's?"

"He parked it back behind the garage, so it didn't get anything but some rain and leaves."

"I appreciate it, Rita. Isa will too. If you change your mind about coming over, you do it."

"I will. Have fun."

* * * * *

Isa and Jilly leaned over the puzzle. The rain continued, finally slowing to a light drizzle a little after seven o'clock. When Will and Tadie stepped out to check for damage, Eb slipped past. He bounded down the porch steps, pausing at the bottom, obviously not sure he wanted to get his feet wet.

Tadie pulled up her hood as she sloshed through puddles that began as soon as she stepped off the porch. Surveying the mess that littered the yard, she groaned. "Oh my."

"Jilly and I can help with cleanup."

"No need. James will be here."

"Who's James?"

"He and his wife Elvie Mae live over the garage. James does the gardening, and he used to drive for my parents. They've been taking care of us forever."

Will raised his brows. "Servants?"

Tadie raised hers right back at him. "Friends. Family."

"How fortunate."

She heard the sarcasm. What did he know? "It has been."

He held out a palm. "I'm sorry. Maybe I'm just envious. Anyway, helping with the cleanup is the least Jilly and I can do. She'll get a kick out of it. It'll be a change of pace from the boat."

"Then I'd appreciate it."

Approaching the south end of the property, they discovered a tall pine that had snapped about twenty feet up. Fortunately, it had maimed only a cluster of azaleas. "I'm glad it missed Mama's bench.

She used to love sitting out here when the azaleas were in bloom. Her grandmother planted some, her mama others. She wouldn't let James come near them, except to water and mulch, but he'd sneak out every so often to prune them so they'd come back fuller the next year. She never knew. She thought if he cut them, they'd be wounded."

"I'll bet they're beautiful," Will said, following her out toward the sidewalk. "Perhaps we'll be here in the spring someday."

She turned to him. "Jilly's special. I hope you do come back."

"She's very much like her mother."

Tadie felt herself relaxing. "Your lifestyle fascinates me. Why did you decide to live on a boat and go cruising?"

"That's easy." He increased his pace to walk beside her. "Because of Nancy. Because she'd always wanted to."

"And couldn't?"

"We'd looked at boats for years, dreaming of the day we'd buy one and head out with Jilly to see the world." He raked his hands through damp hair. "It never happened. One night, a drunk driver hit the wrong pedal at a red light."

Tadie stopped walking as the force of his words hit her, like a fist slamming into her stomach. She'd imagined cancer or some other disease taking this man's wife, Jilly's mommy. Not a drunk driver.

Before she could utter a word, he continued. "You know the ironic thing?"

Tadie shook her head, even though he was staring out at the water.

"She was a school counselor and had been trying to help a number of boys whose fathers went on drunken binges."

All she could utter was a lame, "I'm so sorry." This man needed a hug. She wished someone who knew how to comfort were here to give it. Someone not named Tadie Longworth.

He whispered, "Yeah," and seemed suddenly fragile. "Me too."

Should she leave this wound alone, or would he want to talk about it—about *her*? She kicked a stick out of the way and stuck her hands in her slicker pockets. Her shoulders hunched forward.

She knew parental loss and sibling loss. Sometimes those memories, those endings, turned her into a jellied mass of pain. But the sudden death of a much-loved spouse? How did Will manage day after day, having to be strong for Jilly? What were his nights like, when he'd turn in bed to find his wife gone? "When ... when did it happen?"

"Twenty-one months and three days ago."

She winced. He'd counted the days. They were longer ago than her daddy's death, but obviously not long enough. "I don't know what it's like to lose a spouse. I'm so very sorry."

"Thank you." His expression seemed wistful when he glanced her way.

She started walking again. Perhaps it was time to change the subject. "May I ask you one more thing?"

"Only one?" His mouth curved.

"For now," she said. She liked that, his humor. Perhaps that was how he endured.

"Shoot."

"Do you ever miss having a home—other than the boat?"

He seemed to think about that for a while, peering across the water dreamily, as if seeing past the banks to the great ocean. "I guess, sometimes. But not for a house, more for what home used to be. Now, home for me is wherever Jilly is. I know she misses some things, like having a best friend—and that's your fault."

Whoa. Tadie tried to see his expression, because his tone sounded pretty serious.

"My fault?"

He shrugged slightly and then turned. Tadie's tightening stomach eased. Will's eyes twinkled at her when he said, "She found out from Hannah that the two of you have been best friends since kindergarten. Now she wants one too."

"How sweet. But I suppose that's difficult, traveling as you do."

"She'd love to get to Baltimore and meet up with the children she played with in Charleston. She may not have one best friend, but she makes friends wherever we stop."

Tadie looked away. If only she could suggest they stay. Let Jilly find friends here.

Will began walking again, avoiding broken limbs and debris. "She loves the *Nancy Grace* as much as I do. This is not merely a passing fancy for either of us."

"I'm sure. You're giving Jilly something priceless, even if there are negatives involved. I suppose each choice negates some other one." At the sidewalk, she stopped again. "I had a wonderful father who taught me a lot. I guess the times I miss most are those when we sailed together, just the two of us."

"Your mother didn't like the water?"

"She was afraid of it. She was a lovely, gentle woman, but she had issues—at least that's what they'd be called in today's world. There was a simplicity about her that probably came from some sort of mental illness. It wasn't talked about."

"Why not? Couldn't she have gotten help?"

"Right after Bucky was born, my daddy took her up to Duke. I was very young, but I remember she couldn't stop crying and seemed to retreat inside herself. I think she probably had postpartum depression that triggered something deeper. They gave her medication, but from then on, we spent a great deal of time taking care of her."

"That was a lot to put on you."

"No, we had Elvie Mae and James."

"A good thing, obviously." He shot her a rueful grin.

"Yes sir. A lifesaver."

"I hate it when I stick my foot in my mouth."

"You're forgiven. You ought to meet them sometime, you and Jilly. I think you'd like them—and their daughter, Rita, who is about to take the bar exam. An amazing young woman."

"You got me there. Anyone who can get through law school and still be sane is amazing. My father wanted me to go, but I couldn't imagine anything more boring. I'm much more of a hands-on type of fellow."

"Hands-on doing what?"

"Mechanical engineering. I still get to dabble in it, consulting for my old firm, but the wonderful thing about owning a boat is getting to play with engines and systems all the time. I'm really just a glorified mechanic."

"A handy man to have around."

"I am that."

They smiled in harmony before Tadie stepped out into the road far enough to see that a crew had blocked each end of Front Street. A downed pole obstructed the west end. Debris littered lawns, the street, and the marsh across the road. Her dock seemed to have survived relatively intact, but she couldn't say the same for a small motorboat that had blown off its moorings and landed in the grass. In the other direction, limbs were down in the yards, and next door to Mr. Bobby's, a tree blocked the Nelson's front door. Mr. Bobby and Angie seemed to have fared pretty well, unless there was damage she couldn't see.

"I hope it isn't any worse in other places," Will said, his voice and the lines in his forehead exposing the worry that suddenly assailed them both.

Sensing his urgency, Tadie asked, "You want to call the marina?"

"Think anyone will be around?"

"If they can get through, they'll be there, checking on the boats."

They hurried inside, where Tadie took their jackets and pointed Will to the landline in the hall, before following her nose to the kitchen.

"What's going on in here, ladies? Certainly smells good," she said, hanging their damp jackets on hooks outside the laundry room.

"Spaghetti." Jilly said proudly.

Tadie tapped the child's cheek. "Can't wait."

Sampling the sauce, Isa held up a finger. She tossed in another few pinches of basil and said, "Hannah phoned. I told her we were fine. She said Matt and Alex had a mess to contend with in the driveway, a big tree downed. Otherwise, they're doing well."

"Good thing both of them know how to handle trees." Tadie

turned at the sound of Will's shoes tapping on the hardwood floor.

He rubbed a hand down his face. "No one answered."

"They could all be outside," Tadie said. "We'll try later, but it's possible those downed lines are affecting the marina. They may not be letting cars pass. Surely by tomorrow you'll reach someone."

"I hope so. If not, I'll have to walk over."

Jilly grabbed her daddy's hand. "We're cooking. Isa's teaching me how to make spaghetti."

He tweaked her nose. "I'm so glad, punkin. You know how much I love good pasta."

"Since we're the designated chefs," Isa said, waving a wooden spoon their way, "why don't you two go sit down in the other room and do some grown-up thing. Tadie, I'm using sauce from my freezer, and we're adding things from yours."

"Teach Jilly as much as you can, please," Will said. "I beg you. I'd love to have a budding gourmet."

"Tired of your own cooking?" Isa asked.

"An understatement."

Tadie wished she could let go and relax, but she sure didn't want to go sit in the living room alone with a man who was fretting about his boat and wishing he were anywhere but here. "I think I'll go freshen up," she said, pretending a lightness she didn't feel. "Call me when you're ready for help."

Will seemed as relieved as she was. He grabbed a lit candle and handed her one. "That sounds like a fine idea."

Great, now Tadie had to worry about where to put her free hand and how her feet hit the floor. She didn't want to stumble on the stairs, and she didn't want him staring at her backside. She hoped the stairwell hid her reddening face and awkward tread.

Breathe. Just breathe. Concentrate on walking a straight line and getting into your room. You can do it.

* * * * *

They managed to get through dinner. Well, more than managed, but only because Jilly chattered and Isa told stories and the food really was delicious.

"I'm exhausted," Isa said after they'd used another bucket of water in the clean-up. "You children may stay up all night, but I'm for bed."

"Right behind you," Will said, herding Jilly.

Candles in hand, they headed toward the stairs and had begun their ascent when lights popped on around them. "Goodness," Tadie said, startled by the brilliance. "I thought we'd turned all these off."

"One of us, probably yours truly," Isa said, "must have forgotten and hit switches during the dark day. Sorry. You need help?"

"Not a problem. I've got it." Tadie started toward the hall outside the kitchen.

"You take the back. I'll get the front," Will said, shooing Jilly upstairs with Isa.

"Night, Tadie," Jilly called.

"Goodnight, honey."

Isa's hand was on Jilly's back. Isa would be the one helping Jilly undress. Tadie shrugged back her longing for another, "Will you hear my prayers?" from that sweet little voice. Another, "Can I hug you?" She flicked off the kitchen light, along with the one in the dining room. Will peeked in her daddy's library as Tadie walked through the dark at her end of the house.

"Done," he said when they met up again at the bottom of the stairs.

"Thank you."

They climbed silently. Why did they have to be silent? Couldn't she think of one intelligent thing to say when they were alone together? They'd almost achieved ease as they walked the yard that afternoon. He'd shared his story. She'd shared some of hers. It had almost felt as if they could be friends. But now it was merely awkward. She was too conscious of him, too aware of his male-ness, and she hadn't a clue why. She couldn't be attracted to him.

Not to him. Not to a man who'd soon sail out of her life and never be heard from again. A man who was still in love with his dead wife.

Tadie's feet hit the landing first, and she turned toward her room.

Will headed toward Jilly's. "Goodnight, Tadie. Sleep well." His words sounded soft, easy, in a way she couldn't answer.

She wished she could. She'd like to know how to be relaxed again. "Goodnight," she said, barely glancing behind her. Goodnight.

The water sputtered through the pipes as it got used to flowing. Thankful the gas hot water heater had kept the tank ready for this moment, Tadie turned on the shower and climbed in.

* * * * *

Will lay in the big bed, longing for sleep. He'd been greedy in the shower, letting the spray sting his back, but his muscles still tensed.

It must be worry about the boat.

Jilly's eyes had slammed shut almost before he'd finished kissing her. The other side of the house was quiet, so maybe he was the only insomniac.

Tadie'd seemed different after dinner. Maybe even before. Had he said something during their walk? Something that upset her?

She'd been buddy-buddy all day with all of them, but especially with Jilly. That was good. It was. But he didn't want it to intensify. A little fun passed the time. A little friendliness. He wasn't trying to lock up Jilly. But he sure didn't want her upset when they had to leave.

So it was probably a good thing those lights had gone on like they did so Isa had to corral Jilly toward bed instead of Tadie having another bonding moment with his daughter. Too many emotional weavings between Tadie and Jilly might be Jilly's undoing. He'd seen women, single women, who preyed on motherless children as a means to an end.

That was not going to happen here.

Maybe he was abnormally cautious, but Leslie and others like her had made him so.

Leslie had come to visit her friends on *Sea Breeze* when they were all anchored in Charleston. She'd been so good at the game, Will hadn't recognized her ploys until he'd found her in his face every time he ferried Jilly to the other boat. It hadn't taken her long to sniff out Jilly's weaknesses and try to weasel her way into their life.

He could hear Leslie's sugary voice now. "I'm just taking the children to the yacht club pool, wouldn't Jilly like to go?" And then, wouldn't he like to meet them afterward for dinner? And, where was the *Nancy Grace* off to next? Did they need crew? She'd love to volunteer.

Will had never been happier to see someone's back than when Leslie's vacation ended and she waved a somber good-bye from the *Sea Breeze's* dinghy.

He was not going to be ensnared by any woman. Knowing firsthand what stepmothers were like, he wasn't about to inflict one on Jilly. She was never going to play second fiddle in his life. Besides, they were doing just fine on their own.

Sure, Tadie seemed like a nice person, a friendly sailor and now a hostess without any hidden agenda. But she was single and over thirty, an age when most women were either attached or looking to become attached. And getting pretty desperate about it. Well, she could just get desperate with someone else.

He blew out a puff of air. Boy, wasn't that conceited.

But better to be too cautious than to regret a relationship and see his Jilly hurt. People said a child was better off with two parents. Not true if the child didn't belong to both of them. Any budding expectations? He'd just nip them and run.

Sure, he had needs. He was human. And male. But he'd practiced sublimation now for almost two years.

Just the thought made him grit his teeth.

He missed Nancy so much. Talking about her today must have triggered all that had happened after that walk. Including his aching need as he lay here, his mind switching from Tadie to his own imaginings.

"Nancy," he whispered in the dark. He longed to see her beloved shadow, to feel the whisper of her breath on his cheek. He reached out and slid his hand over the empty pillow, brought it down over the cool sheet. "I need you."

But only silence greeted him. He pulled the pillow over his face and tried to hide from the ache that wouldn't go away.

Chapter Nineteen

Tadie gasped at the carnage, unable to utter another sound after Will's pained, "Oh, no." The *Nancy Grace's* starboard rigging hung, limp and lost, the stainless wire draped over stanchions where it had ripped free of the masthead. The lifelines were down, several stanchions broken. A large gash streaked through the paint along the topsides, just under the porthole for Will's cabin. And about two feet of wooden rail had splinters pointing upward.

Into their silence, the balding yardman droned on, scratching his head between words. "I knowed we shoulda got all that stuff off that big boat. Shoulda said something, but we kinda got caught tryin' to get things tied down all over the yard."

Will stared at him, obviously speechless. Tadie longed to take Will's hand for comfort—his *and* hers. Instead, she balled her fingers into a fist, letting her nails bite into her palms.

The man rambled on. "When that wind came up, it just laid hold of that furling and shredded it, but not before the loosed sails added to that there shade thing of his and that high pilothouse just sent it kabooming right over into the boat between yours and his. That's the one hooked your riggin'."

Will opened his mouth, but no words came out. Tadie tried to wrap her mind around the pain he must be feeling, like coming upon a loved one who'd been assaulted. If *Luna*'d been holed or sunk, she'd feel the blow to her stomach, the squeeze to her heart.

"Sorry about that, mister. Real sorry. Boss is too. He's in there on the phone, trying to get the other owners down here and get the insurance things going. You got insurance?" At Will's nod, he sighed. "Got good photos before we pulled that other boat off'n yours. Boss said he tried the number you gave him. Didn't get no answer."

Will found his voice. "Cell towers must be down."

The man shrugged and walked away, shaking his head.

Will set up the ladder and climbed aboard. "She's got a small hole, probably where the other guy's spreaders slammed down before he lost his mast." He sounded weary. "It could be worse."

Again, Tadie longed to put her arms around him. Just as a friend. For comfort. She pointed at the poor sloop that had suffered the most damage. The crane had righted it as well as the yacht next to it, whose bimini would never be the same. The smaller boat had lost mast and rigging and had dings and dents, as well as a couple of holes in her sides. Her owner was not going to be happy when he got here. Tadie marched around to the stern. Morehead. Okay, a local. Then she checked on the big boat. Nevada.

Nevada? As in desert? No wonder the boat wasn't prepared for a storm.

Will poked his head over the rail. "We got some water inside. I'm going to have to haul out these soaked things and make sure the bilge pump works. I'll need some help."

"Coming right up."

As few boats can seal out water when it's blowing sideways at over 100 mph, Tadie wasn't surprised to see the mess. The hatch over the V-berth had dribbled onto Jilly's bed, but with a waterproof mattress cover, only the sheets and comforter needed cleaning. Jilly's menagerie hung in netting along the side walls and had missed much of the onslaught.

Tadie yanked bedding off the bunks while Will reached into

cupboards and pulled out wet foodstuff. He set the items on plastic bags on the floor and wiped down the damp spaces. Tadie checked the drawers and hanging lockers. Jilly's clothes were damp, so she bagged them and set them on the deck with the bedding. Water seemed to have slithered in through a vent in an aft locker. The hole in the deck was over the head, so rain had merely run into the bilge. Will opened floorboards to make sure the battery-driven sump had done its job.

"Still working." He dropped the board back in place and went on to the next task, grabbing more towels from a dry cubby to sop up water where it puddled near the companionway. He spoke in a monotone, his voice revealing nothing.

If only the *Nancy Grace* had stood alone somewhere. Or if the yard had done its job of preparing the other boats left in its care. Tadie sighed and continued wiping wet walls.

Digging around in a cockpit locker, Will pulled out damp line, which he ran through a couple of boom blocks. "I'll rig this up so we can lower the bags easily. You want to climb down and meet them?"

Tadie untied the line from each sack as Will lowered it. His efficiency impressed her, the way he'd immediately started solving problems instead of moaning. A man who didn't get mad at things impressed her.

All right, fine. A lot about Will Merritt impressed her.

The muscles flexed in his arms as he lifted the bags over the remaining stanchions. Knowing he was immune to her—and unavailable—gave her license to study him, didn't it? Wouldn't he be horrified if he could read her mind?

He'd surprised her many times in the past two days. His smiling eyes, his intelligence, his thoughtfulness. Now she noticed his lean strength.

Deep breath.

She wanted to keep Jilly in her life, at least as much as the cruising lifestyle would permit. She could be an aunt to Jilly. Maybe invite the child to visit and give Will a break every so often. Wouldn't that be fun?

Suddenly, he paused and stared back. She pretended to be studying the sky. He lifted the last bag over the rail. "Here it comes."

"What's next?" she asked, untying the line.

"I'm going to bring all the cushions out to sit in the sun for a few hours, now that I've cleared some deck space."

Tadie climbed back up the ladder as he went below. "Hand them out to me."

After setting out the last one, she leaned in the companionway. He stood, wiping his forehead with a paper towel and surveying the cabin. His shoulders hunched slightly before he straightened them and climbed toward her.

She backed up. "I bet you could use a dehumidifier."

"You think I can find one?"

"In my barn."

"Well, aren't you amazing?"

She shaded her eyes. "You want me to go get it?"

"I'll come and help. We can use my muscles instead of yours."

"And nice ones they are too."

At his surprised expression, she blushed. Maybe she shouldn't have been quite so frank. "You being a man and all."

His face seemed to relax and catch the humor. "Of course. Being a man."

* * * * *

They hooked up the dehumidifier with a few asides about a man's muscles tossed out for her benefit. "Enough," she cried as he fitted "the beast" into place—a small device even she could lift. The teasing seemed to help them both relax.

"Isn't the insurance company going to want to see the 'before' pictures?"

"I'd rather dry the boat than worry about them believing I need to. Besides, if I don't get those wet things to a Laundromat today, I'll have mildew issues, which will cost a lot more."

"No Laundromat. You'll use my washing machine. Why don't we head on back to the house where Jilly and I can wash clothes while you deal with your insurer?" She put her hands on her hips and tried to sound severe. "And don't even think about moving back on board until everything's fixed. Jilly likes my house. Besides, Eb is her new best buddy."

He cocked his head and watched her. "You're going to spoil her, you know."

"My daddy spoiled me because my mama couldn't. I adored him."

"That's what I'm worried about."

"That she'll adore me?"

"She already does."

"Well, the feeling's mutual. You'll have to bring her back every year so her new Aunt Tadie can love on her some more."

Will nodded, but he had a crease between his brows.

She bit her tongue. A little late, but she stilled it. She'd better work a lot harder at keeping her wants from getting the better of her mouth. Wants could land her—and Jilly—in big trouble. But how could she let them run off to a motel when she was having so much fun with them at her house?

The thing to do—maybe—was let them stay at the house, but distance herself. Keep busy in her studio or at the shop. Enjoy them at dinner. Whatever it took to keep that worried look out of Will's eyes.

* * * * *

Tadie's studio door closed as Will and Jilly tuned in to the Discovery Channel. Like the perfect hostess Will had found her to be, she'd set out a bag of microwave popcorn and pointed to the refrigerator, telling them to make themselves at home while she caught up on some work.

So maybe he'd been wrong. Maybe that look on her face wasn't what he'd imagined.

He hadn't been wrong about his own response when he'd caught her gazing up at him. He'd seen her eyes widen. Lust had slammed hard into him, and neither of them had been able to speak, even as her eyes quickly shifted and she pretended she hadn't been staring at him. She'd tried to turn it into a joke.

He'd shrugged off the moment as a normal male reaction to obvious female appreciation. That's all he needed to do. Recognize the problem. Then solve it.

Jilly snuggled deeper into the couch cushions, her sock feet stretched across his knees, the cat sprawled at her side. "Look, Daddy. Zebras. Turn it up."

The doorbell rang as he pressed the volume button on the remote control. Jilly's feet hit the floor and before he could catch her, she dashed into the hall.

"Hold on, kiddo. It's Tadie's house."

Jilly skidded to a halt in front of the door.

At the second chime, Tadie emerged and flipped on the porch light. Will ambled closer as Tadie checked to see who was there.

"It's okay, Jilly, you can answer the door," she said.

Jilly pulled it open and cringed back. Will looked past her to the creep from the store—the fellow who'd asked about Tadie—who'd almost killed Jilly. He pressed his curled fingers against his thighs.

The man peered around Jilly, smiling when he caught sight of Tadie.

"Alex," Tadie said with a loud sigh.

Will didn't have time to analyze the sigh before Jilly ducked behind him, only her head peering around his hip. Tadie made the introductions.

"We've seen him before," Will bit out.

Jilly mumbled something under her breath.

"What, honey?" Tadie bent to ask.

Jilly shook her head against Will's backside, her fists clutching his shirt. He saw the concern in Tadie's eyes, but his attention was drawn to the snide look on the other man's face.

"I thought you would all be gone by now," Alex said, his gaze taking in Will and Jilly.

Tadie glared at him. "What made you think that?"

"The hurricane's over. Anyway, Hannah sent me to see how you're doing. Do you need any help?"

"We're doing fine. But let's be clear here, Alex. She didn't send you last time, so I don't imagine she sent you as her messenger this time either. Besides, she knows not to worry, not with James and Rita around. And now Will is here too."

"I see."

Will bet he did. Bet the creep saw the disgust in his eyes and the fear in Jilly's. Just what was this man's relationship to Tadie that he assumed the right to question—or even wonder—who stayed here?

"Did you and Matt get the drive cleared?" Tadie asked.

"Matt supervised."

Will's jaw tightened at the man's arrogant tone, which the fool couldn't hide even when he tried to massage his sneer into a smile.

"It's clear," Alex said. "They lost the old cedar."

"What a shame. It was a beautiful tree."

His glance again passed over Will. "What are you three up to?"

"Not much," Tadie said. "Jilly and her daddy are watching TV."

He stepped a little farther into the hall, forcing Tadie to back up. Peering into her studio, he asked, "And you?"

"Working." She reached around and closed the studio door. Turning her attention to Jilly, who still hid behind Will, she gentled her voice. "What are you watching, Jilly?"

Jilly peeked up at Tadie, did a quick reconnaissance, then whispered, "Zebras. I love zebras."

"I'm crazy about them too." Tadie reached down and Jilly slipped her hand in Tadie's, edging part way out of her hiding place.

Will remained still.

"Then you better come see these. They're stupendous," Jilly said.

"If Tadie needs to work, that's a lot more important than television, don't you think, young lady?" Alex said.

Will's eyes narrowed when Alex spoke to Jilly. Come on, jerk, he almost said. Take one step closer. He clenched and unclenched his fist. One more word. Give me a chance to rearrange your face.

Will watched Tadie's cheeks color as she reached for the door, gesturing Alex out. She pushed on the man's shoulder when he didn't turn. "You just scoot on back home and tell Hannah I'll talk to her tomorrow." Her voice had risen at least one octave.

It took Alex a moment or two to wipe the surprised look off his face. Will spread his feet apart, ready to boot the fellow out. But he held back. This wasn't his house.

Alex must have noticed the fists and the scowl. "Well, fine," he said, retreating. "I'll look forward to seeing the pieces you're working on. Perhaps in the shop next week."

"Good*night*, Alex."

Tadie closed the door on him, then leaned down to put her arms around Jilly. "Sweetie, I'm sorry he was rude. But we got rid of him, didn't we?"

Jilly gave Tadie a big hug. "He's not very nice."

"No, he's not, but he's Hannah's brother-in-law." She wore a questioning look as she turned to Will. "Is there something going on between you two that I don't know about?"

"He almost ran over me with his car." Jilly hopped sideways and then back. "And he wasn't very nice to Isa in the store."

"No wonder we don't like him. I'm glad we showed him the door."

A little of Will's anger drained out. "I take it he doesn't know you well enough to recognize Mama Bear."

"He's never seen her before." Tadie glanced down at a puzzled Jilly. "Come on, sweetheart. Let's go watch those zebras."

Jilly's heart was in her eyes. Will glanced over at Tadie. Same thing. Not good.

He mumbled, "All I need now is a pipe, slippers, and the big chair."

"Porridge, anyone?" Tadie asked. He caught her sarcastic tone, and the bite of it surprised him. So she could dish it out too, could she?

Jilly's "Yuck!" at least got them all laughing.

But it didn't stop the questions. Will pretended to watch the screen, but he couldn't forget Alex's glances. Or Alex's words.

And there was Tadie, hovering over Jilly with a proprietary air of her own.

Yep, Mama Bear, indeed.

Chapter Twenty

Tadie fell more deeply under Jilly's spell when the child asked for help with her bath. "Come on," Jilly said, tugging at her hand as they started up the stairs.

Later, Jilly's bedtime prayer plaited Tadie's heart strings to her own, and her kiss soldered them permanently. The prospect of Jilly and Will sailing away was already too painful to imagine.

She didn't go back downstairs. She couldn't let Will see her lost state.

His door eventually opened and closed. A few minutes later, splashes sounded from across the hall.

Listening to the spray on tile, Tadie imagined water streaming down his firm body. She fanned her face to cool it. She was a mess. That's all there was to it.

Celibacy hadn't looked quite this bleak in a very long time.

A man like Will Merritt would never be interested in a woman like her—alone, unloved, untouched. Men didn't like women other men rejected. Isn't that what Mr. Darcy had said? They might try to seduce such a woman, but they would never marry her. Never love her.

No one, not even Hannah, knew her secret. Hannah assumed

she'd had sex with Alex—which meant Alex had kept his mouth shut.

Unless he hadn't. She wouldn't put it past him to have strutted around, proclaiming something that hadn't happened. Especially after Matt's early success with Hannah.

Tadie slipped down under the covers and yanked a pillow over her head. She saw the movies. She read the books. No one except Sara Longworth, spinster of Beaufort, had hit this ripe old age untouched.

If only she could blame it on her faith. If she'd stayed chaste out of reverence or obedience, she could feel justified. After all, hadn't chastity been a frequent Sunday school subject? And hadn't her father and Elvie Mae taught her a standard of purity?

But no. She knew her heart and it wasn't pretty.

She'd almost let loose with Alex. It hadn't been God who'd kept her from taking that step. Far from it. She'd lusted and yearned and only said no because she hadn't trusted Alex, not deep down where she'd needed to. And after that, the others, even her erstwhile—and very temporary—fiancé, hadn't tempted her to the tipping point.

There had to be something basically wrong with her—with her appearance or her personality or her psyche. Look at her, imagining her houseguest naked in the shower. That little girl's *father*. And why was she allowing herself to become attracted to a man like Will Merritt, a man who'd never want her?

She was sick. There was no other answer.

And she couldn't tell a single soul.

* * * * *

Will scrubbed at his skin until it hurt. He'd tried to ignore his fears as Jilly and Tadie had cuddled. He'd brushed them aside, sublimated them even, for the sake of his own comfort. What kind of father was he?

Jilly did not need someone in her life who would even consider having someone like Alex as a friend. No, he and Jilly were doing just fine on their own.

Besides, he still mourned Nancy. What kind of man—husband—let a strange woman's laughter sneak under his guard? It was wrong.

All of it. Time to go, and quickly, before Tadie did any more damage to his little girl's heart.

He usually spotted this sort of thing before it got out of hand. What had been different this time?

He knew the answer to that. This wasn't a new discussion between him and his thoughts.

But still. Once more.

Maybe this time he'd hear, put it in perspective, and figure out his next move.

Tadie was a sailor. Since Nancy, all the other women sailors he'd met had been married, safe. Leslie didn't count. She had been a *friend* of sailors, not one herself.

Tadie had opened her home to them. That one had been his fault. They'd needed a place and he'd been lulled by the town, the friendliness of the people at Down East Creations, and his conviction that Tadie was an independent woman who wouldn't use a child to get herself a husband.

Well, he'd been a fool. When her *friend*, Alex, had stopped by, Will had seen the calculating look in Tadie's eyes and he'd known. Yeah, Alex was related to Tadie's friend Hannah, but the man's attitude didn't come merely from being the friend of a friend—or even the brother of a friend.

Maybe Alex was someone she'd dated who just wouldn't come up to scratch, so she figured he and Jilly were a better bet. That way, she'd even get a bigger boat thrown in. She'd absolutely coveted the *Nancy Grace*, oohing and aahing at the woodwork and the layout. She'd stood tall and proud at the helm on the way to the dock.

Too bad. The *Nancy Grace* wasn't hers and never would be.

Instead of sleeping, he strategized. He'd go out early and find a rental car. He could get a loaner from the yard until the agencies opened. Then he'd return Tadie's humidifier, get the rest of their clean laundry, and fetch Jilly.

But he couldn't keep her on the boat while he was restoring it, not for very long. He'd call Jilly's Aunt Liz as soon as he figured out his timetable.

That settled, he dozed fitfully. And in between bouts of sleep, he thought of Nancy. He even tried a half-hearted prayer or two. He was way too upset to make them real.

* * * * *

Tadie headed downstairs the next morning, still looking like a hag in a horror movie. Sure, she'd tied back her hair and done her best to cover up the dark circles and baggy eyes. She'd even put on a bright turquoise shirt. But none of it helped.

A note on the counter greeted her: *Jilly should sleep until at least nine. I'll try to be back by then to take her to breakfast. Please go about your day as if we're not there. You've already done too much for us. Will.*

She sagged against the refrigerator door.

He knew. He'd felt her desperation.

But he was right. She'd get on with her day and forget about them. It was the only thing to do.

She brewed a cup of coffee, toasted an English muffin, and carried them to her studio. As an afterthought, she picked up the portable phone in case Hannah called.

She pulled out her sketches and opened the drawer where she stored some of the amber she wanted to use when she finished the garnet pieces. She was sorting by shape when little feet pattered into the room.

She took a deep, cleansing breath and did her best to smile. "Good morning, sleepyhead."

"Whatcha doing?"

This was Jilly's first visit inside the studio. Tadie understood the child's fascination with a hidden room. "I'm working on some designs for new jewelry."

Jilly leaned forward over the workbench. "Can I see?"

"They're in the rough stage now. I'm waiting for the stones to speak to me."

"Do they really talk?"

"No, of course not. But sometimes a certain stone will just seem to belong somewhere, with a certain chain or in a certain setting."

Jilly wandered the room checking out all the fascinating objects. When she came to Bucky's photos, she stopped.

"My brother took those," Tadie said. "Do you have any idea where that might be?"

Jilly shook her head.

"It's Afghanistan. It's a country that's had a lot of war and some very unhappy people ruling it. But look at the smile on that old man's face."

"He seems happy."

"My brother and some of his friends helped him. I think he was happy then."

"Your brother died, didn't he? Did someone shoot him?"

She started to answer when Will strode into the room and pulled Jilly away from the pictures. Tadie felt the blood drain from her face at Will's hard expression.

"Jilly, sweetheart, go load up your backpack." The glare he gave Tadie couldn't be mistaken.

Jilly looked puzzled. "Is the *Nancy Grace* ready? Is she all fixed?"

"She will be. Now scoot."

"But I don't want to go yet." Jilly grabbed Tadie's hand and clung to it.

It took all Tadie's self-control not to hold the child just as tightly.

Jilly's lip quivered. "Not until the boat's all ready. I like it here and Tadie said we could stay." Her voice sounded panicky.

"Well, we can't."

"Why not?"

Will turned to Tadie, his eyes hard, glinting at her.

She unclasped Jilly's fingers and took her by the shoulders. "Hey, trooper. We've had a grand time. And we'll do it again. But if your daddy wants you to go with him, don't you think you should?"

Tadie recognized the beginning of tears in Jilly's eyes. She knew if she kept looking at them, the cold horror she felt would loose itself in her own tears, and hers wouldn't be silent. She turned the child toward her father and gave her a quick push. "Go, sweetie. Get packed."

Will waited until Jilly's feet hit the stairs. "You've been wonderful to us and we're very grateful," he said. "But I don't appreciate you filling Jilly's head with ugly tales about the world's savagery. She's much too young."

Had she mentioned savagery? Her heart thudded and her hands shook as she raised them to her throat. "I'm sorry. I didn't think."

"Of course you didn't. You've never raised a child. You've no idea how sensitive Jilly is, how a story about war could give her nightmares. She's still getting over Nancy's death, and now you throw images of Afghanistan at her. If I'd seen this room earlier, I'd have warned you to keep it locked and Jilly out of here." At the door, he turned. "I know she's become fond of you, but I'd appreciate it if you didn't try to see her again."

Tadie didn't move. She couldn't. She heard Will climb the stairs, heard him walk into Jilly's room. He must have already packed his things, because he didn't go back into her father's bedroom. He must have been planning to leave since last night.

It didn't take them long to finish and come back into the studio, where Jilly ran and threw her arms around Tadie's neck, burying her face in Tadie's hair. "Thank you so much. I had a wonderful time."

"I had a lovely time with you too, Jilly."

Jilly backed away and wiped the back of her hand across her eyes. She sniffled hard, making herself cough. "Daddy needs me at the boat, so I have to go. But I'll see you later."

"Sure," Tadie said, her voice catching. "Take care."

"Will you hug Eb for me? I couldn't find him. Will you tell him I'll be back?"

Tadie nodded. "Mmm," was all that came out, and she had to turn her head to hide the tears.

As they walked out the front door and out of her life, Tadie dropped into the big chair near her daddy's desk and stared at the walls until she could no longer sit. She rose and wandered back upstairs, where she stepped out of her nice clothes and let them heap on the floor.

She replaced them with a long T-shirt. Without conscious thought, she moved to the window.

The view didn't mesh with her expectations. The water ought not to reflect sunlight. And the sky—how could it be blue and cloudless?

Surely, such palpable changes ought to be visible beyond her ripped and bleeding heart.

Chapter Twenty-one

Tadie finally managed to rouse herself enough to stumble downstairs. She had the refrigerator open and a pitcher of tea in her hand when she heard the sound of flip-flops on the porch steps. By the time Rita stepped over the threshold, Tadie had taken down a glass and filled it, handing it to her without a word.

"They gone?" Rita perched at the table while Tadie wiped the counter.

Tadie nodded and continued to wipe, moving to the stove. When she'd rinsed the rag and folded it over the faucet, she straightened the tea towel and braced her hands against the countertop as she stared out the window and into the backyard.

"Mama's wanting to see you. Can you come up and have lunch?"

"I'm not hungry," Tadie said, this time bending to fetch a spray cleaner, which she squirted on the front of the refrigerator. She wiped it down with a paper towel.

"That wasn't dirty to start with. You sure you're okay?"

"I'm fine. There were some streaks I've been meaning to clean."

"Okay, you've cleaned. Now, will you come see Mama or not?"

Tadie ran a hand over her forehead. Her fingertips felt gritty. How could there be grit left on anything? "I'm sorry. Of course, I'll come."

"Lunch?" Rita rinsed her glass and set it in the dishwasher.

"Fine. Lunch. I'll bring the tea." She forced a smile, but knew it didn't make it all the way to her eyes.

* * * * *

"Hey, child," Elvie Mae said, patting the couch beside her. "You come over here and give me a hug, you hear?"

Tadie set the pitcher on the kitchen counter and bent over Elvie for a proper hug.

"There now," Elvie said. "I had to see you're okay. This is the first hurricane we didn't spend together, helping each other out. I knowed you had help, but it wasn't *my* help."

"Yes ma'am. I surely missed you."

Elvie's gaze pulled Rita and James into her circle. "See, I told you. This child still needs us. See that, James? She's not so grown-up that she don't need the rest of her family."

James nodded. "You're right there, Elvie. Nobody's that grown-up."

They ate and chatted, but Tadie tried to change the subject when Elvie asked about the folk who'd stayed with her. She did tell about Isa's neighbor who'd turned out to be the painter fellow everybody admired so much.

"What's new since your last visit to the doctor?" Tadie asked.

"It was a good report. I got to go back every so often, but I'm not gonna let them talk me into any chemo," Elvie said, her voice fierce. "That'll kill me faster than that cancer and make my life miserable while I'm here." She shook her head of tight grey curls. "No sir. I'm gonna live how I live and trust in the good Lord to do what's best for me. If he wants me home with him, fine. If he thinks I'm needed here with my family, that's fine too."

"Mama!"

Elvie Mae raised her palm, shushing Rita. "You heard me. Hush now."

James scooted closer and touched his wife's hand gently. "It's a whole lot better for you to stay here. We ain't ready to do without you any time soon, you hear?"

Elvie turned her hand over and clutched his. "I hear, old man. I hear."

Tadie used her napkin to wipe at her eyes.

Rita changed the subject. "Guess who's coming to dinner day after tomorrow?"

Tadie snapped her head toward Rita, whose innocent tone told Tadie exactly who would be revealing himself. "Re-ally?" she said, elongating the word, eyes wide.

"Martin wants to meet my folks, and they want to meet him. So, yes. Really."

"Am I invited?"

"If you want to come, you're invited."

"I can't wait."

* * * * *

The sun shone through a gap in the curtains, dancing on the wall with shadows from the oak tree. Tadie lay curled on her side, watching the patterns but not paying much attention. Eb stretched, poked his nose up close to hers, then bounded to the floor when she didn't respond. Normally, Tadie would have cuddled her cat and let the morning stir her imagination. Now, she wished the night and oblivion could last all day.

When Hannah called, Tadie was still trying not to think. They compared hurricane damage and the news that Matt had caught a cold from someplace.

"Why doesn't that man do what the doctor says and rest?" Hannah said, her voice edged with anger, more than likely generated by worry.

"Can't Alex pitch in more? Isn't that what he's here for?"

"Lands, Tadie, he's too busy trying to get Matt to entertain him. He's bored silly and keeps complaining because the land's too soaked to do any logging, no matter how many contracts need filling."

Tadie listened and tried to make soothing noises while Hannah talked of the brothers' latest battle over selective harvesting.

"The owner doesn't want to pay to do it right. Alex drives Matt crazy with his 'who cares, strip them, the trees will grow back.' You know how Matt feels. So he's telling Alex the growth will take too long, making it bad for the land and bad for business."

"Good for Matt," Tadie said, trying for enthusiasm about something that would normally have her up in arms. Strip cutting should be against the law, the way it wasted trees and left the land looking ugly and vulnerable.

"Matt shouldn't get so riled, but Alex's pouts and stomps are going to drive me batty. Was he always like this?"

"Seems so."

"How come we never noticed? Anyway, I think Matt's beginning to wise up about his baby brother, but he still defends him, says we should let Alex stay as long as he needs to. I say he ought to pay rent. But, of course, Matt won't hear of it."

"Maybe Alex will get tired and move on. Or at least, out."

"I heard him on the phone with Bethanne yesterday. There sure is no love lost between those two. I think she's demanding money from him, probably for the girls. He was telling her he can't afford to send more, although I don't know why not. Unless he's spending it on something I don't know about, he should be setting aside a big chunk, living with us."

Tadie had trouble caring about any of this, but she tried to make appropriate noises. It wasn't Hannah's fault Will had run hard and fast.

"Not only does Alex mooch food off us, but he keeps bringing in liquor. Matt won't tell him not to. And the last couple of nights, Alex reeled up the stairs. What a mess. Oh dear. Hold on." Hannah said something offline, then came back with, "Matt needs me. I'll call you back later."

Tadie climbed out of bed, because staying in it just made her mind wobble all over the place, wondering what Will and Jilly were doing, seeing Jilly's impish grin. She turned on the shower to wash off the aches she'd accumulated overnight and pictured Will rounding up supplies, getting started on repairs. She hadn't asked if he planned to contract it out or do it himself. He'd probably pay someone so he wouldn't have to hang around Beaufort and risk running into her.

But hiring out the job didn't sound like Will.

What if she went downtown? Would she see them?

No, that wasn't likely. The boat was across the bridge off the causeway. Will would have rented a car so he could get to supply houses, maybe a grocery store. It would be just as easy for him to go over to Morehead and not come to Beaufort at all.

She towel-dried her hair and ran a brush through her curls. This would teach her to let new people into her life. Never again. She was fine with the circle of friends she had. They wouldn't hurt her like this.

If only the world would return to the simpler place it had been before Elvie and Matt had gotten sick, and Delia—along with Alex, Will, and Jilly—had blown in. She needed to re-launch *Luna*.

That reminded her of their last sail. She heard again the tinkling sound of Jilly's laughter.

The buzz of a saw told her James was out cutting limbs, so she left the shorts where they lay on a chair and got out long pants to go help. Rita joined them after her errands, lightening the workload, but it still took most of the day. Only once did Tadie remember Will's promise to help. And then it replayed as she hefted branches or filled a bag.

James pulled the last large limb free so he could cut it into pieces. "You want to get *Luna* in? We could do it next high tide."

Tadie glanced at her watch. "Not unless you want to go out at ten tonight."

James laughed, shaking his head. She dragged a smaller branch to the pile. "How about noonish tomorrow?"

"Sounds good."

Tadie backed away from the noise of his chainsaw, bending with Rita to grab an armload of brush. "You up for some sailing?"

"Sure am."

"Tomorrow then, if you've got the time."

New memories. That's what she needed. To write new memories.

* * * * *

Dusk settled slowly over the water as Tadie perched on the dock bench, staring out at the empty anchorage. There was a loose board near her feet. And one missing. She should get them fixed.

Maybe tomorrow. Or the next day.

A big trawler crawled by, likely heading for the town marina. How on earth was she going to drive across that bridge and not look over to the left, imagining Will and Jilly on their boat? Would she wonder each time whether they'd fixed the rigging, planked and glassed the hole, painted the topsides yet? With contractors in demand everywhere, hurricane damage took weeks, months to fix. Whether or not he did it himself, the work would take a while. Jilly was bound to ask questions. What would he tell the child?

And why had he been so angry? He'd spoken to her as if she were thoughtless and cruel. As if he hated her.

Darkness began to overtake the day. Scattered street noises included a blaring car radio. Crickets sawed in the marsh. Gentle waves sloshed at the pilings.

She sure could pick them, couldn't she?

"Daddy, how come I keep getting entangled with fools or crazies?"

The breeze carried her words away, but didn't bring back an answer.

* * * * *

As Tadie crawled in next to Eb that night, more doubts crept in like a fog, the kind that slithered over banks and along the shoreline until it shrouded the entire town. Bucky's death had hurt. When grief had taken her mama, followed soon by her daddy, she'd tried to hold on. But losing Jilly in this awful mess she'd made with Will? That felt like the tipping point, where the next degree of heel would land a boat on her side.

Somehow through the years, she'd believed, maybe some days holding onto her faith like it was the tail of a line ready to slip through her fingers, but holding on. Yes sir. She'd prayed for Elvie. She'd been chatting regularly about Jilly and Will. About this *more* thing that troubled her, making her want something but not knowing what.

And where had it gotten her?

Perhaps she hadn't held up her end of the bargain with God in terms of going to church regularly, but what about his part in the whole thing? Wasn't he planning to cut her any slack?

She got up to fetch a wet cloth, glaring at her reflection as the water ran in the sink. "Girl, you're a mess. Look at you. And you're getting worse, not better." If only her eyes would quit leaking.

"Stop it. You don't need that man. Or his daughter."

She got back into bed, laid the washcloth over her eyes, and settled back on the pillow. "Time to quit whining."

She and Jilly would both be fine. She was strong, and Jilly was resilient. Pretty soon Jilly wouldn't even remember the lady who lived in Beaufort.

Chapter Twenty-two

Rita's legs dangled off the end of the dock. "Didn't they say we'd have wind today?" She lifted her hair off her neck and wiped at sweat that had formed there. "You know they lied. That little ripple across the water isn't going to get anyone sailing."

Tadie leaned back on the bench, the brim of her sunhat pulled low. "It's too hot even to think of moving, honey."

"Well, maybe, but it seemed like a good idea when we thought of it. I miss hanging out with you and *Luna*."

Footsteps on the wood meant someone was headed their way. Tadie didn't bother to turn, but Rita called out a greeting to her daddy.

"I brung you some chicken necks." James set a basket between them and the scoop net next to Rita. "You two ain't doin' much. Might as well catch us some crabs for dinner."

Rita was the first to move. James was already back in his garden when she pushed herself up to tie one crab line to a piling. "Come on, lazybones."

Tadie quietly complained, but she picked up the other line and knotted it on her side of the dock. They both sat back and waited.

"Daddy's been trying to make me into a crabber all my life."

Tadie fanned herself with her hat. "He hasn't been very successful with either of us."

"I prefer pots," Rita said, inching her line up through her fingers. "They're a whole lot easier."

"You got one?"

"I think so. Hold the net, will you?"

Tadie bent down, lowering the net slowly as Rita worked the line. She couldn't tell whether there was a crab down there or merely the bait. When Rita eased it toward the surface, she slipped the net down and under, hauling in a dripping chicken neck.

"He was there," Rita said. "Look how the bait's been chewed."

"Toss it in again. Maybe he'll come back."

Rita dropped her line and went to check the other. "This is almost as bad as fishing. Wait, wait, and then—poof. The thing's gone."

"We used to catch a basketful," Tadie said, leaning against a piling. "Bucky and I would come out here and spend all afternoon, then take a basket in to your mama to cook. Nothing better than just-caught crab. Bucky must have been the one who made it happen. You remember those days?"

"Not much. I remember my daddy coming out sometimes to check on you two. Sometimes he'd let me tag along." She got the chicken neck in sight. "Nothing here either. I bet it's too hot for them, so they've backed themselves into that nice, cool mud to wait for night."

"Maybe so." Tadie laid down the net. "Is Martin going to get here early enough to go out if a breeze comes up?"

Rita hooded her eyes as she scanned the water. "I doubt it. He's got rounds to make before he can leave Raleigh."

"Have you told them about him yet?"

"I wanted to," she said, looking sheepish as she smoothed her hands over her thighs, "but how do you say something like that when Mama and Daddy are all excited, thinking I'm bringing home a nice, church-going, dark-skinned doctor?"

"How do you *not* tell them and embarrass everybody?"

"Don't imagine I haven't worried myself nearly sick."

Tadie pictured the scene. "I'll tell you what. Your mama and I have been friends—more than friends—most of my life. Why don't I come up there early, maybe with some things to add to your table, and you tell them then? What are they going to say, remembering how they feel about me and my family?"

"Tadie, would you? That's just the thing. You've never been afraid to speak your mind to Mama—nor she to you—and if you're coping with her, maybe I can get Daddy wrapped an extra turn around my finger."

Tadie could picture Rita doing exactly that. "What're you serving? I need to know what to bring."

"I thought I'd make Daddy's favorite fried chicken and mashed potatoes, 'cause we're not likely to be cooking crabs. You have any flowers that weren't taken out by the storm? Mama was just saying it's going to be a while before she sees any color on her table. I told her I'd buy some, but she doesn't think that counts."

"They've got to be grown right here, don't they? Well, I hauled in a couple of pots of new chrysanthemums in gorgeous colors. I'll repot a small one for her table."

She could do that. And maybe take another of the small pots to her bedside. Something cheery up there would be good.

When a slight movement caught her eye, she said, "Is that line going tight? The one on your right?"

Rita jumped up. "Maybe it's just the tide."

"And maybe it's not."

* * * * *

Tadie climbed the steps leading to the apartment. She couldn't help her frisson of excitement as she anticipated the evening ahead. She didn't imagine sparks would fly—Elvie and James weren't like that. But she, Rita, and Martin would have to exude charm, and she wanted to see how Martin would perform. Because if he couldn't pull it off, well then, he wouldn't be half good enough for their Rita.

Elvie oohed over the plant, her eyes dancing. "Look at those colors, James. Those purple and rose tones, and that yellow thrown in. My lands, missy, you did well. So you saved these from that storm. Good for you." Elvie turned and fluttered her fingers at Rita. "Get out the yellow cloth napkins. Let's celebrate. Aren't you something, Tadie-girl?"

Rita nodded over her shoulder at Tadie. When she'd reset the table with the requested napkins, she offered Tadie some tea.

Tadie took it and eased down on the couch near Elvie's chair. They'd better get this over with, or Martin would be arriving and they'd still be sitting here looking at each other. She tried to make her words sound casual. "Do you all know much about this fellow of Rita's?"

Elvie patted the doilies on the arms of her recliner. "Rita's kept him a secret, seems like. We know he's a doctor, which made Rita's daddy perk up. The only problem with doctors is they work too much."

"He's from someplace up north," James said, as if that were a strike against him.

"Only when he was born, Daddy. He grew up in Raleigh. Like I told you, his daddy's a doctor too."

"His folks still alive?"

"They are."

"Have you met them?"

Rita looked pleadingly over at Tadie. "I told you already, Daddy. I met his father once when he was visiting Martin at the hospital."

"Rita," Tadie said. "Best get it over with."

Elvie sat a little straighter. "Get *what* over with?" She looked from Tadie to her daughter. "What aren't you saying?"

Rita closed her eyes and took a deep breath. When she opened them, she reached out and took her mama's hands in both of hers, then turned to her daddy. "Martin's last name is Levinson."

James rolled that around on his tongue. "Levinson?"

Elvie eyed her sharply. "Say it straight out, Rita."

"Mama, Daddy, Martin's Jewish."

"You mean white Jewish?" James squinted at his daughter. "Not black Jewish?"

Rita's head bobbed and her lip found its way between her teeth.

James groaned. Elvie stared straight ahead. Tadie tried to remember something her father had said when Bucky asked him about Jews. "My daddy once said that believing Christians are grafted to the vine—the one Jews get born into. By faith for us, so we can be children of Abraham and of the promises too."

Rita's head bobbed faster. "That's right. Didn't you read me that? From one of the Epistles?"

"Aside from being Jewish, he's white," James said, a frown furrowing his brow and his eyes open enough to glare.

Tadie waved her arm in front of James's face and pointed to her skin.

Elvie's eyes bugged slightly, but she grinned in spite of her shock. "My goodness, look at the girl, James. You see what Tadie's tryin' to tell us?"

James crossed his arms. He wasn't budging. He obviously didn't like it, and there'd be no shaking him.

"James, we sit here calling Tadie family, lovin' her like she's family. But listen to us."

"Miss Sara is Miss Sara. That don't extend to this Jewish boy."

"Why not, Daddy? You taught me I was just as good as white folk. Are you telling me now they're not as good as we are? That a Jewish boy isn't as good as I am?"

Elvie gasped. "Rita!"

James stood and started pacing. "I just might be." He squared his shoulders and kept his eyes focused ahead instead of looking at any of them. "He's not a church-goer."

"James, honey, you come sit here by me. Scoot over, Tadie. Let the man in."

Tadie moved to the far end of the couch. James was no match for his tiny wife. He lowered himself next to her.

"Now, James, you're not meaning these things you're saying. I know you. You had a different thing in mind for our Rita, and I can appreciate that. But you can't be saying this when all along you've taught the child to be independent-minded. To follow her dream. You can't."

"I surely can."

"I tell you what. This young man's coming in a few minutes. Why don't we pretend he's a friend of Tadie's come to dine with us? Won't that make it a mite easier this first time?"

"Don't see how. I knows who he's come for."

Elvie turned to Rita and Tadie. "You girls go on down and wait for Martin outside. I need a little time alone with your daddy, Rita."

They couldn't get out of there fast enough. As they raced down the stairs, they felt like children escaping from the principal's office. By the time they reached Tadie's porch, they were giggling.

"Oh my, Tadie. When you stuck out your arm like that—"

"Did you see your mama's face? She'd forgotten I was white."

"I know!"

"What do you think she's telling him?"

"If I know my mama, she's telling him to shape up and behave. Can't you hear her? 'We've got company coming, James Whitlock, and you'll not disgrace me or this home.' She'll mimic your mama something fine and sound more like your mama than your mama ever did."

That set Tadie laughing again. "She's something, that mama of yours. I love her to pieces."

A racy black Mustang zipped up the driveway and slowed to a halt near the barn. Rita let the screen door slam behind her and jumped into Martin's arms before Tadie managed to cross to the porch steps.

The way he cradled Rita's face melted Tadie's reserve. That wasn't the embrace of a man in lust. That was love shining in his eyes, and if James couldn't see what was staring right at him, then he needed new glasses.

Rita led Martin over, her expression as brimful of happiness as his. When he shook Tadie's hand, his grip was strong and he looked her in the eye.

"So this is Tadie. You're famous among Rita's Raleigh friends. Rita wears that necklace you made for her and delights in telling everyone all about your shop and your work. I'm glad to finally meet you."

Tadie couldn't help but like him. "Are you ready to beard the lions?"

His arm encircled Rita's back. Looking down at her, he asked, "How're they taking it?"

"I'm not sure which was worse, your skin or your faith."

"Well, I can't change my skin, and I think one is born a Jew and dies a Jew. I may be in trouble here."

He said it with a mischievous twinkle in his eyes. Yes, he'd do well enough.

Upstairs in the apartment, Martin shook James's hand with a steadiness that had to impress the older man. When he bent and kissed Elvie's fingers lightly, she smiled right up at him.

Tadie liked that he did all this with aplomb and what seemed to her a sense of humor. She winked at Rita.

"You sit right here and let me get to know you," Elvie said, patting the couch, "while Rita and Tadie set out the dinner."

* * * * *

Walking back to her house after the early meal, Tadie felt lighter than she had in days. At least things looked good for somebody.

Maybe Martin hadn't completely won over James, but he would. Elvie would pray about it and would secure the backing of God.

Tadie envied Elvie's ability to hear from God. But to get to that same place, she'd probably have to be as good as Elvie. Tadie Longworth, spinster, had never heard a peep from on high.

That thought brought a frown to her face. "With all that hullabaloo, there'd better end up being a wedding," she told Eb as he sped past her into the kitchen. He braked near his bowl.

She shook in some kibble, but he stared up accusingly. "What?" His gaze seemed to darken. "Demanding, are we?"

She breathed through her mouth as she opened a can of smelly tuna stuff and spooned some over the dry food. "Here. Enjoy."

He rubbed against her leg, his tail switching, before he meandered back to his bowl. "Glad you like it," she said, washing her hands, pleased that he'd been gentleman enough to thank her. As she filled a glass with water, she noticed the message light blinking.

"Call me," was all Isa said.

Carrying the portable phone onto the front porch and into the lingering daylight, she punched in Isa's number.

"What's going on?" Isa asked. "I saw Will and Jilly coming from the dinghy dock. He says the boat's still on the hard, but he's working on it. He was decidedly cold. Poor little mite, she didn't seem to know what to make of her daddy's hurry to get past me, and when she asked if she could wait for him in the shop, he spoke sharply to her. I've never heard him do that before. I'm not sure Jilly has either." Isa paused, but Tadie remained silent. "You should have seen that face. I thought she'd bawl right there."

"Isa, it's so awful."

"Tell me."

She did, haltingly at first. Isa's response was a stunned, "What got into the man?"

"That's not the worst. He said I can't ever see her again."

"Oh, Tadie. That child loves you. It's obvious to anyone."

"And I love her. Maybe that's the whole problem."

"How? You think he's jealous?"

"Could he be? But Jilly was drawn to you too. Could he be insecure enough to want Jilly all to himself?"

"I don't know. He didn't seem like that sort of man."

"I've been driving myself crazy thinking I don't know how to judge people. That I let people into my heart, and then they turn out to be different from what I imagined."

"Well, I'm certainly not one to talk. But if it's any consolation, I liked Will."

"So, we're both misguided fools," Tadie said, a catch in her voice.

"That poor little thing."

And poor me. Tadie hated pity parties, but she sure felt another one coming on.

Chapter Twenty-three

Jilly finished her prayers and tucked Tubby under the sheet. Her daddy sat on the edge of the bed, smoothing back her hair. She closed her eyes. It felt good, even if his fingers were rough like his chin when he forgot to shave. Forgot or was too busy. The bristles were all over his face, but it was all the work on the boat that messed up his skin and made him not very daddy-like.

All day he'd grumbled about how long it was taking. He'd crumpled up papers, saying no way was he going to pay good money to have some nincompoop like that yard man do something he could do better.

She had tried to be good and stay out of his way, 'cause he'd talked about sending her to Georgetown. But good hadn't worked. Now he'd gone and done it. He'd called Aunt Liz.

She loved Aunt Liz, but she didn't want to leave Beaufort or her daddy. Why couldn't she just stay at Tadie's house if Daddy didn't want her on board? She was sure Tadie missed her. Hadn't she said Jilly could have the pretty yellow room whenever she wanted?

And Isa had told her she could come help in the store. It would work. She knew it would. She didn't need a babysitter. She was a first mate. First mates knew how to take care of themselves. But when she'd said something about going back to the house, Daddy had gone all red in the face, and his eyebrows had almost hit in the middle. He'd grumbled out a "No," and when she'd tried to argue, he'd only gotten quieter. So the "No" was the kind that meant business. The kind you'd better not argue with.

Now, as he straightened, his hand reaching for the light, she whispered, "Daddy?"

"What, punkin?"

She hesitated. She wouldn't argue. She'd just ask, and maybe he wouldn't get mad. "How come I have to go? I can help you here. I'll be good."

His sigh was so loud it scared her. Sort of like the sighs he used to make instead of getting angry back when they were first learning how to handle the *Nancy Grace* and things didn't go so good. He did it mostly in the beginning, when she didn't know how to be a very good first mate, and he had to steer and trim the sails and tie up and anchor and cook and clean and do the homeschooling all by himself.

He never yelled. He got mad at stupid men who screamed bloody murder at their wife and kids for not doing things right. Daddy *never* did that. He just tried to teach her better. And sometimes he sighed.

She worked really, really hard to learn, because even when Daddy tried not to let her see how much he wished Mommy were here to help him, she could tell. Sometimes he kind of looked off into space, and she'd hear him talking out loud when there wasn't anybody there to talk to.

After tonight's big sigh, he hugged her really tight. "I know you will. You're always good, but things are going to get a lot messier on the *Nancy Grace* before they get better again. I need you to be in a safe place so I won't have to worry about you. Can you do that for me? Be a big girl and not fuss?"

Jilly bowed her head. When he asked like that, what could she do? He was all she had, so it was important to make him happy. And to be good. Whenever he got sad and missed Mommy, she had to be good and stay cheerful and try to help him smile.

She took the hand that now rested between them and clutched it to her cheek. "Okay, Daddy. I'll go."

The hurricane must have upset him. Maybe it was the mess it had made of the *Nancy Grace*. Maybe it was because they'd named the boat after Mommy, so if the boat got hurt, it was almost like Mommy being hurt again.

At least, that's what made sense to her, since Daddy had been angry since they left Tadie's.

There was one thing she had to do before he put her on a plane. She had to see Tadie.

Tadie's house was just across the bridge and then a little walk. Okay, maybe a long walk. But she could do it. She'd sneak away while her daddy was busy tomorrow.

* * * * *

It seemed like hours before her daddy got up. Jilly dressed Tubby in his little coat so he'd be all ready to go on the plane, and she tried not to think about how mad Daddy would be if she couldn't get back from town before he found out.

She heard the water running in the galley and went to help him. While his coffee dripped into the mug, she kept real quiet and got out bowls and cereal. Daddy smiled better after coffee.

He took a sip, poured milk into the bowls, and sat down at the table. "I bought you a ticket to fly from Raleigh late this afternoon. Aunt Liz will meet your plane in Baltimore."

That didn't leave much time. *Please let Daddy be busy.*

"What are you going to do this morning?" she asked around a spoonful of Cheerios.

"I want to get the first layer of fiberglass on that hole."

"Eew, stinky."

"I know. Maybe you can do the laundry while I take care of it. I'll help you get the washers started. You can load the clothes in the dryers."

Jilly tried not to show her excitement. The washers took a long time—plenty of time for her to get to Tadie's and back. All she wanted to do was thank Tadie and give her a hug. That shouldn't take too long. "I'll take my new book and read it while I wait," she said, hoping God wouldn't be too mad at the lie.

"Good girl." He took her bowl, rinsed it, and put the cereal away. "Why don't you get your things together so we can start while it's still cool?"

When they got there, Daddy unloaded the bags of laundry. "How did we make so much of a mess? I didn't even know we owned this much."

"Silly, it's all that sanding and stuff."

His smile was crooked as he helped her sort the clothes and start the washers. He handed her a baggie with all the quarters she'd need and pointed her to a hard plastic chair. "I'll be back in a couple of hours to fetch you and the clothes. Okay, punkin?"

"I'll be fine."

"The manager's right on the other side of that wall. You know him. You need anything, you ask. And you know where I'll be."

"Daddy, I've done laundry before. And you'll be right over there." She waved toward the *Nancy Grace*, whose mast rose behind a big motor yacht.

He bent toward her. "I know. But we usually do chores together."

"I know how to set the temperature, and I have the money. You can go."

She stood in the doorway and watched as he left. When he was out of sight, she stuffed her book into her backpack, put the laundry bags under a table, and headed out, keeping clear of the marina office window and trying not to let any of the other boaters see her. They'd tell if they did, because she was a kid, and boaters were like that. They all watched out for the kids on boats. It felt like she had dozens of parents, which was nice most of the time. Except now, when she wanted to sneak away.

Her heart beat so fast, it might bust open. She squinched her eyes tight and whispered, "Sorry," to God. If this was what being sneaky was like, she wasn't so good at it.

She had to walk out to the highway, turn to the right, walk a little, and cross the bridge. At least it wasn't the big bridge over to Morehead. Just a small one. Well, smaller anyway.

The best thing to do when you had to cross a bridge with cars zooming past was not to look. Just keep your feet moving on the walkway and your head straight, like you know what you're doing. And don't look in the little bridge building. If you stare ahead, the man in there will think it's okay. "That's it," she said under her breath, talking mostly to the bridge railing. "Oh, and there's a boat leaving its slip. Just think about the motorboat and not the cars."

The boat was one of those flashy ones, all front end and loud motor. Daddy called them cigarette boats. She should remember to ask him why.

The boat's driver was trying to back up, but there was a lot of current pushing his backside into a piling. He went forward again, revved his engine, and zoomed out straight. Jilly was glad the *Nancy Grace* didn't have to back out of a place like that. You could see the current whooshing past. She'd hate to get caught in it.

She stepped off the bridge and felt a shiver of excitement. She'd made it across on her own. Now all she had to do was go to the first road, turn right, head to the waterfront, and go left until she came to Tadie's.

* * * * *

Will spread out the fiberglass, measured what he needed, and cut it. This was good. He was being efficient and so was Jilly. They'd get something done before he had to waste an afternoon driving to Raleigh and back.

She'd be okay. Liz was good with her. Liz wasn't Nancy, but she was a good aunt. She'd help Jilly forget this nonsense about Tadie.

He pulled on his gloves and pumped epoxy into a mixing cup. It squirted about an ounce and then only air. He lifted the can. Empty.

How had he let that happen? Hadn't there been plenty the last time he'd used it?

Everything was ready, but not enough epoxy. Great.

He pulled off his gloves, fetched his keys and wallet, and set off for the laundry area. Jilly'd probably be glad to be rescued from babysitting the clothes. The wash load should be about finished, so he could put them in the dryer and take her with him to buy more epoxy. By the time they got back, the clothes should be dry. It was too bad Plan A hadn't worked, but Jilly would have to sit upwind of the curing epoxy.

He parked and went in to get her. She wasn't there. Well, maybe she'd needed a bathroom break. He checked the washers. They had a few minutes left before the spin cycle ended. He'd wait.

Why was it that whenever you wanted a pot to boil or a washer to finish, it took forever? He looked at his watch.

Jilly must be reading in there. He'd give her until the washers finished before he'd call her out. Surely she'd be ready by then.

Finally, the washers clicked off, one at a time. He loaded the dryers, but Jilly had his stash of quarters. He went to find her.

The bathroom door was ajar and the room empty. He walked into the manager's office. "Have you seen my daughter?"

The manager, a normally cheerful fellow from someplace south of the border, glanced up from the papers on his desk. "Jilly? *Si*. I thought she went with you. She followed you out."

"You haven't seen her since I put in the clothes?"

The man shook his head. "Not since then."

Will swallowed the panic rising like bile in his throat. Maybe she'd gone wandering around the yard. She knew she wasn't supposed to, but she was an inquisitive child who made friends easily. She was probably off chatting with some boater. He pictured her tucked on a stool someplace or leaning over someone's project, asking questions.

But what if she weren't? What if …

His gaze circled the yard, but he didn't see a flash of red anywhere. She knew better than to go inside anyone's boat or into one of the offices. She wouldn't have done that, would she?

Why had he left her alone?

He spent the next ten minutes striding the perimeter, asking questions. No one, it seemed, had seen her. He zipped into the yacht brokerage office just at the entrance. No luck. The same with the outboard repair place.

He ran back to his car and drove slowly, stopping frequently. Finally, he headed out toward the highway. There he pulled up next to a fellow selling the day's catch on the side of the road just before the turnoff.

"I'm looking for a little girl who may have come this way. My daughter."

"Red hair and yellow shorts?"

Hope surged. "Yes, yes. Have you seen her? Where was she?"

The man pointed toward the bridge. "She went that way, about an hour ago now."

Will could feel his heart speed and shoot the blood faster. What was Jilly doing on the bridge to Beaufort? Alone.

For the first time since she was two, Will wanted to tan her hide. Didn't she know how dangerous bridges were? Not to mention walking by herself along the highway. Anyone could have snatched her. Anything could have happened.

He drove at a snail's pace, torn between wanting to hurry after her and fear of missing her if she'd hurt herself and was lying in the ditch, or if she'd gotten hot and crawled under one of those big bushes to cool off.

What if he couldn't find her?

That wouldn't happen. Jilly was mature for her age. She'd be careful.

What was he thinking? Jilly, *mature*? A rational, mature child wouldn't go hightailing it off by herself, scaring her father half to death.

At the far end of the bridge, he tried to decide which way she would have gone. She probably wouldn't want to stay on the highway, so he turned off toward the waterfront. But what if she were walking another street and not this one?

He drove to the waterfront without seeing her. How far could her little legs have taken her in an hour? Not this far, surely.

When he still hadn't found her twenty minutes later, he pulled over at the waterfront and laid his forehead against the steering wheel. He prayed, this time with all the force of desperation. And then he went looking again.

* * * * *

Jilly didn't have far to go now. Sweat dripped all over her, and her backpack felt as if she'd stuffed it with bricks. Her legs hurt. She must have worn blisters on her feet where her sneakers didn't fit so good.

She sat on the steps of the Maritime Museum and pulled out her bottle of water. She would have worn a hat if she'd known it would take this long to get here. The laundry must be finished by now. Pretty soon her daddy would come looking for her to carry the clean clothes back to the boat. He'd be mad when she wasn't there and the laundry wasn't finished.

But she couldn't turn around now. Not when she was this close.

She took a deep breath and stood. Tadie's house wasn't more than maybe five blocks from here. She could pop into the store for a second and give Isa a hug.

That thought gave her courage because the shop was only a block away. Hefting her backpack, she stepped out onto the sidewalk—and heard a screeching. She turned to look as her daddy slammed the car door and ran right out in front of another car.

Her heart thunked hard. Oh boy, she was in for it now.

He grabbed her shoulders, stared into her face, and lifted her to him in the hugest hug he'd ever given her. She hugged him right back. "I'm sorry, Daddy. I'm sorry," she wailed as she felt the pounding of his breath against her face.

"I couldn't find you anywhere. Do you know what that did to me?"

"I had to come, Daddy. Please don't be mad."

He set her down. Now he looked angry instead of scared. "What do you mean, you had to come? You had to leave your job, do something stupid like walking across that dangerous bridge all by yourself, and risk having something terrible happen to you? You had to do that?"

Tears coursed down her cheeks. She wanted to wipe them, but he had her arms in his grip. She couldn't look at him, knowing how much she'd disappointed him. She didn't want him to be angry, because what if he got so mad he left too?

"I'm sorry, Daddy."

"Come on," he said. "Get in the car."

He drove them back to the boat, stopping only to put quarters in the dryers. He didn't say anything the whole way there, not even when they climbed on board. He just put away his stuff and got out her suitcase so she could pack what wasn't still wet.

He went by himself to get the dried clothes and dropped hers on the V-berth, leaving her to fold and put them in her soft suitcase. "I think we both ought to go get a shower before we leave," was how he broke the silence.

On the drive, Jilly stared out the window until her eyes wouldn't stay open anymore. When she woke, they were outside some town, and her daddy was pulling into a McDonalds. He ordered for both of them before he parked the car under a shady tree.

Handing her a cheeseburger, he set the fries on the seat between them and opened a pack of ketchup. They never went to McDonalds, and they hardly ever had fried potatoes or a soda. She wasn't sure she could eat anything because her stomach still felt all knotty.

"Why did you go to Beaufort?" This time her daddy's voice was gentle, curious.

She took a big sip of soda. She poked her straw in and out of the plastic top to hear it squeak. "I wanted to see Tadie."

Her daddy didn't say anything. He just waited.

"You wouldn't let me go back, but I wanted to tell her good-bye."

He did that sighing thing again, and her stomach bunched even more. "We said good-bye when we left."

She tried to be brave. "We said we'd see her soon. We didn't. And now I'm going away, and I don't know when I'll be back."

Her daddy stared out the side window. His fingers were tight on the steering wheel for a long time. Finally, he turned. "Eat your lunch. You've got to be hungry with all that exercise you got."

"She's my friend, Daddy."

His face softened. "I know she is, sweetie. But you shouldn't have walked off like that. I've never been so scared in my entire life. I couldn't bear the thought of losing you."

"I was sure I'd be able to get there and back, and you wouldn't have to know."

"But anything could have happened to you. It wasn't safe. Can't you see that?"

She bit her lower lip and nodded. "I won't do it again."

"Thank you. You're all I have. You mean more to me than anything in this whole world. Can you please remember that the next time you want to do something that could get you hurt?"

"Yes, Daddy."

He picked up his sandwich and pointed to hers. "Now eat."

"Yes sir."

It was a little better after that. Not perfect. Not easy between them like it had been. She knew it was because she'd scared him so much. And she was sorry for that. But not so sorry she would take back going to Beaufort.

She pressed her forehead against the side window and watched the land go past. There wasn't anything much to see, not even any cows. Just some dirt and grass, some buildings, a whole bunch of gas stations and food places. Lots of cars. She sighed quietly so her daddy wouldn't ask why.

She knew why. She'd tried to get to Tadie and her daddy had stopped her. Maybe if her legs had been stronger and she hadn't stopped for that drink of water, she'd have made it there before he found her. That's what made her sorry. If her daddy had to get mad, it would have been better—a whole lot better—if he'd done it after she'd found Tadie.

* * * * *

Will watched the flight attendant take Jilly's hand and escort her to the plane before he walked back to the parking garage and turned the car toward Beaufort.

If only he could undo the last few hours. Jilly was the light of his life, and he'd let her get on that plane without showing her. How could he have done that? For the first time since Nancy's death, he'd been unable to get past his silence, past his own pain, to think of Jilly.

What on earth was wrong with him?

When she'd run off to Tadie, she'd triggered some elemental anger—and a profound sense of failure.

What he needed was to get back on that boat and get it finished. Then he'd sail out of North Carolina for good. He'd move the boat and himself to safer climes, where he and Jilly could go back to enjoying life.

They would do just fine on their own. She didn't need Tadie. And he didn't need these complications.

Chapter Twenty-four

Days overlapped, one into the next. Before Tadie knew it, three weeks had passed since Delia had left all that detritus in her life. The rest of the world seemed to be getting back to normal. Too bad she couldn't.

Martin drove over from Raleigh every free moment, trying to get on James's good side. Rita said it appeared to be working. How lovely for them.

Rita sailed with her when she could. Tadie occasionally sailed alone. *Luna*, her *Luna*, felt like a foreigner.

The shop thrived. Hannah's stock sold as soon as she put in something new, and she kept it coming. She probably needed the wheel-time to escape from her houseguest, who showed no signs of leaving. Hannah's phone calls were full of Alex's misdemeanors.

It was after eleven when Tadie emerged from her studio where she'd been trying to do something with the same stones she'd had her eye on the morning Jilly left. Hunger drove her to the kitchen, but lack of energy had her staring at the open refrigerator.

She finally pulled out salad mixings and had just tossed chopped cucumber over a bowl of spinach when the phone rang. She didn't bother to check the caller ID before answering.

"Hey, girl," Hannah said. "You working?"

"Just eating." She dribbled on some olive oil and carried her plate and the phone to the small kitchen table. Trying to instill her words with warmth and enthusiasm, she said, "What's happening with you?"

"I got a few more mugs ready to fire. I'll have a kiln full soon."

"Matt feeling any better?"

Tadie chewed a forkful of greens while Hannah described Matt's latest symptoms.

"He feels lousy, but at least he's leaving work earlier and getting Alex to do more," Hannah said. "Which has Alex in a dither."

"Why? I thought Alex wanted control."

"Control, maybe, but not work. He comes home complaining about how tired he is and slamming cupboard doors while he pours himself a drink. Then he plops down in Matt's den, and turns on Matt's television to some program he knows Matt won't watch. I guess that's why he's not been over to see you. He probably doesn't have the energy to come courting."

"Thank God," Tadie said, meaning it. "I'd have to boot him out if he did."

"Has something new happened between him and you?"

"Nothing new. Last time I saw him, that evening after Delia, he got on his high horse with Jilly. And he'd already scared the poor child to death by almost running over her."

"Oh no. I'm so sorry. You didn't tell me."

"Not much to tell." Nothing at all, really.

"I hear Jilly's gone to stay with her aunt ..." Hannah's voice trailed off, probably waiting for confirmation or denial.

Tadie hadn't told her much about the Merritt's visit—or their abrupt departure—except that it had happened. During most of their conversations, she'd only been able to manage platitudes and talk of Rita's love life or Elvie's improving health. Now she said, "That's what Will told Isa."

"She was a sweetie. But we knew they'd be moving on."

"We did. Cruisers always do."

"You okay?" Hannah asked.

"Of course."

Tadie listened without hearing any more of Hannah's words and was glad when the conversation ended. Her best friend really must be preoccupied if she hadn't heard the lie in Tadie's *of course*.

After rinsing her lunch dishes, she grabbed a sun hat and headed downtown. Haunting the shop seemed easier and more fruitful than staring at her studio walls. Isa smiled when the bells tinkled overhead.

"Hey, lady. Gorgeous day out, isn't it?"

Tadie glanced back out the glass windows. "Ah, yes, it is." Bright sun and lots of tourists in town for the weekend. Odd that she'd walked all the way here and noticed only where she needed to plant her feet so she wouldn't stumble on a crack or miss a curb.

"Perfect sailing weather," Isa said. "I'm surprised you're not out on *Luna*."

Luna sat neglected at the end of her dock, as if the days were breezeless. "I'm not."

Isa stared at her oddly.

Concentrate, Tadie. She drew on a smile and tried to make her voice sound cheerful. "I've come to give you another few hours off."

"Again? You don't have to."

"It'll be fun. Go."

Isa didn't need to be cajoled. She grabbed her purse, said she'd be back soon, and hurried out the door, leaving Tadie to wonder why she'd been so eager and what she'd rushed off to do.

A call came in shortly after Isa left, saying that a quilt was ready for pick-up. The quilter was an incredibly talented paraplegic from Newport. "I've finished the design I told Isa about," the woman said. "You think she'll be able to get it sometime soon?"

"If not, I will."

Tadie mentioned the call to Isa when she came in, flushed and smiling from wherever she'd spent her lunch hours.

"I wish I could get it today," Isa said. "I know she needs the money."

"You can't?"

"Not tonight. I've got an appointment."

When the other woman didn't explain, Tadie's curiosity soared, but it wouldn't do to ask. "I'll go," she said instead. "I'm not busy."

Isa bent to scribble the address on a pad. "It's easy to find. She's out there off Highway 24 in one of those new condominiums."

Taking the note, Tadie collected her hat and bag.

This would be another trip over the causeway. She had to go at least twice a week, either to pick up a consignment or to fetch something in Morehead. And Sundays, of course, when she went to church in Newport.

She got in her car, backed out, and headed west. She hated crossing that bridge, because as soon as she did, the boatyard acted like magnetic north to her compass needle. She had to hold her head rigid and cling to the steering wheel to keep from exiting, just to take a peek. Just to see if the *Nancy Grace* still waited to go in the water.

This time, the compulsion to turn in was almost overpowering. If the boat were gone, she could forget about them. Imagining Will climbing up and down the ladder, working practically within shouting distance, was killing her.

She held her course, although she felt like an alcoholic weaving past an available bottle without stopping to drink. Gone or not, Jilly wasn't going to be forgotten so easily.

Once she entered Morehead, she turned onto Bridges Street and eased on past the city to the outskirts. She hadn't called ahead and wasn't surprised when a stranger opened the door. "I just came for the quilt," Tadie said.

And that was that. She had the quilt in the car, the car headed east, and the causeway to face again.

* * * * *

With Matt's cold lingering, Hannah spent more time closer to home, escaping only occasionally to catch breakfast or lunch with Tadie, which didn't do much for Tadie's loneliness, especially now that Rita had found a job working at the local women's shelter and their sails were rare.

She was almost glad when Alex called the next Saturday, because arguing with someone suddenly seemed better than silence ... at least until he said, "Can I come by in a little while?"

"Sorry. I'm swamped."

"I was hoping we could take *Luna* out. There's a good breeze, and I haven't seen her off your dock recently."

"No, thank you."

"You don't *want* to sail?" His voice sounded incredulous.

Hadn't they had this discussion? "No, thank you." Which wasn't strictly the truth. She'd like to sail. She would. Only not with him.

She spread apart the living room curtains. Sun and a perfect breeze. The idea took hold.

After lunch, she gathered her sailing things and was heading down the stairs when a voice called from the kitchen. "Hey, it's me!"

Hannah. How long had it been since Hannah had popped in like this?

"Hey, stranger," Tadie said. "What got you out of the house?"

"Alex just took off for who knows where—with a suitcase. While that's interesting and very good news in the short term, I don't know what it means for Morgan's. Matt's in denial and has gone off to play golf. Mind you, that nasty cold ought to have kept him off the course in this heat, but will he listen?"

Tadie lifted the pitcher out of the refrigerator and filled two glasses. "The porch or in here?"

"Here," Hannah said, taking a glass and plopping down on the kitchen couch. "I need a little best-friend time with no other distractions." She kicked off her sandals and extended her bare feet onto the table, wiggling unpainted toes.

"You give up the pedicures?" Tadie asked, stretching out her own feet and settling back into the cushions.

"Chipped polish. I'm between colors."

"Well, that's good. You had me worried." She lifted her glass in salute. "I'm so glad you're here. It's been ages."

"Too many." Hannah gulped half her tea. "Lands, Tadie, I'm so tired of worrying about that man. He's a grown-up. He ought to care about his own health."

He should, but this wasn't the first time Matt had neglected himself to the point of getting really ill. Hannah hadn't been able to fix him then, and she wasn't likely to stop him now.

Tadie tried to sound soothing. "He's got to make the decision for himself."

"You're preaching to the choir, except I'm no good at paying attention, am I?" With a huff, Hannah set her glass on the lamp table and laid her head back. "I'm tired of thinking about it and more than tired of moaning." Shifting to the side to look at Tadie, she said, "I haven't been a very good friend."

"That's not true—" Tadie began, but Hannah's hand stilled her.

"It is. Something's been going on with you ever since that hurricane. Does it have to do with those two, Will and Jilly? Isa said—"

"Isa said what?" Tadie sat up straighter. If they'd been talking about her ...

"Calm down. Isa only said Will wouldn't let Jilly come in the store to work, and that he'd sent her off to her aunt's. I thought he liked having her there, hanging around us."

"Yeah, well, I guess he changed his mind."

Hannah's brows hiked.

What? Was Tadie supposed to spill her guts and give Hannah another reason to feel sorry for her?

"He has issues," she finally said. "Something about being afraid Jilly would bond too much and be unhappy when they sailed away."

"The fool. He'll be sorry someday when that child's old enough to make her own decisions. Wrapping her in wool, keeping her from making close friends. That's not smart."

"Isa suggested he might be jealous."

A snort greeted this. "Of his daughter's friends? Good riddance is all I can say."

Absolutely. Good riddance. But Tadie couldn't say those words aloud.

* * * * *

Tadie kicked at a pebble along the sidewalk as she walked home from the shop the next day. Wasn't heartache supposed to render an artist more creative instead of less? Her sketch pad remained pristine, and its naked pages taunted her. Working on pieces she'd already designed was one thing. Her hands could perform in spite of her mood. Tackling anything that required a higher brain function made her gut hurt. It helped that Isa had found a way to fill in the emptying jewelry case with little *objets d'art* from the back shelves.

She paused for a bite to eat at the Beaufort Grocery and brought home leftovers. She always had leftovers these days. After tucking them in the refrigerator, she spied the box of Godiva Stefan Ward had given her—with one each for Hannah and Isa. Her mouth watered. A bite of Godiva was exactly what she needed after that partially eaten dinner. Just one.

Reaching in, a stab of regret assaulted her. She'd left the box sitting on the counter where the sun could get it, and her beautiful truffles had morphed in the heat.

Oh well, they were still edible. She studied the oddly shaped candies and chose one with an orange center, closed the box, and stuck it in the freezer. She chewed slowly, but the pleasure didn't last long enough to be satisfying, so she opened the freezer door and drew out a messy glob of dark raspberryish delight. When she'd finished it, she licked the residue from her fingers and poured herself a small glass of wine, deciding she needed something nutty to go with it.

She carried her glass as she wandered through the downstairs. Her shoes echoed on the wood floors, but muffled when she entered her daddy's library. His desk needed dusting. So did the bookcases. Maybe she'd clean tomorrow, get out the vacuum, the dust rag and polish, and make this place look presentable again.

Setting the glass on the desk, she traced her fingers along the leather bindings, looking for something that might distract her, but the empty chair staring back at her made her chest hurt. She longed to smell Samuel Longworth's distinct perfume again, a smattering of aftershave and a lot of soap. She used to sniff his neck when she was little. He'd laugh and give her a hug.

Oh, Daddy.

Eb padded in her wake as she climbed the stairs. He jumped immediately to the bed, ignoring her as she adjusted the water flow into the tub. Bathing remained her one escape other than sailing. If she couldn't sail—or didn't want to—her big tub eased too-tight muscles.

Her skin pebbled in goose bumps as she stripped. She slipped one toe in and swirled it around, trying to cool the water enough to allow an entire foot to enter. Slowly, she lowered herself into the bubbles and settled against her bath pillow.

Music filtered in from her bedroom, soothing melodies that ought to comfort. She let her arms float at her sides, then pulled bubbles up to her neck until they surrounded her aging and unwanted flesh. Here, at least, she could usually pretend joy in being a woman, even if she were becoming an old-maidish, five-years-from-forty specimen whose sensual pleasures seemed scanty.

Tonight, the seductive illusion of soft water caressing her skin no longer existed, because nothing caressed. Nothing actually seemed to touch her, as if her skin repelled water in the same way that she herself—her psyche and her flesh—repelled others.

The melody changed, recalling her dreams, which seemed to have as much substance as the notes flowing past. Her eyes closed on a groan, and she slid under the water until her lungs screamed for air. She wiped her eyes with a towel and stared at the empty room, at the doorway leading to more empty rooms.

White foam hid her skin, and she knew this was as good as it was ever going to get—her body touched by water. Never by a husband or a baby of her own.

Why not? Was she so horrible? So completely unlovable?

She gripped the side of the tub so she wouldn't scream. Her throat constricted as the furies unraveled. The ache crimped her insides, and tears that had begun as a trickle turned into heaving sobs.

She finally cried out, "No!"

The water sloshed as she bounded upright. She opened the drain and pulled the towel around her, rubbing herself dry. After yanking on a pair of jeans and the nearest T-shirt, she drew a brush through her hair. "I'm going out," she told Eb. He just closed his eyes. Why should he care? Why should anyone?

It was only seven-thirty. She grabbed her keys.

She had to do something. Go somewhere. Be anywhere but here, staring at the walls of this empty house, yearning for Bucky's laughter, for her daddy's smile, for her mama's arms. Yearning for what would never be.

Backing out of the driveway, she pointed the car west, holding steady, not looking left as she crossed the bridge. The beach would do her good. Maybe the pounding surf would drown out her desperate thoughts. If she sat on the sand and waited for dark, maybe inspiration would come blowing in from the ocean. Perhaps she'd hear a whisper from the heavens.

The only thing she knew right then was that she, Sara Longworth, had better do something to change things because life felt nightmarish too much of the time. She didn't like much of anything these days. She certainly didn't like the consumed, self-absorbed person who'd just lost it in the bathtub.

The *more* she ached for had to be out there someplace. It obviously wasn't lurking in her studio while she played at being an artist.

As she cut into the left lane to cross the beach causeway, it hit her like blinders dropping. She braked, signaled, and did a U-turn at the first crossover before the Atlantic Beach light.

She wasn't going to find revelation walking the beach. Hadn't she and Rita sailed to the Cape not very long ago so they could watch the breaking waves? Last Friday, hadn't she anchored *Luna* on a sandbar near Core Banks so she could float and watch the sky, hoping something—someone—up there would speak to her? How much more communing with nature did she need before she understood this wasn't the place where she would find change? It was all too close to home, too familiar. Too static.

No, finding the elusive *more* would require that she get off her duff and do something different. Something that took her away from here and the status quo of small-town Beaufort.

Beaufort coddled its eccentrics, which was probably why she was comfortable here. She had friends and lots to do, but it was unvarying. If she wanted to be something else, do something else, and, yes, find someone else, maybe she needed to *go* somewhere else.

She remembered Rita's question, "Haven't you ever wanted to leave?" For a long time she hadn't been able to. But was anything stopping her now?

She could take a cruise. She had the money. Or—and this came in a flash she decided was inspiration—she could be daring and rent an apartment in some big city—Paris, Rome, or even Manhattan. It might be exciting to spend the fall visiting museums, meeting new people, living a little. She could study the work of other jewelry makers and call it an educational trip. She could decide where she wanted her life to go from here.

When had she ever done anything unexpected?

Her little car crept back through Morehead's slow zone, hit the high bridge, crossed the causeway—she did not look to the right this time—and then crossed the Beaufort bridge. It took her fifteen minutes to make it to her driveway, another fifteen or so to get the computer booted up and begin an Internet search.

Isa didn't need her. Hannah didn't need her. Elvie was recovering beautifully, and James had his garden. Rita's new job at the shelter kept her busy, and Martin visited on weekends. It was time for her to do something proactive to change her life. Something healing. Something fun.

Manhattan was less of a stretch than Europe. She'd spent time in Paris in her youth, but she'd never spent more than two nights in

New York City. She could go and still change her mind whenever she wanted without having to deal with transatlantic travel.

She found several short-term rentals available on the Upper West Side near Riverside Drive, but they were really expensive. She chewed on her thumbnail and weighed her options. Just for comparison, she checked out rentals in Italy and Spain, where she'd never been.

All she found were tiny rooms that cost as much as a New York efficiency. And she'd be too far away to scoot home if anything came up at the shop or with Elvie's health.

Fine. Traveling anywhere cost money, unless she rented a room in the boonies, and then she might as well stay home. No, she needed something radically different. Someplace where she could lose herself if she wanted—or get involved if she wanted. It had to be a city.

She clicked on an apartment a few blocks from the Metropolitan Museum, near the subway. She jotted down the listing and the broker's phone number.

By noon the next day, she'd arranged to lease a one-bedroom apartment for three months, and she'd booked a flight out of New Bern.

"You're what?" Rita asked when Tadie called.

"I'm going to see some of the world, even if it's just New York City. Will you stay over here, take care of the place and Eb?"

"Of course, but are you sure you want to do this?"

"Absolutely."

"Well, then, I think it's thrilling. It will be good for you."

"Would you ask your daddy if he could get me to the eleven o'clock flight tomorrow? I'll need him to take care of *Luna* too."

Tadie heard Rita talking in the background. "He says sure, if you want to, but I'm not at all certain he approves. He'll try to convince you to stay home."

Next, she dialed Hannah and told her the plan.

"Go, girl. I'm proud of you. About time you thought of doing something fun, but make sure that apartment has enough room for me to come and stay. Imagine the shopping we can do."

Her excitement grew at Hannah's words, as if her best friend's approval had been all she lacked. She imagined the two of them strolling through Central Park or catching a Broadway show.

Isa's tone matched Hannah's. "Soon as Hannah gets back, she can babysit the shop and I'll come play with you."

By the time Tadie had made all the phone calls and everyone had encouraged her to leave, she began to hope James would beg her to stay, just so she'd know someone cared enough to miss her.

Chapter Twenty-five

Sandpaper raked across the rough epoxy. Will's electric sander had gone on the blink at precisely eight thirty-five that evening. He knew because he'd checked his watch. It was now a little after nine, and he felt as if he were smoothing millimeters instead of inches. He pressed harder on the sandpaper block and let his shoulders bear the load.

Why couldn't the electric sander have died at six, when he might have found a store open? He switched arms to get at a spot from the other direction.

It was like a sick kid. Jilly never got a fever on a Wednesday. It was always Saturday around midnight, which meant he had to dig out Nancy's old *Merck Manual* and flip through the pages to figure out if Jilly were about to die of meningitis before morning or merely had strep throat. And while he was checking, he had to run a cool bath and get her to lie in it until her 105-degree fever dropped. She hated those baths and he hated making her take them, because that whimper of hers could turn him desperate. Once he got her past the bath, he had to stay up with her to make sure the temperature didn't spike again. The next day he had to decide if she were getting better or if he ought to take her to the emergency room, which, if she *were* getting better, would expose her to a thousand other illnesses and make her *really* sick. That would get them to Monday, when, if the doctor could squeeze them in, would bring them to the place where she no longer had a temperature and was actually almost well.

He was glad Jilly hadn't gotten sick since they'd moved onto the *Nancy Grace*. He could have filled the dinghy to bathe her, but that was as close to a tub as they were going to get.

The only difference between a sick kid and a broken-down tool was that the tool didn't usually fix itself when the store opened.

The sheet of sandpaper disintegrated under his palm. He tore off another, fit it around the wood block he'd made, and started rubbing again. This was 100-grit paper. Next he'd go to 120, then 180.

He slid his hand over the surface. Still knobby. He wanted it smooth and ready to paint by tomorrow evening, obviously an impossibility. He couldn't believe how much there was yet to do before he could get out of here and collect his daughter.

He was tired and it was late. He gazed out over the almost-dark yard. The mosquitoes would be out soon, and so would those nearly invisible, gnat-like stinging insects the locals called no-see-ums.

No-see-ums typified parts of the Beaufort/Morehead area that frustrated the daylights out of him. He also hated that everything took too long to get here after you ordered it. He got the same excuse every time: "There's a shortage on account of the hurricane."

Everything was on account of the hurricane.

He was still here on account of the hurricane.

He couldn't go into Beaufort on account of what happened after the hurricane.

Perhaps he should quit for the day and go read a book or listen to music. He hoped Jilly was happy with her aunt. She should be. Liz was probably taking her all over the place. Maybe they'd even gone boating in Dan's runabout. Dan loved to fish. Maybe he was teaching Jilly.

Will couldn't imagine Jilly sitting still long enough for a fish to bite. Still, who knew?

He couldn't get the picture of Jilly's sad little face out of his mind. Maybe he should have let her go see Tadie, just to say good-bye. It probably wouldn't have hurt.

But he hadn't been able to bear the thought of his daughter latching onto Tadie again, expecting things that couldn't be. And Tadie? What had she expected?

He picked up his tools and carried them inside, where he polished off the last of the iced tea. It was quiet in the boatyard and would probably stay that way unless the yard dog barked or some nocturnal animal came scuffing along. The night watchman walked the yard a couple of times, but didn't make much noise.

Grabbing the hose, he washed off some of the sweat he'd accumulated in the last few hours. He'd already walked down to the toilets, so now he could make do with the portable potty he'd installed in the forward head. He hated not being able to use the boat's plumbing, but there wasn't any place to pump out the holding tank on land. If nothing else, his sanitation needs made him long to get the *Nancy Grace* back in the water.

He'd replaced the rigging and repaired the holes in the deck. He still had to get the new stanchions and lifelines installed, the deck and hull faired and painted. The insurance money would have paid for others to do the work, and he planned to hire professionals to repaint the topsides, but for the rest, he was doing things the way he wanted them done. The cash he didn't spend on supplies and painters was going into the bank to increase his reserves. Other than missing Jilly, he didn't begrudge the time it took to do things right. Not much anyway.

He inserted mosquito netting in the companionway before heading to his bunk. The night was so hot he wasn't sure his little 12-volt fan would do any good, but it was all he had.

Its whirring should have soothed him. The new stanchions had arrived today. He'd finished the basic epoxy work. There'd be holes to fill once he finished the sanding, and then he'd have to sand again, fill again, sand again until it was smooth and ready for paint. But he'd made progress. He ought to be content.

He kicked off the top sheet and turned on his other side. He could see stars through the hatch screen, but no moon. A black, cloudless night. Breathless.

He turned again when his sweat trickled over his chest. Maybe the fan would cool the damp areas.

It did, barely.

He didn't remember falling asleep, though he must have, because the next thing he realized on a conscious level was crying out. He bolted upright, his breathing erratic and his mind a confused jumble.

What had *that* been about?

As his breathing calmed, he groaned and sank back against his pillow, his eyes wide and his senses still reeling. He'd had the dream again. It was the sort he'd often had in the aftermath of Nancy's death. She would come to him and lie with him, and he'd almost be able to feel her warm breath on his cheek, feel her lips joining his. For those first few minutes after waking, he'd be able to feel her in his arms, her fragrance so real he'd shudder with the memory. Then loneliness would sock him with such an intensity that he'd want to scream.

It had been too long since he'd last held Nancy in his dreams. And then, this one had lured his sleeping brain into joy. How? How could he have responded as he used to with Nancy? This time, it had been all wrong. This time, Tadie's long fingers had caressed his face. Tadie's lips had touched his. This time, he'd whispered Tadie's name.

He slammed his fist onto the mattress. What was she, a temptress? Out to steal his peace as well as his daughter's?

He'd seen it at her house. He'd known.

But he hadn't known she'd climbed the barriers, crept in, and could now seduce him in his dreams.

There was no way he was going to close his eyes again that night.

The next day, he worked even more feverishly. If he were realistic, he knew it would probably take another three to four weeks to put everything back together the way he wanted it. But he was going to do everything in his power to keep it from taking longer than that. Too bad he couldn't control the weather or breakages.

Or his dreams.

As he picked up the new sander, the disgust he'd felt last night churned again until he thought he'd hurl. He must really be losing it.

He hoped the rapidly-approaching fall meant he could expect a few more cool days. They'd had a week of rain and then a few days of cool before it had turned hot again. Rain was forecast for Saturday, which meant he'd be delayed yet again.

His hands were deep in epoxy when the phone rang. Stripping off one glove, he inserted the earplug and answered. "Hey, punkin. How're you doing?"

"I miss you, Daddy," Jilly said. "Will you come soon?"

"I'm trying." Since the thickened epoxy would soon set up, he slipped the glove back on and spread on a layer to fill in the dips he'd exposed with the last sanding.

"I know. But could you please try harder? I need you."

And he needed her. "I'm working as fast as I can, baby."

If only things were different. But he was wishing for the impossible.

Chapter Twenty-six

Tadie's feet barely touched the sidewalk. Her arms swung at her sides and her hair caught the wind. The autumn sun was cooler at this latitude than back home, and she reveled in the sounds wafting off the Hudson River of a churning tug and cawing gulls. Multicolored trees along the waterfront path rustled impatiently, as anxious as the people scurrying beneath them, so different from the soft soughing of North Carolina pines and the slower pace of hometown folk.

Everything hurried here. She tried not to get caught up in the bustle, except when she walked for exercise. The rest of the time, Tadie worked at slowing her pace and her heart rate as she moved through the days.

There was so much to see. So much color. She marveled at the variations in skin and hair and language. The cooler air brought out the sweaters and jackets: baggy, form-fitting, long, short, sleeveless, or draped over the fingertips. Piercings and tattoos in every shape and color imaginable, on a variety of body parts, stood next to her on the subway and in the park.

She left her cell phone at the apartment when going out and returned calls when she felt like it. She'd chatted four times with Isa, more often with Hannah, although what used to be once a day had dwindled to once, sometimes twice a week. Her mail arrived several days after the Beaufort Post Office received it. She'd stare at it, and then, when the mood struck her, she'd plop onto either the apartment's big chair or the couch to read it. Most of her bills were paid online, so nothing was urgent. Rita stacked the sailing magazines at the house.

Tadie walked and walked and walked, hopping on the subway only when a destination proved too far or the rain too blighting. Taxis got her where the subway couldn't. There were hours spent at the Met, the Museum of Modern Art, the Guggenheim, and the Whitney. When she found galleries with jewelry collections, she haunted them.

Sometimes she cooked. More often, she ate out, experimenting with Thai, Cuban, Afghan, and Moroccan cuisine. She'd begun dining fashionably late. It gave her something to do, somewhere to be instead of alone, wondering if the phone would ring and whether or not she would answer it.

When she saw a sail raised on the Hudson, she pined for *Luna* and whispered that she'd come back soon, after seeing a little more. When she'd convinced herself that her lonely life wasn't one of default because she lived in a small Southern town.

Perhaps alone was her lot.

There were offers of one sort or another all the time, but none that tempted her. A man eating alone near a woman eating alone seemed compelled to offer the other side of his table. She'd smile and shake her head and concentrate on the food in front of her.

One evening, a handsome man approached her, his hair curling over his forehead in a carefree manner. She had just ordered a dish of *linguine con vongole* in a nearby Italian restaurant that had become one of her favorite eateries.

"Please, signorina," he said, "often I have seen you dining here. Alone, as I am. Would you do me the honor of joining me this evening? Allow me to share a meal with you?"

His accent slipped in under her guard. His hair was smattered with grey. It made him seem at once distinguished and safe. She shrugged and agreed. He beckoned the waiter and asked that she be seated with him. The waiter bowed and obliged.

She loved the curl ... and his eyes, a deep brown that bordered on black, as if there were no pupil, only depth. His name was Massimo Giardini, and he'd come here from *la bella Roma*.

"Do you know it?" he asked, and when she shook her head, he said, "Perhaps someday. My home, it is beautiful, high on a hill, overlooking vineyards and not far from the sea."

The picture he painted and the way his accent filled out the words enticed her. When he spoke of his children, she recalculated. He must be divorced.

"I am here on business often. And you? What is a lovely woman of such obvious quality doing alone in such a city?"

"I longed for adventure," was all she'd tell him, although she described Beaufort and mentioned her boat and her shop. He listened raptly, making her feel as though each of her meager words held value.

Perhaps the glass of wine had gone to her head. Or perhaps his smooth words intoxicated. She felt heat in her cheeks—and wondered.

When the meal ended, he asked to accompany her to her flat. "Merely to assure myself that you are safe."

"You don't need to do that. I'm not afraid."

"Of course you are not. But it would be my honor."

At her door, he bowed over her hand. "May I again escort you to dinner? Perhaps tomorrow evening after I have finished my appointments?"

Tadie felt the rush of heat in her cheeks again and longed to fan them. "I would like that."

The next day, the sky seemed a little brighter as she stepped out for her daily walk. At five-thirty, she showered and chose her clothes. The air had begun to cool in the evenings, and a light sweater seemed appropriate over her red dress. Wouldn't red be fun?

She felt giddy, like a teenager on her first date. Massimo didn't arrive until ten after seven, just late enough that she'd begun to fidget. A last pat of her hair, and she opened the door.

"*Che bella*," he said, kissing her fingertips. "So beautiful."

She wanted to say, "You too." His blue suit and tie were elegant, his shoes a glossy black. But his chiseled bones and the cleft in his chin were what had her thinking movie-star gorgeous.

He took her to a French restaurant. She didn't tell him she found most French food overrated and over-buttered. His stories of traveling the world entranced her. If she'd come to New York to experience a different life, this was it, but in spite of all the flirting and the dancing eyes, she couldn't help a moment or two of skepticism.

What did such a man want with her? He was obviously wealthy and could have his pick of interesting and exciting women. His children were nearly grown, and yet they lived in his villa with their mother. Very cosmopolitan of him, this relationship. Had he actually said he was divorced?

"Shall we finish at a club I know? It is just down the street."

She'd never visited a New York club. "Why not?"

As he helped her from her seat and ushered her into the street, Tadie tucked away her excitement. She could get used to being treated like a desirable woman. It was heady stuff.

She tried to ignore the noise of too many people and too little soundproofing.

"A cognac? It is good for the digestion."

"I think not, but you go ahead. I'll just have water."

He shrugged in a very Italian way, using his lips and eyebrows instead of his shoulders. When the cognac arrived, he offered it to her. "One taste."

She took the snifter and sipped a few drops—and nearly gagged trying to swallow. She tried to cough away the fire and then douse it with water.

"*Mi dispiace*," he said, reaching out to pat her on the back. "I am so sorry. Too much perhaps."

Tadie waved him away. Too much, too soon, Never again.

One could not converse in the middle of this din. Tadie sipped her water, Massimo sipped his cognac, and they stared at the people standing, talking, dancing, yelling. She felt old and was relieved when they left.

He called for a cab and, on the way to her apartment, let his arm slip around her shoulders. She shivered slightly. They still didn't speak.

At her building, he paid the cabbie, but she leaned in the open door. "Wait, please."

She allowed Massimo to walk her to the outer door and then extended her hand. "Thank you for a wonderful evening."

"Ah, my dear Tadie. Let it not end so soon. May I not come up to see where you live and perhaps finish with a coffee?"

Here it was. He'd want to take her to bed. This was the way it was done in the world. Two dinners, a smattering of conversation—and not very much of that—and then sex.

The frustrated, lonely part of her felt momentarily tempted. After all, he was very attractive. But had she waited all these years just to give in to a virtual stranger? Call her old-fashioned. Call her cautious.

"I'd love to, really, Massimo. But I doubt your wife would be thrilled."

His eyes widened, but he covered his surprise with a slight smile and a raised brow. "We have an understanding, she and I," he said smoothly. "She does not tell me of her friends, and I do not tell her of mine. She would not know."

"But I would." Tadie kept her hand out. "I do thank you. I've had a wonderful evening, but I must say good-bye."

He bowed over her hand and kissed her fingertips. "You are quite a woman, Tadie Longworth."

After he climbed back in the cab, Tadie took the elevator to her quiet, empty apartment. As she dropped her purse onto the small living room table and hung her sweater in the closet, she wondered— momentarily—if she'd been foolish to toss away the offer of an affair with no strings attached. To feel, just once, what loving was like, especially as marriage didn't seem to be in her future. But without marriage, could she? Would she?

She imagined the morning after. Massimo would kiss her good-bye and return to his wife. And she would have to confront her reflection in the mirror.

Maybe she didn't want to lose control. Maybe vestiges of her father's teaching, not to mention Elvie's, still held sway. Maybe she didn't want merely to indulge her body and nothing more.

She turned out the lights and stared at the street below her window. There were men out there, multitudes of men, and not one of them to be had for free.

* * * * *

After Massimo, she flirted briefly in galleries when she found herself admiring the same painting as some lone fellow and then found herself in the same room with him a couple of galleries later. They'd laugh, perhaps comment on the work, admit they much preferred the Rembrandt to the Tintoretto, but have you seen ...

It was mildly amusing, but it always ended as one or the other lingered in a particular gallery or headed off in a different direction. She left with a spring in her step because she'd connected on some small level with another human. But these small connections did nothing for her as she ate her lonely dinner or took long walks with only the breeze and falling leaves for company.

When a cold spell slapped the city, she zipped up her jacket, donned a wool scarf, and tucked her hands in her pockets. Slate skies turned the buildings an even darker shade, stones as cold as her bones. She missed Ebenezer, his fur coat tucked next to her skin, the rattle in his throat a comfort in the night.

Her spirit lightened as the weather turned and the sun flung promises of warmth. She found a wonderful display of jewelry down in the Village and planned to meet the designer soon. The thought made her want to skip down the sidewalk.

When she phoned Hannah that evening, her friend's voice

sounded troubled. "We're fine," Hannah said. "I mean, Matt's not. It's that pesky cold he can't seem to shake, and it's gone into a miserable cough. I finally got him tucked up in bed with some aspirin. You know him. He won't go to the doctor, because he won't believe he's sick. At least I convinced him running off to work wasn't the cure-all."

"Tell him I asked about him, will you? And that I want him to get well."

"I will. And don't you worry. He'll be fine."

"Things better with Alex?"

"That's a sore subject if I ever heard one. But at least he's working longer hours and keeping out of my hair. You still having a good time?"

"I am. And I can't wait to see you."

"Get us good tickets, you hear? I'm looking forward to Broadway and shopping. In that order."

"Yes ma'am."

After hanging up from that call, Tadie dialed her house to check on Rita. When no one answered, she phoned the apartment.

"James, hey," she said. "How're you all?"

"We're doin' fine here, Miss Sara, but what about you? When you comin' home?"

"I'm not sure. There's a lot to see up here. Tell me, how're things with Elvie?"

"You want to talk to her?"

She heard Rita say, "Let me have it, Daddy. I'll carry it in to Mama."

"Tadie, I'm glad you called," Rita said quietly into the phone. "Mama's in bed already. She's not asleep, but the doctor says she's got to keep her arm elevated. She's got something called lymphedema. Some word, isn't it?"

"What on earth?"

"It happens sometimes after they take out the lymph nodes, you know, like they did with her. The arm swells because it's not draining properly. Here, you talk to Mama about it."

"Is that Tadie?" Elvie said before clearing her voice. "Oh, Tadie-girl, it's been too long. How is that city treating you?"

"I'm fine. But what's this arm thing you've got?"

"It's not a blessed thing. Just my arm getting a little swollen, so I've got to keep it high a few times a day."

"They're not worried about it, are they?"

"Doctor says take care of it and make sure it doesn't get an infection. That's what we're doin'."

"I'm awfully glad you have Rita there. You need me to come home?"

"What would I need more people around for? To put pillows under my arm? I can fetch my own pillow."

Surely, Elvie's snippy tone meant she was getting better. Tadie pulled her notepad over and dug a pen from her purse. "You take care of yourself, you hear? And let me speak to Rita again."

"I miss you. You get finished up there and come on home."

"Yes ma'am."

Rita came back on. "She's going to be fine."

"Spell the name of that thing again, will you? I'm going to look it up for myself."

Tadie jotted down the word, said good-bye, and turned on the computer. When she finally logged off half an hour later, she felt a little better. The arm thing was a nuisance, but nothing more, as long as Elvie took care of it.

Monday began a week of cold, rainy days. She called to make an appointment with the jewelry designer, only to discover the artist was out of town. Well, that shouldn't stop her from working on new designs of her own. Inspiration enough existed in the city, from both the ancient and the modern. Her pencil flew across the sketch pad, but when she studied her efforts, she flipped to another page. Three sheets later, she sat back and admitted that, without her stones in front of her, the drawings lacked life.

She loved working in three dimensions, manipulating pieces until they appeared as she'd imagined. She sometimes used the lost-wax process. Other times, she soldered or beat metal to form it. Once in a while, she would string together beads mixed with precious stones, a necklace laced with sapphires and gold, perhaps sea shells interspersed with onyx. One of her teachers had said the best artists created their own style, recognizable. So maybe hers was eclectic.

Chewing on the tip of her pencil, she stared out the window at rain dripping off the eaves onto her narrow little ledge. Here she was in New York City, an art mecca, allowing the days to slip past while she embraced sloth. She'd accomplished nothing. If her goal had been to meet new people, she'd failed miserably.

Thirty-five was past time to figure out priorities. Women her age had careers. Look at all those families cheering at soccer games in the park, riding bikes together, and walking the dog. She'd wander past and imagine them chatting around the table about work and school and where they planned to travel for the holidays this year. What was she doing in the midst of all these strangers? At least back home, she had a shop to run and a studio to work in and a boat to sail. And friends.

Yes, in Beaufort, she had friends.

And yet she lingered. Hannah would be visiting in a couple of weeks, and inertia made staying easier than not. The weather meandered between pleasant and downright ugly.

She answered her phone when it rang these days and usually carried it with her. No one seemed to need her, but with Elvie's arm an issue and Matt not well, she thought they might—maybe—at some point.

When she went out to dinner, the phone stayed home. On Saturday evening, she dined at the Thai restaurant and didn't remember to check for messages until quite late. There was only one.

"Hope you're having a grand time," Isa's voice said in that lilting tone of hers. Tadie's pulse quickened as the next words played. "Will came in today. He just finished the restoration and is leaving tomorrow. You knew he sent Jilly up to stay with her aunt a while ago and has been on his own—I suppose avoiding this end of town. He asked about you. I told him you'd moved to Manhattan and he seemed surprised. And sad. His parting words were to thank you."

Listening, Tadie remembered his expression as he'd hurried Jilly out the door. The pain returned like a gut punch.

She hugged her pillow to her chest and fought for sleep. Why did he have to go into the shop and ask about her? Why couldn't he have just gone away and let it be?

The numbers on her digital clock took forever to flip. Her stomach rumbled. Acid burned a hole or two, probably twelve, in it.

She climbed out of bed at dawn. After a bowl of oatmeal, she crawled back under the covers. She kept the blinds drawn and pulled a blanket off the bed to watch DVDs in the living room. She could order from any of the neighborhood restaurants and have a meal delivered. It only took a phone call, and soon a smiling young man would appear at her door. Why go out at all?

What a city. She could order groceries by phone or online. Or she could pick them out herself, and the store would deliver them so she wouldn't have to carry a bag. If she wanted, she could live in the middle of millions of people and never see anyone but the boy handing her the sack.

She phoned down the block for burritos, which gave her indigestion. Curled on the couch, without ambition or even an ounce of oomph, she sailed smack into the doldrums. A slipper remained on one foot. She'd kicked the other at the television when a stupid commercial screeched at her. Bits of cereal floated in a bowl of milk on the coffee table. The remnants of her Mexican dinner took up space next to it. She hadn't washed a single dish.

The next day, Tadie sat with the remote control in her hands and a cramp in her leg. Bending to massage it, she decided she didn't smell very fresh. Her scalp itched and she was bored. She had watched the BBC version of *Pride and Prejudice* twice and a production of *Emma* once. There wasn't enough on TV to keep her entertained, and she'd forgotten to stock up on more books. She had her laptop, but she could surf the Net for only so long before she ran out of things to interest her. Running in place was not going to cut it.

She took a shower, changed into jeans and a clean shirt, and checked her watch. Five-fifty. She'd ordered dinner to be delivered at six.

With three minutes to spare, the boy rang the bell. She let him up, tipped him, and stuck the Moroccan couscous into the refrigerator. If she stayed inside to eat it, she'd probably end up doing violence. This wasn't her furniture and those weren't her walls. She could imagine the stares she'd get if she called a cleaning service to remove the stains of a tantrum.

Not that she'd ever had a tantrum, but she felt on the verge. There was always a first time for most things, wasn't there? *Most*, she reminded herself. Not *all*.

Bundled against the cold, she jogged all the way to the Indian restaurant two blocks over.

Who cared about stupid, mean jerks anyway? Fine, she missed Jilly, but there were lots of kids who needed loving. She'd go find another one.

Maybe she'd adopt those twenty orphans.

Back in the apartment after a less-than-memorable meal of rice and lamb—not because there was anything wrong with the food, but because she'd chewed and swallowed it mechanically—she loaded the dishwasher, cleaned up the litter, and took a long bath. This time, it wasn't to get clean. The tub just seemed like the best place to weep.

Her alarm clock roused her at seven the next morning. She walked five miles along the river until her numbing toes forced her inside a small diner. The chicken-salad-on-a-bagel was fresh, the orange juice just squeezed, the coffee better than her home brew. Paying the bill, she headed out to the street. Five miles back seemed excessive, but she could mosey. Moseying seemed like a better idea than sitting in her apartment.

Sparkles danced on the water as the sun's lower-angled rays raked it. She breathed deeply, pausing to watch a sailboat motor up the river, but imagining those on board, living and laughing and doing what she loved best, just exacerbated her discontent.

It was after one when she exited the elevator and opened her door, shedding her coat and her clothes on the way to the bathroom. She thought she heard her phone ring as she turned on the water. Not that it mattered. At least not for the time it would take her to scrub off the sweat and try for the soul-deep grime.

Chapter Twenty-seven

Will motored out of the harbor toward the Intracoastal Waterway. Going up the ICW wouldn't give him much sailing time, but it would allow him to anchor easily each night, which was a good thing while he handled the boat alone. It would also keep him away from the treacherous waters off Cape Hatteras. This time of year, the Cape, along with the rest of the coastline off the Outer Banks, had reason to be called the Graveyard of the Atlantic.

A fair wind blew as he headed up the Neuse River and into the Pamlico Sound. Turning on the autopilot, he raised sails to take advantage of it and pored over the chart, looking for a good anchorage with enough depth. If Jilly were here, she'd keep him company, but he'd see her in a little over a week if all went well and he didn't run into any storms on the Chesapeake. Although they chatted daily and she still giggled at his jokes, he sensed a distance that wasn't about the miles between them. He had some work to do there.

That night, he dropped anchor in a small creek out of the way of passing commercial traffic and the last of the boating snowbirds fleeing the winter cold. He opened a can of beans, heated it on the stove, and downed it without interest.

His jeans hung loosely on his hips. He ought to eat more, but all he could manage was enough to fill the hole and keep himself going.

He pictured his daughter, saw her bright eyes when she took Tadie's hand, heard her laugh as she and Isa prepared their spaghetti dinner. Flattening his palms against his eyelids, he tried to block the images, especially the one of Tadie's stricken face on that last day. The water lapped gently against the boat's underbelly, but it was hours before it lulled him to sleep.

He upped anchor early and again motored north, munching a cereal bar and sipping coffee from a thermos as he steered. Normally, meandering up the North Carolina waterways delighted him, but not this time. He missed his little chattering bird who always wanted to help, and who did a darned good job when he let her. The silence on board stretched his thinking time, something he didn't need or want.

He had assuaged his conscience in the weeks it took to repair the *Nancy Grace*. The work had occupied his hands and, to some extent, his mind. Now, as he watched out for mud banks and shoals, he had plenty of opportunity to wonder why he'd acted like such a jerk. He'd been furious, believing his anger justified, convincing himself that Tadie had sucked up to him while making much of a lonely, vulnerable Jilly—unconscionable behavior. He'd reared up on his high horse, certain he had to end their relationship before Jilly's heart was broken when Tadie didn't get what she wanted.

When had his thoughts begun to veer in another direction? He hadn't found Tadie particularly attractive the first time they'd met, mostly because she wasn't Nancy. She had none of Nancy's lithe grace or her small dancer's body. As a matter of fact, he hadn't even seen Tadie as a woman until they'd sailed on her small boat and he'd been face to face with her personality. Her laughter had first caught him off guard. Then he'd noticed her sparkling eyes, her wild, precocious brows that shot up in surprise or concern, one at a time when she questioned something he said. As they sat on the floor around the Monopoly board at her house, her long muscled legs had angled in and out of various positions, sometimes curling under her, jutting out from her, corralling Jilly in a tease. He'd noticed those legs all right.

He'd hated himself for noticing and had begun watching to see if she were angling for him. When the creep, Alex, had shown up, Will had been shocked by his own response—which had pretty much sent him over the edge.

And then he'd dreamt of her. Not merely that one time. Oh, no, she returned to haunt him twice more.

Talk about disloyal.

He checked the charts again. It was tricky here, figuring out which direction the markers took as they exited the sound and entered the canal again. He picked out the starboard mark and made toward it.

Amazing how thinking of those dreams provoked other memories. Tadie hadn't ever tried to be alone with him, had she? Or used feminine wiles to lure him. Nothing like Leslie or the others. The only time he'd seen her in makeup had been the morning he'd stood in the doorway, watching her talk to Jilly. She'd been wearing a bright silky thing that slithered over her breasts as she gestured. His physical response had sent him reeling with fury. And he'd blamed it on her.

He wished that morning undone, the words unsaid. But words had power and he'd used his to hurt an innocent woman. He hoped her time in New York would prove healing. Maybe she'd meet a wonderful man, get married, and live happily ever after.

Somehow, that thought didn't ease his conscience as it should have. Or make him stop remembering the taste of her in his dreams.

* * * * *

The Dismal Swamp felt particularly dismal as the *Nancy Grace* motored up the narrow channel. Will sat in the cockpit and watched the moss-strewn trees pass on either side as a hundred eyes followed his progress. He never went this way without imagining the teeming life batting and flapping and crawling and sliding just out of sight. The scent of plough mud was strong. Sometimes a sticky-sweet smell wafted his way, and when the river meandered near farmland, he got whiffs of fertilizer being tilled in for the winter crop.

As he approached Norfolk and hurried on to Hampton Roads, the Coast Guard issued storm warnings. He called ahead for slip space in a marina he'd visited before.

A dock hand waited to take his lines, and Will battened down for high winds before he dialed Liz's house and spoke to Jilly.

"Daddy, where are you?"

"I'm in Virginia, sweetie. There's a storm brewing, so I'll have to stay a day or two."

"I miss you. I want to see you."

"I know. I'm lost without my first mate."

"Goodie. You shouldn't be going anywhere without me."

"I see that. And I especially need you to help with the cooking. Beans are getting old."

"Daddy." She giggled as she said his name. "You should eat more than beans. When you get here, maybe I can remember how to make spaghetti."

"I'm counting on it. I bet your Aunt Liz will help you."

"I miss Isa. We did a good job, didn't we?"

"You sure did."

"Don't be mad, but I miss Tadie too."

He winced. How could he have made his sweet child so wary? He definitely had work to do. "I'm not mad," he said, gentling his tone as he would with a skittish animal.

"Then when can we see her again?" Her little voice changed to one filled with excitement and hope, and Will relaxed, slightly, because what could he say? "Soon?" she asked. He could almost see her dancing on tiptoes.

"I don't know." Probably never. "We've got places to go and lots of people to see before we can stop in Beaufort again."

"But I promised her. She must be very sad because I didn't keep my promise."

Will's heart sank. "I'm sure she understands."

"How could she? A promise is a promise. That's what you always say."

"Ah, yes, well ... we'll have to see what the future brings. Okay?"

Jilly didn't answer.

"Put your aunt back on the phone for a minute."

He heard Liz ask Jilly to go stir the chili. Then Liz spoke into the receiver. "Will, I couldn't help overhearing what Jilly said. The child talks about this Tadie person all the time, about how much fun the three of you had together. She keeps asking if we can call her. Is there some reason you wouldn't let her say good-bye?"

"Only something stupid. A foolish misunderstanding."

"Well, you listen to me. If this has anything to do with loyalty to Nancy, get that out of your head right now. My sister would want you and Jilly to be happy. You hear me?"

He pictured Nancy's spitfire older sister standing there with one hand on her hip, glaring. "Yes ma'am. I hear you."

"All right. Now, when can we expect you?"

"Depends on this storm, but I'm hoping by the end of the week."

"The child misses you. I love having her, but it's you she wants."

Will disconnected and sat in his cabin, thinking about Liz's words. Maybe she was right.

And then he imagined the same scenario, but Nancy widowed and alone with Jilly. What would he want for her?

That's when he picked up a pen and began the letter he should have written months ago. He hoped the Beaufort Post Office had a forwarding address in New York.

Chapter Twenty-eight

Tadie turned off the hair dryer and finger-fluffed her curls. Her cheeks and eyes glowed—finally—which showed how much her body craved activity. What she'd needed had been to get off her duff, walk ten miles, and then stand under scalding water.

No more pining or depression for her.

She pulled on her socks. This morning had also provided another germ of insight.

Germ. Good word. But now was *not* the time to dwell on that one. "If not now, when?"

She glared at the mirror. Soul-searching never offered a compliment.

She wiped down the basin with cleanser and picked at the nasty spot of rust that just didn't want to come up. Draping the bathmat over the shower rod, she noticed her towel hung at an angle. She refolded it.

A second glance into the mirror and her reflection stared back. Had she thought her eyes bright? Now they squinted at her.

The words first choked in her throat. The squint tightened, and out they spewed like seawater from a nearly-drowned man. "Self-absorbed. That's what you are." A deep pouf of breath left her lips.

"Think on that, why don't you?"

She swiveled out the door. She'd been right. Harsh words did not sit well.

"You really do need to get over yourself," she told the body scurrying toward the kitchen and a cup of tea.

Over herself?

Well, yes.

She'd brushed past a homeless man today. Several homeless men, as a matter of fact, along with a bedraggled female panhandler and a blind street musician. As New York had its big-city share of the poor and downtrodden, these weren't the first she'd come across. But today she'd actually *seen* them.

And the now-niggling questions, which grew louder by the moment, required answers. She, Sara Longworth, daughter of Samuel and Caroline Longworth of Beaufort, NC, was not homeless, hungry, ill, or dying. Thanks in part to her parents and forebears, she lived a cushy, self-absorbed life. So where did she get off having a pity party because they'd died and she had no one to take their place?

Look at Elvie Mae and James. At Rita. Elvie called it, "A life well lived."

Tadie had better figure out what that meant, because focusing on her own worries was a sure path to the therapist's couch and only added to the multiplying cells of misery in the world.

The mug sat in front of her, but she couldn't bring herself to drop in a tea bag. If she absorbed that revelation the way the water absorbed the tea, she'd be required to act on it.

Right. There she went again, those twenty orphans. Or something else to get her focused on more than herself.

Her cell phone rang from the bedroom. She dashed to retrieve it, not because she needed a reprieve from those thoughts—although she did—but because the call might be important.

It might.

She answered without looking at the caller ID.

"Where are you?" the voice asked.

Coming at the tail end of the conversation she'd just been having with herself, a strange man asking questions made her angry. "Who's this?"

The voice sounded amused. "Don't tell me you don't know."

She looked at the dial. A 252 area code. North Carolina. It couldn't be.

"Alex?"

"Right the first time. I've been trying to reach you."

"Why?"

"Is that any way to greet me?"

"I'm not greeting you. I'm trying to find out what you need."

"Hannah's with Matt at the hospital. He's not doing well."

Matt? "What happened? Did his cold get worse?"

"That cold turned into pneumonia."

"And she didn't call me?" Hannah had let it get to pneumonia without telling her? Hannah had made light of the cough. Tadie shut her eyes for a moment. Why hadn't she listened more closely? "I'll get the first flight out. Tell her, will you?"

"I'll pick you up. Just let me know when."

"No, don't bother. I need to phone James anyway."

"I'll talk to James," he said. "We'll work it out."

He didn't wait for her response, but she had no time to worry about Alex's rudeness. Instead, she went online and booked a flight to New Bern. Then she phoned James and arranged for a car to pick her up and get her to LaGuardia.

She tossed things in her suitcase and stuffed it closed. Her computer fit in her carry-on bag. The rest would have to wait.

Her driver knew which streets to avoid and got her there with time to spare for check-in and security. The plane took off on time, and all she could do was sit back and wait. There was still a connection to make in Charlotte.

She tried to close her eyes and keep her brain on auto-pilot, but her morning's revelations seemed particularly apropos now. Her best friend had been in pain, and she hadn't even noticed.

* * * * *

James waited just inside the New Bern terminal. She ran into his arms.

"It's okay, Miss Sara. It's going to be okay."

"Do you know anything more?"

"Only what Alex told me." James led her to the baggage carousel. "Fool man tried to say he'd be the one to come get you."

"Thank you. I don't think I could have faced him tonight."

"No, and you shouldn't have to. I had Rita phone over to the hospital to get word to Hannah. Wrote down the room number." He handed her a slip of paper.

"They may not let me in this late," she said, grabbing her suitcase and pulling it behind her, "but I've got to try."

James nodded. "I'll wait for you, Miss Sara. You do what needs to be done."

* * * * *

James dropped her off at the front door, and she strode in as if she belonged, nodding at the security desk. Visiting hours ended at nine. It was eight-fifty.

When she saw Hannah's grief-stricken face, she rushed forward and pulled her into a fierce embrace. "Why didn't you call me? I would have come straight back. Nothing would have kept me away."

Hannah's sobs dampened Tadie's shirt. Tadie tightened her hold, whispering soothing noises. She never should have left town.

Finally, Hannah sniffled and backed up to blow her nose on the already damp tissue she clutched. "The doctor just left," she said, as she tried to gulp air. "They're doing more tests and might have to move him back to the ICU. What if he doesn't make it? What if …"

The sobbing started again.

All Tadie could do was circle her friend's shoulders and hold on. This time they both wept.

* * * * *

Tadie spent as much time as she could at the hospital, holding Hannah's hand or relieving her for a few hours so she could go home to shower or take a nap and catch up on the rest she wasn't getting in the chair next to Matt's bed. Because his room faced the nurses' station, they hadn't moved him to the ICU after all. Something about a shortage of beds. But he lay attached to tubes and lines and things that bleeped and sputtered.

Tadie listened as Hannah spoke in low tones. First, it was of falling head over heels in love with Matthew and marrying him. "It was a beautiful wedding, wasn't it, Tadie?"

"The best."

Hannah's meanderings took in the long years of hoping for a child. Of losing the babies. Of planning to adopt. And of deciding, finally, that the two of them were enough for each other. Tadie listened and sympathized as if she didn't know the story by heart.

"But in these last years, we got too busy. Matt was always at work. I was trying to find enough to do. We missed too much time when we should have been enjoying each other."

Tadie tried to soothe her, but other than whispering platitudes, she didn't know how to answer.

"Dear Lord," Hannah said, choking back tears. "I can't lose him."

"You won't," Tadie said. "Look at all those strong antibiotics they're pumping into him. And all the prayers. You know folk are praying."

Hannah nodded feebly.

"You remember Jilly? That child could pray up a storm. She put me to shame." Tadie didn't mention how their leaving had thrown her faith back in the trash bin and piled refuse on top.

"What happened to them?"

"I don't have a clue." Tadie hoped Hannah wouldn't probe and then felt disappointed when she didn't.

By the time Tadie got home, she felt wrung out emotionally. At least Rita's work schedule gave her time to fix wonderful meals for the two of them and for her parents, making Tadie feel pampered in a way she hadn't since Elvie first got sick. Besides, having someone there at the end of the day, someone with whom she could talk—or not—was a huge comfort.

She climbed the apartment stairs to check on Elvie before going to her own house. Elvie liked to be up doing things when she could, and she greeted Tadie from her post at the stove.

"Sure smells good in here," Tadie said. "Pudding?"

"Yes ma'am. That girl of mine brought the roast, but I thought a little pudding would go down just fine after. I'm making enough for you girls too."

"Yum. I love your puddings. And chocolate?" Tadie's sigh brought a grin to Elvie's face.

"Rita told me about that lift for outside." Elvie shook the pudding spoon in Tadie's direction. "My arm don't keep me from walking or climbing steps. You tryin' to turn me into an old woman? I won't be thanking you if that's what's on your mind, young lady."

"No ma'am," Tadie said, leaning over to hug Elvie.

James wandered in to poke a finger in the pudding and taste it. "Just about right," he said. "Those steps are gonna keep us young, Miss Sara. Livin' long. When these here bodies quit, that's when we can be thinking of ways to ease them." He patted her shoulder. "We appreciate the thought, though. You're mighty good to be thinkin' of us."

Tadie had to turn away to swipe at the wetness she found foolishly pooling in her eyes. Why had she ever gone away? She'd been crazy.

* * * * *

Alex showed up on her doorstep early the next evening before Rita returned home, still in his work clothes and holding out a sack.

"Hey, Tadie. I know you've been in and out of the hospital with Hannah, so I brought something in case you haven't eaten yet."

She let him in, curious now. He'd behaved himself since she'd come home, and Hannah reported that he'd been taking care of everything while Matt was sick. She could at least be civil.

He followed her to the kitchen and unloaded his bag. "Chicken burritos, black beans, rice, and incredible nachos and salsa. Here," he said, pulling out a small container, "is your old favorite, guacamole."

The words made her salivate, not to mention the smells. "Alex, where did you get this?"

"Plaza Mexico. It's a bit noisy and crowded, so I figured take-out would be good."

Mexican food worked. She might even enjoy the meal, as long as he didn't get any ideas. "Water?" she asked.

"Water's fine. I brought limes. Did you know they call them *limons*? But they're green."

Tadie filled two glasses with ice and water and slid one toward him. And then she remembered. "Did you bring enough for Rita? She's due home soon."

His brows tented. "I thought she'd have gone back to her parents by now."

"More room here. Besides, I like the company."

"Then there's not enough."

She merely watched him. Hannah had hinted at changes, but he sounded like his old grumpy self to her.

When he stood and headed to the back door, she continued to wait. His expression hadn't changed, but his words surprised her.

"Phone in an order for her." He flicked fingers toward the bag. "The number's there. I'll go back and get it."

"I don't know what she'd like."

"Then call her."

Tadie picked up the phone and punched in Rita's number. "Hey, it's me," she said. "Alex is feeding us tonight. Mexican. What do you want?"

"Oh," Rita said, sounding as surprised as Tadie had been. "I just heard from Martin and was about to call you. He's got an interview in New Bern tomorrow, so he's on his way there. I'm going to meet him for dinner."

"Lucky you. I'll see you when you get home."

"Be careful, Tadie."

Alex would have a lot of catching up to do if he wanted to win any points from Rita or her parents. "I will. You too."

She hung up the phone and turned back to Alex. "I guess there's enough after all."

His grin lit that too-handsome face as he lifted her everyday plates from the cupboard next to the sink. "O-kay!"

Tadie couldn't believe how much fun they had as they ate the messy food. There was no pressure and no talk about the past or Bethanne. Alex made her laugh with stories from work, even a few self-deprecating ones.

"You won't believe the e-mail I sent out last week." He ran his fingers through that shock of dark hair and loosed his killer smile again. "I'd drafted an order for one of the big distributors at the same time I wrote a notice to our employees to tell them we'd be stepping up the random drug tests and that I expected them to be sober at all times."

"You don't mean ..."

He nodded. "I didn't realize I'd done it until the vice president of the company wrote back to ask what was going on and why I was issuing drug-use warnings to him."

Stories eased their way back to a level of comfort, and he didn't mar it by staying late. "I've been up since dawn," he said. At the door, he paused. "Maybe we can do this again soon."

Maybe so. He'd been the perfect gentleman, and his offer to buy Rita a meal had certainly been more than she'd expected from him. Perhaps the old Alex was back after all.

The pre-Bethanne Alex.

* * * * *

Tadie was in her studio, the soldering torch ready to light, when Hannah phoned. She answered as she eased down onto her studio couch. "Hey, girl. What's happening?"

"They brought food in at noon, hospital food. Horrible stuff, but it hasn't bothered Matt up to now, mostly because he hasn't eaten much of it. Anyway, this time he stared down at his tray and got that look. You know the one—scowling with his eyebrows all squinched. I offered to go get him something that tasted better."

She waited. Hannah's pause was obviously to build suspense, so she wouldn't spoil it.

"He told me I'd better bring enough back for myself, too, because he didn't want to be hugging bones when this is all over." Hannah's laughter interrupted her words. Once she'd calmed enough to continue, she said, "Can you believe it? He told me I should know by now he likes something to grab hold of. Glory!"

Tadie pictured Hannah's fingers fluttering in the air and her arms waving as she did a happy dance. "Of course he does. He loves you just the way you used to be."

"Fat. I know."

"You've never been fat. Just endowed."

"Whatever. But if a man's thinking about you that way, you know he's on the mend."

"Amen," Tadie said, more to agree than because she knew what Hannah was talking about. She whispered another "amen" to the empty room—as a prayer this time that maybe someday she'd know for herself. Maybe someday she'd have a man who would joke about her bones.

After her own lunch, she drove to the shop to work on inventory, which took far longer than she'd anticipated. By the time she pulled in the driveway and parked behind Rita's car, she was too exhausted to notice that Martin's Mustang stood at the curb. Sure, she'd seen something from the corner of her eye, but it wasn't until she approached the back door that her brain linked the image to Martin.

She hated to intrude on so passionate an embrace, but she was hungry. Maybe she could sneak in, get something from the refrigerator, and take it upstairs with her. Or send them upstairs. Or to the living room.

She tried to tiptoe, but Rita turned quickly, her face darkening to a lovely hue.

"Hi, Tadie. Lookee here." She waved her left hand, showing off a big, emerald-cut diamond.

"That's some statement, Dr. Levinson."

"It's meant to be."

"Well, congratulations." She pulled Rita into a hug. "I couldn't be happier for you both. Have you told your parents?"

"Not yet. We're going over now."

Tadie wiggled all ten of her fingers. "Let me know what your daddy says about that, will you?"

Rita grabbed Martin's hand and led him to the door.

"You coming back here tonight?" Tadie asked.

"Are you sure you want me to now that your time's freed up?"

"I told you, there's no sense in you taking up space in that small apartment when I've got a whole house mostly empty. Besides, Eb thinks you're his new best friend."

Rita waved and hurried out with Martin. He must have grabbed her again, because giggles erupted in the back yard.

* * * * *

Sipping her coffee and munching on a blueberry scone the next morning, Tadie felt Ebenezer's tail swoosh over her slippered feet. She looked under the table to see him licking up the big crumb she'd dropped. "Good job, Eb."

Rita padded into the kitchen. "Morning." She took down a mug and poured herself a cup. "Getting cold out there."

The temperature outside hovered in the low fifties. "You only think so because you've been spoiled. When I left New York, it was already coat weather."

"Tomorrow's supposed to be better." Stirring her sweetened brew, Rita grabbed a scone for herself and sat down. The dazzler on her finger winked at them.

Tadie watched as Rita's gaze continued to land on the ring. "I take it your parents are thrilled."

Rita dropped her hand and her face lit up. "Oh, honey, Daddy about swallowed his tongue staring at this thing. But he patted Martin's back and looked pretty pleased with himself, as if he'd hand-picked Martin for his son-in-law."

"No, really? He's actually reconciled himself to the idea of Martin being Jewish?"

"Martin's been visiting church with us. Says he likes the music. So Daddy probably figures he's on the way to converting."

Tadie stopped the scone halfway to her mouth. "You think?"

"Probably not, but I'm not saying one way or the other. If it makes Daddy happy, and it makes Martin happy, then I'm for it. What we'll do later, I don't know."

"And Elvie Mae?"

"Mama just sits there smiling like she knows the truth about life. I expect she does too."

"Don't you wish we could have your mama's faith and her peace of mind?" Tadie bit the pastry, chewed, and thought about how some folk found that contentment—and some didn't.

"How's Matt doing?" Rita said, changing the subject.

"Much better. You know, I think it's taken this to shake Hannah up, make her realize how much she loves that man."

"What? She was getting complacent?"

"That's my opinion."

"And what about you? Did you get New York out of your system, or are you going back?"

Tadie ran her finger around the lip of her cup while she gave the idea some thought. "I'll have to at some point, if only to pick up the rest of my things, but I don't know if I'll stay. You've been there. The city is exciting and busy, and there's a lot to do. But I didn't come away much smarter. No answers, except that I missed home."

"What were the questions?"

Tadie swallowed hard, though by now there wasn't anything but spit to go down. Instead of answering, she held out her mug. "You want a refill?"

"No thanks."

She poured the coffee, added cream and sugar, and turned to leave the room. "I'll just take this into the studio."

Rita held up her hand. "Before you go, Mama wants to know your plans for Thanksgiving."

Hadn't Hannah said something about that, about hoping she'd join them? "I think Hannah's going to need company, but probably not the whole crowd, not with Matt still recovering." That gave her pause. Would Alex be there? They'd had fun—once—but she didn't think she wanted to spend a holiday with him. "What are you thinking?"

"Well, either we all celebrate together, or we go with Martin's idea. He said we should take Mama and Daddy out. His folks will be with his sister this year."

Tadie shook her head. She couldn't picture it. "Take Elvie out to a restaurant instead of her roasting the turkey? Oh, honey, have you asked her yet?"

"I told Martin I didn't think she'd go for it."

"I'd like to hear her response." Who on earth could cook turkey to Elvie's standards? Not even Tadie had ever thought of attempting such a feat.

* * * * *

But Elvie did agree. And Alex would be out of town with his girls, thank the good Lord.

As the big day dawned, Tadie was very glad her first all-by-herself turkey didn't have to face Elvie's scrutiny. Who would have guessed she'd have reached the ripe age of thirty-five without having mastered Thanksgiving 101?

She got the turkey in the oven and set about preparing the stuffing casserole according to Hannah's instructions. Rita had made pies the day before, both for her to take and for them to eat later at the apartment. "Mama wants her own recipe, you know that," Rita'd said.

It really wasn't so hard, not when the bird took hours to bake with only occasional basting in between. When the buzzer rang, she hefted the pan onto the stove top, and put the stuffing in to brown.

The stuffing would be ready in about twenty minutes, so she loaded the pies in the car and readied the trunk to receive the hot food. Hannah was making a salad and green beans. Easy with just the three of them, which was about as big a gathering as she felt up to this year.

She carried the last of her load into Hannah's kitchen. Hannah had already set the table and was fussing and polishing her water goblets to a shine before she filled them with ice and water.

"Wine glasses?" Tadie asked, looking around for their usual Sauvignon Blanc.

"You remember how I got so mad at Alex for bringing hard liquor to the house?"

"Because Matt drank too much of it."

"He was sloshed. So, when Alex moved in, I suggested we make a no-alcohol-in-the-house rule, the only way I'd have some control over what went on at my dinner table."

"That meant you had to quit with the wine?"

"Honey, if that's all it took, I was happy to do it."

"Did it work?"

"Not with Alex. But at dinner? Yes ma'am. I miss a glass with my meal, but nothing was worth seeing Matt like that again. Maybe when he's all well and Alex is gone, we can go back to the way things were. But only if it seems right."

Tadie carried the water glasses to the table. "So, how's it going, having him still here? I thought he was beginning to behave himself."

"I tell you, I was never so glad of anything when he said he was going off." Hannah leaned on the back of a chair. "Having Alex underfoot is getting on Matt's nerves, but every time he asks Alex about his prospects for a rental, his brother says they're all either too expensive, too old, or too far away."

"Maybe we ought to hunt up a place for him."

Hannah grunted. "Haven't I thought of doing just that? Matt's so good-hearted, he lets Alex walk all over him. Alex still spreads himself all over the den and takes control of the TV remote, saying Matt should come join him. But even if it's something Matt wants to see, he knows I won't, so we go upstairs."

Tadie pointed to the food ready to be served. "Come on. I'll carve while we talk."

"How about you and Rita?" Hannah asked, holding a plate while Tadie filled it with white meat for Matt. "You okay with her there?"

"It's fun having someone else in the house. You know how I rattled around alone." Tadie picked up a second plate as Hannah spooned on vegetables and stuffing. "And with her doing a lot of the cooking, I've had time in the studio. I missed working when I was in New York."

Carrying the filled plates to the table, Hannah called for Matt. "Are you pleased with how things are turning out? You seemed pretty frustrated before you left."

"I was." Tadie covered the turkey with foil and looked around the kitchen. "What's next?"

"Gravy," Hannah said, her hands full of salad plates.

Tadie brought in the gravy and waited as Matt lumbered to the table. He surveyed the feast. "Ladies, this looks wonderful."

"Tadie did most of it. Thank her," Hannah said.

"I'll do that. Now you two sit down and let's say grace. Smelling this is making me hungry."

"Thank God," Hannah said. "That you're hungry, I mean."

Matt's blessing varied from his normal short-and-sweet version. He had a lot to be thankful for, he said, but when he got to thanking God for saving his life, the tears spilled onto Hannah's cheeks.

"It's just joy," she said, swiping at them and sniffling.

Matt spooned a dollop of cranberry sauce onto his stuffing and took a bite. "Mmm," he said around a mouthful.

Hannah leaned toward him. "You eat as much as you want, honey, and any leftovers can go to the shelter. Seems the kids like to snack, and there's never extra."

"Those are Rita's words," Tadie said. "She was disappointed they wouldn't have any to take since they're eating out."

"What a hoot that Elvie agreed." Hannah took a large bite of turkey and stuffing, and her eyes lit.

"She said she wanted to try having someone in a fancy restaurant wait on her. Besides, no dishes."

Matt excused himself before they'd even served pie. Once he'd gone to lie down in the den, Tadie said, "You do know I still have to deal with my place in New York."

"Because you've been so busy holding my hand. I can't tell you how much—" Hannah stopped to pull the tissue out of her sleeve and blow her nose.

"You're exhausted. Matt's not the only one who needs to recover. Look at you."

Hannah twisted the tissue and wiped her face. "It's been hard. You know. You've watched it."

"So, drive up to New York with me and help me clear out the place. Take a break." She couldn't keep the excitement out of her voice.

"How can I leave him?" Hannah asked, looking toward the den with a troubled expression.

"You'd better be asking how you can stay. You've lost at least twenty pounds, and you look terrible."

"Thanks a lot."

"You know what I mean. And look at your plate. All you've done is push your food around. You haven't had a moment to yourself since this whole thing started. Matt knows you're devoted. Do you think he's going to begrudge you the time away?"

"But—"

"Hire someone to stay with him. Call the home health people. They'll give you the name of a caregiver. Besides, he's not an invalid anymore. He just needs to rest a lot."

"I know."

"So?"

Hannah shut her eyes momentarily. When she opened them, a tiny smile curved her lips. "Okay. I'll do it. I'll come." Just saying it aloud seemed to loosen her tension, releasing a sparkle that hinted at the old Hannah. "Get your credit card ready, girlfriend. We're going to party."

Chapter Twenty-nine

Tadie slid behind the steering wheel as Alex hefted Hannah's suitcase into the trunk. He showed up at the driver's side window and leaned in before she could turn the key in the ignition.

"You sure I can't drive you two north? I know the way like the back of my hand and, besides, I haven't ever seen the city with you."

"And you're not going to this time either," Tadie said. "You just stay right here and entertain your brother. You owe him."

The flirtatious look in Alex's eyes vanished, replaced by an expression that made Tadie turn her head, put the car in gear, and back quickly down the drive. It seemed the real Alex had returned.

Hannah laid her head back when Tadie suggested they take Route 17 north instead of heading over to the interstate. "That's fine," she said. She napped most of the way up through Little Washington to Elizabeth City and perked up when the road paralleled the Dismal Swamp. After they'd crossed the Chesapeake Bridge Tunnel and hit the Eastern Shore, she began flipping through the radio stations, hunting for some country music. They laughed over an old song about itty-bitty everything, wailed along with an old Patsy Cline tune, then whooped it up with Garth Brooks. They stopped for a barbecue sandwich in some remote place along the highway, where they slurped iced tea and wiped hot sauce off their cheeks.

"Dang, girl, this is great," Hannah said. "You know, I think this is the first adventure we've gone on—just the two of us—since college. We ought to do it more often."

Hannah took over the driving after lunch, and Tadie napped. After the last pit stop in Delaware, Tadie slid behind the wheel again, and trading off like that, they made it to New York City in fourteen hours.

"We'll order dinner in," Tadie said as she collected the mail that had been crammed into her box. "Indian?"

"You can do that? I mean, they'll deliver Indian food right here?" Hannah leaned against the elevator wall looking very pleased.

With a nod of her head, she led the way off the elevator and to her door. "I've got the menu in the kitchen." She unlocked the door, picked up a note that had been slipped under it, and pointed Hannah to the stack of flyers from neighboring restaurants before going to turn up the heat.

"I'm starving." Hannah bit the tip of a pen as she studied various options, then handed her list to Tadie. "Will these work?"

"Good choices," Tadie said after scanning the list. Her stomach rumbled. Time for food, wine, and rest.

While she phoned in their order, Hannah wandered to a window that looked down on a small park and said, "I've never seen anything like New York at night."

"Something else, isn't it?"

The apartment felt different with Hannah in it. Less lonesome, certainly. Warmer. Wasn't it going to be fun, showing Hannah the city that had never quite become hers? Although it felt like a waypoint, it was one she'd explored and Hannah hadn't. Yet.

"Make yourself at home," she called, rolling her bag to the bedroom. "You want the bathroom first?"

Hannah didn't turn. "You go ahead."

"Food should be here in about twenty minutes. I won't be long."

Hannah was rummaging for place settings when Tadie returned

to the kitchen. "What are we drinking?" Hannah asked.

"Shiraz? I know I have that. Maybe a Pinot Grigio."

"You choose. I'll be glad to have a glass of anything."

She uncorked the red and half-filled two glasses. "This is a good one. Or at least its sibling was."

"Thanks," Hannah said, taking hers and sipping as she counted out silverware and napkins.

Her wine in one hand and the mail in the other, Tadie settled on the couch to sort through what had accumulated since she'd left. Some had been forwarded from Beaufort before she'd remembered to tell them she was home. There were statements of bills paid online, several fliers announcing sales or shows, a couple of letters, and an invitation to a bazaar to help fund a homeless shelter.

Their dinner arrived while she was still sifting through the stack.

Hannah tipped the boy and spread the feast on the table. "Look at this stuff. Come on. You've got to be hungry too." She finally glanced up. "What's that?"

Tadie stared at the envelope in her hands. "I don't know. It looks like a letter from Will Merritt. You know, Jilly's father."

"Right. The boater. Nice guy." Hannah sat down and started spooning out portions for herself. "Either open it or come eat. I'm starving."

Tadie still held the unopened letter when she sat down at the table. Hannah passed the rice. Tadie laid the letter by her plate and spooned out rice and *dahl*, adding a portion of curried chicken. She stared at her plate.

Hannah's fork stilled.

"What?" Tadie asked.

The other woman pointed at the envelope with her fork. "You have something going on here you forgot to mention?"

"No, not really."

"This stuff is good," Hannah said around a forkful of lentils. "You ought to try it. What do you mean, 'not really'?"

"The last time I saw Will Merritt, he told me never to contact his daughter again."

"And that was because?"

Tadie told her. At least, she told her most of it. She didn't say a thing about her fantasies or that Will's words had devastated her.

Hannah must have heard what wasn't said. She spoke gently as she stabbed a piece of chicken. "You love that little girl, don't you?"

"Yeah."

"What about her father?"

The heat began its tale-telling climb up her neck to her cheeks. Tadie tried to cover it by cutting into the chicken. "He's a jerk."

Hannah jabbed the fork in her direction, dropping a piece of meat just off her plate. "Sara Longworth, you stop that right now. You can't fool me. So tell." She picked up the lamb and popped it in her mouth.

"There's nothing to tell."

"Excuse me, but that blush means something."

"It's nothing."

"Maybe you can fool some folk with talk like that, but remember me? The person who's known you forever?"

"I hate him."

"Sure you do."

Tadie set down her knife and fork and picked up the envelope, but all she could do was stare at it. It didn't weigh much. It was probably just a thank-you note. Maybe if she let Hannah read it, they could move on to some other topic. Something safe, like what show they wanted to see or where they'd shop tomorrow.

Slipping a finger under one corner, she ripped at the envelope. Still, she hesitated. What if he'd written ugly words like the last ones he'd said? She shook her head.

He wouldn't. No one would commit those to paper.

But what if Jilly were miserable and he blamed it all on her?

"You gonna read it or not?" Hannah extended her hand. "If you want, I'll read it for you."

It was just a piece of paper. Who cared what it said? If Will Merritt wanted to be a creep in writing this time, so what? She yanked out the folded sheet and flipped it open.

Dear Tadie.

"Out loud," Hannah said.

"Shhh."

"Come on, you can't *not* share it."

She clutched the paper to her breast, glaring at her friend. Hannah's eyes widened. Tadie touched her forehead, closed her eyes, and whispered, "I'm sorry." She began reading aloud.

Dear Tadie, I apologize for taking so long to write this. First, I want to thank you for your hospitality to Jilly and me. And for your friendship. Jilly can't stop talking about you and asks me almost daily when we can visit you again. I imagine I have ruined our chances for that to happen, but I promised her I'd write.

"The jerk," Hannah said. "He writes because his daughter wants him to?"

Tadie's lips thinned. She relaxed them before continuing.

I may have misjudged you.

"He *may* have? And he thinks I'm going to appreciate him saying so?"

"Go on," Hannah urged.

Clearing her throat, Tadie picked up the letter again.

I'm sorry if I let my feelings cloud my judgment.

"What feelings?" Hannah wanted to know.

Tadie ignored the interruption, but she'd like an answer to that one herself. Did he mean the feelings of anger—or of something else? And why had he been angry in the first place?

I was wondering if you would ever be willing to see us again, and if so, when?

"I don't *think* so." Hannah's outrage cheered her.

Tadie turned the envelope over and studied the return address and postmark, Georgetown, MD, wherever that was, mailed the day before she'd left New York. It had been sitting here, unopened, for almost three weeks. She guessed Will had his answer.

"The letter says he and Jilly are moving to Baltimore's Inner Harbor on the *Nancy Grace*." Tadie refolded the note and stuffed it in its envelope, which she set aside on the stack of unopened and unimportant mail. Her breathing had started to calm, so she picked up her spoon and took another bite of the *dahl*, but the lentils tasted like paste. She pushed aside the plate and sipped at her wine. "Did I ever tell you how beautiful the *Nancy Grace* is inside?"

"Yes, you did. But don't let a pretty boat seduce you. You've got your own pretty boat. Are you going to write him back?"

"And did I say how much I envy their lifestyle?"

Hannah's long nails tapped on the table. "Why?"

"They get to see the world by sea."

"Yeah. Sounds like they're seeing lots of it. The Inner Harbor of Baltimore. Big whoop."

Tadie couldn't help herself. She hooted. "Big whoop? Where did you hear that?"

"One of Alex's daughters. The little princesses came to see him one afternoon while you were gone. They're exactly like Bethanne—horrible."

"Maybe if their daddy cared more, they'd be nicer people. Poor things."

"Amen." Hannah rolled flat bread around in her curry sauce. "Do you ever think Alex may not have been the person you imagined— even back when we were young?"

"Honey, I found that out back when he gave Bethanne the ring."

"Yeah, but I thought maybe you'd clung to your fantasies over the years. Being with him when you were young might have made it harder for other men to measure up. And now he's back and hanging out at your place."

Tadie shifted nervously in her seat. "He's been over once with dinner. Yes, we had fun, but it doesn't mean anything."

"He seems to think it does."

"How do you know?"

"The way he strutted when he got back from seeing you. Like he knew something we're too dumb to understand."

Tadie ground her teeth. She'd like to grind Alex. Had she encouraged him by having a little fun over that Mexican dinner? Things had relaxed between them because he hadn't pushed or pouted. Sure, he'd flirted, but harmlessly, no more than always. He was still married, and he knew that meant he was off limits. "Maybe he wants you and Matt to think there's something going on because Bethanne dumped him."

Hannah spooned more curry onto her plate. "Since he was your first, you might find it hard to say no to him now, seeing as how the rest of the pickings in town are so slim."

Tadie closed her eyes. Here it was. She could feel herself about to break all the years of silence.

Maybe she shouldn't say anything. Maybe she ought to let Hannah think what she would.

Her eyes opened and the words popped out. "I never slept with him."

Hannah's fork dropped to her plate. "What?"

"You heard me. I never had sex with Alex."

"But he said—"

"I don't care what he said or didn't say. It didn't happen."

"But I just assumed. You never contradicted him. You never told me."

"Because Matt was all you could talk about. How great he was. I didn't want you judging me."

"Me, judge you? Glory, Tadie, you're a piece of work, you know that?"

Tadie pushed her chair away from the table and crossed her arms over her stomach.

"How come you never told me in all these years?" Hannah's eyes reflected hurt. "I didn't think we had secrets."

"You don't know how many times I wanted to say something, especially in college when I was dating Brice. He started pushing me once he gave me that ring. But I couldn't."

"Couldn't tell me or couldn't have sex with him?"

"Both. Either."

Hannah squinted, making Tadie feel like some strange specimen Hannah had never seen before. "Do you mean to tell me, Sara Longworth, that you've never done it with anyone?"

Tadie took a long, deep breath, waited, then eased it out. Finally, she nodded.

"Never ever?"

Tadie shook her head.

"Lord, have mercy. Don't you want to?"

A snort was all she could manage.

"What am I saying? Of course you do. You're not gay. I would have known if you were." Hannah squinted again and peered at her. "I would, wouldn't I?"

Another snort.

"Okay, sorry." Straightening in her chair, Hannah picked up the discarded fork and took another bite. "Well, so what's the plan? You waitin' for God to drop someone through your roof?" She narrowed her eyes. "Is this a sin thing? A ring on your finger before anything else? 'Cause if it is, girl, you better get busy. Wait much longer, and anybody's gonna look good."

It may have grown into a marriage-or-nothing thing with her, but Tadie couldn't be sure it always had been. "I just haven't met anyone, not the right anyone. I mean, I could have done it with Alex or Brice or a bunch of others, but I didn't want to be a notch on their belt, you know?"

"Who would?" Hannah pointed to the rice container. "Any more of that left?"

Tadie slid the food in front of Hannah. "I came here thinking maybe there would be more opportunity."

"To meet Mr. Right?"

"That was part of it, I guess. Mostly to see if I'm single because I live in Beaufort, or because I'm me. Maybe I'm not supposed to be married. I thought I was happy the way things were."

"Until that man came along."

"It was mostly when Alex came back to town and got me thinking."

"Got you going, did he?" Hannah waved with her fork again, but at least it was empty this time. "It was probably that man too. If nothing else, Jilly made you want something else."

"She did."

Shaking her head in disgust, Hannah said, "You need to get a job. Not just your studio and the shop. Find something that would put you in contact with eligible men."

"Good thought. I can just go out and start competing with the twenty-somethings straight out of college." Tadie extended both hands, palms up. Glancing at the imaginary scale in her right palm, she said, "Me," and at one in her left, "a twenty-two-year-old."

"I see what you mean. What about the Internet—one of those matchmaking sites? It worked for Tom Hanks and Meg Ryan."

Tadie hurumphed. "Anything can happen in the movies, which is why we like them." She stood and began stacking dishes. "I moved up here looking for answers."

"And?"

The sound came out as a sort of half-laugh, harsh even to her ears. "What do you think?"

Hannah just waited.

"Obviously, I'm still alone, aren't I?"

Hannah used a slice of *naan* to clean her plate. "Too bad we don't have an Indian restaurant in Beaufort. I like this stuff." She tore off another piece and examined it. "Maybe I can get the recipe. How hard can it be to make flat bread?"

Tadie turned on the water, rinsed her plate, and added it to the dishwasher. "I'm glad I told you, but the way I see it, I'm either meant to die a virgin or the perfect man will come waltzing into our shop one day, offering me a ring and forever. Changing places didn't change me at all."

"So, I'd better get busy."

"Hah! You haven't been able to pull anyone out of the hat in the last sixteen years. Where do you think you'll find him now?"

"I don't know. But you've given me new incentive."

"How?"

"Honey, no best friend of mine is going to die without at least a taste of loving."

"You find a man I want to marry, and we'll see about it. I decided shortly after I broke up with Brice that, as curious as I was, and as much as my body sometimes had a mind of its own, I was not going to take up with some guy just to relieve an itch. If I didn't let myself go with Alex—"

"And why didn't you? I thought you loved him."

"Sure, I loved him. But I wasn't convinced he loved me. It turns out I was right."

"And, obviously, you didn't love Brice."

"Nope. And so far, I haven't found any man I trust enough or love enough to give away something I've held on to this long. It's marriage or nothing."

"In other words, it's got to be great or not at all."

"Exactly."

"Boy, our mamas would have been proud of you. And you ought to tell Father Ames. It would bolster his faith in us."

"Hannah!"

"Well, how many kids listen to him anymore? He might like to know the message got through to one of our generation, at least."

"I'm pretty sure now it was my self-image that got in the way."

"Whatever." Hannah flipped her hand in dismissal. "Who's to say what was behind it?" With one last bite, Hannah picked up her plate and handed it to Tadie. "Is this Will fellow definitely out of the running?"

"He was never in it."

"But that blush?"

"Okay, so I had fantasies while he was staying at the house. But he's still in love with his dead wife. He wrote because he couldn't tell Jilly what a jerk he was to me."

"Fantasies, eh?"

Tadie threw up her hands. "I knew you'd pick up on that. With everything else I've said, that's all you can remember?"

Hannah scooted her chair closer to the table and rested her chin in her palms. "Tell me. I want to know what they were. All the juicy details."

Tadie knew that look from days when they'd sat cross-legged, ready to confide their deepest, darkest longings. "Hannah, you may be my best friend, but I am not going to tell you about thoughts I wish I'd never had."

"You're making me curious to know him better. I've decided you may be misjudging the situation. It's obvious he's no good at communicating, which is probably why I thought him a prick." A Cheshire-cat smile spread as Hannah looked at her, making Tadie nervous. "Maybe you ought to write back."

"I don't think so. If he wants to make up, he can try again."

"It may have taken every ounce of ability he had to get that out," Hannah said, pointing at the folded sheets. "So now he'll give up. What's his job?"

"Mechanical engineer."

Hannah slapped her forehead. "Of course. That explains it. Engineers are notoriously bad at feelings."

"That's his problem," Tadie said.

"Just don't let it be yours too. Anyway, can I at least tell Matt what a liar Alex is?"

"Hannah Morgan, if you so much as breathe that to anyone, including Matt, I'll never speak to you again."

"Okay, fine," Hannah said before trying to cajole her with an innocent look. "You sure? Not even Matt? It would be fun to take the wind out of Alex's sails."

Tadie pulled a catalog from the heap of mail and threw it in the direction of Hannah's face. Her friend ducked, but it was a long time before the twinkle finally left her eyes and she settled on Tadie's couch to channel surf.

* * * * *

Tadie woke to a snore. For a moment, she had no idea who slept on the other side of the queen-sized mattress. Her first-ever shared bed, and there was Hannah, snoring slightly, but with a rattle.

The bedside clock clicked over to three thirty-two. As she continued to watch, the two flipped to a three. She did not want to wait for the green four to stare at her. Closing her eyes, she reminded her body it was supposed to be sleeping.

Her eyelids popped open.

Will's letter sat a whole room away, yet it took up all her brain space. Rolling over onto her back, trying not to disturb Hannah, she replayed every word, especially that bit about letting his feelings cloud his judgment. What feelings did he mean? Good? Bad? Indifferent?

She slipped out to the kitchen and drank a glass of water without even a glance at the stack of mail. Then she tiptoed to the bathroom. Which, of course, flashed her back to a memory of Jilly at her house.

She'd perched on the toilet seat as the child played in the big tub. Slithering around in the bubbles, Jilly had talked about sailing to the Bahamas with her daddy, how big the waves had been on the Gulf Stream, and how their crew, a man her daddy knew from a long time ago, got sick and threw up, and she didn't. Wasn't that something? A grown man who sailed all the time.

Jilly had made Tadie imagine the sailing and the fun when they'd finally reached the islands—the funny accents, all the boats, the food she'd learned to like, riding on the back of a motor scooter hanging onto her daddy. On the night before the disaster, Tadie had let herself—just for a moment—dream of being with Will. As his wife.

Not sleeping in a bed with Hannah, but with him.

She covered her face with her hands. How could she have thought such nonsense only hours before he crashed her dreams with his rejection?

We don't want you.

So reminiscent of Alex's betrayal. *I'm marrying someone else.*

Now Will wrote saying they'd like to see her again, that maybe he'd been wrong.

Why couldn't she meet a man who didn't use words like *maybe*? Who said instead, *I want you.*

No, that wasn't right. Heaven only knew, there were plenty of someones with brains in their pants who'd said just that. Who'd tried to make her believe they meant it.

No. He would have to be the right someone. But it was possible—probable—he didn't exist. And for some reason, she, Sara Longworth, was doomed to remain as she was. Untouched.

The thought brought an awareness to her body, a longing for something she'd never known. To feel a man's fingers trail down her cheek and slide across her jaw, seeking more, taking more—because he was hers and she was his.

What would it feel like to belong to someone and have him belong to her?

Tadie rubbed her palms across her eyes. She wouldn't weep. She wouldn't.

Not for him, the him who wasn't.

Did they still refer to unmarried women of a certain age as old maids any place but Beaufort? She loved the French words: *Les dames d'un certain âge.*

Here in New York, single women of means were merely independent. One could be an independent woman for her entire life, surrounded by fascinating people who never once felt pity for her. A woman of means must certainly have chosen to remain single. She must enjoy her solo state.

Not in Beaufort. There, a woman might make it to thirty—or even to thirty-five these days—before people took pity on her. But after that, she was doomed to spinsterhood. The spinster aunt of somebody. Aunt Tadie, they'd call her, if she could find anyone to do the honors.

Hannah had no offspring, and Bucky hadn't married before he died. Unless he'd fathered someone as yet unknown to her, there would be no help from that quarter. Her other friends from school had more family than they knew what to do with and certainly didn't need another member, honorary or not. Her only hope was Rita.

Those thoughts tumbled unhappily around in her foggy brain until just past four o'clock. She climbed back under the covers and found her eyes unwilling to close. Once more she begged for help as she watched the bright green numerals click over to four thirty-eight.

Peace, please. That's all she wanted. Peace.

Hannah woke her at eight, pulling back the curtains to reveal a dismal sky. "What are we going to do today?"

Tadie yanked the pillow over her head and groaned.

Chapter Thirty

Will had hoped for a reply when he mailed his letter. At least something—*Don't ever write again*, or better yet, *I forgive you, when can you come?*

But no answer had arrived at Liz's house or at the post office box after they left Georgetown. He tried to shrug it off as he and Jilly settled into winter quarters in Baltimore. His old boss had sent some consulting work his way, so he was back at the computer on his CAD program. The Internet was a marvelous tool, allowing him to work from the boat and be with Jilly.

His daughter continued to amaze him. He'd set up her work station near his, and when he turned on the computer, she pulled out her school books. She usually finished before he did, which was not surprising, considering how many of her projects required teacher/ parent input. At least three afternoons a week, they took time to do something special together. Part of her schooling—the part he believed made homeschooling superior—involved individualized research, even for grade-schoolers. For science, they had the National Aquarium and the Maryland Science Center right in the Inner Harbor. A MARC train and subway ride took them to the Smithsonian in Washington for her studies of American and natural history, art, and science. Once or twice, he considered moving the boat to a DC marina, but they'd have a long trip down the Bay, then another long trip up the Potomac, plus having to deal with the Wilson Bridge clearance. No, they were better off where they were. Besides, Jilly enjoyed the train ride. They were close to BWI and flights anywhere, and the Inner Harbor had a lot to offer. Also, when he needed to fly to jobs, he could always take Jilly over to Liz's place on the Eastern Shore.

They were busy and having fun. A lot of fun. They were.

And, no, he wasn't protesting too much. It was true.

Jilly had stopped asking about Tadie, although he occasionally caught her talking to Tubby about Beaufort. Yesterday, she'd said something about Jasper the toad and Penelope the fish, but he hadn't caught the details. And she always asked God to bless Tadie and Isa.

Fortunately for his peace of mind, he'd slept dreamlessly for the past month.

It would soon be Christmas. They'd shared Thanksgiving with Liz and her husband, and they certainly had the option of going back there. But did he want to?

"Jilly, honey," he said, interrupting her math work. "I was thinking about Christmas. What would you like to do this year? You want to go back to Aunt Liz's?"

"We could." She hesitated. "Do you want to?"

"I'd like to do something special, but I'm not sure what."

"Is it supposed to snow this year?"

"Let me see what the weatherman says." He went online and hit the button for the extended forecast. It went out only ten days, but that was close enough. "I'm sorry. No snow. Rain, though."

"Baltimore is yucky when it rains."

"Shall we take a trip somewhere? Maybe the Bahamas?"

"I don't know, Daddy. The Bahamas without the *Nancy Grace* doesn't sound like much fun, and we couldn't sail there in time for Christmas."

"You're right. What about finding someplace that has snow?

Maybe the Poconos?"

She tilted her head as if thinking about it. "You know where I'd *really* like to go?"

He shook his head, waiting for her answer.

"I'd like to go see Tadie."

Will's heart sank. How could he tell her they'd never be able to go see Tadie again—all because he had been such a jerk? "I don't know where Tadie is right now. Remember what Isa said? Tadie moved to New York."

Jilly nodded.

"I wrote to her to say how much we appreciated all she'd done for us and how sorry I was we didn't see her before we left. I'm afraid I haven't heard anything back, so I don't know how we can possibly visit her."

"Maybe Isa knows where she is. We could ask."

"If Tadie wanted to see us, don't you think she'd write back?"

"Of course she wants to see us. She likes us!"

"I'm sure she does, but maybe she's busy right now. Maybe she's met some new people and is having fun with them."

"You mean, like a new little girl, someone she likes better than me?" Jilly lowered her voice and focused on the paper in front of her, probably afraid of the answer.

"Of course not. How could anyone like someone better than you?"

Her eyes brightened at that and a grin curled her lips. "You're so funny, Daddy."

"I know it. The bane of my existence."

"The what?"

"Never mind. Okay. The Poconos is out. Bahamas, no. The rest of the Caribbean, no for the same reason. Hmmm. Maybe we ought to go visit Aunt Liz."

"Dad-dy."

"You don't like that idea?"

"It's okay. But that's where we started. You said, 'What shall we do?'" At the shake of her head, her pigtails shifted and one of her rubber bands loosened. He resisted the urge to fix it as she continued.

"I said what I want, and you said we can't."

"That about sums it up."

She put her elbows on the table and her chin in her palms. "I still think you haven't tried hard enough. I think you should call Isa."

"Oh, Lord."

"Daddy," Jilly said, shaking her finger at him. "You're not supposed to say that. Not unless you're praying."

"I know. Sorry." He reached out to tug the loose band free, and she shifted to accommodate him. "Okay, kiddo. I'll think about it."

"Just think quick, or it'll be Christmas already."

* * * * *

Jilly climbed on Will's lap and grabbed his cheeks, turning his head in her direction. "What did Isa say?"

He tried to bring his attention back to his daughter, but the coldness of Isa's response had disconcerted him—even if he deserved it. "She said Tadie was home for a while because of family issues and now is back in New York, but she doesn't know how long she'll be there."

"Can we go to New York?"

Will ran his finger down Jilly's nose and rested it on her chin. "No, honey, we can't. We don't even know where in that huge city she might be. If she wants to talk to us, don't you think she'll answer my letter?"

"But if she came home and then went back, maybe she never got it."

Will closed his eyes. This was *way* too hard.

He felt the touch of her hand on his cheek. "It's okay, Daddy."

His eyes slowly focused on his daughter's face. What lay beneath her words sounded weighty, much too weighty for a child. And he'd done it to her.

"If you feel so strongly about it, why don't you write to her? Maybe she'll answer you."

Her lips opened slightly on an, "Oh," and then, full of exuberance, she said, "I will. I'll write to her right now."

She climbed down and went in search of her notebook. Taking it and a pen, she tucked into one of the settees and started writing.

It took her three hours to get her thoughts on paper. She wouldn't accept help with more than the spelling of a few words, and she kept it far from his eyes. "It's between me and Tadie," she announced as Will handed her an envelope. He printed out Tadie's name and the Beaufort address for her to copy and tore a stamp out of the book in his wallet.

"Can we—I mean, may we—go mail it now?"

"If you want to. I was thinking we might eat out tonight anyway. Why don't we wander down to the ferry and hitch a ride across the harbor?"

"O-kay!" She added a few more lines to her paper, sealed the envelope, and grabbed her jacket.

He sure hoped Jilly would receive some sort of reply. Even if Tadie had to let her down gently.

Chapter Thirty-one

"We're leaving much too soon," Hannah said as she and Tadie fought traffic south, a cappuccino for each of them in the cup holder. "I haven't even been to Broadway yet."

"You were too busy at Barney's, not to mention H&M. They're going to miss your credit card."

Seeing pre-Christmas New York with Hannah had been a completely different experience from being there on her own. Hannah had agreed to zip through a couple of museums, but she'd wanted to shop. So shop they had.

Now they had to figure out how to get on the turnpike and away from the money pit. "You keep an eye out, please."

"I am." Hannah studied the map and watched for directional signs. "Next exit."

"I sure am glad you started shipping stuff home," Tadie said, flicking her turn signal to ease onto the ramp. A taxi honked, but not at her. At least, she didn't think he meant her. She accelerated into the flow of traffic.

"Are you going to give up your lease?" Hannah asked. "I mean, maybe if we plan ahead, we can find something we want to see that isn't sold out."

"You can't expect me to keep an apartment just so you'll have a place to shop and see musicals. You want a *pied a terre* in the city, you'll have to rent it."

"Like I can afford one."

"You think I can?"

"You did."

"I rented the apartment instead of going to a shrink. It's not something I'm going to continue doing."

"What if you'd decided to stay here?"

Tadie shot a quick eyebrow hike in Hannah's direction. "Then I'd find some way to augment my income. I can't imagine keeping the Beaufort house and a New York apartment going full-time. That's an absurd waste of money."

Hannah finished her coffee and dug in her bag for a tissue. Tadie pointed to a supply between the seats and held out a palm for one to wipe her own lips.

"I'm glad you're coming home," Hannah said. "I missed you terribly when you were away."

"I missed you too."

"You've certainly spoiled me on this trip. I can't believe I'm going back so Matt can yell down the stairs for his slippers."

"You love it."

"It's true. He's turned into an old coot, but he's *my* old coot."

Several hours later they had to make a directional choice. "I vote I-95 this time," Hannah said. "See something different."

"Fine, but we ought to take 301 to by-pass the DC-Richmond mess."

"What do I know? I've never driven that way." Hannah laughed at herself. "Well, I've never driven any of it. I was just thinking two lanes on 17 late in the day didn't sound like a good idea."

As Baltimore loomed to their right, Tadie glanced over at Hannah and quickly scanned the city skyline. She couldn't stare, but her thoughts were certainly centered on one red-haired child.

And the father?

Of course not.

It wasn't until they were approaching the exit to I-97 that Hannah said, "I wonder if they're still there."

"Who?" Tadie asked, knowing, but wanting to hear Hannah say it.

"Will and his daughter."

"That's the address he gave. A post office box in Baltimore. But maybe he just uses it to check in. I don't know much about him ... uh, them."

"But you liked them."

"Jilly. I liked Jilly."

"I liked them too. Both of them."

* * * * *

"What do you think Matt's going to say about all your loot?" Tadie asked, bags hanging from both arms as she followed her equally laden friend to her door.

"He'll be so happy to have me home, he won't care. Besides, don't you think he'll enjoy seeing me dressed in something stylish for a change?"

"You always look good."

"No I don't. I've looked like a frump for years, and you know it."

"Well, honey, if you have, I have."

"We both needed a change."

"Maybe so." Tadie set the things down inside the front door and leaned over to give Hannah a hug. "Call me."

Her own porch light greeted Tadie as she parked around back, but the house was quiet. Flipping the switch in the kitchen, she breathed deeply of cinnamon and picked up a note from the counter next to the pot of cider: *Gone to meet the Levinsons. Be back Sunday. Please pray.*

"They'll love you," Tadie told the note. "How could they not?"

She called to let Elvie and James know she was back, then filled a mug and set it in the microwave to warm while she carried her bag upstairs. Ebenezer greeted her at the landing.

"Hey, big boy, how's it going?" He rubbed against her shin as she stroked him, his tail flicking and curling around her calf. "Did you miss me?" she asked that swishing tail as he padded down the hall in front of her.

Orange, yellow, and white mums winked from her bureau. Lovely, Rita.

She ran her hand along the banister as she went down to retrieve her cup and returned to draw a bath. Easing into the foamy water, she picked up a book and settled back against her neck pillow.

She was home.

* * * * *

Isa fluffed the feather duster in her direction when Tadie pushed open the shop door. "Good morning. You look like your trip did you some good this time. No more dark circles, so maybe Hannah wasn't the only one who rested."

"Well, honey, I'm not sure how much resting we did, but we sure did shop. And eat."

"You needed to. And if shopping bought you that, you did well." Isa looked her up and down. Twirling a finger, she said, "Turn."

Tadie modeled the fitted jeans and black suede jacket that zipped up the front. "Hannah talked me into it. You don't think it's too much?"

"I like it. You won't find anything like it in Belks, that's for sure, but isn't that what you wanted for the new you?"

"Did I need a new me?"

"No, but I got the feeling you thought so."

"Maybe I did." Tadie unzipped the jacket. "The suede is so soft, but I wonder how often I'll wear it."

"Does it matter? Wear it whenever you want."

"I could." She glanced around the store. "So, what's been happening?"

"Did you see Rita before she left? She bought Jamie's fish sculpture."

Tadie's eyes widened, and she whistled a few notes. "To take to Martin's parents? That was brave of her."

"I can't wait to hear how they like it." Isa tucked away the duster and pulled up a stool. "I got the feeling she wanted something to take their attention away from her, and this seemed perfect. Either they'll love it because they have taste—which means they'll love Rita—or they'll hate it because they have none, and Martin will have to deal with that."

"So will Rita."

"She's strong."

"Yes, but I wouldn't want to face that kind of disapproval. We never have, you and I." Tadie headed into the office to drop off her bag, thinking the conversation over.

Obviously, it wasn't. Isa's voice stopped her. "No, but then, you've never had to face anything other than being the rich, white valedictorian."

She turned to find Isa behind her in the doorway. Where had that come from? Was this their normally cheerful Isa?

"Who told you that?"

"What, the valedictorian part?"

"I know Hannah said that. But you talk as if I'm some spoiled woman who never had any troubles."

"I'm sorry. That was rude." Isa didn't sound particularly repentant.

Well, she certainly didn't need Isa's grousing, not on her first morning home. She'd just head on back to her studio and her work.

She slipped around Isa into the shop. "Fine. Whatever. I just wanted to see how things were going here."

"I'm sorry," Isa said, scooting to block her exit. "I don't know what got into me."

"I don't either."

"Can we forget it, please?"

With a nod and a muttered, "Sure," Tadie took one last look at Isa. Had those circles been there at Thanksgiving? Those lines around Isa's mouth?

She pointed Isa to the stool. "I'm the one who ought to be apologizing. You just sit yourself down right there."

"What are you talking about?"

"I don't know why it didn't occur to me. We dumped it all on you, didn't we? First when I left, and then when we both took off." Tadie waved at the computer and toward the shop, all the things they'd piled on Isa. "I may have come back with circles under my eyes last time, but you've got them now. Why didn't you complain? I can't believe we took you for granted like that."

Isa tried to brush off the idea. "I didn't mind."

"You must have on some level, or you wouldn't have snapped at me. That wasn't like you." She retrieved Isa's large bag from behind the office door and shoved it into her lap. "I want you to take off. Go do something fun this afternoon."

Tears pooled in Isa's eyes. She swiped at them and said, "You really don't mind?"

"Of course not. We should have thought of getting you some help while we were off gallivanting. Especially the months I was gone." Tadie felt a pang of guilt. Isa had always been there for them. And she and Hannah had barely given her a passing thought after they'd left. They hadn't even bought her a gift.

"Stefan invited me to go to the theater in Greenville, but I told him I couldn't leave early enough to make it."

"So, things are going well with you two? Wonderful. Now call and tell him you're coming. Go on, pick up the phone."

Isa wiped her face again, grabbed the phone, and punched in numbers. Tadie left the office to give her some privacy. What had happened to change Isa's mind about a church-going man? As much as she'd like to know, this didn't seem like the time to bring it up.

"All set?" she asked when Isa replaced the handset.

Isa nodded. "Thank you. I mean it. I'll be back in on Monday."

"If you can't make it—or don't want to—just call me. It won't hurt me to keep shop for a day or two."

"No, I'll be here." Isa fished what looked like a lunch sack from under the counter and reached up to hug Tadie. As she pulled on the front door, she turned. "I almost forgot. Will Merritt called. He wanted to know when you'd be back."

"He wrote to say Jilly misses me. I haven't answered him."

Tadie surveyed the shop as the door closed behind Isa. She checked inventory, picked up Isa's logbook, and went into the office. While she waited for her computer to boot, she called Hannah to say they needed to give Isa more time off.

"What do you think about a raise?" she asked, distracted by a message box asking if she wanted to install some sort of upgrade to something she'd never heard of. She clicked *Don't Install*. "And I don't know why we didn't bring her anything from New York."

She heard Hannah's indrawn breath. "You're right. I can't believe neither of us thought of it. Look, why don't I find something from my stash? Some of my stuff has already been delivered, and more's on the way. Things I don't even remember buying. Why did I?"

"Greed?"

"Lust. Pure, unadulterated lust."

"Among your lustful purchases, can you come up with something Isa will like?"

"I will. And we'll leave it for her to find on Monday."

"Thanks. I've never seen her wound so tightly."

"We did sort of dump things on her, didn't we?" Hannah said. "Ever since you left the first time, because I was so caught up with Matt."

"What about an assistant for her? We could let her pick someone. That would make her feel she has some authority."

"I like that. You want to take care of it?"

"Sure. In the meantime, get some pots in here, will you?"

"Soon as I can."

Tadie walked home in the early dark of evening, pacing herself, her hands tucked in her jacket pockets. Much of Beaufort closed down in the winter, including many of the restaurants, but not the new Mexican one. Light flooded the sidewalk in front, and she paused to check the menu. Sharing a meal from here with Alex had been fun, but she didn't want to repeat it. Not after what Hannah said.

She unlocked her front door and turned on a light in the hall.

Hanging her coat in the closet, she meandered back to the kitchen where she fixed a salad of spinach, sliced oranges, walnuts, and dried cranberries. Eb raced out the back door and meowed to come back in, all before she'd set her plate on the table.

Between forkfuls of dinner, she sorted through the mail she hadn't yet tackled. She'd left specific instructions not to save the junk, but these days it was hard to tell, so she ripped up the standard number of credit card offers. Of the two invitations to dinner, one was for yesterday, and the other would be next week at the country club. She should have sent an RSVP days ago.

Her fingers stilled when she flipped over an envelope with her name printed in childish scrawl. She stared, unseeing, before she tore it open.

> *Dear Tadie, I miss you so much. Daddy says he rote you but you did not rite back and he says maybe you dont want to see us. But I said no you jus didnt get the letter on* ~~acownt~~ *ACCOUNT of Isa telling him she didnt no where you are New York or* ~~Bofort~~*. BEAUFORT. I told him I promised you we wood see you soon and we have to keep a promise so I no you are waiting. It is almos Christmas and Daddy asked where I want to go and I said Bofort but he said we cant coz your most likely not even there. So if you get this letter plese tell me where you are so we can come see you. If you are in New York maybe somebody can tell us where. I have ben to New York befor and it is a big place. So maybe you wood like to have some friends keep you company. Daddy said maybe you have found other friends and I asked if he ment another little girl you wood like more than me but he said no you wood not like another little girl more. Wood you? I hope you get this letter. My daddy has not smiled much since he came up here from Bofort so I think he misses you too but he wood never say so. My Aunt Liz says that is the way men are so we have to do the saying. Your friend, Gillian Grace Merritt*
>
> *PS We are going to take the ferry across to diner. Have you ever*

been on the ferry?

PS again Daddy showed me how to spell Beaufort and som words and I fixed it once but I sort of ran out of space to fix it the next time. Is that okay? I didnt let him reed it. This is a girls letter I said.

Tadie felt the tears, but she couldn't move to wipe them. Only when one dropped on the precious paper in front of her did she run her hands over her cheeks to stop the flow.

She didn't have Will's cell phone number, and she really needed some way to reach them that didn't require a post office box and days of waiting. Almost-eight was not old enough to have much patience, and this poor child had been waiting since the promise of *soon* they'd given in August. Christmas was only a week away. That didn't leave much time.

She examined the envelope. Jilly had mailed her letter on Tuesday. Will had called the shop before then, and today was already Saturday. How long did the caller ID keep numbers? It probably depended on how many calls had come in since then. The phone in the shop rarely rang. Maybe ...

She grabbed her coat and sprinted out the back door to the garage. It took only five minutes to drive downtown. She had the door open in two more—keys never worked when you were in a hurry. She bit her lip, reached for the phone, and retrieved the IDs from the last callers. Scrolling down, she looked for an out-of-town area code. Thank heavens they all had cell phones, so Isa's personal calls came to hers. She saw where she and Hannah had called on their way home.

There. She didn't recognize that one, not the area code or the number.

She pulled her cell phone out of her purse and dialed. And then she hung up.

What would she say if Will answered? She wanted to yell at him, but that wouldn't do any good. She could ask to speak to Jilly.

That's what she'd do. She'd just politely ask for his daughter.

She dialed again and it went to voice mail. She hit *End*.

But at least it had sounded like his voice. So now she had a number.

She wrote it down for good measure and headed back home, wondering if she ought to leave a message. A message would give him time to recover—to give the phone to Jilly and let her call back.

Then what would she say?

Well, she'd cross that bridge when she came to it.

She pulled back in her drive, parked in the garage, and was on her back steps when the apartment door opened and James stepped out. "That you, Miss Sara?"

"Hey, James. I had to go check on something at the shop. How're you all doing?"

"Just fine. Elvie says come by tomorrow if you have the time."

"I do. You all going to church?"

"You think she'd miss it if she wasn't dead?"

"Well, why don't I come with you? I could use a little of that good gospel singing."

"You know that will make Elvie mighty happy."

"Okay. See you around ten. I'll drive."

"No ma'am. I'm the driver here."

With a wave, she went back into her warm kitchen, turned off the porch light, and picked up her unfinished salad. Eb lay curled on the couch across from her, oblivious, but she didn't mind. Occasionally, his tail swished along the chintz cover, or a paw lifted to rub his nose. She was glad for his company, remote as it was.

Her mama had often sat in this big chair while Elvie fixed something for their dinner. Supervising, she'd called it, though she didn't pay much attention to the preparation. Now Tadie swallowed the last few bites and remembered the then and the now while she put off the phone call.

Finally, she punched in the numbers. When Will's voice again asked that she leave a message, she cleared her throat. "This is Sara Longworth calling for Miss Gillian Grace Merritt. Could you please have her return my call at her earliest convenience?" She gave the number so he wouldn't have any excuse, then she closed the phone. Jilly wrote as Gillian Grace. Wouldn't she think it fun that Tadie answered with her real name?

Of course, Will might think it snooty of her. And if he did? Too bad. That man had a lot to answer for already. What was one more issue between them?

When Alex knocked on her door, Tadie had just loaded her plate in the dishwasher and did not want company. What she wanted was a hot bath, a good book, and perhaps a piano concerto. "Don't you ever call first?" she asked, opening the door.

"Why should I? You might tell me not to come." He obviously imagined himself irresistible as he waltzed right in and checked the coffee carafe. Finding it empty, he took down a glass and filled it with water from the dispenser in her refrigerator.

Tadie watched, fascinated. The man acted as if the years between their youth and the present hadn't happened. "Please," she said with as much sarcasm as she could muster, "make yourself at home."

He peered over his glass. "Thank you. I have," he said, toasting her.

She had to laugh. What else had she ever been able to do when he acted like that?

"Tell me about your trip," he said, turning the chair and throwing his leg over the seat so he faced its back. "Did you and Hannah have a great time?"

"Didn't she tell you?"

"Sure. But I want to hear your version."

"We had a great time shopping and eating."

He looked her over. "I like the effect. You were too thin before." He concentrated his gaze.

She brought up her arms and crossed them. "I haven't gained that much."

"Only where it counts. Your cheeks are fuller. Much sexier and healthier. It's good."

Drat the man. Why did he do this, make her face heat and her heart pump uncomfortably? No, why did she *let* him do this to her?

She stood and wiped her palms on her jeans. "Look, Alex, thanks for stopping by, but I'm tired."

"That was quick."

She held the door open. "I'll see you later."

He bent toward her, but she backed away. The smirk back on his face, he asked, "What's wrong with a brotherly kiss?"

"You're not my brother. Goodnight, Alex."

His shrug seemed intended to say it didn't matter, but she noted the slight pout as he pushed open the screen door and before he whispered, "Goodnight, beautiful."

Standing with her back to the closed door, Tadie fanned her face. She hated that whispery voice, caressing her and calling her beautiful.

Chapter Thirty-two

Will listened to Tadie's message twice. Such a formal greeting. *Sara Longworth calling.*

But she obviously wasn't going to blow Jilly off, and that was the most important thing. He'd caused enough trouble and wasn't about to let Tadie add to it. Not if he could help it.

Maybe he should phone her first. Talk to her. Apologize in person.

She'd asked for Jilly. What had Jilly written in that letter? Probably stuff about missing Beaufort. He glanced toward the V-berth where his daughter lay tucked up in bed, talking to Tubby. Her prayers had been full of Christmas and of going to see Tadie, and she'd sounded happy, expectant. Maybe he should get her up to return the call.

No, that wasn't a good idea. She'd never get to sleep after that.

Slipping on his down jacket, he climbed out into the cockpit. With all the city lights, he couldn't see a single star. It made him suddenly long to be elsewhere, someplace warm, someplace where the horizon filled with sunsets and stars winked overhead. Where the noise came from birds and jumping fish instead of planes, trains, and automobiles.

He blew into his hands to warm them. He should have brought

out his gloves and a hat.

Tadie might be getting ready for bed. He imagined her cleaning up the kitchen, wiping down the counters, and turning out the lights before heading up those wide stairs. She'd walk into her lovely room with no need to close the door. Maybe she'd turn on music. She seemed to like music, much as he did, even many of the same pieces.

Of course, maybe she wasn't alone. Maybe that dark-haired jerk, Alex, was there. The one who had the manners of a toad. The thought conjured an image of those smirking lips.

But if the creep were Tadie's lover, would she have left him to go traipsing off to New York? Not likely.

Will pulled the phone from his pocket and flipped it open. All he had to do was scroll down on missed calls to find her number. He hit *Send* and waited.

It seemed to ring forever. When she answered, her voice sounded lazy. He heard music—he'd known he would—playing in the background and then a splash. What? Was she taking a bath?

Warmth snaked up his body. Her voice spoke again. "Hello?"

She must not have looked at the caller ID before answering or she'd have known who was calling. Should he say anything or just hang up?

"Tadie?" He thought his voice cracked. It certainly didn't sound like him.

Water sloshed. "Wi-ll?"

He knew hers cracked. Good. "How are you?"

"I'm ... why, I'm okay. How are you? How's Jilly?"

"You got her letter?"

"And yours, but not until a couple of days ago."

"I heard you were in New York. Why?"

She was quiet for a moment. Perhaps he shouldn't have asked.

"Why? You mean, why did I go?"

"I'm sorry. It's none of my business."

"No," she said. "It's not. You made sure it wasn't."

"I know. Look, Tadie, I'm sorry about that. I was a jerk."

He heard the sound of air through pursed lips. Lots of air. "Yes.

You were."

"I know you didn't mean to upset Jilly. I can't believe I behaved the way I did."

"I can't either. You hurt me, Will."

"I know."

"I love Jilly."

"I know."

"Can you please quit saying 'I know'?"

Now he'd exasperated her. This was not going well. "I'm sorry." He should never have called.

After a long pause, she came back with, "Good. You should be."

He heard gurgling, like water going down a drain. She was definitely in her bath—this was not a good idea at all. He could picture it, and that was the last thing he wanted, to imagine Tadie naked and dripping.

His eyes slammed shut and then opened abruptly. Think of something else, anything else. Look, someone was climbing on board that big Hatteras. A new neighbor?

It didn't work. The water continued to slurp. "Look, Tadie, should I call back at another time?"

"Oh, no." The no sounded like an embarrassed whisper.

Quickly, he said, "It's okay. I mean, I don't want to bother you. I can call later when you're ... when you're not ..."

Suddenly, she started laughing. It began as small gasps, morphed into a giggle, then bellowed forth in a full-throated laugh. A smile spread across his face. He couldn't help it. And then he was laughing too, caught up with her in the absurdity of it. Both of them embarrassed at an idea. He was hundreds of miles away and couldn't see a thing. And yet ...

"Hold on," he heard her say between guffaws. She must have put down the phone, because things in the background became decidedly muffled. Maybe she had set it on a towel or her clothes. He imagined her pulling on a robe. Maybe even a nightgown. Did she sleep in a gown or pajamas? She'd always been dressed when they stayed with her, always fully clothed before she left her room.

"I'm back," she said, calmer now though her voice still held a hint of humor.

"Decent?"

"Yes sir. Completely."

"What are you listening to?" he asked.

"Brahms. Shall I turn it up?"

"No, then I wouldn't be able to hear you. I'd rather hear your voice."

"You would?"

Boy, was he surprising himself tonight. "Yes." He coughed slightly. "You know where I am right now?"

"No, where?"

"In Baltimore, sitting in the cockpit, trying vainly to find a single star. I don't know whether there's a haze or just too many lights."

"Probably the lights. Why are you in Baltimore?"

"Right now, I haven't a clue. It was someplace to go when we left the Eastern Shore. I didn't have anywhere else I wanted to be."

"Nowhere?"

"Not then. I was too angry. Too upset."

"At yourself?"

"Yep." He couldn't believe he was having this conversation.

"Tell me why, exactly."

"Because I hurt you. Because I messed up a great friendship. Because I did something that would hurt Jilly a lot if she knew about it, and I didn't have a clue how to fix it."

"Why did you do it? It couldn't have been because of what I said to Jilly. You'd already packed."

"You noticed." He paused, trying to find the words. "I was scared. Terrified. I didn't want you getting so close to Jilly. I was afraid she'd be hurt when we left, so I thought I should take her away quickly, before it got worse."

"That's all? That terrified you?"

"Maybe terrified is too strong a word."

"Maybe you're not telling the whole truth."

"Look, the main thing is, Jilly misses you. I was wrong to keep you apart, and I know now it doesn't have to be an either/or thing."

"I never thought it did."

"Well, look. I'm embarrassed to say this. I mean, it sounds ridiculous, but I was afraid you might be playing up to Jilly to get to me."

"Will!"

"I know. But it's happened before, lots of times."

"You think I'm so desperate for a man I'd use a little girl to get one? That I was after *you*?"

"I'm sorry. I was wrong."

"Way wrong, buddy. Way wrong." He heard an intake of breath. "Listen. I'm ready for bed now. You have Jilly call me sometime."

"Sure."

"Goodnight then." She ended the call.

Way to go, Merritt. Way to go.

* * * * *

Tadie turned out her light and lay staring at the dark room. The rat. The self-absorbed, self-centered creep.

Fine. He admitted he'd been a fool. But why had he even thought it? Because she wasn't young and beautiful? Did she give off some sort of scent that screamed *needy*?

Horrid thought. She didn't need any man. Much less a man obsessed with his dead wife, afraid to share his child, who attacked and ran when faced with things he didn't understand or like.

She pictured Alex standing there, calling her beautiful. If anyone, Alex ought to know beauty. He was a whole lot better looking than Will Merritt.

Of course, Alex was married and was a snake.

A rat and a snake. Weren't there any nice, sane, normal, unattached men around?

Maybe she ought to let Dave Fargo, the elementary school principal, take her out. He'd been hinting for ages. But he sported a crew-cut, had beefy arms and no chin—and there was no getting away from it—his jokes embarrassed her.

No. What she needed was to spend more time in her studio.

She did not need, nor did she want, a man.

As she snuggled down under the covers, she remembered the timbre of Will's voice when he'd called. When he'd said he wanted to hear her voice. Not the music. Her voice.

Maybe Will Merritt didn't know what was really bothering him.

What if ...

Chapter Thirty-three

Christmas lights dangled from masts or stays around the marina, and garlands draped a sloop docked next to the *Nancy Grace*.

"Daddy, we need to decorate too," Jilly said.

So Will bought them a wreath to hang from a stanchion. On the table, he set up the little plastic tree laced with white lights. It should have felt festive.

He caught Jilly looking wistfully at the other boats. And dancing on her toes whenever they checked the post office for mail. Maybe today there'd be something.

This had always been his and Nancy's favorite holiday. When they'd first dated, he'd gone to church with Nancy's family on Christmas Eve, then with Nancy, then with Jilly and Nancy. Jilly loved the candle lighting. He remembered holding her candle for her and watching her eyes reflect the light. She'd always been such a happy child.

She was obviously trying to be happy now, switching on a smile when she saw him looking.

That she felt the need to pretend with him hurt.

This year, they'd attend Liz and Dan's little church on the Eastern Shore. And the ache would be worse because the seat on his other side would be empty again.

But he'd blown it with Tadie, so there was no going there.

"Hurry, Daddy, it's cold," Jilly said, bringing his attention back to the present. They'd run out to pick up a last-minute gift for Dan's mother, who was flying in for the holidays. Jilly had chosen a package of sweet-smelling soaps.

They stopped at the post office. Will noticed the postmark and tucked that envelope at the bottom of the stack so she wouldn't see it. Jilly hurried them back to the boat, where he unlocked the companionway door and slid back the hatch.

It had been three days, and still he hadn't mentioned Tadie's call. Did he dare steam open the letter before he gave it to Jilly?

No, that was absurd. He helped her shed her outerwear then hung her jacket with his. "Go turn up the heater, will you, punkin?" he asked before sitting down to sort through the letters.

Jilly stood at his side, watching as he pulled Tadie's letter to the top. "Here. This one's for you."

Her eyes glowed. She grabbed the envelope and tore it open. "It's from Tadie. I knew it. She says thank you for my letter, and she's sorry she didn't write sooner." Jilly turned breathlessly. "I knew she wasn't mad." She read more. "Tadie says she didn't get your letter in time. And listen to this. 'I'm sorry we didn't talk early enough for you to make Christmas plans that included Beaufort—'" Jilly looked up to say, "I can read that now. I can spell it."

"You certainly can."

Jilly continued. "She says maybe we can come later. 'I want to see you whenever you can come,' she says. I knew it. She even says she misses me."

Will gazed out the salon porthole. "I'm sure she does."

"You were wrong, Daddy."

"I guess I was."

"We could still fly down and surprise her."

Will turned up her chin so she could look in his eyes. "I'm sure she has plans and besides, we've promised your Aunt Liz we'd drive over."

"I know. But we were going to do something different this year. Something fun."

"We'll have fun with Aunt Liz, and then maybe next year we can branch out and be different."

With a downcast look, Jilly went back to the settee and studied Tadie's letter again.

Will closed his eyes. *Nancy, what should I do?*

If only he could ask. She'd know. She always knew.

The hurt grabbed at him again, tightening his chest. Getting through this Christmas would be especially hard. Last year they'd been in the Bahamas. This year the memories would be right on the surface. Liz would make the same vanilla flan Nancy used to—their mother's specialty. The ham and turkey would taste the same, and so would the gravy. Why hadn't either daughter established her own traditions? If they had, maybe this one wouldn't be so much like all the holidays of his married life, only this time without ... without ...

He hurried out to the deck so Jilly wouldn't hear him lose it. The wind slapped his face, tightening his skin, clouding his breaths. He wrapped his arms around himself to ward off the cold, and there, in the middle of wanting Nancy, he saw Tadie's stricken face watching him leave. He wasn't sure which hurt most.

* * * * *

James dragged in the tree and set it up in the living room before lighting a fire in the fireplace. "I'll go fetch Elvie," he said, returning with her some twenty minutes later.

Tonight was their traditional decorating party. Elvie sat in one of the large wing chairs, her bad arm propped on a pillow, and directed the production. As they laced garlands on the staircase and mantel between sips of cider or eggnog, they sang carols, and Rita's rich contralto kept Tadie's voice in tune.

"It looks as good as ever your mama used to have it," Elvie said, rubbing her hands and beaming proudly.

James handed her a refill of cider. "Yes ma'am. It sure does."

When they finished, Tadie plopped at one end of the couch

and extended her legs. The tree blossomed with lights, and the ornaments winked their reflection at the room, which smelled of pine and burning logs. "Let's talk about Christmas Eve," she said. "I'll do prime rib and you all can bring what suits you."

Elvie settled her hands and nodded. "My sweet potatoes in orange juice."

"Rita—" Tadie began.

"Of course, Rita will help," Elvie interrupted. "Lands, girl, don't make me an invalid."

"Yes ma'am," Tadie said, even though she hadn't meant to suggest any such thing. Best move on and talk to Rita later. "Hannah's bringing oysters and lots of hors d'oeuvres, as well as a Christmas pudding. Isa said her mashed potatoes—red potatoes in their skins with chicken broth and garlic—will knock us out."

"Yum," Rita said. "How many are you thinking?"

Tadie started counting. "You three. Martin's coming too, isn't he?"

Rita nodded. "He bakes a fantastic apple pie. I bet he'll want to bring one."

"Excellent. So, that's five of us, plus three from Hannah's house, Isa and Stefan—I can't wait for you all to meet him. He's a darling. That's ten. Considering we easily seat twelve, we're golden."

* * * * *

She'd slept well enough. Not great, but she hadn't had to count sheep. No, instead she'd counted knives and men who'd look good with one sticking out of the chest. And then she'd laughed at herself for being so gruesome.

She picked up the newspaper from the front porch and was sipping coffee and reading the paper when Rita padded into the kitchen. "Morning," she said as Rita filled her own mug.

"I was wondering," Rita said as she stirred in sugar and cream. "Martin's folks are going to be alone this year. Bobby and Beverly are too far away to come."

"I hope you invited them here."

Rita sipped, watching her over the mug's rim. "I didn't want to say anything without asking you."

"I'd love to meet them. What fun."

"What should they bring?"

Tadie thought over the menu. "Whatever they'd like. I'm thinking you and I can add a light salad, but we don't have any other green vegetables. Find out what they want to do, then we'll fill in the gaps."

"Are we cleaning today?"

"And polishing the silver."

When Elvie said she wanted to help, they hauled the large coffee service up to the apartment so she and James could feel a part of the preparations. Elvie thought of that silver as hers because she'd been polishing it for the past thirty-five years.

By ten-thirty on the morning of the party, they had added two leaves to the table, set it with Caroline Longworth's linen tablecloth and napkins, placed the silver around, and set crystal glasses at each place. Hannah had brought over an arrangement of forced tulip bulbs for the centerpiece. The roast was ready to go in the oven, the Boston lettuce washed and drying. Tadie sent Rita off to help Elvie and went upstairs to rest for a while. Having the house to herself all afternoon seemed like a gift.

She had just brushed out her hair and was smoothing moisturizer on her face when the phone rang. She answered with a lilt, imagining Hannah or Isa with a last-minute question.

"Yes ma'am?"

A little voice spoke her name tentatively. "Tadie?"

"Jilly, hey, baby, how are you?"

"I'm fine. Daddy and I just left to go to my aunt's house, but he said I could call and wish you a merry Christmas."

"I'm glad you did. I wish you were here with us."

"Are you having a party?"

Tadie rubbed the rest of the cream under her eyes. "I am definitely having a party. Lots of guests."

"Who?"

"Well, Isa's coming and bringing a new friend."

"A man?"

"How did you guess?"

"I could tell. The artist man who helped her, right?"

"She told you?"

"Uh-huh."

"And Hannah will be here with her husband and his brother. Elvie and James are coming, and Rita, along with Rita's fiancé and his parents. I think that's all."

"Oh my. That's a big party. Do you have to cook everything?"

"Not I. I'm too smart for that. Everyone is going to bring the thing they most like to make. I have to do very little, just the salad and roast beef."

She heard Jilly's sigh, deep and long. "I love roast beef. I wish I could come help you. I wish we were there instead of in this stupid car."

"Jilly!" Will's voice carried easily, though the reprimand wasn't spoken harshly.

"I'm sorry, Daddy. It's just ..."

"I know. I'm sorry too."

"I wish your car was pointed this way. Maybe next year."

Jilly didn't speak. When Tadie heard a sniffle, her heart melted. "Jilly, honey, are you okay?"

"Tadie, this is Will here. I'm sorry about that. Jilly and I just wanted to wish you a happy day."

"I wish you one too, Will. I'm sorry you can't join us. We're going to eat lots and be very merry."

"Well, you have fun. We'll talk to you later."

"Bye. Hug Jilly for me, please."

"I will."

Tadie stared at the phone in her hand for several minutes before replacing it in its holder. A pall had fallen over her celebration. If only Jilly could be here to dance around the table, settling that winsome smile of hers on the guests, making everyone laugh.

She screwed the top on the face cream and grimaced at the mask in the mirror. When had she started looking so old? The cracks near her eyes and the smudges under them reflected more than just her thoughts. She glanced toward the ceiling. "Why does everything have to be so hard?"

* * * * *

Jilly had dried her tears, but she continued to stare out the window into the bleak sky, her head resting against the glass. Will checked the lock again and glanced down at her seat belt.

He had heard the list of guests. Liz would have a crowd too, but they wouldn't be his and Jilly's friends. Isa had such a lovely laugh. He wanted to meet the artist she was dating. And Elvie and James, who obviously loved Tadie.

His fingers tapped on the steering wheel, and he ground his teeth. That fellow Alex would be sitting down to eat with Tadie while he and Jilly celebrated hundreds of miles to the north.

Suddenly his reasons for heading east seemed as lame as his excuses.

He pulled the car into a gas station. Jilly ignored him as he got out and moved slightly away, opening his phone and digging out his wallet as he walked.

When he climbed back in, he pointed the car in the opposite direction and took the ramp onto the parkway. Jilly didn't pay any attention until she noticed the exit he took. She sat straighter in her seat, her fists balled in her lap.

She still didn't speak when he drove into the parking garage. As he flicked open the trunk, she was right there to get her bag and coat. Her eyes were big and round.

Maybe she was afraid to find out where they were going. Maybe she thought by asking, she'd break whatever magic had captured their car and taken it to the airport. He offered his free hand.

At the US Airways ticket counter, they walked right up to the first-class agent. Will handed over his license. This had better be the right move, because it was costing him a fortune.

Jilly's eyes were still big when they passed through security and headed almost immediately to boarding. If both flights kept to schedule, he and Jilly might make Beaufort in time for dinner. Of course, he didn't have a clue what time Tadie planned to sit down to eat. Maybe they were the early-evening types who had the kitchen cleaned by six and then sat around opening gifts or watching whatever came on television. Well, if that were the case, maybe there'd be a few leftovers for two starving waifs.

Jilly picked up his hand again as soon as they found their seats. She still hadn't asked him anything, which he found both odd and comforting. Maybe she trusted him again.

Liz had been wonderful. All she'd said was, "About time. Go catch that plane and call me when you get back. And tell Jilly I'll keep her gifts safe."

"I don't know what she's going to think when she finds out she won't even have the ones I shipped to your house," he'd said. But Jilly would probably be too excited to care. Besides, they could shop for others on Monday.

There was always that plant in Atlanta—the one whose system he'd designed last summer. If they called back and said they needed more help, well, he'd be that much closer to Atlanta in Beaufort than on the Eastern Shore of Maryland.

Chapter Thirty-four

Tadie couldn't rest. Her guests would start to arrive in—she looked at her watch—a little under five hours. What was she supposed to do with herself until then?

She went to the closet, pulled out a coat, and headed out to the sidewalk. The cold bit her cheeks. That was good. She'd have some color in them.

Twice down to the west end of Front Street, around the block and back, and she still had four hours to go. An hour before she had to put the roast in. She retreated to the living room, laid another log on the fireplace, and plopped down on the couch, picking up the new *Cruising World* magazine she hadn't seen yet. After adjusting a pillow at her back, she flipped through the pages until she came to an article on watermakers. Everyone should know something about watermakers.

She scanned a paragraph. Nothing. She turned the page. The latest electronic aids to navigation weren't needed on *Luna*. She tossed the magazine to the floor.

Why did she subscribe to all these glossy bits of useless information? She'd never get to any of the cruising places or use any of the gadgets displayed on their pages.

A shower. She should be clean for tonight. The house was.

She trooped upstairs, turned on the hot water, and took a new razor in with her. By the time she'd shaved her legs, pushed back the cuticles on her toenails—my, how they grew—and washed her hair, the water had begun to cool. She dried and slathered cream all over her body.

Pointing the blow dryer at her head, she fluffed her curls without paying a whole lot of attention to how they fell. Next, she added a little something to her eyes and a dab of blush to her cheeks— because the color from her walk had melted to nothing. She dressed as slowly as possible in her new white wool dress, which made her look washed out in spite of the brushed-on pink. Digging around in her drawer, she pulled out a silk scarf, all greens and blues. It took four tries before she was satisfied with the way it hung on her shoulders, fastened with a mother-of-pearl pin.

It was time to get the roast in. She ran her hand along the banister on her way downstairs, remembering Jilly's delight in it, her small hands caressing the highly polished wood.

O … kay. On to other things.

She donned an apron, turned on the oven, and, while it was heating, straightened the silverware and wiped smudges off the glasses as she circled the table. When the buzzer sounded, she maneuvered the big roast into the oven before heading to the living room. She poked at the fire, waited for it to rouse itself, clicked on the stereo, and did a surface check throughout the downstairs—just in case she'd missed a speck of dust.

"Get hold of yourself," she whispered, settling back onto her daddy's big wing chair and checking her watch. Still over two hours to go. She tried closing her eyes. Eb wandered in and leapt onto her lap. She pulled him close to her chest and bent to lay her cheek against his soft fur. "It's Christmas Eve. Did you know that?" He nudged her chin. "It's supposed to be one of the happiest times of the year."

Her voice changed to a whisper as she said, "It's *supposed* to be."

Finally, it seemed late enough to set out the nuts and cheese.

She wished her stomach would unknot. All she had to do was smile and welcome everyone when they arrived, make light conversation through the evening, none of which should cause all this turmoil. They were friends, coming to spend the evening. It would be fun.

When the doorbell rang, she noted it was only ten to five. Martin's parents. They were the only ones who wouldn't just walk in the back door.

She slipped on a smile, took a deep breath, and pulled open the door. Small arms flew around her waist, and a red head crushed against her. "We came."

Tadie stood momentarily frozen as she stared at Will's apologetic face. Then she burst into tears and bent to embrace the child. "Jilly, sweetheart. You did come."

Jilly's arms moved to her neck. Tadie could feel Jilly nodding against her shoulder.

"I'm so happy to see you," she whispered to the child. Suddenly embarrassed, she straightened and swiped at her eyes, sniffling until she could get to a tissue. "I can't believe you're here. And look at you, all dressed up and beautiful. How did you do it?"

Jilly seemed to understand exactly what she was asking. "My daddy turned the car around, and we got on a plane. Isn't he wonderful?"

Wiping the wet remnants from her cheeks, Tadie nodded at Will. "He's definitely amazing." She remembered they were standing in the doorway. "Come in, you two. I can't believe it. What a wonderful Christmas gift you've given me."

She helped Jilly take off her coat and waited as Will shed his. "There's room in the closet," she said, pointing the way in case Will had forgotten. She ducked into the powder room to grab something to blow her nose. "Now, Miss Jilly, you told me you wanted to help me get ready, so come on back to the kitchen with me."

"Where's Ebenezer?"

"I think he raced upstairs to hide when he heard the doorbell. You can see him later."

"I'm glad you haven't eaten yet."

Tadie touched the tip of Jilly's nose. "I'm glad too. Everyone should start arriving soon."

"Aren't we lucky?" Jilly asked, turning toward her father, who handed her a wrapped box. Jilly held the box in front of Tadie. "This is for you. We wanted to bring something too."

"How lovely." Tadie glanced at Will then back to Jilly. "Thank you."

"You've got to open it. It's dessert."

"Is this all right?" Will asked. "I mean, us showing up like this?"

"I'm thrilled," Tadie said, tearing off the wrapping paper on her package. "Oh, just what I love. Godiva." She gave Jilly another hug. "Thank you, sweetie. This is a grand treat."

She turned to Will. "Thank you too. And don't worry. I told Jilly I wished you'd come. And here you are."

He looked relieved. "What can we do to help?"

"You can hunt up two more chairs. I think the small desk chairs upstairs will be best, so we can fit everyone at the table."

"If it's too tight there, we can sit someplace else."

Tadie waved him off. "Don't be silly. Jilly and I can squish together, can't we, young lady?"

"Yes ma'am!"

"Let's get out more silver. This is where I'm sitting, so we'll turn it into two places, okay?"

"Okay!"

"And we don't have to give everyone so much elbow room. Help me fit another place over there."

They did it, but barely. Tadie left a couple of larger spaces because Rita had said Martin's parents needed spreading room, but Rita was tiny and so was Elvie. Fitting the old-fashioned chairs was the biggest issue.

Will had just slipped the last of the small desk chairs into place when Hannah and her entourage arrived, carrying in their offerings.

They stopped abruptly when they saw Jilly.

"Tadie? Keeping secrets?" Hannah asked.

"Jilly and her daddy just arrived."

"We surprised Tadie," Jilly said, bouncing up and down.

"I bet you did," Alex said.

Tadie glared at his sneering face, silently daring him to utter another word. "It was a wonderful surprise."

Will tucked Jilly in front of him and reached out to shake the hand Matt offered. "Good to see you again."

Alex didn't even excuse himself. He just pushed past Will and left the room.

"Brat." Hannah leaned close enough so only Tadie heard her words.

"One more outburst," Tadie said, "and I'll boot him out."

"You have my permission. But about the other," Hannah said with an elbow pointing toward Jilly and Will, who still chatted with Matt, "you must be ecstatic."

Tadie didn't have time to answer because Isa's voice sounded at the back door, which led to more welcomes, more introductions, and more happy hugs for Jilly.

"Okay, you all," Hannah said. "Make yourselves scarce. I'll bring in the drinks." When Matt had wandered out of earshot, Hannah announced she was pouring Matt a soda. "Anyone else want one?"

Isa looked at Stefan. "Will you join the other men or stay in here with us?"

He tickled her chin. "I'll go do some male bonding. Will, you coming? We're in the way here." To Hannah, he said, "Give me something to carry."

Hannah handed full glasses to each of them, turning to Isa when they'd left. "It's exciting to have Stefan here with you. It's like having a celebrity in our midst."

"Isn't it fun?" Isa blushed, but her smile was a lovely thing to see. Tadie accepted the nod sent her way and returned it with a little wave and a grin.

"What's he like?" Hannah asked. "I mean, with you?"

"Gentle. Lovely."

"You needed that, didn't you?" Hannah brushed her hand up and down Isa's back.

"After Ben? Absolutely."

"Who's Ben?" Jilly asked, slipping under Tadie's arm so that it rested around her shoulders.

"Once upon a time," Isa said as she looked down at Jilly, "Ben was my husband."

"Did he die?"

"No, sweetie. But he wasn't a nice man."

Jilly seemed to think about that. "And Mr. Stefan is?"

"A very nice man."

"Good."

"Hey, everybody, here we come," Rita said, holding the door for her mother and father. "Martin called to say they're driving through Morehead now."

"Wonderful." Tadie pulled Jilly forward. "See who flew in for the party."

"Look at this sweet child," Elvie crooned. "You come right on over here and let me hug you." Jilly scampered over and threw her arms around Elvie's neck. "James, you ever seen anything as beautiful as this child's hair?"

"Sure haven't. Glad to see you, missy. You brung your daddy too?"

Jilly nodded. "He's in with the other men. You going to join them?"

"I suppose I could."

"No, Daddy," Rita said, grabbing his arm. "Not yet. I don't want you lost when Martin's parents get here. Can you wait to meet them first?"

"Sure, honey. I can do whatever you want." He turned to Tadie. "You need the candles lit yet, Miss Sara?"

"Soon. I'm thinking we ought to wait for the ones on the table until right before we sit down. But I sure could use some help taking this roast out. Will you do that?"

James's eyes twinkled and he stood a little straighter, obviously pleased to be asked. She handed him potholders and shooed everyone else into the far end of the kitchen or out to the rest of the house. Hannah and Isa busied themselves plugging in hotplates for the potatoes and vegetables and finding a place for the oysters.

Rita helped her mama ease down onto Miss Caroline's chair near the loveseat. "I'll get your water, Mama."

Jilly tugged on Tadie's sleeve and whispered, "That man, Mr. James, he called you Miss Sara."

"He usually does."

Jilly nodded, looking pleased to have gotten it right. "Like your mama."

"Yes, Jilly, just like my mama." That child sure did make her feel like she'd bust open with happiness every time she looked at her.

Rita and James went off to answer the doorbell, but only Rita and an older woman returned. "We lost the men to the front room, Tadie, but this is Martin's mother, Doris." She finished the introductions, ending with her mama.

Tadie suggested the tall, large-boned Mrs. Levinson sit and visit with Elvie Mae while Rita helped put the finishing touches on the salads.

"If you need a carver," Doris said as she dropped onto the couch, "I'm your gal."

Tadie pointed to the carving knife and fork. "Excellent. A much better idea than disturbing the testosterone party in there."

Oysters slid down throats and conversation hummed in the other room. In the kitchen, Doris carved, Tadie made a rich gravy from the drippings, and Hannah and Isa handed out plates.

James took this as his cue to light the candles. Will filled the water glasses and poured wine or iced tea upon request. Jilly waited and scooted in next to Tadie, with Will tucked in on her other side. There was laughter and jostling, but soon everyone had a place and a plate.

"James, will you say grace for us?" Tadie asked.

He bowed his head and gave thanks with a booming eloquence that made Tadie want to clap. She looked around at the people she loved, at her new friends, and even at Alex, and felt so full and rich she had to lower her head so they wouldn't see more tears that needed wiping.

"You okay?" Jilly whispered.

"Very okay. Just happy you're here," Tadie whispered back.

The only downside to the party was Alex. He alternated stares her way and glares in the direction of Jilly and her daddy. At one point, she heard him say, "Ow!" and glance accusingly at his sister-in-law. When Tadie caught Hannah's eye, Hannah winked, and Tadie had to cough to cover her laugh.

* * * * *

Finally, the last dish was loaded into the dishwasher, the silver and special china hand-washed, the leftovers stacked and ready to go, some in Tadie's refrigerator, some to be sent home with guests. Doris and Larry declined, saying they'd booked rooms on the ocean for themselves and for Martin. "We love the sea in winter," Doris said. "We're going to stay all weekend."

Larry beamed and cuffed Martin's shoulder. "I think Martin may have other plans than being quiet with us, honeybunch."

Martin rubbed his shoulder, backing out of his father's way. "You've got that right. James and Elvie invited me to hear their church choir in the morning while you decadent folk snore at each other."

"Make your exit, Mother," Larry said. "I don't want any more insults from your son."

Rita pulled Tadie aside while Martin helped James get Elvie down the porch stairs. "I'm going to Mama and Daddy's for a little while, help get them settled," she said quietly. "You want to go with us to church in the morning? You and your guests?"

"I need to ask them. I'll let you know in the morning."

As Hannah scurried about, collecting everything and loading packages in her husband's arms, Matt asked, "Why isn't Alex here helping with this?"

Stefan turned from chatting with Will. "He's laying siege to the living room couch."

Hannah's eyes narrowed. Catching Isa's grin, Tadie followed in Hannah's wake, pausing with Isa in the doorway as Hannah, carrying a plate of foil-wrapped meat, marched right up to Alex. For a moment, Hannah stared down at him while Alex ignored her, then she dropped the plate in his lap. "We're leaving. You bring that," she bit out and turned on her heel.

Alex's expression reminded Tadie of a spoiled child readying himself for a tantrum, but when he noticed his audience, he waved toward Hannah's back. "Sure thing. Coming."

"See you real soon," he told Tadie as he followed Matt out the door.

"I've done my best," Hannah whispered. "If he sneaks back over here, don't let him in." At Tadie's nod, she waved toward the room. "Bye, all. You take care, Miss Jilly, you hear?"

Jilly nodded, but her hand was tucked securely in her father's, and she stood with her back against his legs. She stayed there as Isa and Stefan donned their coats, releasing Will's hand only long enough to hug Isa and promise to visit the shop.

"Good girl." Isa turned to Jilly's daddy, whose hand was now clasped in Stefan's large one. "You bring her by."

"I'll sure try." Ending the handshake, Will said, "It was fun chatting with a fellow sailor."

"We'll have to repeat it."

Tadie handed Isa a plate of leftovers and let Stefan carry the empty pan. She waved them off and turned to see Will helping Jilly into her coat.

They were leaving.

Perhaps they *should* leave.

She tried for a casual tone when she said, "Do you have a reservation somewhere?"

Will didn't make eye contact. "We'll find a room."

"But you don't have to." Her cheeks must have turned scarlet, but she couldn't fan them. Not in front of him. *Her. Them.*

"Y-you." She stopped on the stutter, cleared her throat, and tried again. "You know where your rooms are here."

Jilly danced on tiptoes in front of her father. "See, Daddy, I knew she missed us. I knew she wouldn't have another girl she liked better."

Jilly's words offered the perfect distraction. "Of course not, silly. How could I?"

Will looked into her eyes. "You sure about this?"

She straightened her shoulders and nodded. "I'm positive."

"Then I'll go get the bags." He tugged on Jilly's pigtail. "We don't have gifts."

"I know. It's okay. I brought Tubby. And we gave Tadie the candy."

Tadie bent down. "I'm glad you brought him. I've missed Tubby too."

"May I have another bath? We don't have a tub on the *Nancy Grace*."

"Of course you may. Bring your bag up, and I'll run the water for you."

Tadie headed upstairs while they fetched their suitcases. The beds all had clean linen, but she set out towels for Will and took one into the bathroom for Jilly.

As she poured bubble bath into the water, she thought she heard male voices coming from below. Perhaps James had forgotten something.

"It's all ready, sweetie," Tadie called when she heard footsteps in the hall.

Will poked his head in with a look Tadie could not quite identify. "Your friend Alex would like a word with you."

Startled, she stood and wiped her hands. "What's he doing here?"

"He asked me to tell you he'd like to talk to you. Jilly and the cat have reconnected, but I'll see to her bath."

She frowned at the thought of Alex. "I'll be right back."

She hurried downstairs and confronted Alex at the living room entrance. "Did you forget something?"

"What are *they* doing here?" His tone reflected the scowl on his face, which deepened when he asked, "Wasn't he the reason you hightailed it to New York in the first place?"

Her fists curled at her hips. "Is that any of your business?"

Shoving his hands in his pockets, he puffed out his chest. "I overheard Hannah talking to Matt. I don't want anyone to hurt you, Tadie. I don't think you ought to let them stay here."

"Alex, will you listen to yourself? You're calling the kettle—"

He jerked his hand up and waved her to a stop. "That was a long time ago. We were kids. Now's different."

"Now you're married."

Raking his fingers through the thatch of hair hanging on his forehead, he said with a hint of anger, "Stop throwing that in my face. I won't be married much longer."

"That's your choice. But you've got to quit pretending we can pick up where we left off all those years ago. I'm not the same person and neither are you."

"I'm better now. I wouldn't do that to you again."

Tadie held up her palm to stop him. "Alex, go home. I don't want to have this conversation with you."

He crossed his arms and glared. "I'm not leaving while that man is in this house."

What was with this guy? She walked right up to him, her anger making her feel tall enough to stare him down. "You *are* leaving. Right now. You cannot dictate who stays here, do you hear? You have no right to say anything about my life."

"Tadie, don't."

"Good-*bye*, Alex!" She moved to the front door and held it open. "And stop acting as if this is one of your homes, you hear? I don't want you coming back."

"You don't mean that. I know you don't," he said, easing past her. "I'll see you soon."

She shut the door after him, locked it, and went to lock the back door as well. Alex's behavior frightened her. She tried to shake off the worry, to tell herself this was only Alex, Matt's brother, but it didn't work. His eyes had held a fierceness she'd never seen before.

Chapter Thirty-five

Jilly lay on her back in the tub, her hair floating out in a halo, singing a song Tadie didn't recognize. Her eyes were closed, and a look of pure happiness lit her face.

Tadie passed through to her father's room, where Will rested one ankle on a knee as he thumbed through a magazine, looking as if he belonged in the big leather wingback. She stood in the doorway and asked, "Are you comfortable?"

Laying the open pages against his chest, he looked very content. "I see why your father loved this chair."

"I'm sorry about the visitor. Alex had no business showing up here."

"He's a bit possessive, isn't he? Do you two have something going on?"

Tadie glanced behind her, but Jilly was still playing happily in the tub, so she perched at the edge of her father's bed. "It was over a long time ago."

She studied Will as she smoothed the spread out on both sides. Sitting there with the light shining over his shoulder, he seemed more relaxed than he had in August, more comfortable with himself. Maybe he'd come to terms with a few things. She wondered what they were.

When Will didn't comment, she said, "Alex and I dated in high school and during our first year of college, before I went to France to study. By the time I got back, he was married. Now his wife has left him, and he thinks he can move right back into my life."

"He seems to be succeeding to some extent." He spoke calmly, but with a question in his voice.

It brought a certain flutter to hers. "Hannah's my best friend, and he's staying at her house for a while, helping with Matt. You heard, didn't you? At dinner?"

"That Matt's got to be careful?"

"He nearly died while I was in New York."

Will set the magazine on the table. "I'm sorry." Resting his elbows on the arms of the chair and lacing his fingers together under his chin, he focused entirely on her.

His concentration pulled the same from her. Awareness quickened as she noted that strong chin and those long fingers, the lips beginning to curl slightly, the straight nose, the eyes.

Oh ... his eyes.

She dropped her gaze, suddenly aware of the bed under her and the man watching her. She tried to remember what she'd been saying.

Oh yes, Matt. Matt and Hannah.

"When Matt finally got home from the hospital, Hannah needed a break, so she went back with me to New York. That's when I found your letter. I didn't know what to make of it."

"I probably didn't word it well. I'm not always good at saying what I mean."

"I gathered that after your phone call."

"I wish I could go back and change that."

"At least you came."

"Tadie—"

A loud splash followed by a plaintive cry got them both up and running to the bathroom. Jilly was leaning over the side of the tub, reaching for her towel. "I got cold."

Tadie draped the towel around Jilly, willing her heart to slow as she patted the child dry. "Here you go," she said, trying to keep her voice light. "You had a nice long bath, and I'll bet your fingers are all pruney."

Jilly inspected her hands. "They are."

"I'll get you some lotion." Tadie glanced over at Will, who leaned against the door jamb, watching them.

He nodded, and she fled to her room to grab the scented body lotion, trying not to focus on his look or the sweet feeling of holding that little body. She'd better pack as much mothering as possible into these few days. And later, she could do that auntie thing, having Jilly visit sometimes. Or often.

She took a deep breath as she rounded the banister and through Jilly's room to the bath where Jilly stood, still wrapped in the big fluffy towel. Will must have gone back to his chair. Her father's chair.

"Okay, missy, you just climb up on the seat there. Keep the towel over your shoulders." Tadie knelt and began rubbing the lotion into Jilly's feet and legs.

"Umm," Jilly said, sniffing the air. "It smells like you."

"My mother used this lotion. Look at the label. It's French, and it says water of green orange—*l'eau d'orange verte*."

"I like it."

"Here, put some on your hands," Tadie said, squirting it into the child's palm. She looked around the bath. "Did you bring your jammies in?"

"I have them," Will called from the dressing room. "Here you go." He held out some pink flannel pajamas. "The cat sniffed at me, but he dashed past to your bed, punkin."

"I think he missed you." Tadie found a hair dryer in the cupboard and directed the air toward the child's silky hair as she finger-combed it.

Long before they'd finished, Jilly started bouncing on the balls of her feet. "I need to brush my teeth and go see Eb. He's waiting."

"You take care of your teeth and I'll tuck you in, if that's okay with your daddy." She glanced at Will, who waited by Jilly's door this time.

He nodded, and his eyes held that peculiar intensity that brought a flutter to Tadie's stomach. She quickly turned to hang Jilly's towel.

After she'd heard Jilly's prayers and received a goodnight hug, she said, "You just scoot Eb off if he bothers you."

"He's a good cat. He can sleep right here." Jilly curled around Eb as she pulled him closer. "He's my friend."

Tadie smoothed her damp palms down the side of her dress before knocking on Will's door. "She's waiting for you," she said, indicating Jilly with a wave of her hand. "I'm going downstairs for a little while."

"I'll be right there."

The water had come to a boil by the time she heard his footsteps on the wooden floor. She braced herself for his approach.

Breathe, just breathe.

Over her shoulder, she asked, "Tea? It's herbal."

"Thank you."

She poured the boiling water into a second mug and handed it to him. "Shall we sit by the Christmas tree?"

He followed her. She focused on the door ahead, on moving gracefully, on not shuffling her feet, but it wasn't easy.

Setting his mug on the coffee table, he bent to check the fire. "It's almost out. Shall I build another one?"

A fire would be a focal point, a distraction. "Please." And then, just so he'd know, "I suppose we can sit up and wait for Rita to come back. If you want. She's staying in the room next to mine. Where Isa slept." Boy, wasn't she smooth?

"I like her," Will said, rolling newspaper and tenting the kindling over it. "And Martin. All of your friends, except Alex."

"Well, yes. But he's not really a friend anymore. I'm glad you like the others."

As the flames caught and crackled in the hearth, she hit the *Play* button on her CD player, not remembering what she'd loaded, but longing for music. A fire, the lights on a tree, beautiful music. She could close her eyes and let it ease her.

"Ah, Respighi," Will said.

Her eyes snapped open. His head rested against the back of the couch with his eyes closed and his fingers laced lightly across his lap. He'd recognized Respighi. And now he looked so comfortable sitting in her house. With her. What had happened to him in the past months to change him so radically?

As the flames danced, she remembered her father's trick log, the one that made the fire multi-colored. Her daddy would have enjoyed the feast today, although it would have been too much for her mother. Too many people, too much noise, way too confusing. Mama wouldn't have remembered everyone's name, and that would have upset her.

Will remained motionless. She turned back to the fire. She mustn't think about him sitting next to her, or how attractive he now seemed, or how much she'd like to ...

Stop it.

Elvie had enjoyed herself, hadn't she? And she'd looked good, all gussied-up in her navy flowered dress. The swelling had gone down in her arm, and her face had filled out a little. And wasn't that mother of Martin's a hoot? Doris and Elvie had chatted like good friends with no cultural, ethnic, or racial barriers between them. Rita must have been in seventh heaven.

She felt Will's gaze. The pull of it turned her. *Oh, my.*

Treacherous heat rose up her neck, flaming her cheeks.

"You look beautiful tonight," he said.

Her breath caught. Her lips parted, but she couldn't seem to close them.

"I love the way the fire brings out the highlights in your hair and makes your eyes sparkle."

She caught her bottom lip between her teeth. She wondered if he could see the pulse throbbing in her throat.

The music changed to Strauss. She didn't remember putting that disc in the changer.

He stood and took her hand, easing her to her feet. "Dance with me."

"Here?" She hesitated, but let him pull her into his arms.

They fit so well, his shoulder and her cheek, his hand on the small of her back, her hand resting lightly in his. The blood pounded in more than just her neck now, and he must have felt it. Or maybe that was his blood, because the hand on her back eased her closer until she felt his breath caressing her hair and his heart *thurumping* under their joined fingers.

The music swelled, pressing on her insides until she wanted to burst. She had to break away, otherwise she would cling to him and embarrass herself.

She stopped dancing, but as she did, he pulled her closer, dropping feather kisses on her forehead, her eyelids, her cheeks. She heard a groan and thought maybe it had come from her throat. But she didn't care, especially when he moved to touch her lips with his. She was sure she'd fall apart from the pleasure of it. He deepened the kiss. When his hands roamed her back and then moved down her hips, pulling her closer, she'd passed into swooning territory.

He pulled back enough to rest his forehead on hers. "Dear God, what have you done to me?"

Her breathing still seemed awfully fast, but so did his. A detached part of her thought of what he'd just said. Had he really asked God, and if so, had God orchestrated their encounter? She hoped so. She hoped it wasn't her neediness that had made it happen, or her obvious availability.

What if it were only that? Who was needier than a spinster? She couldn't let him see her face. She probably exuded take-me vibes— even if unintentionally.

But this time she had meant them. Hadn't she?

His hands slipped down her arms and entwined with her fingers. "I can't stop wanting you. I want to touch all of you."

When she could speak, she asked, "Me in particular?"

"What do you think?" he whispered.

"How can I know what to think?" She eased away from him. "I barely know you."

He watched her, his face intent. "You know how you feel."

She looked away, staring at the floor, at the geometric reds in the oriental rug, at the dark blue woven into it, and shook her head. "Maybe. I don't know."

"I'm rushing you. I'm sorry."

Wasn't this what she wanted? But she couldn't. Shouldn't. She tossed up a prayer for help. "I suppose you are."

He moved away and slumped back onto the couch, looking deflated.

She found a spot at the other end and leaned forward, bracing her forehead in her palms, her elbows on her knees, so she wouldn't have to look at him.

"Tadie, I've had a lot of time to think about this, about my fears and why I didn't want to admit my attraction to you. You obviously haven't."

Wasn't that what she'd just been doing? "That isn't completely true."

"You've thought about me?"

She nodded, but did not raise her eyes to his. What was she doing? Admitting her feelings made her vulnerable, because what if he were only talking about sex? Men did that, didn't they? Made promises, spoke of romance, just to get what they considered the gold. And then they left.

Or, they left if you didn't give it to them. Either way ...

"I've been moving beyond simple attraction for some time now." His voice brought her head around, and she saw the twinkle in his eyes that she found so adorable.

"But I shouldn't rush you. Although I'd like nothing more than to take you upstairs and show you how much I want you, I also know it would be wrong."

The heat gathered again. She couldn't look at him. She couldn't look anywhere.

She just *couldn't*. And how could she say so without giving away her secret?

Out of the corner of her eye, she saw his hand rake through his hair. "I said I'd slow down, and now listen to me."

"It's, uh ... okay."

He took her hand. "I want to make love to you, Tadie."

Those words again. They were hard to ignore and hard to answer. But he'd said he wanted to make love to her, not that he loved her.

"I can't."

"I understand."

"I think I'll go to my room now." She tried to withdraw her hand from his.

His grasp tightened. It didn't hurt, but it forced her to stay. "Tadie, do you love me at all? Even the tiniest bit?"

Love? He wanted to know if she loved him? What about if he loved *her*?

She bit her lip again to keep from saying those words.

Again, he did the raking thing with his free hand. He had such luxuriant hair. "I keep bungling this, don't I? But I need to know, because I have fallen in love with you."

Her head shot up, eyes wide.

"Deeply, irrevocably."

Whoa. "You have?"

He nodded. A crooked smile played over his lips. "So?"

"So ... what?" Did he mean, did she love him too? Or was he asking if she wanted to make love with him? Now. Here. Upstairs. Hadn't he said he knew it would be wrong?

"So, do you?" he asked.

Is this what men did, give conflicting messages? She continued to look at him, trying to see into his soul.

His smile faded and he placed her hand on the couch between them. "It looks as if I presumed again."

"Oh ... no. No, I do love you. I mean, I think I do. But—"

"You do?" That brought back the twinkle. "But what?"

"I've no experience with this."

He grew very still. "With what? Falling in love?"

Tadie lowered her head again and pointed from him back to her. "With what exactly?"

Wasn't it enough that she'd admitted she loved him? Why did he need more? Where was Rita or Elvie Mae, to tell him to go to bed and be good, that they shouldn't have this talk?

She *never* wanted to have this talk. Certainly not with a man who'd been married, and who, while making her want him, scared her to death.

He must have read her mind. Or maybe her scarlet face and hidden eyes gave her away. "Did I turn you off by saying I want to make love to you?"

She shook her head.

"Did it scare you?"

Oh, God, please. "I have no experience." She sneaked a peek and saw his puzzled frown.

"What about Alex?"

She shook her head.

"What about since then?"

She wanted to dig a hole and drop right into it. What must he be thinking?

"I'm sorry," he said. "I just assumed."

She felt the tears and jammed them back as best she could. She did not want to be the object of any man's pity.

"Excuse me," she said, fleeing with as much dignity as she could muster. She half expected him to follow her—the poor spinster lady who loved his daughter. Of course, she would want a man, any man. And wouldn't he be doing her a favor, after all?

Either that or her inexperience must seem so odd that he'd reevaluate the love he'd proclaimed. And he'd be glad of the escape.

Perhaps he would think to bank the fire and turn off the lights. She certainly hoped so, because no way on earth was she going down there again.

Eventually, footsteps climbed the stairs and paused outside her door, but soon they crossed the landing to his room. And then there was silence.

Chapter Thirty-six

Tadie woke to dark clouds pressing toward earth. It was Christmas Day. She tossed back her bed covers and struggled to ease her legs over the side. The hall barometer probably echoed her mood—storm imminent.

As she padded into the bathroom, she realized she'd forgotten to ask Will if he and Jilly wanted to go to church. It didn't matter. Not after last night. She could go without them, let them sleep. Or whatever.

Rita had come in shortly after Will's retreat to his room. Tadie had heard water running, then the soft closing of a door. And finally, quiet had stolen over the house again, disturbed only by the hum of the furnace when it kicked on sometime later.

Jilly in one room. Rita in another. Innocent and oblivious.

Tadie reached into the shower to flip on the faucet. While warm water meandered through the pipes, she brushed her teeth and glanced at her reflection. That was a mistake. The mirror was definitely not her friend this morning.

The shower washed her hair and skin, but didn't do much for her attitude. This was obviously the wrong time of the month to have houseguests. That had to be it. She was PMS-ing. She yanked a brush through her wet hair and plugged in the dryer, fluffing her curls under the hot air.

Fine. It had been awkward last night, but recognizing the problem armed her to deal with it.

After pulling on leggings and a dark turquoise sweater that hung almost to her knees—bought at Hannah's insistence during the marathon shopping spree at H&M—she straightened her shoulders and whispered to her reflection, "You're a strong, independent woman. You do not need to cower or act all miss-ish."

Miss-ish? Listen to her. Too many Jane Austens?

But hadn't she been exactly that last night? Running away like a scared teenager instead of a grown, in-control-of-her-life woman.

She edged her lips with gloss and tried to breathe out the knot tying both her stomach and her lungs. She'd go downstairs and make a lovely breakfast for Will and Jilly, then she'd see what else the day brought. If they declined her invitation to church, she wouldn't worry about it. She'd don her red-and-black suit and slip in next to Elvie. It was Christmas, after all, and that choir was beyond comparison.

She found Will leaning back at the kitchen table with a mug of coffee clamped between his hands. He didn't look as if he'd had a whole lot of sleep either, but he certainly seemed more relaxed than she felt.

"Merry Christmas," she said, trying for a lilt in her voice as she took down another mug and filled it.

"Merry Christmas to you."

She stirred in creamer and stretched her lips, but the effort to form a smile of her own seemed unusually difficult.

"I'm surprised Jilly didn't beat us down here," he said. "Rita came through a short time ago, said she was going to have Christmas breakfast with her parents. She wants us all to go to church with them. I told her Jilly and I would love to, but that it's up to you."

Her coffee needed a dollop more honey. The spoon made lovely swirls as she stirred. "Thanks for making the coffee. I'm glad you found everything you needed."

"I remembered."

Why did that make her stomach flutter? She wished Rita were still here. And that was strange. How had Rita finished in the bath without her hearing anything?

She opened the refrigerator door, which gave her something to look at other than Will. "Jilly's bound to think the pickings are slim here in Beaufort, considering Santa's sleigh was limited to the size of your suitcase."

Maybe she should make spoonbread.

"Jilly will be fine."

Spoonbread needed eggs. She should get out the eggs.

"Tadie, will you come over here and sit down? Please?"

Her brows arched. Of course they did. Whose wouldn't, a man using that tone of voice, tacking on a please at the end for form's sake? Still, she closed the door and wedged herself in across from him, adjusting her chair slowly, concentrating on setting her mug in the center of a paper napkin to prevent rings on the antique table.

He cleared his throat, but she merely drew her cup closer. When he spoke, his tone had gentled. "I'm sorry about last night."

She waved off the words, catching his eye momentarily. "It was nothing."

"To me, it was."

"I understand. We don't have to talk about it. Why don't I just fix some breakfast?"

"Please, not yet. I don't think you do understand."

"I do. Perfectly."

"Then tell me."

She shook her head. "Look, let's not." She wasn't doing very well in the take-charge-of-her-own-emotions department. Time to change the subject.

"You and Jilly will enjoy the church service. Elvie used to sing in the choir. It's—"

"You surprised me last night. That's all. I had no idea."

"So you said."

"It's unusual in today's world."

"That's me. A throwback. Queen Victoria would have been proud." She raised her hand in salute to the late queen.

His long arms stretched across to take her hands, holding gently when she tried to pull away. "Tadie, honey," he began, and that word flowing off his tongue sent a surprising jolt of pleasure through her.

Heat must have betrayed her again. She could see it in his face. That smile.

His voice cajoled her to believe his silky words. "Please don't be embarrassed. It's obvious you're a woman of passion who values herself and doesn't give herself lightly to anyone. Frankly, it makes you more of a prize for the man who wins you."

Her pulse quickened, but her chin jutted slightly. "I've had lots of offers."

"I'm sure you have. The delight is that you haven't accepted any of them." Standing, still holding her hands, he edged around the table. "Come here."

She hesitated, but not because she didn't want to obey. She just hated to give in too easily. One more nudge and she stood. Watching his chest, which was where her lowered gaze rested, she felt the flutter low in her stomach as his thumbs traced circles on her palms. Her eyelids lifted slowly. She noted the collar of his shirt, how it opened to a strong bronzed neck, how its points forced her gaze up to his firm jaw. His lips parted over fine, straight teeth. His nose was just a shade long for perfect harmony, yet everything fit together— his dark eyes crinkling at the corners, his full brows slightly raised in question, his hair just long enough to make her want to run her fingers through it.

"Will I be one of the rejected ones, Tadie?" He continued to speak gently, though the humor remained. "You need to know my intentions are honorable."

Honorable? What did he mean by that? It sounded so wonderfully antiquated. She looked into his eyes and took a deep breath. "It doesn't feel like it right now," she whispered.

His head bent and his lips touched hers, one of those feather kisses so seductive it made her hungry for more. His lips slipped over hers lightly, taking their time, moving to a place just below her jaw.

Oh my. She had no idea that spot was so sensitive.

His mouth hadn't quite reached hers, though his hands did cup her face, when a little voice croaked, "Daddy!"

They jumped apart.

She'd forgotten Jilly. Well, so had Jilly's daddy—obviously. Tadie expected to see horror on the child's face. Instead, the green eyes shone.

"Oh, Daddy, you're going to give me what I want most in the world, aren't you?"

Tadie stared at the child, who didn't seem at all distressed to have found her father embracing someone other than her mother. "Jilly, honey, Merry Christmas!"

"Merry Christmas!" Jilly said, her gaze darting to Tadie and back to her father.

He looked about to say something, but Tadie rushed in with, "We're going to have something special for Christmas breakfast, and your father's going to help make it. Would you like to help too?"

"Sure," she said, but her focus was on her father. She grabbed his hand and tugged him down to her level. "Daddy," she whispered, "are you going to marry Tadie? I prayed for a new mommy—for Tadie to be my mommy. That's all I asked God to bring me for Christmas."

He reached out to stroke Jilly's hair. When he answered, he didn't bother to lower his voice. "So, you'd really like me to marry Tadie?"

Jilly's eyes sparkled as she rocked up on her toes. "Yes, Daddy. So much."

"We need to ask her, don't you think? To see if she likes the idea."

Jilly spun around and walked straight up to Tadie. "Do you want to marry us? We really want you to."

Tadie felt the tears. She couldn't talk. There was no way words were going to make it past her lips. She sniffled slightly and hoped no one noticed.

Jilly slipped a hand in hers. "Don't cry. It's okay. We love you."

"You do? You're sure?" Her gaze shot from Jilly to her father and back.

"Don't we, Daddy? We wouldn't ask her to marry us if we didn't."

"No, we wouldn't. But don't you think, First Mate Extraordinaire, that maybe you ought to let me take it from here?"

"Sure," Jilly said, backing away.

"Then how about you go get some clothes on. When you get back, we'll be ready to start breakfast."

His daughter looked at him suspiciously, probably wondering if he could manage on his own.

Will raised one brow, pointed to the doorway, and said, "Scoot."

"Do it right, Daddy." Her laughter lingered as she fled up the stairs.

"And don't rush," he called after her.

Tadie didn't take her eyes off Will's as he moved toward her again, but when he stood right there in front of her, she couldn't sustain it. His second button suddenly seemed fascinating, and her heart was back to pounding in her throat.

"Tadie," he whispered, waiting silently until she raised her chin. "I know this is sudden, and I wasn't going to do it like this."

"She forced your hand."

"No, she merely brought things to a head sooner than I would have. I had planned to court you."

"Court me?" She heard her voice crack between words.

He nodded, taking her hands again. "Nancy and I were very young when we met, fifteen and sixteen. She was my first love. She said I was her second because she liked to count her seventh-grade romance with the boy next door." He let his fingers roam over hers as he continued. "We married very early, and because we waited until after marriage, we learned about love from each other. Since her death, it's been difficult for me to even look at another woman."

Tadie's gaze fell again, back to that fascinating place on his chin. He had a slight dimple there, but it was a strong chin. Strong chins showed character, didn't they?

His words reclaimed her woozy thoughts. "Last night I told you I'd fallen in love with you. It took me completely by surprise. While I worked on the *Nancy Grace*, I caught myself thinking about you and dreaming about you as I'd only dreamed about her."

"You fought it?"

"Valiantly. Although I didn't know it at the time, that was probably the major reason I acted so badly."

Tension built as he stroked her hand, then his fingers tightened slightly. "Now I'm hopelessly in love with you."

She searched his face. "Alex was my first love, and a very disappointing one he was."

"And you were never in love again?"

"I imagined I was, once. I got engaged, but decided it was never going to work. He hated sailing. To this day, Rita says she warned me. I wouldn't listen."

"I finally listened to Jilly. And to my heart."

"That sounds a lot like courting to me."

"I was imagining roses and long dinners."

Tadie laughed. "I'm not saying those wouldn't be nice."

"The logistics may be difficult."

"Mmm."

"What would you think of life with us, with Jilly and me on the *Nancy Grace*?"

Tadie bit her lower lip before admitting, "I've fantasized about it."

"You have?" He looked both surprised and pleased.

"Of sailing places with you. First, I imagined coming on board as galley maid, one of the crew. Then I pretended you let me come as a sort of mother/companion to Jilly. Then ..." But emotion overcame her and she couldn't finish.

"Then?"

She shook her head.

"Did you ever imagine being with me? As my wife? In spite of how I acted?"

"I couldn't help it."

He cupped her face, looking deep into her eyes. "It's crazy, isn't it? Neither of us can help wanting the other, in spite of our prejudices. I love you, Sara Longworth. Will you marry me?"

Jilly's voice came lilting in from the hall. "You finished yet, Daddy?"

"Not quite. How about if I call you?"

"I'm getting hungry."

"Okay. Just another minute."

The top of a red head peeked around the door frame. "Have you asked her yet?"

Will burst out laughing. "Minx, get out of here. I was just doing it."

Tadie grinned at the pair. "Oh, let her in, Will. She deserves to hear my answer too."

"Yeah," Jilly said, climbing up on the chair Will had vacated. "I asked her first." She kept her eyes on Tadie and waited.

Looking from Jilly's expectant face to Will's, Tadie extended a hand to each. "I would be proud to marry both of you."

"Now?" Jilly grabbed Tadie's hand with both of hers and used it to focus Tadie's attention where she wanted it—on her. "Can we get married today?"

Will swatted at her playfully. "Don't be greedy, young lady. You got your Christmas wish, but these things take time. Tadie may want to have a big wedding."

"No thank you. Simple and easy, with just enough fuss to make my friends happy." Bemused, she wandered over to the refrigerator and opened the door, but couldn't remember what she'd wanted in there. "What was I looking for?"

"Breakfast?" Jilly asked, climbing down from the chair.

"I guess. Yes, of course." That must have been what she intended. But the sense of being caught in a whirlwind persisted. "I can't believe this. It's amazing."

"I know." Jilly bounded over and threw her arms around Tadie's waist. "I'm so excited. We're going to have a wedding."

"You ladies need some help over there?"

Will's expression made Tadie's knees weak again. She eased Jilly around to her front so they could both examine the refrigerator contents. "I think I was trying to get milk and eggs. Can you hand them to me?"

Jilly passed out the eggs first. "What are we cooking?"

"Well, it was going to be spoonbread, but I think pancakes will be faster."

"I love pancakes."

Tadie brought the bowl, whisk, and ingredients to the table so Jilly could help. While Will manned the spatula, they planned a wedding.

* * * * *

Will's cell phone blinked when he checked it after breakfast. He almost didn't retrieve the message, because, really, today? On Christmas?

Of course, not everyone celebrated the holiday, but he'd have thought even non-believers would be eager for a break. Obviously, not the plant in Atlanta.

They'd been having problems running one of his systems. He returned the call, offered to troubleshoot over the phone, but they'd tried everything he'd suggested and were in a bind with the government contract. Every day of downtime was costing a fortune, and old Uncle Sam didn't care what day of the year it was. The plant manager's voice sounded testy. His maintenance crew was ragging on him for keeping them there, and if Will would come, they'd make it worth his while.

None of that mattered to Will, but the guy's desperate, "Please," convinced him to see what he could do. At least Jilly would be happy hanging out with Tadie. That is, if Tadie didn't mind.

"Of course not," she said when he explained the situation. "But can you get a flight today?"

"I've already arranged it, though I'll have to leave from Raleigh. That's what, three hours away?" At her nod, he looked at his watch.

"I'll have to go soon. I'm sorry."

"I hope you won't be gone long."

In answer, he pulled her close.

* * * * *

When Rita phoned to ask about church, Tadie said she and Jilly would meet them there, hoping a quick explanation of Will's absence would suffice. It did during the service, where Jilly sat wide-eyed. She loved the singing and clapping, the gaily-hatted ladies, the white-gloved ushers. At the end of the message, everyone wanted to meet the lovely child wearing the green plaid jumper.

"You come on and eat with us," James said after the service. "You know you can't take that child away yet, Miss Sara. She's brightening Elvie right up. Look at her now."

Tadie carried the rest of the roast beef upstairs, enabling them to eat way too much. "It was good last night. It's just as good today," Elvie said, pointing to the heaps of food and telling Martin he'd better get his fill.

Martin rubbed his stomach after his second helping of sweet potatoes. "I'm convinced. Christmas feasts in this family are worth the extra pounds."

"We're mighty glad you joined us," James said.

While Rita made coffee, Jilly nudged Tadie out of the room. "Can we tell them?" she whispered. "Please?"

Tadie didn't move. Tell? Already? "You don't want to keep it a secret for a little while longer?"

The red hair swished back and forth.

Tadie's slight shrug was all Jilly needed. She bounded back to the dining area and stood next to Elvie's chair with her hands folded in front of her.

Elvie's face glowed as she looked from Jilly up to Tadie. "Child," she said, "you got something you want to say? Either one of you?"

"We're getting married," Jilly announced, clapping her hands and bouncing on her toes.

James grunted. "Who you marrying, little missy?"

"Tadie! Tadie's going to be my new mommy."

"Lands, Tadie-girl," Elvie said. "You sure do know how to keep things quiet from folk. When did you decide this?"

James crossed his arms, looking suspicious. "Can't have been before supper last night. We'd of knowed."

Rita hugged her. "I'm *so* happy for you." Bending to clasp Jilly, she said, "And you, sweet thing. Tadie will make you a wonderful mother." As Jilly's little arms tightened, Rita glanced up at Tadie, mouthing, *Oh my.*

Tadie nodded, swallowing at the knot in her throat.

They spent the afternoon talking weddings, and before Tadie knew it, Jilly's eyes had begun to close. Elvie was the first to notice. "That child should be home in bed."

That was all Tadie needed to hear. She was more than ready to go back and spend a few hours alone with Jilly, reading, snuggling, and waiting for Will to call.

She ought to phone Hannah, but she felt all talked out. Tomorrow would be soon enough.

* * * * *

That evening, Will's declaration that he couldn't wait to get back to his girls had made Jilly giggle and Tadie hug the unfamiliar joy to herself. Now the child's sleepy voice told secrets to Eb as Tadie wandered back downstairs to daydream on the living room couch with the Christmas lights as a backdrop. Rita should be home soon from dinner at the beach with Martin and his parents. The picture of Martin's face as he'd kept time with the music at church this morning encouraged Tadie. The man had been having fun, no doubt about it. And as important as church was to Elvie and James, Rita wasn't going to escape the need to be there too. It was her heritage.

Besides, the girl sang like a nightingale. She'd want to use that gift, just as her mother had. Elvie's voice didn't have the vibrancy it used to, but she could still carry a tune. And hadn't Martin's voice rung loudly when the choir led them in *Joy to the World*? Martin had probably heard the song on the radio all his life, but never had the occasion to belt it out.

That made Tadie's romantic heart flutter. She closed her eyes. How different this night was, how peaceful and full of love she felt.

She must have dozed, because the doorbell woke her with a start. Who on earth? Rita had her own key, but maybe she'd forgotten it.

Peeking behind the curtain, Tadie recognized Alex. Why hadn't she turned off the lights earlier and gone to bed? She opened the door to tell him to go away, but he pushed right past her.

Chapter Thirty-seven

"What do you think you're doing?" Tadie demanded as Alex headed for the living room.

"I take it he's gone."

"What business is it of yours?" She tried to get in front of him, to stop this madness. "You have no right to come bursting into my house. And you've been drinking. I can smell it."

He waved that away. "I saw you with him last night."

"What do you mean, you saw me with him? Were you spying?"

"I wanted to find out what was going on. You've kept me at arm's length ever since I got back, even though I told you I was getting a divorce. You know how I feel about you, how I've always felt."

Was he functioning in some alternate universe? "You dumped me to marry Bethanne."

"Only because she was pregnant."

"And who got her that way?"

He dragged his fingers through his hair, pulling at the front. How had she ever thought that attractive? "The point is," he said, "you've waited all these years for me, and now I'm free. I told you we could take it slow, but, no, you go and wrap yourself all around this fellow just because you want to mother his little girl. Listen, Tadie, you don't want to go there. He's obviously out looking for someone to take care of her, and you've fallen right into his trap."

She backed up two steps, edging toward the door. "I haven't, and he doesn't."

"Then what was all that about last night? My kisses were never good enough for you? You'd never do it with me, but you let the first drifter on a sailboat into your bed?"

He didn't allow her to respond, just grabbed her upper arms and yanked her to him, pressing his mouth to hers with enough force to draw blood. She tried to push him away, but that only enraged him. His arms encircled her, and he lifted his head long enough to growl out, "You're mine, Tadie. You're mine."

His hands pawed her. His legs forced her back into the living room and toward the couch. Alex? This was *Alex?*

He was so intent on getting her flat on her back that he didn't realize what hit him when she kneed him in the groin. He cried out and she jerked free. As he doubled over in pain, Tadie raked her nails down his cheek, ran to the fireplace, and grabbed a poker.

She brandished the iron rod above her head and said, "Get up," with as much disgust as she could pour into her voice. "Get up, get out, and don't you *ever* come near me again."

He hobbled to his feet, cupping his groin and moaning.

"If I see your face within ten feet of me or find you anywhere near my house, my shop, or anyone I love, I will report your behavior to enough people to get you run out of town. I don't care how much Matt thinks he needs you. And don't even imagine he'll take your side against me. Do you understand?"

He didn't answer, but he looked at her with a hatred she'd never expected to see on his face. As soon as she locked the door behind him, she headed to the phone. If Alex started whining some sob story, there was no telling where this would end.

Hannah picked up on the second ring. "Hey, girl. I was wondering how your day went."

"Can you come over now?"

"Sure. You okay?"

"No. Is Alex still staying with you?"

"He's out right now, but, yeah, he's still living here. Why? You need him to come too?"

"No! Just you. You can tell Matt about it when you get back home."

"You want me to bring him? He's in bed, but he could get dressed."

"Just come on before Alex gets back there."

Tadie was leaning against the kitchen counter, waiting, when Hannah jiggled the back door handle.

"What's going on?" Hannah asked, tossing her jacket over a chair. "You've got me scared, so spit it out." Then she really looked at Tadie. "Lands, girl, you're shaking. Come on, let's go sit down." She led Tadie to the couch. "Now, tell me."

"Alex. He—he attacked me." Tadie tried to spit out the words, but the shaking only intensified.

"*Alex?*" Hannah stilled for a moment. "He *hurt* you?"

"He ... he tried." Her teeth chattered. "I ... I got the poker."

Hannah's face darkened and her words turned ugly. "That sorry, low-down *bastard*. He *can't* be related to Matt."

Tadie seconded her, but silently. She couldn't have spoken right then.

Hannah's arms pulled her into a hug. "Oh, honey, are you sure you're okay? You want something hot? You're still trembling."

Tadie started to shake her head, but changed her mind. "Hot water and lemon."

Rising, Hannah busied herself filling a mug, putting it into the microwave, and slicing a lemon. "You tell me when you're good and ready. I'm not going anywhere."

It came out hesitantly once Tadie could cup her hands around the hot mug. How Alex had behaved the night before and what had transpired between her and Will—which sent Hannah into whoops before she calmed down enough to listen to the rest.

This time, Hannah said, "The *snake*. Matt's going to tar and feather him."

"Tar a snake? I wish he could."

"I'm going to call Rita to come down and stay with you, but I need to get home to see what's happening there." Hannah pulled her cell from her purse. "I never imagined anything like this from Alex, even as spoiled as he's been all his life. But after I tell Matt, no way is that man going to have bed and board at my house. Not and act like that."

Tadie set the mug on the table. "Don't call Rita. She's with Martin, but she'll be here before long. I'll be okay, and they don't need to know about this up at Elvie's."

"James does, so he can watch out for you."

"Not tonight. Alex won't come back, not when he's had a chance to think about it. Especially when he finds out I called you over. It was just fool's courage from too much liquor."

Hannah finally nodded. "Fine. We don't want to get Elvie all upset. Let them have their Christmas night. But tomorrow, you hear?"

"I hear."

Another hug and Tadie got up to lock the door behind Hannah. She turned out most of the lights as she went upstairs, trying to control her emotions, because she expected Will to call before he went to bed. It was part of the courting process, he'd said.

She warmed at the thought as she climbed into the shower. Maybe she didn't need another one, except to wash away Alex's odor and any memory of it. Better to think of Will's kisses instead of ...

Stop it. She couldn't go there.

But it was hard not to hope the creep still hurt from her nails and her knee.

When the phone rang, she was tucked up in bed, staring at her book. Will began with the business of the day. "I think I've found the problem at the plant, so maybe I'll be able to make it back by tomorrow night."

"I hope so."

"We'll test the system in the morning, and if all goes well, I'll catch the first flight out."

Tadie sympathized, but wanted other words.

And then his voice changed. "I miss you," he whispered. "I can't believe how much I miss you."

Ah, there it was. She eased under the covers as the power of his voice settled through her body. "I know. How can things change so quickly?"

She heard a chuckle. "Amazing, isn't it?" Then he sobered. "I had this horrible thought on the way here. What if I hadn't turned the car around? What if I hadn't let down my guard?"

"It would have happened later."

"I've been stubborn, clinging to the past, to my fears. I might have missed you."

Boy, he was good. He seemed to know just what she needed to hear. When she didn't respond, he said, "Thank heavens for Jilly. She saw through it all, right to the heart of the matter."

"She brought us together."

"In spite of my fears, she certainly did."

His voice had grown husky on that last word. She slid her hand over the cool sheet, imagining him next to her, gazing at her with the same yearning she felt now. Still, one hurdle remained. "I'm not Nancy. I never will be."

"No, you're not. I loved her—I won't deny it. I'll always love the memory of her. But for some reason, you've gotten to me, past all my defenses, and made me love you, Sara Longworth. Not a shadow of someone else, but you."

Mercy. Her throat went all tight.

"You okay?"

She tried clearing it. "I'm more than okay. You know what you're doing, don't you?"

"What?"

"Making me fall more in love with you by the minute."

"Isn't that the way it's supposed to be?" The love in his voice warmed her even as her belly shivered with joy.

For a moment, he became quiet, but it was a comfortable silence.

And then he said, as if the inspiration had just dawned on him, "You need a ring. What kind would you like?"

"I haven't thought about it."

"You make such beautiful jewelry, but I want to buy you something special, something you haven't had to create yourself."

She tried to picture an engagement ring on her finger, remembering the early days with Alex when she'd dreamt of a huge diamond and the later days with Brice when she'd had one.

"Maybe just a wedding band. I have a lot of stones and rings that belonged to my mother and grandmother. I would like something simple."

"Should we choose rings together when I get back?"

"Oh yes."

"I love you, Sara Longworth."

"I love you, Will Merritt."

"How long do we have to wait? I'd like to get married soon."

"Me too."

"And Jilly."

She heard the humor as he spoke, the affection. "Then," she said, hesitating only a moment, "why not next weekend?"

"New Year's? Could you pull it off that quickly?"

"I don't know why not, if our priest, John Ames, is willing and the church is free. He'll have to meet you. I hope there aren't rules and things we'd have to do first. I'll call him tomorrow and ask."

"Where are you now?"

"Snuggled in bed. Wishing you were here."

"You keep talking like that and I won't be able to wait a week."

Tadie laughed softly. "Oh, you'll wait."

"Yes, of course I will. I believe if we do it right, we'll be blessed. I want this to be special for you, darling girl."

Tears sprang to Tadie's eyes. "My daddy used to call me that."

"Darling girl?"

"Yes."

"It's what you are."

Chapter Thirty-eight

Tadie carried her morning coffee into the library. Upstairs, Jilly slept, but here in this quiet room, Tadie pivoted her daddy's chair toward the window and caught the faint whiff of cigar smoke. "Daddy, do you see how blessed I am?"

Did she imagine him here, watching out the window with her as the shadows changed? She could almost feel the solid muscles of his thighs under the linen slacks he always wore. He never minded that she'd crease them when she climbed into his lap. He'd point out the different birds that splashed or merely dipped their bills into the birdbath just there, near the big azaleas. Now, she thought she heard a whispered, "I do, my darling girl. I couldn't have wished for better."

She sat in the quiet room and let the image of her father morph into a longing for Will's voice and his return. Sipping, she waited for the phone to ring. Surely he'd call.

But it was Hannah who disrupted her peace, Hannah's words that made her choke on her coffee.

"Alex did *what*?"

"He broke into Matt's safe. Soon as I got home, I caught him with the door open, holding a bunch of bills and certificates. He'd probably have dug out my jewelry next."

"He's full of surprises, isn't he?"

"Well, he's gone now. Matt fired him, threw him out of the house, and said he's going to make arrangements to get Alex out of the business."

"I'm sorry Matt had to find out what a cad his brother is."

"We're best rid of him. Bethanne's not likely to take him back. Maybe he'll go live near his daughters, Lord, help them." Hannah paused and her tone changed as she said, "On another subject, Matt's thrilled about your news. When's the wedding?"

"We're thinking New Year's Eve."

"Tell me you're kidding. That's less than a week away. How are we going to manage so quickly?"

"With your help, kiddo. You're wonderful at that sort of thing."

"It will take a lot of phone calls. What about the church?"

"As soon as nine o'clock rolls around, I'll find out."

"If you can't get the church, we could have it here."

"Lovely idea. I want it simple. Just a few friends and a nice meal afterward."

Call waiting cut in. It was Will.

"Hannah, I'm going to take this. Catch up with you later."

She clicked over to the voice she wanted to hear.

"Good morning, bright eyes," he said, and she melted.

"Bright eyes? Aren't you the charmer?"

"I'm missing you so much it hurts, but I'm sorry, it looks like I'll be stuck here until tomorrow morning."

"Oh, Will."

"I know, love. But here's my thought. If I fly directly from Atlanta to Baltimore, I can pull my car out of hock and spend Wednesday getting the *Nancy Grace* ready for you. She won't know what to do, having a grown woman on board."

"What, you mean none of your other girlfriends fixed a meal there?"

His voice felt like liquid honey pouring over her. "I told you there haven't been any girlfriends. And the only crew we've taken on board were men."

Words she'd wanted to hear repeated. "No ghosts then?"

"None. Except her name. Will that bother you?"

"Nancy was your wife and Jilly's mama, and she deserves a special place in your life."

"How'd I get so lucky?"

Now his sigh sounded like pines in a light breeze, a soft soughing that brought comfort and peace. How had *she* gotten so lucky? Or blessed? Or whatever one wanted to call it?

Little footsteps sounded in the hall outside, and Jilly peeked around the open door. Tadie motioned her in.

To Will she said, "I don't think luck has much to do with it. That's one thing I've learned about loving. The more folks you give it to, the more you get back." She pulled Jilly closer and held out the phone.

"Daddy?" Jilly asked.

"Come say good morning."

"Is that my girl I hear?"

Jilly's face lit up. "Hi, Daddy. When're you coming?"

"Soon, punkin. I'm going to go pick up our car and drive it down, so it might take a little longer than I thought."

Tadie eased out from under Jilly, leaving them to chat while she carried her mug into the kitchen. Cowardly, perhaps, but she didn't want to tell Will about Alex's visit—not when he couldn't come racing to her rescue. And he'd definitely want to do that, but it was so unnecessary.

Alex was long gone.

* * * * *

An hour later, Jilly shadowed Tadie into the office building of All Saints Anglican Church. The church secretary and a couple of the other women working that morning heard the chirpy little voice and came out to meet Jilly, while the rector, John Ames, ushered Tadie into his office. Now she had to tell this man, this Anglican priest, this grandfather who'd known her all her life, why she'd finally shown up at his door after such a long dry spell.

He listened without a lot of comment as she asked him to marry her to Will on Saturday. "What about premarital counseling?" he said when her narrative slowed. "That's how we normally do things here."

Tadie tried to sound coaxing, because who wanted to wait through weeks of counseling? Of course, if she said that, he'd probably mention patience and virtues and things she'd heard all her life. The way she looked at it, patience was something she might never acquire. And after all these years of waiting? Enough was enough. She wanted marriage and soon.

Not to mention what came next.

Finally, John pressed his palms on the desk and said, "I need to meet this fiancé of yours. Is he a believer?"

She hadn't considered that. Her hands flew to her cheeks. "I think so. He's bound to be. I mean, I'm sure he's not an atheist."

John hiked those bushy brows, making her feel about ten years old. "That's something you need to know before you marry him, my dear. It won't be much fun for either of you if you're coming from different perspectives about God."

"He'll be here Friday. You can ask him." She should have asked. Why hadn't she?

True, it had all happened so suddenly. But the way Jilly prayed must mean someone in her life knew God. That child hadn't picked up her faith by whimsy. "I'll ask him when he calls tonight. But we might as well be realistic about this. I've not exactly been holding up my end either."

John steepled his fingers over his broad chest. "That's another thing. You want to talk about it?"

Fiddling with the hem of her shirt, Tadie tried to gather her words. "I almost lost my faith with all the deaths. You saw that. Then something else happened that hurt so badly, I ran as far as I could. Something with Will. But I shouldn't have been afraid. It all worked out."

Understanding filled his kind eyes. "Doubting's not wrong, Tadie. It's what you do with it, how you struggle through it, that brings you peace or not."

"I know, but it scared me. I was alone, dealing with the what-ifs. Things don't always come together, do they?"

"Sometimes they don't. But if we trust, they always work out for good—maybe not the way we want them to, but for the best. And, ultimately, for the greatest happiness of everyone concerned. That's something we can hold on to." His voice held such certainty. It always had, which may have been one of the things she'd run from these last few years.

"Your father would have wanted to know the man you plan to marry, so I hope you will be guided by me. If for some reason I sense that all is not as you've been led to believe, will you listen to a man who has only your best interests at heart? One who has known and loved you since you were a babe?"

Tadie felt a rush of tears and swiped at them quickly. "I will."

He rose and came to her, resting a big hand lightly on her shoulder. "I miss them, you know. Few men could offer so fine and stimulating a friendship as your father. And his faith was a great thing, though usually quiet."

"I often talk to Daddy while I'm sitting in his chair or on *Luna*. I desperately wish he were with me."

"I've wished him here many a time." He released her and moved to the window, staring out over the yard as if into his memories.

She waited, caught up in her own. They shared so many, she and this priest.

Finally, he turned. "You have Will here at eleven on Friday. If all is well, I'll open the church and marry you on Saturday. Just don't forget the license."

* * * * *

A whirlwind swirled in their midst, with Hannah at its vortex pulling together a catered brunch. "And you won't believe this," Hannah said, "but Isa put me in touch with a friend in the North Carolina Symphony, and he's willing to bring three friends—an entire string quartet. I've spoken with the florist, who's coming by tomorrow with some ideas. Are we having it at the church or here?" With barely a pause for breath, she continued, looking up from her list of to-dos. "And, no, thank you, but I don't want to go shopping in Greenville. I spent my wad in New York."

Tadie smiled at that, because Hannah had spent several wads while in New York. "I won't know about the church until Friday. That's when Will has his big interview."

"Well, if you can't get the church, you can always go to the courthouse."

"Thanks. Not exactly the most romantic spot for a wedding."

"Well, no, but we'll have a very romantic party afterward."

"I love you, Hannah, but let's not even think about John saying no."

After she'd disconnected from that conversation, Tadie approached Rita about the shopping spree.

"A girls' day out?" Rita said. "Count me in. Mama too."

"You don't think it's too much for Elvie?"

"If it gets to be," Rita said, "I'll take her someplace to rest."

* * * * *

Greenville couldn't compete with Raleigh for stores, but it was hours closer and provided what they needed. Tadie's new cream-colored wool suit made her feel slim and attractive.

Elvie Mae, approving, said, "You need a hat. Miss Caroline would have said so."

Tadie imagined the hats Elvie might want. "None of those British aristocracy confections," she said. "How about one of the new veils? Instead of a hat?"

"You gotta at least look."

Elvie led them to the hat department, where Rita stopped in front of a simple, big-brimmed white hat. "Killer," Rita said. Her mama just raised her brows, but Tadie bought it.

Elvie Mae chose a turquoise wool suit for herself with a small-brimmed hat to go with her tiny size, but Rita declared she already had the dress she planned to wear and needed only new shoes.

Jilly bounced in her seat on the way home, bubbling about her deep blue velvet dress with a creamy satin sash. "My bow will match yours," she told Tadie. "Can I hold my box now?"

"We'll open it when we get home. You don't want to get your pretty dress dirty."

Jilly looked at her hands, which had been passing grapes and cookies from baggies to her mouth. She wiped them on her pants and checked again. "I guess you're right."

* * * * *

Tadie tucked Jilly in bed with Eb at her side and returned to the kitchen to fix a cup of herbal tea while she waited for Will's call. She sipped it as she listened to him speak sweet nothings in her ear, and as she whispered them back into his.

My, could that man make her yearn.

Saying goodnight, releasing him to sleep, took a ridiculously long time, but she eventually hung up the phone and climbed slowly to her own room, dragging her fingers along the banister, her entire body delighting in the thoughts she captured.

She brushed her hair and stared wistfully at nothing. She heard Rita in the bathroom not long after she'd slid beneath the sheets, and then there was silence, with only the occasional old-house moan or the soft whir of the furnace to disturb it.

One more day and she'd have Will across the hall. Three more days and she'd be Mrs. Will—William?—Merritt.

My goodness. She didn't even know his full name.

Staring at the darkness, she sifted that thought. Did not knowing bother her?

She turned on her side, smoothed her fingers across the sheet, and imagined him there beside her. She saw Jilly, perched up on her knees between them. Jilly with her little-girl smells and giggles.

No, it didn't matter. Because, deep down, Tadie knew Will.

She was drifting on the edge of sleep when her door opened. She patted the mattress and said, "Come in, sweetie," and then wondered why Jilly didn't answer.

Loud breaths followed the click of the door latch. Tadie tried to silence her own rapid breathing, but she couldn't stop the blood pulsing loudly in her ears. She recognized the scent of the man, the stench of alcohol that oozed through his pores. She opened her mouth to scream for Rita—then closed it. She didn't want to wake Jilly.

"Who's there? Is that you, Alex?" Maybe if she seemed unafraid, he'd leave her alone.

Right. He'd broken into her house and crept to her room. Was he likely to slink away now?

She could sense him approaching, but saw only an outlined form, black against black. She didn't move.

Lord, help me. Please, help me.

Her bathroom door closed quietly, and the light flicked on behind it. Rita was up, just behind the door, unaware of the danger here.

Tadie opened her mouth to cry for Rita when a hand clamped over it. She tasted dirty sweat as he forced her jaw shut. "Get off me," she screamed behind the hand, but it came out in muffled yelps, pitiful even to her ears.

She slapped at him, tugged at his fingers, tried to bite.

Water ran in the bathroom as she clamped down on a finger. His other fist connected with her cheek. Agony shot through her, making her feel woozy, disoriented.

And furious.

She flailed her arms, batting at him as he climbed on top of her. When she tried to kick, blankets tangled around her legs. He plopped down on her thighs to still them, then grabbed one of her wrists and forced it against her side, wedged beneath his knee.

She groaned and tried to pry open her lips so she could bite him again even as she clawed with her free hand at the fingers covering her mouth. Failing that, she reached for his face.

He cursed when her fingernails pulled at the ski mask and caught his lip. She'd hoped for an eyeball.

Was that a noise from the bathroom? She was thrashing too much to be sure. Then he had her other hand. His fingers twisted against her skin, burning her, pinching. Pressing down on it with his knee, he leaned forward and hissed. His breath suffocated her.

"Stop ... fighting ... me!"

Stop fighting? Did he think she was just going to lie here and let him do whatever he wanted? Hannah'd been right. The man was a fool—a dangerous one.

She heard what sounded like a length of tape being pulled from a roll. She tried to yank her hands from under his knees while he was distracted, but he only pressed them more deeply into the mattress.

He was going to break her wrists. And the hand on her mouth pressed her lips so tightly against her teeth they were probably bleeding.

The tape thing wasn't going well with only one hand and those teeth. He obviously hadn't thought this through. If he'd been smart, he'd have brought a gun and kept her silent with it. Thank the good Lord, his only forethought had been the mask and the tape.

Of course, maybe he did have a gun but hadn't thought he needed it yet.

The tape ripped. She could just make out the shine of his teeth against that partly-masked face. Teeth she'd once admired.

He needed pointers, but they wouldn't come from her. Instead, she readied herself to scream when he moved the hand on her mouth and before he brought the tape to take its place.

As he began to lift the one hand, he slammed an elbow into her stomach, whooshing out all the air she had in her lungs along with a garbled whimper. Slapping the tape on her lips, Alex grabbed her chin with one hand to hold her still and pressed the tape securely against her skin with the other. She tried to jerk her head away, but his fingers dug more tightly into her jaw, and she felt the bite of his fingernails.

Dear God, I'm going to suffocate.

"Hold still. I mean it," he hissed next to her ear. "I don't want to have to hurt you, Tadie. You keep quiet and you'll be fine."

Fine?

He withdrew one of her hands from under his knee and taped it to the brass headboard. Then the other. She tried yanking free of the tape and of him. The pain knifed through her.

Alex was a sadist. How had they all missed this?

As he leaned toward the headboard, she tried to kick him off, but she was so tightly tangled in blankets she barely accomplished anything before he was back, sitting on her thighs, his weight pressing her flat. He slid down to her knees.

He was going to break her legs. He'd failed to break her wrists. Now he was after her legs.

She squirmed and arched her pelvis, trying to buck him off, but she could barely hike up more than a couple of inches. Yanking up one side of the cover, he grabbed an ankle and pulled it free while he sat on her other leg. If she survived, she'd probably require knee surgery.

She almost loosed a kick, because his angle wasn't as good as hers, but he clawed her bare foot.

Either that, or he bit it.

She'd kill him. If she ever got free of this, she was going to make sure Alex suffered—big time.

There. She managed one good blow with her probably bleeding foot before he got it laced to one side of the brass rail and went after the other one. If her feet hadn't been bleeding before, they were now.

She was bound, gagged, and spread-eagled.

Oh, God, no. Help me, please.

She felt his hands on her thighs, pushing up her gown. "I couldn't let you get married without knowing what you're missing," he whispered into her ear. "Without experiencing a real man. Oh yes, I heard about the wedding. In a hurry, are you?"

She wanted to yell in *his* ear and remind him how much fun prison was going to be when *he* got to be someone's lady friend.

Please, God, not this way.

He'd have to kill her to keep her still and quiet.

Maybe that's what he meant to do. But Alex, a *murderer?*

No, he couldn't. He wouldn't.

She heard his zipper.

He yanked her nightgown all the way to her neck and climbed on top of her. Again, she tried to buck him off.

He moaned and grabbed her breasts. His fingers dug into her flesh as if he needed something more to get him going. He seemed to be having trouble there.

She wondered why, but was grateful for small favors.

Still, it wouldn't be long. Not the way he was panting.

Why wasn't someone coming? Surely, Rita must have heard something.

Oh, please, let her have heard something. Let her even now be summoning help.

Before he went from mauling her to more.

Please ...

Suddenly, her door burst open. The overhead light flipped on, and Alex gaped as he stared down the barrel of James's shotgun.

James motioned Alex away from the bed. "You move one inch except to climb off there and back away from Miss Sara, and I'll shoot you right where you don't want to get shot." James spoke over his shoulder. "Rita, honey, you go tend to Miss Sara. Just do it from this side so you don't get anywhere near that man. And keep your eyes off'n him."

Alex ripped off his mask and backed up, tripping over his pants. When he bent to straighten them, James barked. "Nope, no way I'm letting you diddle with the evidence before the police get here."

"I was just—"

"Ain't no question what you were just doin'. Now get your hands up."

Rita pulled Tadie's gown down over her legs and set about freeing her mouth. "Your face. Oh, Daddy, look. He hit her."

James didn't take his eyes off Alex. "Rita, girl, you keep your attention where it's at. And you, Alex Morgan, got a whole lot of somethings to answer for."

Tadie couldn't see beyond Rita's hands working at the tape, but

Alex must have tried to lower his, because James said, "No you don't. You keep them arms up high so's I know you can't get up to any tricks. Even if I wasn't so good a shot, I could do plenty of damage between here and you. And I tell you this without bragging—I can get me a duck at fifty yards."

Tadie cried out as Rita yanked the last of the tape from her mouth. As soon as she could gasp out the words, she said, "In the night table."

Rita rifled in the drawer until she found a pair of scissors to cut the tape off Tadie's hands and feet. "The police are on their way," she said, slipping the scissors between the tape and the bed frame. "I was so scared, I didn't know what to do first when I heard noises in here—and not ones you'd normally make. I'd have barged in to find out, but I figured if he had a gun, I'd just make things worse. Sorry we took so long."

"I'm just glad you made it."

As each of Tadie's hands fell free, Rita cradled it and set it down gently. "Oh, honey, your poor wrists." Tadie's ankles brought another sympathetic groan. "I'll get you some compresses and aspirin."

Tadie waited with her eyes closed until Rita returned. Rita helped her sit up and handed her two aspirin and a glass of water. Those swallowed, she let Rita drape her wrists in a warm washcloth.

"Now you're untied," James said, "you young ladies need to go on outta here and let me wait with Alex till the police come."

"No, Daddy. He might try something sneaky. I'd rather you not have to shoot him."

"Then you two sit on this side of the bed lookin' elsewhere while you take care of Miss Sara, Rita."

A car door slammed. "That'll be the police," Rita said, heading down to let them in.

She returned with Clayton Dougherty and another officer.

Clay had been in the same class as both Alex and Tadie. He nodded at James, who'd lowered the shotgun and set it out of the way. "What do we have here? Tadie?"

"Hey, Clay," Tadie said hoarsely, holding the cloth to her face. "It's like this ..."

She began to speak, but Alex came up sputtering and denying, until Clay quelled him with a finger pointed at his face. "I wouldn't," Clay said.

They told the story while the other policeman shot photographs of a cuffed and exposed Alex, with a knit mask on the floor beside him and the cut tape still hanging off the bed. Clay told his partner to haul the now-dressed Alex downstairs.

"I never liked him, boy or man, Tadie, but I'm sure sorry he hurt you," Clay said. "You need a doctor?"

"I'm okay. Nothing a few compresses and a painkiller won't cure."

"It's a good thing you didn't destroy *all* the evidence."

Rita glared at him. "You didn't expect me to leave Tadie lying here like that, did you? You've got enough evidence and you've got our word, which ought to be good enough, even for you, Clayton Dougherty."

"Oh, it is. No problem here. I figure we got him red-handed." Clay slapped James's back and winked. "Oh, man, red-something'd all right."

"Tadie, what's going on?" Jilly slipped in, rubbing her eyes. "Eb and I woke up. Why are all these people here?"

Ebenezer jumped up beside Tadie, and Jilly ran into her arms. "It's nothing, sweetie. Everybody is leaving now."

"But you're hurt. Who hurt you?"

Tadie looked pleadingly at James and Rita. Rita knelt in front of Jilly. "It's all taken care of now, Jilly. This nice man came to get rid of someone who wasn't being kind to Tadie."

"Who?" Jilly asked Rita, turning from her to James and back to Tadie. "Who was it?"

As the child obviously wasn't going to drop that bone, Tadie said, "You remember Hannah's brother-in-law, Alex?"

Jilly nodded her head. "Him?"

"I'm afraid so."

"I told you he was a bad man."

"Yes, you did. I should have listened better." She certainly should have. She hated that Jilly had to know about any of this.

Jilly nodded as if that were all the explanation she needed. She climbed up on the bed with her feet hanging off next to Tadie's, and pulled Eb into her lap.

Clay crouched down in front of Jilly. "Who's this young lady?"

Tadie circled Jilly's shoulders with her arm and drew her close. "This is my soon-to-be-daughter, Jilly. Gillian Grace. Jilly, Clay is an old friend of mine from school." She left off Clay's status as a detective.

"Glad to meet you, Miss Jilly. I heard tell you were getting married, Tadie. Congratulations." Clay stood and headed toward the door. "I'll talk to you more later. Hope you can get some sleep now."

James had moved the shotgun out of Jilly's line of sight as soon as he'd heard her voice. Now Rita stood between him and Jilly, and together with Tadie, occupied the child's attention so he could whisk it out of the room. When the coast was clear, James poked his head back in to say, "Rita, you come down and check on the doors when I leave, hear?"

"James, thank you," Tadie called. "I can't tell you how grateful I am that you did battle for me."

"You'd of done the same for me and mine, Miss Sara. Now you git on back to bed, all of you."

Jilly cuddled closer. "Can Eb and me sleep with you now? Just so you won't get scared?"

Tadie smoothed the soft hair. "I would like that. You climb right on in. Eb's already waiting."

She tucked covers up around Jilly's shoulders and leaned down to kiss her. Jilly made it all better. All of it.

Rita stuck her head in the door after saying goodnight to her daddy. "You two need anything more? You need to soak anything? A hot toddy to drink?"

"As good as a toddy sounds, what I really need is a hot shower.

The aspirin is helping already."

"How about I bring up the toddy for you to drink when you get out?"

Tadie relaxed for the first time since Alex had entered her room. "Thank you," she told Rita. One more kiss to Jilly's head, and she said, "I'm going to have a quick wash. Can you keep Eb company while I do that? And then I'll climb in here with you."

"Kay," Jilly said, snuggling deeper under the covers as Eb circled to make a nest next to her. "Love you."

"I love you back, sweet girl."

In the bathroom, Tadie examined her wrists and ankles. They were merely abraded and would heal. Her face would heal too, but it might sport some color first.

She turned on the shower to let it run, accepting the toddy at Rita's knock and pulling Rita close. "Thank you. So much."

"Oh, honey, I'm just glad something woke me and I heard you." Rita wiped her eyes. "You need anything else, holler, will you?"

"I will."

Tadie closed the door, sipped the hot liquid, dropped her gown, and climbed under the steaming water. If it was the last thing she did tonight, she'd get rid of Alex's stench from her skin and from her mind.

At least she'd never have to resort to another shower because of Alex and his maulings, not with him locked up and rotting among like-minded souls. Too bad for him.

She closed her eyes, pulling in images of Jilly and Eb on the other side of that door. No more Alex. Never again.

Maybe one day she'd have it in her to feel sorry for him, for his daughters, for Matt. But not tonight.

Chapter Thirty-nine

Tadie tried to keep the good side of her face turned toward Will as he hugged Jilly and then reached for her. He'd driven all day through both wet snow and pounding rain, but exhaustion obviously hadn't dulled his vision.

"You bang into something?" he asked, holding her off so he could look.

"Seems like I did. Now, sit down and let me feed you." She shook her head so he wouldn't ask more questions and mouthed, *Later.*

"Hey, Will," Rita called from the couch where she was watching television.

"How're you doing? You guys have a good Christmas?"

"We did," Rita said.

"I was sorry to miss church. Jilly said she had a fun time."

"She was a big hit. Made friends with some of the children too."

Tadie set a plate of curried shrimp in front of him and turned back to the sink. She was fussing with the pans when Jilly grabbed the chair next to her father's and blurted, "Daddy, you missed all the excitement. The police came while I was sleeping. They took the bad man away."

Tadie winced at Jilly's words. She took a moment to dry her

hands before turning.

Will emptied a spoonful of chutney carefully next to the rice, set the spoon on its plate, and looked up, his head tilted slightly. "What happened?"

She chewed on her lip. "We need to discuss this later. Please?"

"You're all right? Both of you? Is that what you ran into?" His voice increased in intensity as he spoke.

"Mr. James came, Daddy. Rita went and got him. He had a big gun, but he didn't want me to see it."

"Mr. James had a gun? Tadie, what the—"

Tadie laid her hands on Jilly's shoulders. "Honey, I think your daddy wants to eat his dinner now. Rita and I will tell him all about it later, after he has digested his food. It would be better." She spoke this last to Will, hoping he'd be satisfied.

His brows tented, but he didn't comment, merely pulled a pouting Jilly to his side. "I hear you bought a fancy dress to wear on Saturday." While Jilly regaled him with details of their shopping trip, he shoveled in the food like a man who was either starving or wanted the whole thing over with. Tadie tried to keep out of his way, but once, between bites when Jilly glanced away, he raised those brows again and mouthed at Tadie, *A gun?*

After his dinner, Will announced that he'd be right back, looking pointedly at Tadie as he herded Jilly upstairs to bed. Tadie rinsed his plate and said over her shoulder to Rita, "You'll help him understand, won't you?"

Rita shook her head. "Girl, you're going to have to pull this one off on your own."

"You came to my rescue last night. Won't you do it again?"

"Think about it. That would just embarrass you—and Will—even more." Rita turned off the television. "Honey, you've got a good man. Just give him the story and let him cuddle you a little, make him feel like a rescuer."

Will passed Rita at the kitchen door. "I'm glad you and your father were around to come to Tadie's aid."

What Tadie wanted to do right then was rest in his arms and listen to his tales of the trip and the things he'd done in readiness for their honeymoon on board the boat. The idea of being mistress of the *Nancy Grace* thrilled her. The idea of confessing everything to him did not.

"Come over here," Will said, leading her to the couch. "Now. Spit it out."

She first told him Hannah's story of Alex with his hand in Matt's safe. Then she tried to make light of the two episodes she'd survived. Will's fists balled, and a vein throbbed in his temple.

"I'd have killed him."

"I know."

He took a while to unclench both his fists and the tightness around his mouth. When he finally spoke, his voice was more controlled, but held hints of what seemed a puzzled sadness. "Why didn't you tell me about the first episode? Why did you wait?"

"Because I didn't want you all upset that you couldn't be here."

"I would have come. I'd have left everything on the boat until later. The rest wouldn't have happened if I'd been here."

Perhaps this was the worst thing, making Will feel this way. "I'm sorry. It never occurred to me he'd come back." Or that not calling Will would hurt him. She'd been so used to coping on her own.

"It should have." He had a strange edge to his voice.

She shook her head. "No, I've known Alex all my life. I couldn't imagine he'd try again. We all assumed he'd left town after Matt threw him out of the house."

"Tadie, be realistic. He was thwarted and angry and was bound to blame you for it all. You could have at least called the police to report him."

"I guess I should have."

"You put yourself and everyone else at risk."

She had. She'd risked Jilly. And Rita. She'd wanted to be strong. In control.

My God. She could have gotten Jilly killed. The sick feeling that rose in her throat nearly overwhelmed her. She shuddered and covered her face as the tears formed and fell. "I'm sorry. I'm so very sorry."

He drew her close. "We're in this together, Tadie. You and I. We're a team. We don't keep secrets." He hesistated. "And you can't leave me out of the decision-making process like you did on this. I deserved to know."

"You did. You do. I'm *really* sorry."

She hadn't let him be a man, *the* man. She'd emasculated him, hadn't she?

She pushed herself up. Sniffing and swiping at the tears that hadn't spilled onto his sweater, she said, "I'm not used to relying on anyone. I mean, other than James and Elvie." She looked over at him. "Can you be patient while I learn how to do this team thing?"

"I'll try. But you do have to figure it out, you know. It's what marriage is about."

She nodded and swiped at more tears. "I get that."

"Good. I'm trusting we won't have to worry about Alex again. Not if he's behind bars."

"I'm trusting he'll stay locked-up for a good long time."

He pulled her back into an embrace that left her breathless and in no doubt about the kind of teamwork she could look forward to after Saturday. "I love you, Tadie," he whispered when they came up for air.

"Mmm," was about all her lips could manage, and it took a few minutes for her breathing to slow. She longed to pull him back for more, but figured she'd better lighten the mood and get all the rest said.

"You won't believe the picture James made, aiming those two barrels straight at Alex's privates. When Alex begged to cover himself, James told him not to diddle with the evidence."

"Diddle?" Will repeated. "No way."

"That's what James said. And he kept telling Rita and me to turn our eyes away. It wasn't seemly, us not being married women."

"Good for James. Of course, I wouldn't want you looking even if you were married," he said, pinching her chin. The scowl had vanished with their kisses, and finally humor lit his eyes again.

Tadie playfully swatted at his hand. "Clay Dougherty—the detective, an old friend of mine—got pictures. He couldn't keep a straight face once they'd taken Alex off. It seems Clay doesn't remember Alex all that fondly." She pursed her lips, remembering high school and how stupidly in love she'd imagined herself. "I wish someone had clued me in when I was seventeen."

"You probably wouldn't have paid attention."

She snuggled back on his shoulder. "Probably not. Anyway, just so you know, they hauled Alex off before Jilly woke up."

"I'm glad of that. Think of the nightmares she might have had otherwise."

"I know. It wasn't a pretty picture."

Will kissed her forehead. The scene had ended on a ridiculous note, but what if rescue hadn't come?

"You want to know another funny thing?" Maybe telling him this bit would get them back to the fun part of the evening and off this horrible topic for good.

"Tell me."

She sat up, but couldn't look at him. "Alex really wasn't very good at it."

"What makes you say that?"

"Well, don't you think a true rapist would have found his victim's subjugation exciting, instead of, shall we say, deflating?" She bit her lip, peeked at Will, and described the moments when Alex tried—and failed—to make things happen.

Will howled as he yanked her back into his arms. "Only you, Tadie. Only you would think like that the day after an attempted rape." Tadie felt his rumble of laughter until he took a deep breath and said, "You, my darling girl, are a treasure. If I'd been standing in James's position, I don't think I'd have just pointed the gun. Castration is too good for Mr. A. Morgan." Touching her chin with gentle fingers, he lifted it so he could examine her face. "You sure you're okay? He didn't hurt you too much?"

"He just wanted me to shut up. And the rest of me is already healing. Anyway, you want to know what I imagined while he was trying in vain to get with the program? It was very naughty of me." She paused for a moment and watched his brows arch in question. She liked the way they became so expressive.

"Yes?"

She grinned wickedly. "I wondered how Alex would like being someone's girlfriend while he rots in jail."

"Much better than castration."

"But not at all nice."

"No," he agreed. "Not nice, but Alex Morgan has proven himself not very nice—in every sense of the word."

"I suppose I have to forgive him."

"I suppose you do. I'll have to work at it."

"I guess we both will."

He nuzzled her neck. His words were muffled, or perhaps her hearing had blurred due to the attention he was paying that especially sensitive spot just below her jaw. "I suppose," he dipped to kiss just below her ear, "I suppose I can manage the forgiveness thing because he's there and you're safe and here. Ah, Tadie, so sweet. I'll keep reminding myself that he obviously came out way on the minus side." His lips roamed her face before stopping right where she wanted them to, so she could get into the act with him. My goodness, but he was good at this.

She felt her limbs turn to putty. If Will didn't quit ...

He must have realized things were moving rapidly in a direction that would make control difficult, because he stopped, took a few deep breaths, and suggested they watch the lights in the living room and perhaps listen to Handel's *Messiah* again. Tadie curled next to him with her head on his shoulder, grateful that Rita had promised to take care of the Christmas decorations while staying at the house until her own wedding in June.

All these weddings. So many changes.

"Beautiful," Will said, and she had to look up to see what he meant. He watched the flickering lights. "This will be a good place to have our Christmases. A wonderful home base."

Tadie's heart expanded. He hadn't said much about spending time in Beaufort, though he certainly knew she planned to keep the house. "I'd like that. I think Jilly would too."

"Mmm," he murmured, his hand stroking her hair, tracing lines down her cheek. "I can't quite believe all this."

"I want to pinch myself. Me, getting married."

"That's not the amazing thing. It's that you're marrying me, especially after the way I behaved." His hand played along her neck. When he turned her chin toward him, she lifted her fingers to his cheek. "I think perhaps we ought to go off to our own rooms now," he said, "because all I want to do is kiss you senseless."

It sounded wonderful. And frightening. "Two more days." She sat straight and looked at him. "I wish ... "

"What do you wish?"

"I wish I knew—about everything. Is it always good? I mean, what if I can't?"

He kissed her gently. "You'll be fine. Have a little faith. We'll be wonderful together."

* * * * *

Tadie sat on the side of her bed, brushing her hair and pondering Will's words. All her adult life she'd suppressed her sexuality. Okay, granted, not always with perfect success, but obviously well enough. The rest of the adult population seemed to take physical relationships for granted. Not even Christians seemed immune to premarital sex.

That thought stopped her. According to statistics she'd read somewhere, the ones messing around with other people's bodies these days weren't waiting much past puberty. Maybe that was full circle. Hadn't girls once been given in marriage in their early teens? According to Bucky, good old Mohammed only required they hit the ripe age of nine—the age of his last wife. No wonder the women in the Middle East had issues.

Okay. She took a deep breath and rubbed her temples. What on earth was she supposed to do on her wedding night? In fiction, everything worked perfectly. He did this, she did that, and everyone was blissfully happy. Tab A into Slot B. But Tadie didn't think it always worked like that in real life. Otherwise, bookstores wouldn't stock all those how-to books, would they?

She should have asked Hannah for details way back when. Hannah had tried to share experiences, but Tadie always changed the subject before Hannah had the chance to ask her to reciprocate. Now, she'd just have to wait and see—and try during the next two days not to worry herself sick about it.

They trooped to the courthouse Friday morning for their marriage license. "You're okay doing this in an Anglican church?" Tadie asked. "Meeting with John Ames?"

"I'll marry you anywhere. But as for attending that particular church? I'll have to ask your priest a few questions first and then make my decision."

She'd have to trust God with this too, because she loved John Ames. Tadie watched the clock while Will was gone. Either the interview was going really well, or they were arguing religion. But she couldn't imagine anyone arguing with John.

Will stepped inside the back door several hours later. "Hey, where are my girls?"

"I'm in here," Tadie said, stepping out of the pantry with a new jar of pickles. "Jilly's still up with Elvie and James. She's learning how to crochet."

Will took the jar out of her hand and pulled her against him. "And what are you doing?"

"Waiting for you to tell me how it went." She backed away so she could look at him.

"I passed." He led her to the couch and eased her down beside him. "We had such a great discussion about all sorts of things that we continued it over lunch." He looked around. "I take it you ate without me."

"You knew we would."

"Once I assured him that I'm madly in love with you, it got serious. I don't think I've ever been grilled so thoroughly on my beliefs, attitudes, and financial status, not in all my thirty-nine years."

"You poor thing."

"Not at all. I'm glad you have someone who cares so much about you. In the absence of your father, I think he wanted to make sure I wasn't after your money or hunting up a mother for Jilly. And once we got past that, we started talking shop."

"Whose?"

"His. I wanted his take on faith."

"And?"

"I may have to get used to some of the practices of a liturgical church, but I admit, I'm intrigued."

Tadie leaned over to plant a kiss on his cheek. "I'm glad."

"He also made me promise to get you to come more regularly. I said we'd attend whenever we're in town. We can listen online from the boat."

"Won't that be fun?"

Will tweaked her chin and nodded. "And—just to show you what an *in* I have—he insisted I call him John as he regaled me with wonderful stories about your father. I wish I could have known your dad."

"He would have liked you," Tadie said, poking him in the ribs. "I'd have been jealous. You two would have talked a blue streak and spent all your days examining boats and systems."

"But, Tadie, honey, that's what you and I'll be doing. Didn't you know?"

Chapter Forty

Will helped Jilly pack her suitcase that evening. "Why can't I stay with you and Tadie?" she asked, a whine in her voice. "I can see Aunt Liz and Uncle Dan anytime."

"Because when a man and a woman get married, they need to spend a little time alone to get to know one another."

"But you already know her."

"In some ways. Other ways are just for married people."

"What about Eb?"

"He'll come with us. Don't you worry about him."

"He'll be okay on the trip?"

"Tadie has already talked to the vet. She has a carrier for him. And he'll have you once we all get to the *Nancy Grace*."

"I hope he likes it."

"Cats acclimate. He'll be fine. So, missy, for now, you'll get to go to Georgetown and have a second Christmas. There are gifts waiting for you there, you know."

Her eyes lit. "I forgot." She picked up Tubby and hurried downstairs to see her aunt and uncle.

While Dan visited with Tadie in the kitchen, Liz took Will aside. "This is perfect," she said. "Nancy, if she's watching, must be very happy for you and Jilly."

Will hugged her tightly. "Thank you. You don't know what that means to me."

Liz wiped her eyes. "Well, there. I love you both, you know that," she said, heading toward the kitchen to collect her husband.

Dan shook Will's hand. "Glad to be here to wish you well, old man."

Will liked Dan well enough, but the good-old-boy affectations sometimes got to him. Still, he thanked his brother-in-law and happily sent him and Liz off to Hannah's, where they would spend the night in preparation for the big day tomorrow.

* * * * *

Tadie carried her coffee to the front porch to watch the sun inch up over the horizon into a blue sky. The creek was quiet and still, the temperature a balmy sixty-four. She wanted to capture what might be her last still moment of the day.

The sun shone. Sparkles danced as a slight breeze wafted out of the south. Tadie hoped it would blow away the vestiges of fear that lingered.

Jilly's excited voice came from inside. She heard Will answer and got up to join them.

Jilly wanted to get dressed before breakfast, but they convinced her to wait so she didn't spill anything on her pretty clothes. While Will and Jilly sat with Rita to devour a bowl of cereal each, Tadie nibbled on a piece of toast.

"That all you want?" Will asked.

"I'm eating this much only so my stomach won't act up during the ceremony."

James stuck his head in the back door. "Just thought I'd let you know I'll be driving Miss Sara and Jilly in the Lincoln and bringing the couple—sorry, little missy, the family—back to Miss Hannah's after the ceremony. Rita, honey, you take your mama with you."

"Yes sir."

As James backed out the door with a wave, Tadie said, "He's as nervous as I am. He did tell us that yesterday, didn't he?"

"Walking you down the aisle is a big thing for my daddy."

Tadie reached across to touch Rita's hand. "I'm glad you share him with me."

"Hah. Seems you had him first."

Hannah and Matt arrived to pick up Will at nine-fifteen. Hannah fussed over Tadie, promising to wait right inside the church for her. They hadn't practiced, so Hannah was full of instructions for Jilly—when to walk, where to stand.

"She'll be fine," Tadie said, her hand resting gently on Jilly's shoulder. "It's just going to be us there—all friends and family—so we don't need to worry about protocol. Let's go have fun."

* * * * *

It was done. They were married in the sight of God and man. Will leaned forward to kiss her, and everyone cheered.

The party blurred for Tadie. Congratulations rained on them from everyone.

Isa stood with Stefan. "I'm the matchmaker here, and I'm happy to take my share of the credit."

Tadie hugged her tightly. "Thank you," she whispered.

"And you'll be back in a few months so we can put on that show of Bucky's work?" Isa asked. "And I can have more of your jewelry?"

"I promise. Will doesn't want me giving up my life here, so we're going to live two places. Isn't that exciting?"

"I'm glad. I'd miss you terribly if you stayed away long."

Matt's face looked ready to crumble when he pulled Tadie aside. "If I'd had a clue ..." He hesitated, and she was sure there were tears in his eyes. "I'm sorry, Tadie, really sorry."

"None of us knew. But I'm sorry you've lost a brother."

"I want you to know we love you, and I'm glad about this man of yours. You made a good choice."

She reached up and kissed his cheek. "I always envied you and Hannah. Now I've got a good man of my own. And let me tell you again how pleased I am that the doctor has given you such a good report."

"I haven't taken very good care of myself for years. All that's changed now. So maybe the time in the hospital did some good."

"We've got to grow old together, all of us. Whatever it takes."

Hannah came up and slipped her arm in Matt's. "What are you two yakking about?"

"Mutual admiration society," Tadie said. "I've been telling this handsome husband of yours I expect us all to be playing together in our old age, so he's got to stay healthy."

"Amen to that. Now that Alex has gone, Matt's been interviewing candidates to help manage the company."

Tadie gave Matt's arm a squeeze. "Good for you. Maybe you'll free up enough time to come sailing with us someday."

"I hear Will's boat is big enough to be comfortable. None of your little tippy things. And you'll be living here part of the time?"

"Of course. Jilly's bound to want a house before very long so she can bring friends home."

"And when you give her a little brother or sister," Hannah said, stepping right in front of Tadie's face, "you'd better do it from here. You got that?"

Tadie pulled her friend into a hug and felt the tears begin as she remembered Hannah's lost babies.

"Oh pooh," Hannah said. "Don't get all mushy on me. I'll love being an aunt."

When Jilly slipped between them, Tadie rested her hands on the girl's shoulders. "You can start with this one," she said, pulling Jilly back against her and crossing her hands over Jilly's chest. "Aren't we blessed to have such a beautiful little girl to love up on?"

"Jilly and I are going to be great friends, aren't we?" Hannah bent to Jilly's eye level.

Jilly glanced up at Tadie, then back to Hannah. She nodded as her hands fastened themselves over Tadie's, gripping hard.

"You remember how I told you Tadie is my very best friend?" Hannah asked, touching Jilly's cheek. "That makes me your new auntie."

Jilly's hands loosened on Tadie's as Hannah stood and said, "You've just come into a wonderful family of aunts and uncles." She pointed at Matt and over at Rita and Martin. "Isa too, but you already knew that. And Elvie Mae and James will spoil you like they spoiled Tadie and me."

"Don't you believe her, Jilly," Tadie said. "Elvie Mae's a hard taskmaster."

"Aw," Hannah said. "She just pretends to be. Elvie and James will be putty in Jilly's hands."

Jilly grinned from one to the other.

"You like having all these new relatives?"

Jilly's head bobbed. Tadie hugged her closer and turned to look for Will. She caught him winking at her from across the room.

Hannah must have seen the exchange. "Jilly, baby, come visit with me for a few minutes, will you?" She reached for Jilly's hand. "Let's go see what Isa's up to."

Tadie mouthed her thanks and detached herself from her new daughter. Moving close to Will, she whispered, "How soon?"

"Mrs. Merritt, I'm surprised at you."

She jabbed his side. "Sure you are."

It took another two hours to finish visiting with everyone and to see Jilly off to the airport with her aunt and uncle. When Jilly teared up, Will took her in his arms. "Remember the presents, punkin, and think about all the fun we're going to have. Tadie and I will be there to get you before you know it. We'll all go sailing for a while, and then we'll come back here. Won't that be fun? You have two homes now."

"I love you, Daddy. Thank you for giving me a mommy."

"One who loves you, you know."

She turned to hug Tadie. "Can I call you Mommy now?"

Tadie could barely hold in her own tears, so she pulled Jilly close and whispered in a choked voice, "Yes. Please."

Hannah reached out to Tadie as Jilly climbed into the car and waved from the backseat. "Okay, your turn. Go."

Matt agreed. "There'll be folks staying to listen to the music and eat for a while yet, but you two need to get going. If you go back inside, you'll never get away."

Will extended his hand. "I can't tell you how much I appreciate all you've done for us."

"Our pleasure," Matt said, shaking hands with gusto. "Tadie is pretty special to us."

She laid her head on Matt's shoulder. "You're going to make me cry, so stop it." She hugged him, then Hannah, whispering to her friend as she held her, "I'm scared."

Hannah whispered back, "You'll be fine. Of course, you'd better call me with details as soon as you can."

* * * * *

Tadie's hands were shaking and her stomach queasy. No two ways about it. Will had left her at her door and gone to his room to get ready.

What did a man have to do to get ready? She shivered as she took off her hat, set it in its box, and slipped out of her suit.

What was she supposed to wear? Jeans? Maybe she should just go out in her robe. Would that be too suggestive? Maybe Will wanted to wait until after dinner.

Was it always so difficult? Did other women go through this on their wedding day?

No, of course not. Most modern women had already done the deed before they got married. Nothing new to them. Maybe a few married young enough to be virgins on their wedding day, but probably not many. None she knew. She supposed she'd hung out with the wrong crowd.

Did Will have a clue how awkward this was? What was he thinking?

Okay, she'd just get dressed again. She'd find something alluring yet casual. She had a caftan someplace.

There it was, on a hook at the back of the closet. She pulled the green silk over her head just as Will knocked softly on her door.

She ran her fingers through her hair, patted her cheeks, and called, "Come in."

He shut the door behind him. His hair was damp, his feet bare, and he looked so adorable in his terry robe that the butterflies flapped from Tadie's stomach right up to her throat. Her fingers splayed in the folds of her gown as he crossed the room, his gaze unwavering. Nodding at the caftan, he said, "I like that." His voice softened, and he traced a line down her cheek. "I like this."

Her pulse quickened. Both his hands came up to cup her cheeks, to draw her face toward his. He lowered his head so that his lips hovered and, drawing out the moment, brought them close to toy with hers. She'd never thought her lips so sensitive, but all her thoughts centered there. That is, until he increased the pressure and the movement, and her lips parted under his. She'd had no idea erogenous zones existed in such odd places.

"I love you." His voice caressed her. His voice and his eyes told her she was beautiful. Perhaps, to him, she was. She felt so at his touch.

When he helped her shed the caftan and then dropped his robe, there was no thought of embarrassment, only wonder. His touch gentled her fears and awakened things in her she'd only dreamed of. If there was pain, it was only momentary and soon forgotten. He took them both to places that made her imagine magic.

She lay in his arms afterward, her free hand gently tracing circles across his chest. So that's what it was all about. A little taste of heaven right here on earth.

Will stroked her back as she listened to the beat of his heart thurumping under her, slower now, steadier.

"You are a wonder, Mrs. Merritt."

She hiked up on one forearm, looking down into eyes that made her insides turn to mush again. "Ah, Mr. Merritt ... " A sigh fluttered past her lips at the thought that surfaced.

"What?" he asked.

"I think married life is going to be perfectly delightful."

Wasn't it grand? She didn't have to die an old maid after all. She bit her lip to keep from giggling like a silly schoolgirl.

His brows rose slightly, but instead of questioning her, he focused on the path his hands took as they roamed across her skin. "So soft, so smooth, so very lovely."

A quiver slipped up her spine. "Amazing. I'm a wife, a mother, in love, all in one fell swoop."

Will watched her as he inched toward her lips. "Let's see if we can do some more swooping."

"Swooping?"

"Hush, Mrs. Merritt."

Disclaimer

While all the characters in this story are fictional, the town of Beaufort, NC, isn't. Yes, I've taken liberties with some locations. I reinstituted flights from Raleigh to New Bern, which once existed but are no more. I added a boat yard in a convenient spot. Down East Creations is a figment of my imagination, as are Tadie and Hannah's homes. Most of the other named places—the restaurants, the bookstore, the museum, and the dinghy dock—all exist, and I picked them as hangouts for my characters because they are just the sort of places I enjoy. Cruisers from all around the world actually anchor in Taylor Creek or back in the anchorage off Town Creek Marina, and Michael and I serve as station hosts for the many-membered Seven Seas Cruising Association. Even if you're not a member of SSCA, let us know if we can help you in any way, whether you visit our area by boat or by car.

All Saints Anglican Church is also the worship home for a lot of wonderful folk—including the Fischers—but David Linka, the real rector, isn't old enough to serve as the parish priest in this story. Hence, my creation of John Ames. But Dave's a wonderful preacher and a true man of God, so anyone visiting the area ought to join us for one of the three Sunday services. If you're coming by boat and don't have a way to get there, just holler at me (by email), and we'll make sure you have a ride. Oh, and the talented worship leader, Elana McClure, also owns (along with her husband and business partners) both Clawsons and Aqua Restaurant in Beaufort. Jilly loves Clawsons, and Tadie and Hannah both enjoy Aqua, as well as many of the other incredible eateries I've mentioned—or missed. (And the ones I've missed will probably show up in the next Beaufort book.)

Awards ...

1994 Alpha Award as best new fiction writer, Sandy Cove Writers Conference (*Two from Isaac's House*)

2011 Marlene Award for Women's Fiction from Washington, DC, RWA (*Heavy Weather*—Book 2 Beaufort Stories)

2011 Catherine Award for Women's Fiction from Toronto, RWA (*Becalmed*—Book 1 Beaufort Stories)

2011 Fab Five Finalist, Wisconsin RWA (*Heavy Weather*)

2011 Rocky Mountain Colorado Gold finalist for Mainstream Fiction (*Sailing out of Darkness*)

2011 Semi-finalist, Genesis Award, ACFW, Women's Fiction (*Heavy Weather*)

2011 Semi-finalist, Genesis Award, ACFW, Women's Fiction (*Becalmed*)

2012 Semi-finalist, Genesis Award, ACFW, Romantic Suspense (*Two from Isaac's House*)

CPSIA information can be obtained at www.ICGtesting.com
Printed in the USA
LVOW11s1922280515

440292LV00008B/1044/P